Tench rounded a corner. Ahead, a crumbling staircase led to a higher level of the city.

From a different vantage point, she might understand why everything here was a ruin. Perhaps they were just redeveloping this part of Transtromer.

Then Tench saw a body.

It was withered, skeletal, slumped in the shadows of an archway. A hole punctured the body's chest. A man, not too old, shot through the heart. A cruciform mark had been gouged into his forehead. Bloodless, so a post-mortem wound.

"Mark for evidential sequestration," she told the whiphound.

The whiphound fixed its eye on the corpse, nodded.

"Tench to Panoply." She spoke so fiercely that her own spit rained against the bracelet. "Something's wrong with my comms, but maybe you can still hear me. We have an emergency in Transtromer. Request immediate escalation to a Heavy enforcement action. Send Heavy Medicals, ships and prefects, as many as you can find. Petition for instruments of mass control. I'm seeing—"

Tench fell. She looked down, shocked and surprised to be granted an unfamiliar sensation this far into her life. She understood soon enough. It was a thing called agony, and it hit her brain with all the multicoloured novelty of a psychedelic drug.

She had been shot.

Praise for

Alastair Reynolds

"A leading light of the New Space Opera movement in science fiction."
—*Los Angeles Review of Books*

"An adroit and fast-paced blend of space opera and police procedural, original and exciting." —George R. R. Martin on *Aurora Rising*

"Absorbing...gripping in the extreme....A fine provocative portrait of utopia on the brink. The relentless narrative momentum it employs simply underscores the pertinent urgency of that topic. The resulting mixture of space opera and police procedure is sublime entertainment."
—*Locus* on *Aurora Rising*

"This is solid British SF adventure, evoking echoes of le Carré and Sayers with a liberal dash of *Doctor Who*." —*Publishers Weekly* on *Aurora Rising*

"*Elysium Fire* is a tremendously assured read, a fast-paced page-turner that delivers a well thought-out story and characters you'll come to care about." —*Guardian*

"[An] utterly brilliant exploration of life, death, and consciousness....It's his most ambitious, certainly, and at the very least, one of his best. Required reading for SF fans." —*Booklist* on *Eversion* (starred review)

"Reynolds packs plenty of emotion into this mind-bending plot....The result is an excellent adventure that's sure to keep readers on their toes."
—*Publishers Weekly* on *Eversion* (starred review)

"*Revenger* is classic Reynolds—that is to say, top-of-the-line science fiction, where characters are matched beautifully with ideas and have to find their place in a complex future. More!" —Greg Bear

By Alastair Reynolds

THE INHIBITOR TRILOGY
Revelation Space
Redemption Ark
Absolution Gap

REVELATION SPACE UNIVERSE NOVELS
Chasm City
Inhibitor Phase

Century Rain
Pushing Ice
House of Suns
Terminal World
Eversion

THE PREFECT DREYFUS EMERGENCIES
Aurora Rising (formerly *The Prefect*)
Elysium Fire
Machine Vendetta

THE REVENGER SERIES
Revenger
Shadow Captain
Bone Silence

SHORT STORY COLLECTIONS
Diamond Dogs, Turquoise Days
Galactic North

MACHINE VENDETTA

A Prefect Dreyfus Emergency

ALASTAIR REYNOLDS

orbit

orbitbooks.net

Copyright © 2024 by Alastair Reynolds
Excerpt from *Eversion* copyright © 2022 by Alastair Reynolds
Excerpt from *Translation State* copyright © 2023 by Ann Leckie

Cover design by Alexia E. Pereira
Cover images by Shutterstock
Cover copyright © 2024 by Hachette Book Group, Inc.
Author photograph by Barbara Bella

Orbit
Hachette Book Group
1290 Avenue of the Americas
New York, NY 10104
orbitbooks.net

First Edition: January 2024
Simultaneously published in Great Britain by Gollancz, an imprint
of the Orion Publishing Group Ltd.

Orbit is an imprint of Hachette Book Group.
The Orbit name and logo are registered trademarks of Little, Brown Book
Group Limited.

The publisher is not responsible for websites (or their content) that are not
owned by the publisher.

The Hachette Speakers Bureau provides a wide range of authors for speaking
events. To find out more, go to hachettespeakersbureau.com or email
HachetteSpeakers@hbgusa.com.

Orbit books may be purchased in bulk for business, educational,
or promotional use. For information, please contact your local
bookseller or the Hachette Book Group Special Markets Department at
special.markets@hbgusa.com.

Library of Congress Control Number: 2023944054

ISBNs: 9780316462846 (trade paperback), 9780316462853 (ebook)

Printed in the United States of America

LSC-C

Printing 1, 2023

For Bill Schafer

CHAPTER ONE

Something terrible had happened in Mercy Sphere.

Thalia Ng was the first on-scene. She touched a hand to her throat, stifling nausea. With her other hand she slipped on a pair of goggles, feeding her observations back to the Supreme Prefect.

"I'm inside, ma'am," she said. "You should have a clear view of the scene."

"Pan around for me," the voice in her ear instructed. "Slower. Slower still. Why isn't it in focus?"

"It is, ma'am." Thalia coughed. "There's a lot of smoke in the air. The circulators are struggling to clear it."

"Do you need a breather?"

"No, ma'am. It's pretty bad, but if these people are managing without breathers, I think I can as well."

Mendicants—the order who operated Mercy Sphere—were busy fixing damage, clearing bodies and tending to the few souls who had survived the conflagration. Humans and hyperpigs alike made up their number, dressed in green and white clerical outfits.

As Thalia tracked around, her goggles placed reference tags on the fallen and sick.

"It's vile, ma'am. That someone should do this deliberately..." She trailed off, the horror too unwieldy to be carved into words.

"Detachment, Ng," Jane Aumonier said. "Record and assist where you can. Medical and forensic squads are inbound."

Thalia coughed again. Some part of that smoke haze came from the burned fabric of Mercy Sphere, but the rest was a sooty suspension of barbecued flesh. The flavour of it was new and ancient at the same time, as if her brain had always been primed to recognise it.

"Ma'am," she said, swallowing hard.

"Why haven't they sent a hyperpig?"

The question came not from Jane Aumonier, but from the Mendicant who had arrived alongside Thalia. A middle-aged human woman with

1

ash-smeared skin and eyes slitted and inflamed by the smoke.

Her goggles brought up her name from Panoply's register of citizens.

"I was the nearest when the alarm came in, Sister Drusilla. It could have been any one of us, a human or hyperpig prefect. We make no distinction."

"Words for my benefit, or is your superior listening in? Let me address Jane Aumonier personally." Staring directly at Thalia, Sister Drusilla pushed steel into her voice. "This attack against us was a foregone event. We've been warning of such a thing for six months, begging for greater protection. Why did you not listen?"

"Tell her that we did listen, but that our resources are not infinite," Aumonier interjected.

"There are just a thousand of us," Thalia offered. "That's a thousand of us to cover every possible threat in the Glitter Band, anything that can't be managed by the constables. With the best will in the world, we can't be everywhere at once. And since the Cranach crisis blew up…" She winced at her own ill-judged choice of words. "We're tallying multiple threats and multiple possible targets, and with each escalation the problem gets worse."

Sister Drusilla surveyed the carnage surrounding them: the burned, twisted, charred and smoking bodies, the melted architecture, the damage caused by secondary fires and explosions as the chain of destruction played out.

She touched a hand to the snowflake stitched across her chest.

"So, your policy is to stand back and observe…until such threats are acted on?"

"I wish I could offer more, Sister."

"That's the best you have, a wish?"

"Do not apologise for a system forced on us by the democratic will of the citizenry," Aumonier interjected.

Thalia salted some authority into her reply. "Be grateful that we're here at all, Sister. My colleagues will shortly be arriving in force. Rest assured our investigation will be extremely thorough. I must ask: did you have much warning before the capsule docked?"

"What difference does it make, now that the harm's done?"

"With respect, Sister, that's for me to decide. Was there anything unusual?"

A sigh. "We had a few minutes' warning—the usual pattern. When escapees flee to us, they rarely have time to put elaborate plans in place. Of course, our suspicions have been heightened with the threats made against us—that's why we've been pleading for more protection—but everything about this capsule seemed genuine." Despair broke through her mask. "If there's something we missed, something we should have seen..."

"There won't have been," Thalia said firmly. "The ones who did this to you would have made sure of that."

"How long will it take you to identify them?"

"We're already working on that problem. We think they used a non-velope to conceal the capsule's movements until it was very close to you."

"I have no idea what that is."

"A sort of invisibility screen, made from a quickmatter shell. It's contraband technology, but easily within the grasp of hundreds of families and concerns in the Glitter Band."

"But you will find them."

Thalia groped for an answer that was neither a lie nor promised too much. "This attack was part of a pattern of escalating grudges, drawing in many actors. We'll seek to identify all culpable elements. Our greatest concern, though, is to stop the violence on all fronts."

"You've dodged my question."

"We will bring our resources to bear," Thalia affirmed. "And none of us will rest until you have an answer."

"Well handled, Ng," came the voice in her ear.

Thalia unholstered her whiphound, displaying it to Sister Drusilla. "I'm going to send this device off to gather evidential traces. You needn't be alarmed by it."

Sister Drusilla scoffed. "I've just seen my best friends burn alive, Prefect Ng. They're in my nostrils. Do you imagine much is capable of alarming me now?"

Thalia didn't answer. She flicked out the whiphound's traction filament and sent it scurrying away, a busy blur of flickering silver.

Jane Aumonier floated weightless, taking in the audiovisual stream from Thalia Ng.

The large, spherical room in which she hovered had a single continuous inner surface, wrapping it from pole to pole. A mosaic of feeds quilted the surface: images and status summaries of the ten thousand orbital habitats under her responsibility. She even allowed room for the dozen or so that had seceded during the breakaway crisis. Panoply had no formal jurisdiction over those wayward states, but she still considered them her children.

Behind the quilt, algorithms churned ceaselessly. They evaluated metrics from each feed and assigned an attentional weighting to each habitat. As events played out, certain feeds swelled and magnified, while others shrank into the background, diminishing to tiny chips of colour. If

3

a development demanded that a feed be brought to her immediate notice, then the entire quilt would move, creating a dizzy sense of the entire universe spinning around the floating woman at its focus.

That was exactly what had happened with Mercy Sphere.

The structure was an outstation of Hospice Idlewild, operated by the same order of Ice Mendicants. It was a beacon of kindness, a shrine to a way of living in which hyperpigs and baseline humans were considered equals, and given every opportunity to coexist, thrive and prosper. Tolerance, openness and forgiveness were the norms. It was a model of a better Glitter Band, one Aumonier hoped to live long enough to see.

Naturally, it had become a target.

Six months earlier, one of their own—a hyperpig prefect named Mizler Cranach—had launched a murderous and unprovoked suicide attack on a habitat. As the spill-out from the incident intensified, Aumonier had naturally moved to upgrade her surveillance on potential targets like Mercy Sphere. The problem was that there were just too many plausible candidates for any one of them to merit special attention. Too many candidates, too few prefects, even fewer ships to move them around in.

Hindsight was a wonderful thing.

"Completing sweep of segment one, ma'am," came Ng on her earpiece. "The worst of the fatalities were here, but segment two also took a lot of damage. There are reports of fatalities right through to segment three. I'm moving through now."

"Thank you, Ng. You won't be on your own in there much longer. Heavy Technical and Medical squads should be clamps-on inside..." Aumonier stopped. "I'll call you back, Ng."

"Ma'am?"

"A situation, Ng. Continue as you were."

Between one second and the next, an entirely different feed had swelled up to dominate the room.

It was impossible. The algorithms had made one of their rare glitches ...surely?

Because what could possibly overshadow the events at Mercy Sphere, not even an hour into the atrocity?

Something had, though.

"Stadler-Kremeniev," Aumonier said, reading aloud as the feed helpfully annotated itself. "I know you," she mouthed, some faint connection pricking her memory. "Now what is it..."

But she did not need to speculate. Next to a real-time image of the grey, wheel-shaped habitat, the annotation was already answering her next question.

A prefect—Ingvar Tench—was on her way to Stadler-Kremeniev.

And Jane Aumonier's blood ran cold.

She tapped her earpiece.

"Aumonier to Ingvar Tench. Respond immediately, please."

Silence.

"Ingvar. Answer me. If you can't answer me, change course."

She eyed the status summary, willing some alteration.

Nothing changed.

"Dock Attendant."

A thin male voice answered her immediately. "Thyssen, ma'am. How may I help you?"

"Very quickly, I hope. Ingvar Tench appears to be on her way to a watchlisted habitat, Stadler-Kremeniev. Were you on duty when she signed out?"

"Yes, ma'am, eight hours ago. I was keeping an eye on the schedules, making sure we had a docking slot available for her."

"Did she go out alone?"

"Yes. Tench was her usual talkative self. And she didn't make any mention of visiting anyone or anything on a watchlist."

"Thyssen, I need you to take control of Tench's vehicle. Do it immediately. Get that ship steered onto any heading except Stadler-Kremeniev."

"One moment, ma'am."

She heard Thyssen delegating to subordinates in the docking bay. Voices batted back and forth. They were normal at first, but after a few exchanges she detected a gradually rising concern.

Something wasn't right.

"Thyssen?" she pressed.

"We can't stop that cutter," he said. "She's going to dock."

Dreyfus was knee-deep in a mob of angry babies.

Technically they were not babies at all, but rather adult-age humans who had undergone forced developmental regression to an infant body-template, surrendering most of their higher mental faculties along the way. They lived in a world of basic needs and responses: hunger, joy, rage, with just a thin smear of language and comprehension on top, just enough to satisfy the basic requirements of democratic participation, and to earn reciprocal status as full and valued citizens of the Glitter Band, with all the rights that came with that association.

Dreyfus knew all that. As far as he was concerned, though, and especially now that he was in the thick of them, they were still angry babies.

He had planned a straightforward in-and-out, no complications. The

5

thoroughfares of the Grevenboich Spindle had been almost empty when he came through on his way to the polling core. He had gone about his business without molestation. The checks had come back clear, and he had begun the journey back to the docking hub.

Which is when it had all gone wrong.

Without warning, thousands of infant-sized citizens had spilled into the civic core of the habitat. At first, Dreyfus had assumed that he was the object of their concern. But as more and more of them arrived—coming in on moving walkways, escalators and miniature public transit systems —he realised that their interest in him was transitory, a mere detail to be absorbed on the way to something else.

Each toddling, infant-sized citizen carried a toy of some sort, either clutched possessively or itself clinging onto its charge with soft furry limbs and tails. The toys murmured to their human companions, worry forming in the exaggerated wideness of their eyes and the quivering curves of their mouths. Dreyfus had his whiphound sniff the local cybernetic environment, detecting many epsilon-grade artificial intelligences. He felt their synthetic anxiety crackling in the air, boiling off them like a faint electrical haze. They craved some reassurance that their human keepers were incapable of offering.

Or unwilling.

The babies pressed in, squeezing in from all directions. It had been getting harder and harder to walk, and now it was a struggle not to trample tiny toes or trip himself up. Dreyfus was not a tall man, but compared to the babies his heavy-set frame might as well have been that of an ogre.

He stopped, cupped a hand to his mouth and exclaimed over the rising rage of the crowd:

"Citizens!"

No reaction, so he sucked in all the breath he could muster and bellowed:

"CITIZENS!"

His voice turned hoarse. The best he could manage after that was a broken declamation.

"Allow me through. You are under Panoply observance and I—" He had to stop to catch his wind. "I will not be obstructed in the execution of my duty!"

"Too big, too clumsy!" yelled one of the citizens. "And you smell wrong!"

Dreyfus felt his hand drifting in the direction of the whiphound. He hoped that the gesture would be seen and understood by the bawling mob.

His bracelet chimed, loudly enough to snag his attention. He touched a hand to his throat microphone.

He wheezed out: "Dreyfus."

"Are you all right, Tom?"

He cleared his throat.

"I'm fine, just caught in the midst of two thousand bad-tempered toddlers."

"Toddlers?" asked Jane Aumonier.

"Big-headed, thick-necked, belligerent toddlers."

"You must be at the Grevenboich Spindle. The Obligate Infantile State?"

"One and the same."

Down the length of the thoroughfare—behind him, thankfully—the babies and a number of animatronic robot helpers, essentially larger, adult-sized toy animals, were wheeling a movable stage into position. It supported a squat, boiler-like machine with a hopper near the top.

"Is there a difficulty?"

"Nothing that a whiphound won't solve."

"Good. I'd like you to get out of there as quickly as you can. We have a developing situation."

Babies fussed around the machine with the hopper, using ladders to climb up its sides. The hopper was already jammed with a squirming, pleading mass of sentient furry toys. Babies leaned in over the top, using rams to press down on its thrashing, desperate contents.

"What is it?"

"Ingvar Tench is about to get hurt. She's taken it upon herself to make a solo visit to a watchlisted habitat. Stadler-Kremeniev."

A baby pulled a lever on the flank of the machine, making it throb and grind. The hopper was discharging into its guts, a flurry of colourful body parts beginning to spew out from a spout.

"Remind her it's out of bounds."

"Tench isn't answering, and Thyssen can't override her ship. It looks bad."

"Has she arrived?"

"According to our tracking she's close to docking. She'll likely be inside within ten minutes, unless someone stops her."

The hopper was emptying, the first batch of toys were nearly destroyed, but now the mob was moving into its second phase. By a formalised, ritualistic process Dreyfus could not quite follow, babies within the crowd were being singled out and having their toys ripped from them, then passed hand-over-head to the shredding machine.

"I'll get there as quickly as I can. Is anyone else closer?"

"No. Our positioning puts you twenty minutes away, with an expedited crossing."

Dreyfus nodded, bleakly resigned to the worst. He unholstered his whiphound, holding up the truncheon-like handle with its filament still spooled in. The babies pressed around him like a living, squirming sea.

"I'll call when I'm near Stadler-K."

CHAPTER TWO

Ingvar Tench sighed, closed her compad and slipped it into the stowage pouch next to her seat. She had been engaged in research on the way over, trying to find a glimmer of interest—the tiniest hint of a challenge—in the latest addition to her task list.

"Confirming acceptance of updated schedule," she reported for the second time. "Am on normal finals for docking. Will advise of any anomalies once I've completed core inspection."

The habitat was lined up ahead, its rotation neutralised now that the cutter had accepted the local approach-and-docking handshakes, allowing it to be reeled in like a fly on a tongue.

Tench thought this visit was a first time for her. Not that the view through the window told her much: grey, wheel-shaped habitats were hardly a rarity in the Glitter Band. This was a small one, but there would still be hundreds just like it, scattered through different orbits, some closer to Yellowstone, others further out. Some rich, some poor, some home to relatively normal communities, others functioning as theatres of the absurd or grotesque. The habitat's name, Transtromer, rang no bells whatsoever. At some point it must have crossed her attention—lost in a rapidly scrolling list, perhaps—but she was confident that it had never done anything, or had anything done to it, to cause it to rise to any higher prominence.

Given that it *was* a routine inspection, it was a little odd to have had it added to her task schedule at such short notice, when she was already meant to be on her way back to Panoply. Tench was troubled by this for only about as long as it took to flick a loose hair out of her eyes. There was a good reason for it, no doubt. Perhaps it was as simple as saving time and fuel, given that she was already in the right sector when the reassignment came in.

She docked at the wheel's hub, noticing—with no more than mild puzzlement—that there were no other ships latched on. Curious, because the briefing indicated Transtromer had decent ties to the rest of the Glitter

Band, with the expectation of trade, inter-habitat travel and even some low-level tourism. Perhaps she had just arrived at a quiet hour.

Tench unbuckled into the near-weightlessness of the docking hub. She looked around the stowage racks at the limited assortment of equipment carried by the cutter. Breathers, tactical armour, hardsuit vacuum gear, emergency medical supplies, evidential preservation packages. Nothing that was likely to be the least use to her in a routine call.

Tench pushed through the yielding membrane of the m-lock, finding herself in a cold, damp space that in no way fitted her expectations for the habitat.

Oddly, no one was there to meet her.

"Hello?" she called, feeling faintly ridiculous and wondering if there had been some simple mix-up—the welcoming delegation on the wrong side of the hub or similar. Her schedule had been amended at short notice, it was true, but the citizens of Transtromer had still had fair warning that a prefect was about to dock. Time to scrabble together at least a few civic functionaries to meet her at the hub, help her to the core and offer a few crumbs of hospitality.

"All right," she said to herself. "So, they're too busy to send anyone, or they're still on their way, or somehow the message didn't get through."

It was a tissue-thin rationalisation, but it served her needs for the moment.

Tench moved through the hub in long, arcing drifts. Less accustomed to weightlessness than her longer-serving colleagues, she was nonetheless getting better at it all the time.

The hub, she quickly established, was deserted. Not only was hers the only ship docked, but the place had a neglected, decaying feel about it, as if it was only very rarely used.

Clearly no reception party was imminent.

Tench scouted around for a means of getting to the rim, where her briefing told her the polling core was kept. Two connecting spokes thrust out from the hub in opposite directions. The first was just an empty tube stretching away with a set of parallel rails diminishing into the distance. In the absence of handholds, Tench knew better than to just drift into it. She would not have needed to go far before the spoke's inner wall kissed against her and centripetal force took hold. If that happened, she would be on an unchecked one-way slide all the way to the bottom. Bones broken at the very least.

She went to the other spoke and had better luck: there was a simple but functional vehicle fixed onto a similar set of rails to the ones she had just seen. Tench climbed into the open cockpit of the beetle-shaped body, secured herself to one of two spartan bucket seats and pressed the sole control, a bulky start button. With a buzz, the vehicle lumbered into unhurried motion.

Tench was increasingly aware that things were not quite right with this assignment. Panoply briefings could be slightly out of date, especially in the cases of the more insular habitats, but a prefect would normally have made a routine visit within the last couple of years. Unless Transtromer had gone to seed very quickly, it was hard to see how reality and the briefing could be so divergent.

Presumably, she told herself, it would all make sense when she got to the hub.

Thalia had completed her inspection of the third segment of Mercy Sphere, recording fatalities, injuries and structural damage. Beyond the third segment, the harm done to the station was relatively minor. She had no doubt that it could be repaired speedily, especially as there had been no loss of pressure integrity in any part of the facility. The psychological toll would be much harder to heal.

A picture of the atrocity was coming into focus. When the Mendicants had opened the capsule, they had found the four hyperpigs onboard alive but unresponsive. They had barely begun disconnecting the pigs from the capsule's life-support systems when the implanted bombs had been triggered. They had been incendiary devices, designed to cause death, mutilation and terror, rather than the total destruction of the station. Anyone with the wherewithal to arrange for the pigs, the transit capsule and the nonvelope device could easily have planted more potent weapons. That they had not done so demonstrated a repulsive, reptilian restraint.

"Ng to Panoply," she said, aware that she no longer had a direct line to Jane Aumonier. "I've reached the limit of my usefulness here, without additional support. I was promised Heavy Technical and Medical squads were on their way. That was ten minutes ago. Where are they?"

"This is Clearmountain," came the reply. Gaston Clearmountain, Senior Prefect and one of the highest-ranking operatives beneath Aumonier herself. "The support you have requested will arrive in good time, Ng. But we are now facing a two-pronged situation. Enforcement, technical and medical resources are also required elsewhere. Our assets have been re-tasked accordingly."

Thalia spluttered: "What's more important than getting prefects into the immediate scene of a terrorist incident?"

Clearmountain's answer was disarmingly unruffled. "You worked closely with Ingvar Tench, didn't you."

"Ingvar? What the hell has Ingvar got to do with this?"

"Tench has chosen to walk into a watchlisted habitat, without additional equipment or backup."

Fingernails glissaded her spine.

"Which habitat?"

"Stadler-Kremeniev."

The fingers squeezed, wringing marrow out of her.

"Oh, no. Oh, hell, *no*."

"You mentored Tench after her transfer from internal work to field duty. Is there anything that might shed light on her actions?"

"No, sir." Thalia had to compose herself. "That was nearly four years ago, sir. I shadowed her for six months, until it was clear she didn't need any more guidance. It was a routine transition, and she already had years of competent service behind her, as you well know from your time with her in the tactical room. She already had a seat at the big table; all she needed was some reorientation into the practicalities of field service."

"Then you had no misgivings?"

Thalia felt the faint, prickling onset of something. Still surrounded by the workers and injured in the third segment, she dropped her voice to a hush. "Sir, with respect, I was only required to submit observations on a colleague who was already my effective superior. I didn't make the final decision on Ingvar Tench's future." She clawed her hand, nails biting into flesh. "What's happening now?"

"We won't know until Dreyfus is there. He's on his way to the scene, trying to catch Tench before she gets into serious trouble."

Now Thalia was pincered between two anxieties. Concern for the woman she had mentored, and also for the man who had mentored her.

"I should be with him, sir. If those reinforcements can be sped up—"

"You sit tight in Mercy Sphere, Ng. I just wanted your viewpoint on Tench."

"I've got nothing, sir. She was as good as any of us, and the least likely to do something reckless or suicidal."

"Be that as it may, much the same was said about Mizler Cranach. Others might say that there's a conclusion to be drawn."

Thalia bit back any answer that might land her in trouble further down the line. If Ingvar Tench had indeed gone rogue, then Thalia could be hung out to dry for signing her off as fit to serve as a lone field operative. The last thing she needed was to make things worse for herself by getting brusque with Clearmountain.

What was the bastard trying to suggest, anyway? That Tom Dreyfus's mentees were having a bad run of luck with the candidates they had themselves mentored?

Clearmountain closed the call. Ng stared around, eyes still watering from the chemical haze of scorched materials and burned bodies.

Dreyfus jerked forward in his restraints as the cutter slowed down, eighteen minutes after his departure from Grevenboich.

The Stadler-K wheel loomed ahead, face-on and rotating steadily. A chime from his console indicated the habitat's automated systems negotiating with his avionics.

"Jane."

"Listening, Tom."

"I have approach handshakes from Stadler-K. Nothing out of the ordinary. Have we heard from Ingvar?"

"Nothing, and Thyssen still can't override control of her ship. Do you have eyes on it?"

Dreyfus magnified the view with a pinch of his fingers, zooming in on the hub at the middle of the wheel. A cluster of docking positions lay close to the rotational axis, with just the one vehicle throwing an angular shadow off to one side. He watched the shadow's projection alter with the angle of the wheel.

"I see her cutter. She's already docked. Lights are out, so she's likely already inside."

A soft nasal sigh: disappointment, but not surprise. "Proceed, if you're satisfied with the risks."

"Proceeding."

Dreyfus allowed the cutter to accept docking guidance.

Besides the navigation system, the only signal emerging from Stadler-K was the standard housekeeping pulse of abstraction, the universal information protocol which permeated the entire Glitter Band. The threadbare pulse indicated the lowest possible level of engagement short of an enforced lockdown. Still, there was enough information in that flow to indicate that the citizens still had theoretical access to the democratic process, even if that right was going almost entirely unexercised.

That was not a Panoply problem. The point of prefects was not to force citizens to exercise their rights, but to ensure that nobody was denied them.

Dreyfus unbuckled and prepared his equipment. He patted the whiphound at his side and removed another from stowage. Thus armed, he surveyed the options for defence. Full, hard-shell vacuum gear would defend him against a variety of anti-personnel weapons, but it would be

13

intimidating and cumbersome. Light tactical armour was his best option. He buckled the quickmatter tabard and spinal shield over his uniform, grunting as he strained the fastenings together. He waggled his neck, freeing a roll of flesh pinched under the rim of the spinal shield.

"Too big, too clumsy," he murmured to himself.

The cutter clamped on. Capture latches secured, and suddenly all was still and silent. He moved to the nose-facing m-lock, gathering reserves of focus and preparedness. He had the ship conjure up an apple, took a bite from it, contemplated whether it might be his last, and tossed the mostly intact fruit back into the recycler.

"Jane?"

"Yes, Tom."

"I'm about to go inside. Besides my usual good humour, I'm carrying tactical armour and dual whiphounds."

"Take two minutes to go back and put on hard-shell gear, please. I'd like you back in as few pieces as possible."

"I think it might help if my face is easily read. Everyone looks shifty through a visor, and if we end up negotiating..."

"And if we're past the point of negotiation?"

Dreyfus smiled grimly. He had no answer but to sign off and continue through the m-lock, into Stadler-Kremeniev.

Tench got out into something close to standard gravity.

It had taken about four minutes to descend the spoke, the open-bodied car juddering to an unceremonious halt. She straightened her uniform, patted the whiphound against her thigh and moved to an upright slit of narrow light, where two sliding doors had not quite met in the middle.

The doors did not open as she approached. She squeezed through the gap, puzzlement modulating to disquiet.

She had emerged into the city, in a low atrium at the root of the spoke. Pale-clad buildings rose around her on ascending steps and levels. High above, far beyond the tallest rooftop, hung the artificial sky. The spoke—the only really tall structure—emerged from that ceiling, before merging into the ground at her location. There were no windows to the outside world, and the only light came from blue-glowing panels stitched around the ceiling. The majority of them had gone dark. A dusky light drizzled down, inking deep shadows.

The city was a ruin. The pavements were cracked and sprouting weeds. Gardens, set between the walkways, had gone dusty, wild and colourless with neglect. Ornamental fountains stood gape-mouthed, long dry. The buildings were scabby with broken masonry, scorch marks, ominous

14

clusters of close-set holes and toothless expanses of shattered windows. Symbols had been daubed across walls—hasty indicators of some drastic breakdown in social control. Here and there she spotted a broken robot or inert vehicle. Weeds curled possessively around these immobile fixtures.

Nobody moved, nobody made a sound. Tench's footsteps crunched and echoed along the atrium. Her eyes and ears told her the city was deserted.

Yet she felt observed.

"This is Prefect Tench," she called out, fighting to keep a quaver out of her voice. "You are under Panoply observance. Show yourselves. There is no cause for concern."

Her call echoed back, unanswered.

Tench walked on. She unholstered her whiphound, the grip slippery in her palm, spooled out the filament and set the whiphound patrolling a few steps ahead of her. The whiphound slinked from side to side, making a dry whisking sound as it proceeded.

Tench lifted her bracelet. "Tench to Panoply. Our data on Transtromer is ...not consistent with what I'm finding inside." She paused, waiting for some acknowledgement of her transmission—the reassuring voice of some other field or senior prefect on monitoring duty, safe inside Panoply yet still able to offer some understanding of her concerns, if not an explanation. "Tench," she went on. "Field Prefect Tench to Panoply? Please respond."

She glanced at the diagnostic readouts on the bracelet. It was showing normal comms, normal abstraction activity.

"Answer me, damn it!"

Tench rounded a corner. Ahead, a crumbling staircase led to a higher level of the city. From a different vantage point, she might understand why everything here was a ruin. Perhaps they were just redeveloping this part of Transtromer.

Then Tench saw a body.

It was withered, skeletal, slumped in the shadows of an archway. A hole punctured the body's chest. A man, not too old, shot through the heart. A cruciform mark had been gouged into his forehead. Bloodless, so a post-mortem wound.

"Mark for evidential sequestration," she told the whiphound.

The whiphound fixed its eye on the corpse, nodded.

"Tench to Panoply." She spoke so fiercely that her own spit rained against the bracelet. "Something's wrong with my comms, but maybe you can still hear me. We have an emergency in Transtromer. Request immediate escalation to a Heavy enforcement action. Send Heavy Medicals, ships and prefects, as many as you can find. Petition for instruments of mass control. I'm seeing—"

Tench fell. She looked down, shocked and surprised to be granted an unfamiliar sensation this far into her life. She understood soon enough. It was a thing called agony, and it hit her brain with all the multicoloured novelty of a psychedelic drug.

She had been shot.

CHAPTER THREE

Dreyfus moved in near-weightlessness, drifting more than walking. The excess body fat he carried ballooned around his midriff as he glided from one footfall to the next. He kept the first whiphound holstered to his waist, the other in his hand.

He had come through the lock into a cold, windowless reception area. Nobody was there.

"Dreyfus to Tench," he said, speaking into his bracelet. "Are you there, Ingvar? It's important that you respond."

There was nothing.

Dreyfus used his authority to open her ship and peer inside. Beyond a few storage lockers, the single control compartment offered few opportunities for concealment. It only took him thirty seconds to confirm that Tench was absent, and that she had left with nothing in the way of special equipment or armour.

He let the second whiphound loose inside the ship, instructing it to gather a forensic profile. It sniffed around inside for a few moments then came back, puppy-eager.

He sealed up the ship, and then told the whiphound to locate a trail matching the forensic profile. It skittered ahead of him, agile in the near-weightlessness, using its extended filament as a snapping propulsive tail. He watched it patiently as it scurried back and forth, knowing it might take a few moments to isolate Tench's signature from those who had come through before.

Quicker than he had expected, the whiphound froze, staring back at Dreyfus with its single red eye. Confirmation that it had locked onto an evidential trace.

No need to crosscheck the DNA itself with Panoply's records: it could only belong to Tench.

"Lead me."

The whiphound skittered on, out of the reception area and into a much larger hexagonal space. Two of the inner surfaces were blank, sheathed in

17

rough, crumbling masonry. The wall facing Dreyfus was a mirror of the one at his back, feeding into a second reception area with its own set of locks, corresponding to the far side of the hub.

The whiphound showed no interest in that section.

Dreyfus followed the whiphound until it stopped on the threshold of one of the spokes. He looked through the opening, into a long, dim tube stretching away into darkness.

"The trail goes cold here?" Dreyfus asked.

The whiphound nodded.

A hunch took him to the opposite spoke. There was no forensic lead here but there was a travel-pod, perched just beyond the red-lit maw. Dreyfus retrieved the second whiphound, clambered into the open-bodied pod, buckled in and started the pod in motion.

He balled one fist and tightened the other around the second whiphound. In less than twenty minutes he had gone from the business-like calm of a job well done to irritation at the babies in Grevenboich, to a hardening anxiety about Ingvar Tench.

"It's getting to you, I can tell."

The voice was quiet, adolescent, female. He recognised it instantly. For the sake of doubt, he slipped on his goggles. He could see her now, sitting next to him, primly dressed, an auburn-haired girl in green brocade.

"Another time," he mouthed tersely.

"But when is it ever a good time? It's almost as if you don't like seeing me. Don't like being reminded that I exist." She made a careless gesture. "Oh, speak as easily as you like. I've made sure this remains a strictly private conversation."

"There's nothing to say."

"What about our little arrangement? I help you, and you help me?"

"I gave you what you needed."

"Oh dear, Dreyfus. You *are* in a surly mood. Well, let me brighten your day minutely, before I let you get back to your present business. I'm in trouble."

"Pity. Poor you."

"It's started again."

"What has?"

"The thing that came along to upset the easy, carefree years we were both enjoying after that unpleasant business with Devon Garlin and the Wildfire crisis. You remember, surely? Or is your recall failing you in your advancing years?"

He frowned despite himself, despising the way he was being lured into a conversation he wanted no part of.

"You're surely not talking about Catopsis?"

"I surely am. At least, something like it. But cleverer, more subtle than their first crude iteration. I can feel the twinges of it. They're using network latency metrics to localise me based on my distributed processing needs. That's phase one. Phase two will be using routers and nodes to contain me in an ever-diminishing volume of space. Phase three will be shutting me down, or destroying me outright."

"Can you see my tears?"

"Even a man of your limited imagination knows this isn't a good thing, Dreyfus. Have I meddled in human affairs since our last interaction?"

"Would we even know?"

"I haven't," she asserted. "I'm busy enough being me. And, of course, fending off *his* advances, crude and predictable as they may be. Six long years since Wildfire and the last time he dared provoke me. That's been more than enough to be getting on with. But now this! It's a destabilising development. If they trap me, there's nothing to stop him becoming as powerful and dangerous as he likes."

"And I suppose you'd be the very model of restraint, if they trapped him instead?"

"Let's just say it suits neither of us to put that experiment to the test. Believe it or not, this stalemate suits me quite well. It gives me time to contemplate, to reflect on things, to plan. To play a longer game than he could ever undertake."

"There's no second Catopsis. Grigor Bacchus was lucky to keep his neck, let alone a place within Panoply. His team was dismantled and dispersed. The checks and balances we put in place ensure that no such operation could be executed within Panoply ever again."

"Then whoever is running it now is doing so from somewhere beyond your oversight." She nodded down the length of the spoke. "This Tench, the one you're going after. She's the one you used the first time around, isn't she?"

"As if you need to ask."

"Something of a coincidence, wouldn't you say?"

His self-control snapped. "What do you want, Aurora?"

"Your attention, Dreyfus. You'll seethe and sulk, but deep down you know that a reactivated Catopsis is a very bad thing for us all. You need to find out who's behind this madness and shut them down. By any means necessary."

"Find another stooge."

"What would be the sense in that, when we already have an excellent working relationship? Look, I can see you're busy at the moment. I do hope things work out for dear Ingvar Tench."

19

"Do you really?"

"I haven't travelled as far from my human origins as you imagine. I still remember what it's like to be one of you. Small, powerless, vulnerable. In my weaker moments I can even muster a tiny flicker of empathy for what you are, and what I once was."

"In your weaker moments," he echoed.

"At least I still have them. Do you think my adversary feels any remotely similar sentiment?"

"I'll worry about that the day I have to choose between you."

"Oh, Dreyfus," she said, shaking her head fondly. "You put up a good front, but deep down we both know where your sympathies would fall."

The figure vanished. He stared into the vacant space for a few moments, half expecting her to return, then slipped the goggles back into his belt pouch.

"Tom?"

It was a different voice this time, and one he was much happier to hear. "Yes, Jane."

"We lost you for a minute or two."

"Comms are a little ragged," he said, trusting that it really was the Supreme Prefect he was addressing. "I'm ascending one of the spokes, out to the rim."

"Do you think Tench went that way?"

"I'm almost certain she went by the other spoke. Once I'm at the rim, I'll circle around to the other side."

"Understood. The first wave of our response will arrive in seven minutes. After that, there'll be a continuous build-up of resources. The moment you deem an enforcement action necessary, I'll send them in."

"Good. Wait for my instructions, though."

"Of course," she said dutifully, taking his remark as if he were the superior.

Dreyfus shifted uneasily as his weight began to push down on the seat. "Is there anything I need to know about Stadler-K, beyond the little I remember from Dusollier's class?"

"Did you have a chance to brief yourself on the way over?"

"I tried, but I find it a little hard to read with my eyeballs half out of their sockets."

"There isn't a lot to go on. They've kept themselves to themselves for fifty-two years, with little trade or traffic with the rest of the Glitter Band. I'm afraid the stigma of lockdown is a lasting one, even when our own side of the affair could have been handled differently."

"What's the current picture?"

"Sixteen thousand four hundred and thirteen living souls, based on abstraction diagnostics. Baseline human, little to no augmentation beyond the basic neural enhancements needed to participate in polling. There may be children or unaugmented adults we can't track, but Stadler-K couldn't support a significantly larger population, not unless they all became heads in bottles. Population on a declining trend over the last couple of decades, and we think there may be an ongoing breakdown of internal civil order, up to and including an attempted insurrection."

"How did you arrive at that?"

"The abstraction diagnostics show sudden coordinated drop-offs in the number of voters. If it was ones or twos, we'd put it down to accidents or illness. We see those as well, but these mass die-offs seem more systematic. They look like staged executions, anything up to a dozen people at a time. Probably public affairs, to deter anyone else."

"Not good for Tench." He glanced down at his paunch, squeezed beneath the tactical armour. "Or for anyone wearing a Panoply uniform."

The electric car rumbled on. Even if he had wanted to stop it and turn back, it was far too late for that.

The agony faded quickly, not because Tench's wound had become any less serious, but because her suit had detected the injury and begun secreting topical painkillers, antiseptic agents and coagulants. The lower part of her right leg felt numbed and bloated, but the pain was no longer blocking out every thought in her head.

The shot—whether it was a projectile, beam or energy pulse—had gone in just beneath the knee. It had blown away a chunk of flesh and muscle, exposing bone but not—so far as she could tell—actually breaking anything. Still, the leg was now all but useless. Tench tried struggling to her feet, but the instant she put any load on the leg she collapsed again.

Now all she could do was crawl.

"Tench," she tried again. "Tench to Panoply. Answer me, anyone. I'm hurt. My injury is stable, but I need extraction. Please, send everything to Transtromer." She grunted, heaving herself along by her elbows and the one good leg. "I'm at the rim, near one of the spokes. I'm going to attempt to return to my ship and hope my whiphound can form a cordon."

She gave it the order through gritted teeth. The whiphound began to orbit her, cycling around almost faster than the eye could see. It would take a brave soul to cross that flickering, razor-sharp boundary, but it would not stop a weapon. If she could reach the relative cover of the spoke, though, at least she would be protected from most angles.

"Whoever you are," she cried out, her voice breaking with the strain,

21

"you are in violation of the Common Articles! Don't make it worse by killing me!"

Movement flashed along the top of one of the ruined buildings. She saw it only for an instant, just the faintest impression of a head and shoulders bobbing in and out of view.

A shot sounded. She had not heard the first one at all; the sound had been eclipsed by the pain. Not this time. It was a bang, hard and chemical.

Something metallic dinged off a nearby wall.

"Where are the others?"

She searched for the voice, squinting through the silvery fence of the circling whiphound.

"What do you mean, others?"

"You didn't come alone, Prefect. No one would be that stupid."

"You are under Panoply observance," she answered, before pausing to recover her strength. "This was a routine inspection. Why have you attacked me? I was only here to examine Transtromer's core."

Two figures came into clearer view, picking their way down the staircase. A man and a woman, both armed with long, stick-like weapons. Their dishwater-grey garments were heavy, augmented by patches of makeshift armour, sewn or buckled on. Scarves wrapped their faces, save for a narrow band across their eyes. Each wore a grubby orange sash and armband.

They edged toward Tench, keeping close to the bases of the buildings, where the shadows were deepest.

"Don't cross the cordon," Tench advised.

They stopped ten paces from the whiphound, glancing nervously over their shoulders all the while.

"You said Transtromer," the woman spoke. She turned her eye-slot toward her comrade. "She did, didn't she?"

The man edged a step closer. "Where exactly do you think you are, Prefect?"

Tench was still crawling. It was all she could do. But the distance back to the spoke seemed much further than when she had walked it.

"This is Transtromer," Tench said.

The woman gave a mad cackle, as if half her brain was already maggot-ridden. "She really believes it!"

"I've never even heard of Transtromer," the man answered, his tone cooler, less impressed.

"Nor me! But I bet she's heard of Stadler-K!"

Tench slowed. She could not stop herself.

"This is not Stadler-Kremeniev. I was tasked to Transtromer. My cutter

22

accepted the task update. I reported that I was about to dock with Transtromer. No one contradicted me."

Tench had already known she was in trouble. Now the scope of that trouble expanded panoramically, becoming a sunless landscape of limitless horror.

"Someone got their schedules wrong," the man said dryly.

The woman cackled. "Better'n wrong!"

"Listen to me," Tench said, pushing up on an elbow. "Render me assistance, help me back to my ship. There'll be an enforcement action, I can't stop that, but if you help me, I'll make it clear that there were cooperative elements within the citizenry—"

The man stopped her. "And if we don't?"

"You will face shared responsibility for the consequences of violence against Panoply. The Common Articles allow for severe collective punishment."

"Worse'n lockdown?" the woman asked, a mirthful twinkle in her eyes.

"They'd have to put some effort in to make it worse," the man said. He raised his weapon, sighting along the long shaft of its barrel. It had a roughly manufactured look to it, crudely machined and scabby with bright silver weld-work. "What do you think we should do with her?" He fired an experimental shot through the whiphound's cordon, aiming over her head. "It'd be fun, killing a prefect. But not half as much fun as taking our time over it."

"Maybe she's worth something," the woman mused. "If they know we've got one in this sector, that'd play well with the Blues, wouldn't it? They'd give us something for her."

"We'd have to prove it to them that we've got one. Cut a bit off, send it over the barricades."

"Try it," Tench hissed. "I'm one second away from instructing my whiphound to mark and kill you both."

The man fired a few more shots into the cordon. His bullets sailed through. He was learning, though. Now he timed his shots more methodically, allowing for the delay between his brain and finger, between the bullet and the whiphound.

A shot sparked against the whiphound, throwing it off its rhythm. The cordon became lopsided, and the man's eyes flashed in triumph.

He raised the weapon again.

Something sounded. A low, ponderous rumbling, coming nearer. The citizens looked toward the ceiling where an ugly, wart-like machine was emerging into view around the curve of the habitat. It was the size of a house, fixed to the underside of the ceiling, sliding between the lit and unlit sky panels. A former maintenance platform, Tench decided, now serving some darker purpose. Guns bristled out of ports in the belly of the machine, sweeping to and fro, occasionally emitting a crackle of bullets. A loudspeaker was broadcasting a garbled recorded voice, its echoing threats barely comprehensible.

"We'll be back for you," the man snapped.

They scampered off, glancing back at her but more concerned about the slow-moving gun platform. Now that she was no longer the immediate focus of anyone's attention, Tench saw figures slip along the rooflines and deliver retaliatory fire against the platform.

It was her chance to crawl again. The whiphound held its defensive cordon, but it was slower than before, sparking and humming as it moved.

CHAPTER FOUR

Dreyfus emerged from the spoke onto a dusty apron surrounded by a series of windowless buildings: minimalist silos with large sliding doors set at regular intervals. Resting close by was a fierce-looking multi-bladed agricultural machine, partly dismantled. Dreyfus walked to a row of sacks, piled high against the side of one of the silos. He kicked at one, which had already burst open, dislodging a grey slurry of spoiled grain, husked out by some unseen pest.

Beyond the roofline of the silos was the first indication of ongoing human presence. Agricultural cultivation areas, organised in rows, with service roads creeping around them. They rose up in steps, climbing a long way up the curving sides of the rim. There were agricultural work parties in some of the fields, toiling in long, organised lines. The workers were on their knees, inching forward in near unison. Dreyfus watched impassively. Along the line of workers stood figures in blue, carrying sticks. If one of the workers began to lag, deflecting the progressing line, the stick-wielders stepped in smartly. Cries and crackles tumbled down from the terraces.

He released the second whiphound. "Forward scout mode. Ten-metre secure zone. Non-lethal force authorised. Proceed."

The whiphound slinked ahead, dust arcing up from the continuous lashing contact of its filament against the ground. It made a sweeping arc, tick-tocking from side to side, defining an area of ground free of immediate danger, and led him out of the silo complex, onto one of the lanes threading between the plantations.

Dreyfus lifted his bracelet to his mouth.

"Jane. How are my comms?"

"A little faint, but we still have you."

"Not quite the answer I was hoping for. If you can still hear me, then there's no reason we shouldn't be able to communicate with Tench as well."

"What have you found?"

25

He kept his voice low. "That rosy picture you painted of the place? I've a feeling it's a bit out of date."

"Actions have consequences," Aumonier reminded him darkly. "Have you made contact?"

He eyed the nearest work party, grubbing through an acre of drab soil, where just one overseer was in charge of the kneeling labourers. "I'm about to make some introductions. How are my reinforcements shaping up?"

"Satisfactorily. Three ships are now standing off from the wheel at two kilometres, sufficient to muster Medium–Heavy enforcement."

"Instruct them to dock at the hub and hold position. Have twenty prefects prepared with hard-shell vacuum gear, but on no account are they to leave the ships until they have my authorisation."

"Our lack of contact with Tench may mean it's already time to move in."

"Let's make one last attempt at diplomacy."

He signed off and moved purposefully toward the wire boundary demarking the area being worked by the nearest party. No one was speaking, not even the overseer. The kneeling labourers had their heads down, creeping slowly forward with hoods over their faces. The soil ahead of and behind the line looked exactly the same.

His whiphound scissored through the wire boundary, triggering a distant bleating alarm. The overseer peered around with a dull, indolent look.

He spied the whiphound approaching diagonally across the field. A little beyond it stood Dreyfus, a second whiphound in his fist. The overseer raised his stun-rod, levelling it.

The tip of the rod flashed orange and something punched Dreyfus in the shoulder, knocking him over onto his back.

Dreyfus felt the hard thud against the ground first, then a bolt of pain shoot through him.

Too slow, too clumsy, the baby mocked.

Tench crawled through the still-open doorway into the gloom of the spoke's lower end. She was exhausted and pain-racked, humiliated and perplexed by the encounter she had just survived, and yet she knew one thing with supreme, crystalline clarity.

She had not made an error.

The task update had been clear: her destination was Transtromer. She had inputted it, and the cutter had not complained. But instead, the ship had taken her to Stadler-Kremeniev.

That was no accident, she now believed. It had been arranged for her, as had the comms blackout that prevented her signalling Panoply.

In a moment of lucid calm before she gathered the last reserves of energy needed to climb back into the spoke transit, Tench reflected on what it would have taken to hoodwink her so effectively. A thorough knowledge of Panoply's systems, to be sure. And suitably covert access to those systems, so that none of the usual security measures were triggered. That was next to impossible for anyone outside Panoply, and difficult even for someone embedded within the organisation.

It would have taken someone extremely well-versed in the organisation's operational protocols.

Someone much like Tench herself.

And with that came a crueller understanding: she was meant to die here. And for it to look like that death had been self-inflicted.

Tench crawled on. The grey gloom was unforgiving. Surely she should have come within sight of the transit by now, waiting just where she had left it?

Tench stilled. An awful realisation took form.

The transit had gone. It had returned up the spoke, to the hub. It would be waiting there now, a kilometre above her.

There had to be way to summon it.

She looked around, quickly picking out an upright metallic column with a single glowing button on its angled top.

Tench crawled over to it. She reached for the top, fingers stretching to make contact with the angled surface. She could not reach it. The button was a good fifty centimetres beyond her fingertips. It might as well have been fifty light years, for all that she could lift herself from the ground.

"Here," she grunted. "Break cordon. Come here."

The whiphound slinked over to her. The single red eye of its handle seemed to regard her with concern and something close to animal loyalty. It was confused and distressed, pushed far outside the boundaries of its usual programming.

Tench felt curiously reciprocal feelings. The whiphound had been damaged. There was a gouge in its casing, a burning smell and a lack of coordination in its movements.

"Mark this," she said, glaring in the direction of the button.

The whiphound curled its head, following the angle of her gaze. It nodded jerkily, accepting—to the best of its understanding—the instruction.

"Press the target. Press it. Do not destroy it."

The whiphound positioned itself before the column. It angled back its head on a swanlike curve of its filament, and dabbed at the top of the column.

"The button," Tench grimaced. "Press the button."

The whiphound missed again, missed a third time. On the fourth attempt, it struck the button.

Nothing happened. The button kept glowing the same colour. Tench had hoped it might change, letting her know the transit was beetling its way back down the spoke.

Tench listened. She strained into the silence, hoping to hear the distant movement of the transit.

And heard voices.

It had been a while since she'd noticed the gunfire or the low rumbling of the overhead platform. She presumed that it had moved on, traversing through this part of the rim.

From the angle where she lay, she could still see the slitted doorway and a narrow slot of city beyond it. Figures crept back into view, crouching low, advancing cautiously. They carried weapons. Their clothes were drab, except for flashes of orange. They were coming back, now that the immediate threat had passed.

Tench opened her hand, took the whiphound. The filament twitched, ripples of uncoordinated movement sliding down it.

"You can't defend me from this," she said. "So don't try. I need you in one piece. You have to carry a message for me, back to Panoply."

The whiphound waited for her instruction.

Dreyfus lay still, recovered his breath, dabbed cautiously at the spot where he had been hit. The shot had missed his tactical armour, striking him on the less protected area around his shoulder.

The good news was that his arm was still attached to that shoulder. He explored further, fingering a gash in his uniform. The shot, whatever it was, had clipped him through the fabric, tearing in and out of his flesh on its way. He moved his arm and fingers, testing their grip on the whiphound.

He grunted back to his feet, favouring the other arm. The wound was numbing over, his uniform re-knitting to preserve a sterile site around the injury. Dust curtained off him.

The blue-clad overseer was still levelling the rod. Dreyfus observed a dim, mechanical process play out on the shooter's face.

Dreyfus said: "I wouldn't."

"You're a...you're a prefect." The overseer's hand quivered on the rod.

"I know, and now that you've shot me once you're wondering if the

28

smart thing is to finish me off." He resumed his walk, the ache in his shoulder already becoming soft-edged. "Don't try it, is what I'd advise. My whiphound has a threat-marker on you. You might get a shot off, but there wouldn't be much left of you to enjoy it."

The overseer dipped the rod a fraction. "You shouldn't be here."

"And you shouldn't have shot me." Dreyfus flicked at the injury site, the fabric now fully consolidated. "We'll put it down to nerves. You just saw a stranger and made a professional miscalculation." He nodded encouragingly. "Now drop that toy."

The overseer lowered the rod to the soil. The labourers continued their work, not a single hooded head rising in curiosity or defiance. The alarm continued its distant bleating.

"They said you wouldn't come here alone."

"Ordinarily they'd be right." Dreyfus was only paces from the man now. "There was another, not long ago."

"Not long?"

"I mean a few minutes ago."

"There hasn't been another. I'd know."

Two overseers had broken away from their work gangs to approach the first. Burly, booted men carrying rods and dressed in a similar blue outfit to the first. They stepped over the electrical fence and trudged toward Dreyfus, carelessly kicking over the soil that had already been worked. One was shorter and meaner-looking than the other.

Dreyfus raised a sharp commanding hand, wincing as the wound reasserted itself.

"Stop right where you are. You're under Panoply observance."

"I shot him," the first one said, as if he needed to get some grievous burden off his chest. "I didn't mean to. I just saw him and did it."

"Only you could shoot a prefect and not kill him, Jarrell," said the shortest of the pair. He had a scowling set to his features, with liverish skin and deep V-shaped grooves in his forehead.

"What's your business here, Prefect?" asked the other. He had a strained look to him, weary eyes and a shock of white hair sagging down from a high forehead.

"I've come to find a friend."

"Not much chance of that here," smirked the mean one.

"I know your history," Dreyfus said. "I just want my colleague alive. Her name's Tench. She'd have docked a short while before I arrived. I think she used the other spoke to reach the rim."

Dreyfus flicked out the filament from the whiphound still in his hand. The men flinched. Dreyfus tipped the filament down and scratched a circle in the dirt. Two quick, rapier-like strokes added the spokes. He stabbed the filament at the middle, making a bullseye.

"I have three vehicles docked at your hub, with more on the way. There are twenty prefects inside those ships, with tactical armour and whiphounds, waiting on my word. They can be down those spokes in about sixty seconds, using monofilament drop lines." He nodded back in the direction of the real spoke. "They'll be through those doors with dual whiphounds set to autonomous lethal force." He twirled the whiphound handle in his hand, the stiffened filament snapping the air. "So, I'll clarify my position. Get me to my colleague, or I'll give the word."

The taller, shock-haired man said: "I don't want an enforcement action."

"Sensible. What's your name, citizen?"

A heartbeat's hesitation. "Cassian."

"And your role here?"

"Taskmaster First Class, Talus Sector, Agrarian Priority Initiative, Department of Work and Punishments, Central Authority."

Dreyfus moved to one of the hooded workers. They were still toiling, shuffling in a long, ragged line even without direct supervision. He reached with his empty hand to tug back the hood, wondering what level of social control might enforce such grim obedience.

He was not prepared for it. The shuffling figure—he thought she was a woman—had a hairless skull criss-crossed with crude sutures and a pale tracery of older scars. She had ears, for it would have been difficult to take orders without them. She had eyes, to do the work asked of her. She had a nose, to breathe with. Her mouth had been stitched shut.

Her sleeve lifted from her wrist. It had been bandaged over, the plastic nub of a catheter protruding through sweat-soiled fabric.

Revulsion shot through him, His hand closed on the whiphound as fury gripped Dreyfus. His every human instinct told him to do something. But there was nothing he could do.

"You're worse than dirt."

"We're trying to hold together a world that was already broken by Panoply," Cassian answered. "We're a pariah state because of your organisation's mistakes. No one will trade with us, no one will communicate with us. We're on our own, just as if that lockdown was still in force."

Dreyfus seethed. "You didn't have to become monsters."

"No one chooses to become a monster," Cassian answered placidly. "We become what we're made to become." He paused, nodded at the shuffling line. The hoodless woman moved on, seemingly oblivious. "Before you judge us, understand that our crops have been failing for years. The rules of rationing and distribution must be obeyed by all. When insurrectionist elements within our society threaten to disrupt the already fragile processes that keep us alive, extreme measures must be taken."

"Who are these insurrectionist elements?"

"Orange Faction. They're small in number, but organised, armed and vicious. There's a good chance your friend walked right into their territory. They're holding a sizeable part of Alvi, our largest town." Cassian dipped his eyes to Dreyfus's wrist. "Aren't you in contact with her?"

Dreyfus eyed the man. "How high up the chain are you, Cassian?"

"High enough."

"Get me as close to Alvi as you can. I suppose we can walk there quickly enough, but a vehicle would be better."

"I can't guarantee your safety."

Dreyfus smiled. "I can't guarantee yours, either."

They quickly passed out of the plantation sector, slipping through sickly, parched scrubland and into an area where there were more buildings. One of the other overseers was driving, Cassian and Dreyfus in the rear seats of the government-issue buggy. Cassian told the man to take them via back roads as far as possible, so there was less chance of the citizens noticing the prefect. From a distance, squatting next to the blue-clad Cassian in his own dark uniform, Dreyfus might just pass as another Central Authority functionary.

"You have guts, coming here alone," Cassian remarked.

"Let's just say it wasn't the plan." Dreyfus winced as the buggy hit a particularly deep pothole.

"Do you know this woman well?"

"Not closely," Dreyfus said, considering his answer. "Well enough to have complete confidence in her abilities."

"Whose idea was it to send her in here alone?"

"Nobody's. Our rules wouldn't allow it, given the trouble she was likely to run into."

"Then what made her do it, besides a death wish?"

"If I find her alive, I'm sure she'll have an explanation. That'll depend on your continued cooperation."

"I hope there's something in this for us, Prefect."

"Don't push your luck, Cassian; the best outcome you can expect today is avoiding an enforcement action." A chime sounded from his bracelet. He lifted it warily, ruling out any possibility of a private conversation. "I'm here, Supreme Prefect. With company."

"What sort of company?"

He glanced at Cassian. "Cooperative, for now. We'll see if that lasts."

31

"Good. Assuming you're not speaking under duress...are you all right?"

"Yes, I'm fine."

"I have a feed from your bracelet which says you've been injured."

"A flesh wound, from a minor misunderstanding. We've put it behind us. Please don't be concerned. I'm still focussed on finding Ingvar."

"You've not made contact?"

"I'm on my way to an area of the habitat where anti-government forces may be holding Tench, assuming she's alive."

"Give me one good reason not to send in our people immediately."

"Let's see how this plays out. I'm with a man called Cassian who's doing his best in a difficult situation."

Her silence stretched his nerves.

"Supreme Prefect?"

"I'm only one more provocation away from sending them in. Let this Cassian understand that."

"Oh, he's more than grasped the picture." The other spoke was coming into view around the rim, a pale tube thrusting down from the ceiling, its flared roots lost in a dense, smoke-hazed clot of streets and buildings. "I'll report back in when I have something concrete," Dreyfus added. "I think we must be approaching the outskirts of Alvi, where the anti-government crowd are dug in."

"Be safe, Tom."

"Worry about Ingvar, not me."

Cassian indicated for Dreyfus to keep his head beneath the armoured visor on the front of the buggy. The rim's curvature meant that that walls and ditches offered only limited cover from snipers.

"Tom?"

"My name," he answered tersely.

They approached a tall, fortified wall enclosing a large area of the town on this side of the spoke. The buggy stopped at a checkpoint.

"Say nothing," Cassian instructed.

Guards converged on the vehicle. They wanted to examine the dark, slumped passenger in the seat next to Cassian and once they realised the nature of the man, their curiosity curdled to scorn and hostility. Cassian was already deep into a dispute with the main guard, some technicality about the limits of Talus Sector jurisdiction. The impasse was only resolved when the guard came back out with a clipboard and pen, shoving both into Cassian's lap.

"This blows up, it's all on you."

Cassian flourished his name, signature, rank and the date at the bottom of a long list of similar inscriptions. He handed back the clipboard with more grace than it had been presented to him. A guard spat on Dreyfus. He looked down at his sleeve, observing the saliva as it vanished into his uniform.

Formalities observed, the barrier went up.

They drove down a narrow, winding alley between damaged buildings. After a few turns the buggy arrived at a dead end formed by a street-wide barricade composed of rubble, broken vehicles and countless dirt-filled bags, piled five or six metres high. Ladders and cross-walks pressed against the barricade's slope, with blue-uniformed guards squatting low behind patchy defences, taking the occasional shot into the contested territory beyond.

Dreyfus looked up as they climbed off the buggy. Fixed onto the ceiling above Alvi, about one hundred metres overhead and positioned a block or two further down the street, was a barnacle-like gun platform. Gunfire crackled out of the platform, aimed into the areas of the city beyond the barricade and to the left and right of the secure zone. Now and then a shot went in the other direction. The platform presented an easy target, but it was too well armoured to be threatened by the reprisals coming from below.

Cassian spoke to a woman, slump-shouldered and with dirt ingrained around her weary, fatigue-reddened eyes. "Signal the mayor that I need the secure line."

The woman glanced at the flashes of rank on Cassian's clothing.

"On whose authority, Taskmaster?"

"On mine," Dreyfus cut in.

"That's a—" the woman began, shooting Dreyfus a hateful glance as she noticed him for the first time.

"I know what I am," he answered, purposefully stone-faced. "The sooner you do as Cassian requests, the sooner you can go back to shooting your own citizenry."

The woman went into a small, dust-sheeted communications shack. Some exchange took place and she returned, gazing up at the platform. Emitting a low, throbbing, grindingly unpleasant noise, with black smoke pulsing from its flanks, the machine laboured in their direction until it was exactly overhead. A cable reeled out from the bottom, weighted at the end. Cassian snagged the weight as soon as it was within reach and dragged it to his lips.

Sporadic gunfire continued all the while. Now and then a looped message boomed out from speakers under the platform.

Cassian went through several cycles of speaking and listening. The noise was so bad that he kept having to ask for things to be repeated, or kept needing to repeat himself. Dreyfus heeled the ground, restless and worried. His shoulder was hurting again now.

"I saw eight of you once," the woman commented, as if they were just picking up the thread of a normal conversation. "Ten the time before. You never come alone." Her eyes searched him, his mere presence a grotesque affront. "*Never* alone," she repeated.

"I decided to come on my own," Dreyfus answered. "I thought it was a shame that your hospitality had to be spread so thinly among all those prefects."

Cassian walked back over, the communications cable still dangling down from the platform. They had not started reeling it back in.

On the barricade, the guards, repositioned and re-stocked with ammunition, lifted up the ladders in buckets.

"I spoke to Mayor Dokkum. They're monitoring Orange chatter all over Alvi. So far there's nothing about another prefect."

"There will be."

"The mayor is trying to open a line to Tillman Drouin, the Orange spokesman. It's not guaranteed. They only speak when they have something to lose."

"Perhaps Dokkum could impress on them that they have a lot to lose today."

His bracelet chimed. Dreyfus walked a few paces away from Cassian, answering grumpily.

"I don't have anything to report."

"Where are you?"

"Behind government lines in Alvi. Cassian is in contact with his superior, someone called Mayor Dokkum. Dokkum is attempting to open a channel of negotiation with the rebels. There's no guarantee that they'll answer."

"Then I'm not prepared to wait a moment longer."

"Please allow me a few more minutes. Things are already bad enough here. Sending in prefects will only raise the temperature even further."

"How much longer?"

Dreyfus looked back to Cassian. The other man was back on the communications cable, glancing anxiously at Dreyfus as he listened. Dreyfus went cold. He could already read the bad news in Cassian's manner.

Dreyfus signed off from Aumonier, saying he would be back in touch shortly. He sauntered over, every stride hammering a nail into his shoulder.

"What is it, Cassian?"

"Drouin's side are issuing demands."

Dreyfus permitted himself a last flicker of hope, however illusory he knew it to be.

"To release my colleague?"

"No, to hand over her body." Cassian swallowed hard. "I'm afraid she was dead when they found her. Drouin's side will deny responsibility, but she died in an area under their control."

Dreyfus processed this. It was exactly as he had feared, but he still needed time to absorb it into his mental picture, so that he could begin building out from this new truth.

"What demands?"

"A ceasefire. Free movement. Prisoner releases. The usual. Obviously we don't negotiate with murderers."

"I must have her body. Instruct Dokkum to give them whatever they want."

"She's already dead, Prefect."

Dreyfus hardened his tone. "Meet their demands. Exceed them if necessary. But get me that body."

They brought Tench through twenty-five minutes later. There was an exchange, complicated and fraught. Prisoners had to go up and over the barricade, and then the stretchered body had to come back over the same way.

When it had been brought down, Dreyfus walked slowly to the stretcher, each step harder than the last, as if a weight were settling steadily onto him. He gestured for the guards to step aside. He lifted the sheet away from the body's head, savouring the last possible instants of hope.

He surveyed Tench's face. Even in death, even allowing for the way her attackers had treated her, before or after her murder, there was not the slightest room for doubt.

"I'm sorry, Ingvar," he mouthed.

He drew the sheet off her completely.

The cause of death would have to wait for the medical experts in Panoply. But there was no shortage of possibilities. From the evidence of the injuries before him, Tench had been attacked in many different ways. She had been shot, bludgeoned, strangled, stabbed and lacerated. Those were just the most obvious assaults.

"I failed you," he said quietly. "You never knew it, but I failed you all the same."

Cassian neared his side. He had given Dreyfus a few moments alone with the body.

"Is it your colleague?"

"Yes. This is Ingvar Tench."

After a silence Cassian said: "What will happen with her?"

"She'll be returned to Panoply. They'll determine the exact mechanisms of death. I wouldn't worry yourself too much about that."

"And after that—will there be another version of her that carries on?"

"A beta or alpha-level, you mean?" Dreyfus nearly laughed at Cassian's no doubt well-intentioned ignorance. "That's not how it works for us."

"I'm sorry."

"That she died, or sorry that this might be a bad day for the rest of you?"

Something flashed in Cassian's eyes, some defiance that was nearly admirable. "She wouldn't have got a warm welcome if she'd come through the other spoke, I can promise you that. But she'd still be alive."

"Just shot in the shoulder, you mean."

Cassian looked at the body. "There's really nothing you can save of her?"

"If we'd got to her quickly, there are things we could have done. It's too late for any of those measures now."

"Again, I'm sorry."

"This won't be the end of it." Dreyfus eyed the man, wondering if he had the measure of him yet. "I'll make a deal with you, Cassian. You don't want an enforcement action, and frankly I don't want the paperwork."

"What are you proposing?"

"I have the body, but I don't have the crime scene. Secure that for me, and I can downgrade this to a Heavy Technical action." He met Cassian's eyes, willing him to accept his offer. "Believe me, it's in your best interests."

CHAPTER FIVE

Dreyfus hesitated at the entrance to the tactical room. The hammered bronze doors flashed his reflection back at him, pensive and deep-shadowed, a man already condemned.

He pressed his hands to the gauntlet motifs on the doors and pushed through into the dark, solemn space beyond. Varnished walls, a black conference table and the ever-changing Solid Orrery off to the left, the evolving, three-dimensional quickmatter model of the Glitter Band at that exact moment of time, rendered in fastidious detail.

Jane Aumonier was just taking her place at the middle of the wide, oval table, flanked by Senior Prefects Lillian Baudry and Gaston Clearmountain. Sparver Bancal had already taken his seat next to Baudry, to Aumonier's right, and Dreyfus walked to his customary position next to Clearmountain, two seats from Aumonier's left. Next to him was a supernumerary analyst whose name he had forgotten, and next to them was the chair that ordinarily belonged to Ingvar Tench, a legacy of her earlier stint as an Internal Prefect, working closely with Aumonier and the others on matters of high sensitivity. Owing to that technical seniority, she had continued to report to the tactical room even after her reassignment to field duties. Her expertise and insights had still been valued.

Now the chair was empty.

"Tom," Aumonier said, before he sat down. "I'm glad of your presence, but you should still be resting. Twenty-six hours is nowhere enough time to recuperate."

Dreyfus grunted into his chair, his shoulder aching but no longer painful. "I'll mend. More than can be said for Ingvar."

"Thank you for supervising the return of her body. It's with Mercier as we speak." Aumonier's gaze drifted around the table, fixing on the nineteen prefects and analysts gathered before her. "We lost one of our very best in Stadler-Kremeniev. Regardless of the reasons for that loss, I want to stress that one mistake doesn't negate a lifetime of dedicated service to our organisation. Her expertise—her in-depth knowledge of our history and systems—was unequalled. And I include myself in that calculus."

No one raised an eyebrow at that. Aumonier was known for many things, but false modesty was not one of them.

"One might say," Lillian Baudry remarked, "that it was slightly more than a mistake. This was...a wild provocation."

"Lillian, please," murmured Gaston Clearmountain.

"If I don't say it, no one else will," Baudry countered sharply. "With one reckless act Tench has undone years of work in fostering good relations with our more difficult clients. It's a miracle that we didn't have to send in a massed response. The death toll could have been—"

Dreyfus cut her off. "You're insinuating that it was a suicide bid, Lillian. How do you know it wasn't an honest error?"

"There's no way that she walked in there without knowing the consequences," Baudry said. She turned in her seat, stiff as a finger-puppet. "They still teach the history of Stadler-K in induction. Besides, this was Ingvar Tench. What she didn't know isn't worth knowing."

Dreyfus bit into an apple, the crunch audible across the table. "Perhaps she didn't realise where she was until it was too late."

"With respect, no one just stumbles into a watchlisted habitat," said Baudry. "Our systems ensure that."

Dreyfus shrugged, slumping deep into his seat. "Systems go wrong occasionally. Isn't that half the reason we exist?"

"We have her vehicle," Aumonier said, directing a sideways nod at Dreyfus. "Which is already more than we had when Mizler Cranach died. The Heavy Technicals are bringing it back to Panoply under tow; they won't risk activating any of its systems until they have it fully secured."

"There has to be a reason why we couldn't override her control," Baudry said.

"And we'll find it." Aumonier's gaze swept the room, lingering on the half-dozen or so attendees who were relatively new to the hallowed cloisters of the tactical room. "Now, I must mention something else in connection with Ingvar's service. What I'm about to discuss goes no further than this room."

Dreyfus put his teeth to the apple, but refrained from biting.

"A little more than four years ago," Aumonier said, "Ingvar was pursuing an investigation into an unsanctioned operation within Panoply code-named Catopsis. Following Tench's investigations, I had it shut down completely and instigated disciplinary procedures against the ringleaders, including Grigor Bacchus. No one was forced out of Panoply, but shutting down the operation left a legacy of ill will, most of it directed at Tench. It was her suggestion that she be transferred to field duties, and I consented. I did not relish losing a gifted IP, but I had no doubt that she would make an equally effective, dedicated field agent."

"Forgive me, but may I ask the nature of this operation?" asked one of the newcomers, an analyst called Jaffee.

"Tom?" asked Aumonier.

Dreyfus straightened in his seat. "Catopsis was a project to trap and contain one or both of the hostile artificial intelligences known to be loose in the Glitter Band."

"Why would that be a bad thing?" queried Jaffee.

"There was merit in it," Aumonier said. "But the practicalities were hazardous. If it failed at any point, Catopsis would have risked destabilising the situation, potentially allowing one intelligence to grow more powerful than its adversary."

Jaffee was enjoying his moment in the limelight. "The people behind Catopsis didn't see that?"

"Grigor Bacchus and his associates were confident that their trap could neutralise both adversaries in one stroke. I was less so. There's something to be said for a predictable status quo; while those two damaged gods are fixated on each other, we can go about our lives."

No one argued with Jane Aumonier on that point. It would have been extremely unwise to do so, given she had been the prisoner of one of those malign intelligences.

"You think the lingering ill will may have continued until the present day?" asked Clearmountain.

"I don't know, Gaston. But I do want the matter looked into." Her eyes settled on the only hyperpig in the room. "Sparver, I'm putting you on this case immediately. You're to dig into Ingvar's actions over the last few weeks and months. You may find nothing, but if there's anything in her recent history that might shine a light on today's events—even if it turns out to be nothing more complicated than suicide—I'm counting on you to find it."

"I feel I could be of more use in the Mercy Sphere investigation," Sparver said.

"Nonetheless, Thalia Ng will remain in charge of Mercy Sphere, and the wider operation into containing the fallout from Mizler Cranach. I'm authorising her to return to Valsko-Venev, to liaise with the lemurs and view the original crime scene with a fresh pair of eyes."

"Mine weren't fresh enough, ma'am?"

"I don't want either of you getting too emotionally invested in the actions of your mentees."

39

If Sparver was not exactly satisfied with this explanation, he had the good sense not to challenge it further. Dreyfus met his eye, nodded his approval and support, and willed his friend not to dig a deeper hole than he was already in.

"Fine," Sparver said off-handedly. "I'll take Ingvar."

"Indeed, you will." Aumonier paused, looking down at her fingers before resuming. "There's another matter which has only now come to my attention. I think it would be fair to say that we considered Ingvar a dedicated loner, loyal to Panoply, given over to her work to the almost total exclusion of a private life?"

No one had anything to offer by way of contradiction.

"Tench has a daughter," Aumonier continued. "She's an ordinary citizen, down in the Glitter Band. Someone needs to let her know what's happened."

Aumonier and Dreyfus used a passkey to access Tench's rooms. They stepped through, subdued lighting springing on at their arrival. Surveying the uncluttered ambience, the bare furniture and unadorned surfaces, Dreyfus stopped in his tracks.

"Some idiot's already been here before us. They've cleaned the place out."

"I don't think so," Aumonier said. "I've a feeling this is just as she liked it."

Dreyfus glanced at his superior. "You visited her, when she was alive?"

"No. She wasn't one for tea and sympathy. I knew Ingvar, though, and this is exactly how she'd have lived." Aumonier gestured at the surroundings, lit in warm shades of ochre. "The spartan life. No distractions, no complications. Nothing except the barest essentials."

"I thought my surroundings were minimalist," Dreyfus answered.

Aumonier scoffed lightly. "You're not even in the running."

Now that he had adjusted his perceptions, he realised that the rooms were not completely lacking in personal touches. There was a handful of possessions, arranged squarely and deliberately like exhibits in a gallery. They would all have been removed, archived, or destroyed had the room really been swept before their arrival.

His fingers settled on a heavy black book, a bound volume of historical lecture notes by Albert Dusollier. He leafed through the thin, durable pages, reminded of when he had attended the same classes and surprised by Tench's attachment to such an archaic format. At the front of the book was a personal dedication by Dusollier himself, Supreme Prefect at the time that he had made the inscription.

To Ingvar. Brightest of us all. Go far, but not too far.
Albert.

"Light bedtime reading," Dreyfus remarked in a low voice. "The life and times of Panoply, including our biggest screw-ups."

"It fits."

"Dusollier saw her talent early on. And maybe something else."

"That'd she'd invest herself too heavily in her work, sacrificing all else in dedication to Panoply?"

"Hardly the worst crime." Dreyfus moved on. At his approach a vertical surface whisked open, revealing a small but ordered wardrobe of pre-conjured garments. These were her civilian clothes, but in their formality, funereal hues and total absence of frippery they could easily have served as operational garb. "Did you ever see Ingvar out of uniform?"

"I don't think I ever saw her except when she was on duty. It's as if she didn't exist outside the hours of service."

Dreyfus wondered if he had ever seen Tench in the refectory, or in any of the recreation areas.

"I should have made more of an effort," he said, imagining Tench spending her off-duty hours eating alone in these rooms, with only Albert Dusollier's gruelling tutorials for company.

"Each of us chooses our own path," Aumonier said, before he sank too deeply into self-recrimination—on that score, at least. "We mustn't look at all this and conclude that she was unhappy, or that there was some absence in her life. This may have been all that Ingvar needed to feel complete contentment."

Dreyfus nodded gloomily, hoping she was right but far from persuaded.

"How do you feel about Baudry's theory?" he asked.

"Lillian's just voicing a suspicion that most of us have entertained. I attach no stigma to suicide. Voi knows I considered it often enough when I was under the scarab. If Ingvar did choose to end her life, then she would have had my sorrow but also my understanding."

"But you can't see her choosing that particular way to do it."

Aumonier looked back at him. "Can you?"

"Not really." He nodded back at the book. "Not with that dedication to our values. She'd have done nothing that inconvenienced or embarrassed you or Panoply. And she'd have completed her shift and filled in her daily report first."

"I concur. It wasn't suicide. The problem is, you and I can't prove that."

"It's early days."

Dreyfus's hand alighted on a sturdy black chest resting alone on a bare

41

shelf above the small, neatly made bed which was tucked into an annex of the room. The chest had a brass clasp and a fold-up lid. He opened it and peered inside.

The clutter of its contents was in striking contrast to the order beyond it.

He fingered through the items. Images, jewellery, keepsakes. A child's painting, two adult figures daubed in primary colours. Scraps of poetry, a multicoloured feather, a hair-clasp. A lock of hair. He extracted one of the images, feeling the glossy texture. It was a still capture, chemically bonded to paper. A little girl, sitting on the edge of a lake with her legs dangling into water.

He offered the archaic memento to Aumonier. She took it, examining it with her usual judicious eye.

"It could be Ingvar herself, or the daughter."

"Do we have a name?"

"Hafdis. Hafdis Tench. I've checked our citizen records: she's in Feinstein-Wu, a cylinder habitat."

"I don't know it."

"It's never given us a headache, just one of the thousands of places that only need occasional visits from prefects. If our records are correct, Hafdis has never been anywhere else. She'll be a young woman now, in her early twenties."

A cheerless premonition settled over Dreyfus.

"I wonder how she'll take this."

"I'm afraid you'll be the one to find out. If I can't stop you working, at least I can give you an assignment that won't be too hard on your shoulder." She eyed him with an authentic concern. "Is that all right, Tom? Or would you rather I sent Gaston or Lillian?"

Dreyfus had been expecting this, even though Ingvar Tench's daughter was the last person in the world he wanted to meet.

"It'll be fine," he said. "You need your seniors here, putting out these fires caused by Mizler Cranach."

"If only we were putting out fires."

Aumonier returned the picture to him. Dreyfus replaced it in the box and closed the lid, as silently and softly as if he were sealing a coffin. "Hafdis might want these things," he speculated.

"She'll be shown them in due course, but you shouldn't be lugging a chest full of knick-knacks around in your condition. They can wait here; there's no pressing need to recycle this room. If Hafdis wishes to have any of the items, they can be shuttled over easily enough."

Dreyfus agreed. Break the news first, then deal with the personal effects later.

"Odd that none of us knew about this daughter."

"I've checked the timeline. Hafdis was born a couple of years before Ingvar submitted her application to Panoply. If it was anyone else, I'd say it was unusual that she never disclosed the daughter to us, nor requested any special arrangements for childcare during Hafdis's early development. But she violated none of our disclosure policies and it's also completely in keeping with the total privacy Ingvar extended to all areas of her life."

"Was there another genetic contributor?"

"Yes. Citizen records show a father, Miles Selby."

"Then he should be informed about Ingvar, and made aware of any responsibilities pertaining to Hafdis."

"I'm afraid there's no way to inform Miles Selby of anything. He left the system on an outbound lighthugger shortly after Hafdis was born. Records show no other close relatives around Epsilon Eridani. We'll signal him, of course, but it'll be decades before we can expect a response. I'm afraid this one is on you." Aumonier regarded him with the fond concern she afforded a handful of her closest confidantes. "And there's no one I'd rather have delivering that news. When will you be able to leave?"

Dreyfus looked at his bracelet. "If there's no other pressing business, and Thyssen can provide a cutter for me, I can be on my way immediately. I don't know what sort of hours they keep in Feinstein-Wu, but I'm sure I can adjust accordingly. Do you have an address for Hafdis?"

"Yes, and her work contact. She's in—"

His bracelet chimed. Dreyfus frowned as the status update spilled across the thumb-sized display.

"What is it?" Aumonier asked. "I'm guessing it's not a major crisis, or mine would be going off as well."

"It's just a call from Necropolis. Seems one of my dead would like to make a confession." Dreyfus nodded to himself, realising that he could call Thyssen, have a cutter readied and delay his departure only slightly by first attending Necropolis.

"Rather you than me," Aumonier told him. "I hate that gloomy, ghost-haunted place. I fear the day I wake up there, like all the rest of them."

"It grows on you," Dreyfus replied.

Dreyfus wandered the quiet paths and empty pavilions until he found the ghost he sought.

Victor Muya sat on a white wooden bench, waiting patiently for him. He had a paper bag in his lap and was dipping into it to toss breadcrumbs to the immaterial birds pecking around his feet.

"I was wondering when you'd have a change of heart," Dreyfus said, his shoes crunching on gravel. "You're too sensible not to have come around in the end."

"It wasn't an epiphany, Dreyfus, just a dull realisation that my options had expired." He tossed a last crumb. "I'm used up."

Dreyfus faced the man, squatting down on his haunches. "Everyone can do some good, Victor. Even the dead."

"Easy for you to say, from the standpoint of the living."

Dreyfus was addressing a beta-level emulation of the once-real, once-alive Victor Muya. It was a predictive model of the original man, a library of algorithms trained to behave like him, based on a lifetime of self-directed surveillance. Panoply had sequestered the beta-level after Muya's death in one of the tit-for-tat episodes spiralling out from the Mizler Cranach crisis. Now the beta-level existed only in Necropolis, the virtual environment Panoply had created for those victims and witnesses it wished to interview after their corporeal deaths.

"Give me their names," Dreyfus urged. "You've nothing to gain by protecting them now. They used you, Victor. They knew those weapons were faulty, and that just handling them was going to be risky. They were prepared to let you take that fall."

Muya had been the designated handler for an illegal cache of foam-phase armaments, being stockpiled for use against hyperpigs and the human sympathisers aligned with them. The weapons had malfunctioned, blowing up prematurely—leading to further escalation when the incident was perceived as pig-sponsored sabotage.

Dreyfus just wanted to identify the ringleaders who had provided the grisly armaments in the first place.

"They'll get to me here," Muya said. "You think I'm safe, just because I'm dead? There's nowhere they can't reach."

"Then they underestimate Panoply, to their cost," Dreyfus said. His knees were aching from the squatting stance already. He was goggled up, pressed into an ill-fitting immersion suit, alone in the blank room prefects used to access Necropolis. "You're safe here, and safe from any reprisal. Once I have their names, my operatives can move quickly." He shook his head regretfully. "You never wanted any part of this bloodbath, Victor. I've studied your biography: no history of anti-pig sentiment at any point in your life. You were just looking for a few thrills, and playing terrorist for a day seemed like a fun diversion."

"If I give you something…"

Muya began to blacken, like paper held too near a flame. He crisped, soot coiling off him at the edges. Dreyfus fell back, startled and alarmed.

The immaterial birds scattered in alarm. Muya was smoking away, dissipating by the second. The soot rose off him in a tight-coiling column, like a dark waterspout. Scrambling to right himself, Dreyfus tracked the column as it angled overhead, becoming horizontal. It led to a white teahouse: a pagoda-topped structure with open sides.

In the teahouse, a hooded form sat with its back to Dreyfus. The soot column was drawn to it, hooking around as if it were being sucked into the hooded figure's face.

Dreyfus detected a terrible low humming.

He staggered to his feet, sweat sloshing within the immersion suit. "You can't be here."

The humming became a voice. It was calm, measured, almost amicable.

"I don't know why you're surprised. You've long known I could reach you whenever I wanted to."

Dreyfus flashed back to the events of the Wildfire crisis.

"You left a message for Aurora. That's not the same as manifesting yourself."

"To me, the distinction matters little." The figure patted the bench next to the one it was seated on. The soot flow was ebbing, almost nothing left of Victor Muya now but a wraith-like residue, thinning out by the second. "Come, Dreyfus. Sit with me a moment. There's something we must address."

The hood turned in his direction, but not enough for him to see a face. "Oh, I'm not going to hurt or kill you. I had the opportunity on Yellowstone. I didn't take it then, so why would I take it now?"

"What have you done with Muya?"

"Digested him. Who will miss him now, but you?"

Dreyfus approached the teahouse. There was no point denying the Clockmaker. If it could insert itself into Necropolis, then it could find him anywhere.

Better to be done with whatever it wanted.

"I've heard from your adversary. She sends her fondest wishes."

"Does she?"

"Not really, Philip."

"That name belongs to a dead man. Please don't use it in my presence again."

Dreyfus sat down on the bench opposite the Clockmaker, rather than the one he had been invited to use. The Clockmaker kept its hood dipped, a sort of mercy. Cradled between its iron hands was a complicated mechanism: a box of brass and glass alive with a busy, flickering metabolism of levers and gears.

"It's been a long time since I heard from Aurora, and even longer since I had any contact with you," Dreyfus said. "It doesn't take a detective to work out the connection. I suppose this means she wasn't lying?"

"What did she tell you?"

"That something is using network latencies to detect and quantify your activities, as a prelude to capturing you. I suppose you're aware of these interventions?"

"How could I not be?" The hooded form leaned in, its whirring toy seeming to shimmer between its prisoning walls of brass and glass. "They've learned from their earlier mistakes. Their methods are cleverer now, less easy to game."

Dreyfus echoed the words he had used against the Clockmaker's adversary. "Pity. Poor you."

"You saw once that I was capable of mercy, Dreyfus. Even in my cruelty, there was restraint."

"You just killed Victor Muya."

"I erased the shadow of a man already gone. It was nothing, like drinking air. There are many others I could start on. Few would miss any of them. But I won't, for now. I understand self-denial. That can't be said for Aurora. You've never glimpsed her true intentions."

Dreyfus shrugged his indifference. "I take my monsters as they come. You're no better or worse than each other."

"Think that if you must, but even you'd have to agree that it would be very bad for one of us to achieve dominance."

"So, what's your point?"

"You'll act to stop this reckless experiment. Find out who is behind this new version of Catopsis and stop them."

"That's exactly what Aurora wanted of me."

"And did she threaten you if you failed her?"

"We discussed terms."

"Then so shall we. I'm here now, able to do as I please in Necropolis. I can make the dead disappear for ever. Some might say...what does it matter, if they're already dead? But you wouldn't, Dreyfus. They mean too much to you."

"For all I know, you're just Aurora wearing a different face."

"I might be her, and she might be me. That's a question you'll have to live with. But it won't be enough to stop you taking the necessary measures. Tench's death proves that this isn't mere fearmongering. Something is happening, something that needs to end, urgently. You're just the man for the job."

"Two votes of confidence from disembodied super-intellects," Dreyfus remarked. "I must be going up in the world."

"End this," the Clockmaker instructed him. "And don't take too long doing it."

The hooded speaker set the brass-and-glass construction down on the table in the middle of the teahouse. Just as Victor Muya had done, the hunched form started smoking away at the edges, becoming ash, until eventually there was nothing left but the new clock, ticking and whirring like the most sublime embodiment of inanimate malice.

CHAPTER SIX

An approach handshake came in.

"We have you, Prefect," came the clipped, not exactly welcoming voice. "Clarify your intentions, please."

"This is Prefect Ng," Thalia replied, fighting the instinct not to explain herself, for which she would have been entirely within her rights. "I'm returning to Valsko-Venev to carry out a secondary review of the events surrounding the Mizler Cranach incident."

"And by incident, you mean the unprovoked murderous attack? You'll find that all relevant records are in Panoply's possession, Prefect."

"Indeed, and we thank you for all cooperation to date. I'd still like to make sure there's nothing we missed on our first evidential sweep. You understand, of course."

"A perfectly reasonable request, Prefect." Although the voice managed to make it sound as if her request was anything but reasonable. "All necessary assistance will be rendered. Continue your approach at your discretion."

The fat, wheel-shaped carousel was a hubless toroid, twenty kilometres in diameter, with bi-curved windows on the inner rim. The interior landscape turned before her, partially obscured by a lacy fretwork of windowpanes. She saw exactly where the weapons had touched. The cutter's armaments had gouged a line in the windows almost a quarter of the way around, shattering and puncturing them in a narrow strip, straight except for a wayward kink at one end, as if an otherwise perfect brushstroke had been disturbed.

They had fixed it now. Glass panes and structural supports had been replaced all along the line of damage, but since these were new components, they stood out against the old. The fresh panes of glass had not had time to acquire a frosting from exposure to micrometeorites. The scaffolding gleamed brightly, not yet tarnished by cosmic radiation. It would weather down in time, but it would be a long while before the scar faded to invisibility.

She came in and allowed herself to be vectored to one of the many berths spaced around the outside of the torus. Thalia climbed up and out through the dorsal lock, then ascended a short distance by elevator, until she emerged into warm, humid air and dusky daylight. She felt bouncy on her feet, only a quarter of her normal weight, and unencumbered by armour or special equipment.

The elevator had disgorged her out of a tree trunk, into a shaded dell hemmed in by dense vegetation and soaring trees. A chatter of whoops and trills filled her ears. Each breath was heady with fragrance. Every possible shade of green splintered against her eyes. It was beautiful, primal and totally overwhelming. She stared up, peering through the scissoring, rustling canopy a hundred metres or so above her head, and could barely make out the glass ceiling that formed the inner rim of the torus. The trees around her pressed in thickly, with tunnels of inviting gloom threading away in all directions.

Movement caught her eye above. A creature glided across the clearing, its four limbs stretched with an aerofoil membrane growing between them. She watched patiently as more of these creatures flitted through the air. They made it look easy. In a quarter of a gravity, with standard air pressure, perhaps it was.

There were other beings in the trees, not all alike. Some flew, some swung from prehensile tails, some brachiated. They were furry, generally about half her size, and they all had humanoid faces, albeit with faintly canine features and exuberant black and white patterning around the eyes, nose and snout.

She waited. Eventually something or someone scampered down to the forest floor and bounded over to her in a lolloping sideways gait. It was one of the long-tailed variants, abundantly striped, black daubing the eyes. Clad as it was, only in fur, the only indication that she was dealing with an intelligent, tool-using creature was a sort of waistcoat made of hand-sewn material, bulging with pockets and pouches.

"Hello," Thalia said guardedly. "I'm Prefect Ng."

"Good afternoon, Prefect," her host said, skipping to a halt. "How was your journey?"

"My journey was fine, thank you." Thalia smiled tentatively. "And you are...?"

"I'm Minty Green Grass, Dew At Morning, Who Finds Only The Good Berries, Mostly At Dusk." The chest-high creature had a piping, child-like voice, yet spoke with a distinct authority. "You may call me Minty. Procurator-Designate Minty, if you insist on formality."

"Perhaps we should stick with titles, Procurator-Designate. May I ask your role here? I hope it isn't rude, but it helps to know what level of administration I'm dealing with."

"Oh, it isn't rude at all. My role encompasses a number of spheres, including official coroner for incidents involving mass casualties. Thankfully we hadn't had many of those. I mean, not until *lately*." Minty dug into one of its pouches and scooped out a palmful of gleaming red orbs. "Would you like some? These are really good, and freshly picked."

Out of consideration for her host, even though it was against field protocol, Thalia took a few berries. She popped them down and made a dutifully appreciative sound before her taste buds had really had time to comment. They were sweet, with a slightly metallic aftertaste.

"Thank you."

"Just ripe for eating now. Notice that greenish marbling to the crimson, shading into a faint coppery-pink?"

"I will have to take your word on that."

"It's not your fault," Minty said pityingly. "We've been raised from birth surrounded by family and friends who make a point of differentiating an immense variety of colours and textures in berries, nuts and leaves—and that's aided by the extra receptors in our eyes."

"I see," Thalia said doubtfully.

"It matters!" Minty declared, pointing to a cluster of berries blooming on one of the trees hemming the verge. "Do you see those? A sort of deep black, with a purple shimmer? Totally delicious, and at the peak of ripeness. Really, really good. We'll try some later. Now see those off to the right, a little higher? Past their best. That's more a dark purple frosting into black. They'd be immediately and fatally toxic to our young, and quite bad for an adult."

"Best skip those, then."

"Definitely. But you won't be leaving us without a gift of some rare and delicious specimens of perfect ripeness."

"That will be very kind, but please don't go to any trouble." Thalia set about the difficult task of getting to the point of her visit. "After all, I'm not really here on any sort of pleasant business."

"Yes, that. I'm not terribly good with baseline faces, but do I remember you from the original investigation?"

Thalia shook her head earnestly. "No, I wasn't involved. I don't know if you heard about the events at Mercy Sphere, but it's kicked off an even worse spate of terrorist acts. We have to get to the bottom of it, Procurator-Designate, which is why I've been assigned to return to the scene of the original crime and see if there's anything that can turn the tide."

"We've been following developments," Minty said. "Don't get the idea we aren't fully engaged with the outside world, just because we mostly hang around in trees, make babies, eat berries and sing. We follow the news. We vote. We watched with horror as each atrocity unfolded, and we understand that it began here. But I'm not sure that raking over it will help very much, so many months after the original incident." Minty made a beckoning gesture. "But come. Let's walk. The transit will take us to the scene."

"You've got a mass-transit system?"

"I wouldn't say 'mass.'" Minty had set off on its sideways gait, arms spread for balance, tail erect. "Most of us are quite happy to take the slow way anywhere, through the trees or on the ground. So what if it takes an hour or two to get anywhere? Best way to forage."

"Of course."

"But now and then officials and emergency response crews have to move more quickly—such as when someone attacks us with no warning."

Thalia was puffing already just keeping up with the bounding creature. They were heading out of the clearing, down one of the tree-shrouded passages.

"I'm sorry about what happened. I've no wish to pick over a fresh wound either. That said..." She paused to collect her breath. "That said...Minty. Procurator-Designate. Could you...slow down a tiny bit?"

"Of course—thoughtless of me! And here I am rushing past some good berries!" Minty slowed down just enough to scoop a handful from one of the bushes along their way. "These are a bit early, but if you press them, they make a good salve for insect bites. Are you really hoping to find something new, Prefect? I thought your colleagues picked over everything pretty thoroughly the first time around."

"So did we." Thalia fanned her face, already perspiring. "But not everything fits."

They continued, Minty bounding at about ninety per cent of their earlier speed. The passage widened out into another clearing, this one set with towering stone statues. Some of them were very old, cracked, vine-shrouded and beginning to crumble back into the greenery. They told a condensed history of the habitat, beginning with the oldest human-baseline founders and tracking the forced genetic changes that had been applied from generation to generation, culminating in the range of arboreal forms now evident. In the middle, going back a century or so, were the intermediate cases: furry people who were smaller than baseline, with longer, springier legs and arms, the beginnings of tails and other specialised adaptations.

"We understood that the case looked pretty straightforward."

"It did. Mizler Cranach even left a suicide note." Thalia nodded at the largest and oldest of the looming, green-tinged statues. "It says that he attacked you in vengeance for the sins of your founders. Your habitat was built on tainted capital: profits from the early genetic prototyping of pig-human chimeras."

"You could say that about many habitats."

"Agreed, but Mizler didn't have the luxury of attacking them all. That's if his attack was anything of the sort."

"I don't mean to argue, but is there any debate about that? He had the means, motive and opportunity."

"All of that's true, but it doesn't tally with a personal view of Mizler Cranach."

"Your view?" Minty asked, glancing back.

"No. I didn't have much to do with Mizler. But a friend of mine did."

"Was this friend of yours a hyperpig, like Mizler?"

Thalia had the feeling that she had just been baited.

"Yes, but he's also an extremely reliable judge of character. His opinion matters to me. Besides...a fresh pair of eyes never hurt, which is why I am here."

"A dreadful crime happened here, Prefect. Please do nothing to diminish that."

"I won't, I promise." Thalia slowed, her ears pricking at a distant but rising wail, like some kind of emergency siren. It reached a whooping crescendo, faded, then began to build again, as if on a recorded cycle. "What's that sound? Are we in trouble?"

"That's singing. A family group, probably the Speckled-In-Lights showing off again." There was a scathing edge to Minty's voice. "Yes, we know you can harmonise well. That's all you ever do."

Thalia listened, adjusting her mental filters. She began to hear mournful undercurrents, hints of a developing melody.

"It's rather lovely."

"It's loud and forceful, certainly. We must see if the Noon-Baskers are passing on one their foraging sojourns. They'll show what singing's *really* like—if you've got the ear for it. They're among the best we have. Good berry-finders, too—unlike those Speckled-In-Lights, who are very good at turning up just after someone else has done all the hard work."

Minty slowed, bent down and tugged at a pair of handles jutting from the lawn. A grassy hatch lifted up. Thalia followed her host down a short flight of musty steps to a gloomy vestibule where a small, beetle-shaped car rested on a transit rail, dark tunnels stretching fore and aft.

52

"I said it wasn't mass-transit," Minty said, hopping into the car and tucking its tail through a hole in the back of the seat.

Thalia sat next to her host.

"Where are we going?"

"Where it all started—to the place where Mizler Cranach's weapons first touched our paradise."

Minty touched a control. The car moved off into the tunnel, gloving itself in darkness.

Making a conscious decision to leave his whiphound behind, Dreyfus exited the cutter and moved through a low-gravity immigration facility, drawing glances from citizens, tourists and officials moving through the same space, while doing his best to project calm authority and reassurance.

"It's all right. I'm here on routine business, nothing to be alarmed by. You are not under observance."

He moved out of the immigration complex into the main core of Feinstein-Wu. It stretched away, five kilometres of rolled-up landscape, a kaleidoscopic vista of greens, blues and paler accents, transected by the window strips and their complex, glittering frets of directional mirrors. It was daytime, by the internal clock.

Transits shuttled up and down radial tracks, connecting the docking axis to the cylindrical landscape. Still conscious that he was drawing attention, Dreyfus wandered around the circular plaza, moving in long, bouncing strides, studying the illuminated signs which indicated the routes of the individual transit lines. The presence of physical signage was a strong hint that the citizens of Feinstein-Wu participated in abstraction at a relatively low level, and this was confirmed when he slipped on his goggles. Provided all was functioning well, they simulated the view that any ordinary citizen would have enjoyed, via neural implants and layers of augmented reality. The view that—ordinarily—prefects were denied.

There was little to choose between the two. The signage had been tidied up, some coloured threads overlaid the paving, and a few citizens wore plumage over their physical forms, concealing degrees of nakedness, or in some cased adding to it, but there was no jarring disconnect between the two views.

Dreyfus glanced at the address he had retrieved on his bracelet, comparing the residential neighbourhood to the intermediate stops on one of the transit lines. He was confident that he had it now, and even if he made a mistake, it would not be the end of the world. The cylinder's length was criss-crossed by numerous roads and transit lines.

"Prefect. May I help you?"

It was a constable, one of the yellow-garbed officials Dreyfus had been doing his best to avoid since his arrival. Dreyfus smiled tightly at the young woman who was staring impassively back at him from under her yellow-billed cap of office.

"It's all right, thank you, constable. I'm not here on business." He corrected himself. "I mean only that it's a semi-private matter, an internal matter for Panoply."

"Nonetheless, may I be of assistance?"

"Just confirm to me that I'm not about to step onto the wrong transit. I think I have the right one for Causley and Strugnell?"

She nodded peremptorily. "Yes, you have the right line. Is it Causley or Strugnell in particular that you want?"

"Causley. A dwelling in Holdenhelm—that must be a sub-district?"

"Yes, and I know it quite well." She pointed out down the tube, into the haze of detail about halfway down its length. "It's that terrace of red-roofed houses, overlooking the kidney-shaped lake. You can't miss it from the transit stop."

"Thank you. You've been most helpful."

"I'll ride with you, Prefect. I'm nearly off-shift and my own dwelling is in that direction."

"There's really no need."

"I insist. We get few enough visits from Panoply—the least I can do is make sure you're taken care of when you do arrive."

Dreyfus relented. He had not been in a hurry to reach the habitat, but the truth was, now that he was here, he just wanted to get the whole awful business over with.

They bounced and drifted to the transit and buckled into seats in an empty section. The transit accelerated away from the hub, riding the concave curve of the endcap's inner surface.

"You *are* Dreyfus, aren't you?"

"I'm just a prefect," he said, without contradicting her.

"Your name kept coming up during that affair with Devon Garlin. You set yourself against him, becoming something of a celebrity in the process."

"I suppose I only have myself to blame." He sighed, accepting the inevitable. It was true: his name had been out there as far back as the Aurora–Clockmaker affair, well before the business with Devon Garlin and the breakaway crisis. But he had hoped that recollections would have dulled in the intervening years. "May I know your name, Constable?"

"Constable Sistro."

"You said you were familiar with Holdenhelm. It's a long shot, but would you know a citizen called Hafdis Tench?"

She gave him a look of mild reproach. "There are two hundred and twenty thousand of us in Feinstein-Wu, Prefect."

"I said it was a long shot."

"Funnily enough, I have crossed paths with Hafdis Tench. She's involved in volunteer community work, something of a model citizen. Quite well known in Holdenhelm." She looked at him with quiet concern. "She's not done something wrong, has she? We try to stay on good terms with Panoply, but it only takes one bad apple."

"She's done nothing wrong. I was just hoping I might get an impression of her before we meet. If we meet. I have no idea if she'll be at home."

"And if she isn't?"

Dreyfus looked around as the transit levelled off, speeding through verdant gardens at the leading edge of the cylinder. "I'll wait. This seems like a pleasant place to be stuck for a few hours."

"I suppose you tend to see the worst face of the Glitter Band in your work, not the best."

"There's some truth in that. But I try to remember that there are millions of citizens going about decent, fulfilling lives, accepting the system, content with the choices available to them."

"And yet you always see the problem cases."

"We do."

"Doesn't that grind you down, after a while?"

Dreyfus thought of the reflection he had seen in the doors to the tactical room, like a premonition of some weary, over-burdened version of himself. He had got used to catching sight of that older man, but lately the gap between the present and the future had been narrowing. Time to consider an exit from Panoply? The possibility had been distant for years, easily dismissed from his thoughts. Lately it had moved much nearer to the foreground of his concerns, requiring acknowledgement. The constable was right: it would grind anyone down, unless they were already emotionally cauterised. Leaving came freighted with complications, though. Valery was his first consideration. She depended on the care of the Ice Mendicants for her rehabilitation. Within Panoply, Dreyfus could keep an eye on the welfare of the Mendicants and their hospice, orbiting high above the Glitter Band. Each month, when his stipend arrived, he sent as much of it as he could spare to the Mendicants, anonymously and untraceably. It was a tiny contribution to their running costs, but it helped his conscience during the intervals when he was able to visit Valery less frequently. What remained of his stipend, he put into a private fund for the day when Valery and he could live together again, beyond the care of the Mendicants. It was a pitiful amount even now, but then no one went into Panoply to make themselves wealthy.

His other consideration was Aurora, and the equally vexing question of her adversary. He had played his part in the destiny of each. Because of his deeds, public and private, he owed a debt of responsibility to both his colleagues and the wider Glitter Band. Something would have to break before he walked away from that.

"You can't grind something down to nothing," he answered, just before the silence between them became uncomfortable. "There's always something left, some residue. You cling to that."

"You become the grit, you mean. Well, I suppose there are worse things."

"Much worse." He tensed as the transit arced over a lake, slowing down for the first of its stops. It was not in his usual habit to speak so candidly to a virtual stranger, but some part of him needed to rehearse the difficult encounter ahead. "Do you know much about Hafdis Tench?" he ventured. "Her mother was also a prefect. A very good one."

The constable was silent for a moment. "You say 'was.'"

"I'm afraid I don't have the best news for her."

"What kind of news?"

Dreyfus was already regretting the overture: the latest in a series of misjudgements. "I've said too much, forgive me."

Their conversation dried up for the next two stops. As they were approaching the third, the constable unbuckled from her seat and bid him to rise. "Causley is next."

"Thank you. You've been very helpful."

"I'll walk you to the house."

"I assure you, it's really not necessary."

But she would not be discouraged, and with a rising gloom Dreyfus accepted that he had gained a guide whether he wanted one or not. They were in full gravity now, and he had to catch his breath once they had gone up a couple of levels from the stop. It was a pleasant, leafy neighbourhood: the close-packed mass of red-roofed dwellings he had seen from two and a half kilometres away turned out to be not nearly as hemmed-in as they had looked, with ample gardens and public spaces between each property.

A breeze lifted off the lake, where pastel-coloured sailing boats circled like shark fins.

They reached a dwelling: smaller than most, but perfectly comfortable in its own right. It was far roomier and airier than his own quarters in Panoply. Dreyfus wondered if it was the kind of place that might be within reach of his fund, if he kept topping it up for another decade or so.

"I'll see if she's in," he said, knocking on the door.

"I can tell you that she isn't," the constable said. She pressed past him, touching a hand to a slate-coloured panel on the door. The door clicked open and the constable went straight on inside, leaving Dreyfus standing at the threshold.

"You're Hafdis," he said belatedly, half smiling through his own confusion and embarrassment.

"For an investigator, I have to say that you're a little slow on the uptake."

"Possibly because of the completely different name you gave me."

"I didn't lie. I took the name Sistro in recognition of an older constable who took me under his wing."

"Rather than take the name of Miles Selby?"

"That man contributed some genes to me and nothing else. As soon as he felt the first brush of responsibility, he was on a lighthugger heading out-system. I've no reason to give him a second thought, and certainly no reason to commemorate him." She turned back to invite him into the hallway. "I had no problem with my mother. We got on well enough without being in each other's pockets."

"But you didn't use her name either."

"I didn't want to walk around with an obvious link to Panoply. Do you have a son or daughter out in the world? I bet they wouldn't want to be called Dreyfus, given the baggage it carries."

"Your mother kept a low profile within our organisation," Dreyfus replied, ignoring her question. "The name Tench wouldn't have meant much to the average citizen of the Glitter Band."

"Call it a precaution, then. I didn't want the risk of a connection being drawn. Nobody fears your organisation here, but that's not the same as everyone being comfortable with it."

"I understand," Dreyfus said.

They went into a lounge, small but cheerfully furnished, with one wall given over to a coloured mural showing jungle creatures against a dark, velvety background. Hafdis went to an alcove in the wall and poured out two glasses of some rose-coloured drink, setting them down on a small table between two chairs. "Please." She beckoned for Dreyfus to sit.

"I don't believe in coincidences."

"Nor did my mother."

"You knew I was here. You met me deliberately."

"We monitor all traffic approaching Feinstein-Wu, and of course we have systems to alert us when a Panoply inspection is imminent. We want to put on the best reception."

"But you didn't know it would be me."

"Not until you emerged. Then you were recognised, an alert came through to me, and I had about ten minutes to get to the hub while you were blundering around looking for the right transit."

"I'm sorry that you found out about your mother like that. It wasn't how I meant it to happen."

"I was forewarned," Hafdis said, sitting opposite him. She removed her yellow cap and scrunched her fingers through an explosion of black curls glistening lightly with perspiration. "I always worried that there would be bad news one day, and I had a feeling you'd be the one to deliver it. It was a little unkind of me to string you along like that, but I didn't think you'd speak freely if you knew who I was."

"I'd have told the truth. Your mother was as good as I said." He watched her guardedly, measuring her reactions. "I am very sorry, Hafdis. Please take as long as you need to process this news."

"You're surprised that I haven't broken down into a ball of tears?"

"Everyone handles bad news differently. There's no right or wrong way." He sipped at the drink, tasting strawberries. "And as you say, you had reason to assume my arrival might be connected with your mother."

"Are you ready to tell me happened?"

Dreyfus put down his glass. "Ingvar died in the execution of her duties. But there's a question mark over the circumstances. We're trying to get to the bottom of that right now. One of my best operatives—Sparver Bancal—is taking personal responsibility for the investigation. And, of course, I'll be fully involved."

Hafdis frowned beneath her curls, her interest sharp and unwavering.

"Why a question mark?"

"Had you been in contact with your mother lately?"

"Not for a few months. I know that must sound cold, but that's how it was. I've learned to be independent of her, almost from the time she joined your organisation. It doesn't mean we'd fallen out or anything; it's just that we had different, equally busy lives."

Dreyfus nodded, casting no stones. "I know how the time can fly."

"When we were in contact, all was well. Mother wanted to know how I was doing, and I was interested in her welfare. Of course, it tended to be a one-sided conversation. There wasn't much she could ever tell me about her work in Panoply. But I was happy if her work was going well and she was satisfied, and she was happy that I was doing well here."

"Did your mother tell you about her transfer to field duties?"

"Yes. About four years ago, wasn't it?" Hafdis looked at him with dawning concern. "Was she allowed to tell me?"

"By all means. Did your mother share the reasons for the change?"

"She didn't go into details, and I didn't press her. I gathered there'd been some internal matter that had put her on the wrong side of some people. She liked her work too much to give it up, so she decided to become a field prefect, an FP-I."

Dreyfus noted her uncommon knowledge of Panoply's organisational hierarchy. "Yes, that's it. Your mother's experience meant she could come in at that level, which meant she had a high degree of operational freedom. She could pick and choose her investigative priorities and task subordinate prefects to assist her." Dreyfus shifted in the chair, which was a little too low and narrow for his bulk. "But she didn't mention any recent difficulties? Anything that might have indicated she was under pressure?"

"No, not at all. But—as I said—she didn't talk about Panoply in any detail."

"Thank you, Hafdis."

"What happened, Dreyfus? I mean, exactly what? Because you wouldn't be asking these questions if there'd been an accident."

"It wasn't an accident." Dreyfus considered his answer carefully. "Your mother made an uncharacteristic error. She went somewhere she shouldn't have done, somewhere very dangerous for a lone prefect."

"Why?"

"That's what we need to understand. If it was a mistake, then our systems should have prevented it. If it was suicide, then it runs counter to everything I know about Ingvar. No matter how troubled she was, she would never have done anything that caused difficulties for Panoply."

"So, what does that leave you with?"

"That some people may have still wished to hurt her and this is how they did it. But that raises many questions as well. I thought that if you had been in contact recently, and she'd mentioned any concerns, that might give me a lead."

"I'm afraid there was nothing. Now that you're here, though, can you tell me what got her into trouble in the first place?"

"Not at the moment." Dreyfus toyed with his empty glass. "Perhaps later. It's still operationally sensitive. All I can say is that your mother's conduct was exemplary."

"Am I in danger as well?"

"It's not likely, given how little your mother shared with you. But I can understand any concerns you might have. Normally I'd ask the local constabulary to arrange for enhanced security measures around a person such as you, until you felt safe. But since you are already a constable, you might not feel that you gain very much by that."

"Could I come to Panoply?"

"Indeed. In fact, I recommend that you do. Not just because we can guarantee your safety, but because you'll be close to my colleagues and me, should you remember anything."

"I don't know if there'll be anything else. But I do have an ulterior motive. I want to come to Panoply because I'd like to follow in my mother's footsteps." Before Dreyfus had a chance to register concern or surprise, she pinched at the sleeve of her uniform. "This isn't some whim. I've demonstrated my commitment to public service in the Feinstein-Wu constabulary. You can review my record if you wish."

"I imagine it's excellent."

"It was only one step along the way. Mother's advice, actually. Learn the ropes in local enforcement, put in the hard hours, then apply for Panoply."

"It's one way into our recruitment selection process," Dreyfus admitted.

"And not an uncommon one, from what I can gather. I've kept myself free of implants for exactly this reason: so there's one less obstacle to joining your organisation."

He nodded, sympathetic but concerned that she was rushing into this.

"Why today of all days?"

"I would have thought that was obvious: I was never certain I wanted to come to Panoply while mother was still on active duty." She gave a bittersweet smile. "That's moot now. I don't have to worry about my being there complicating things for her, or vice versa."

Dreyfus looked down. "I see."

"At the very least allow me this chance."

"I don't want to set you up for a disappointment. You seem well suited, but there are a hundred things that can get in the way of candidacy. Even if you made it into our induction stream, that's still no guarantee that you'll graduate to prefect."

"I'm aware of that, and I don't mind."

Dreyfus smiled softly, sensing that her decision was already made, and admiring her for it. "I suppose Ingvar gave you a realistic idea of the challenges."

"I just want to serve." She leaned in forcefully. "Don't deny me this chance, Dreyfus—not today of all days."

Dreyfus sighed, beginning to push up from his seat. "All right, Hafdis —you've every right to put yourself forward. But your mother's seniority won't confer any favours. If anything, you'll have to work harder to prove yourself, just because of your name."

"It's human nature. When can I begin?"

He raised a cautioning hand. "I'll need to make a few calls. Our normal induction process only opens twice a year. There's some flexibility for exceptional cases, but it will need to be agreed by the senior prefects. In the meantime, that offer of sanctuary still stands."

"I won't need long to tie things up here. If I asked you to send a ship in fifty-two hours, would that be possible?"

"We'll make it happen. I must warn you that I'm working on a number of difficult enquiries at the moment. I'll support your application and do all that I can to help with the induction process, but there'll be a limit to how involved I can become."

"It's all right. I wasn't expecting you to mentor me."

Dreyfus prickled. She had surely meant nothing by it, but the question of mentorship, and his competence in the selection of his deputies, was far too raw in his thoughts.

"Just so long as that's understood."

"I have to ask this. Did she speak of me much?"

Dreyfus searched within himself. Sometimes a white lie made a better universe. Sometimes even the kindest lie could make things much worse, in the long run.

"Not to me. But then, she wasn't one for small talk. I only really knew her professional side."

"Yet you won't rest, will you? I can see it in your eyes. Not until you know why this happened, and who is to blame."

He glanced aside before she could meet his eyes.

"I won't."

She rose as he rose. "Thank you for taking the trouble to come in person, Dreyfus. You must be busy, so I don't take it lightly."

"It was the least I could do."

"I have one other question before you go. How exactly did my mother die? You said she went somewhere she shouldn't have gone. What happened to her?"

"We can go over that later."

Her voice firmed. "I'd rather know now."

Dreyfus steeled himself. The calm, homely nature of the room pressed in on him like a barbed vice. He wanted to be out of there, away from pleasant things and kind hospitality. He wanted to be away from Hafdis Tench, her aspiration to follow her mother and the guilt that had stuck to him like a shadow. He was in the presence of the daughter of the woman he had betrayed, and he felt it would only take one word, one slip, for the truth to reach Hafdis and lay him open and defenceless.

"A mob caught her," he answered. "They shot her, then attacked her with

61

knives, blunt instruments and their own hands. She died alone, knowing she was beyond any help. I'd love to tell you it was a good death, Hafdis."

"Did you see her afterwards?"

He met her eyes again, nodded once. "I was the one who brought her home."

CHAPTER SEVEN

The car had been moving horizontally for several minutes, speeding beneath the soil and roots of the forest above, when the tunnel split into two forks. Minty touched a control and the car veered into the rightmost tunnel, climbing suddenly. Thalia expected them to burst out into daylight at any moment, but instead the tunnel kept ascending, winding gently, the car's speed dropping as it toiled uphill. They were surely above the forest floor now, higher than their boarding point, but still there was no sign of the ascent's end. Thalia sat demurely, trusting her host that there was a point to this odd excursion.

There was, but she only understood when the car finally whirred to a halt at a dead-end terminus. They climbed out into a dry, rock-walled cave, quite unlike the humid vestibule where they had started the journey. Minty led Thalia out of the cave onto a rocky, granite-coloured prominence with daunting drops on three sides. They were far above the forest now, standing on the edge of a boulder-like mass thrusting nearly all the way to the glass ceiling that formed the inner rim of the habitat.

Minty side-skipped to the edge, arms and tail projecting for balance. The black-and-white face called encouragingly: "Come nearer the edge."

Thalia edged closer, thinking that it was easy for a small, arboreal creature to be so fearless around heights. The view was worth it, though: a panorama along a great arc of the habitat's curvature, her line of sight unobstructed until the rising floor eventually climbed beyond the ceiling. She could, in fact, see the continuation of the floor by looking directly through the ceiling glass, out across several kilometres of space and through the ceiling glass again, but it was difficult to make out more than a few hazy details, especially given the patchwork repairs that had been done to the ceiling in the wake of the attack.

"This is where it started?" she asked, looking down a long, scorched clearing racing away from the foot of the boulder.

"Yes. Cranach was above us when he started firing, just a little way beyond the window glass. His weapons penetrated the ceiling and struck the forest just beyond the base of this outcropping. Decompression start-ed immediately, through the lengthening rent in the ceiling. That doesn't mean the air left all in one go. Even as his attack neared its end—at the far end of that blackened ribbon—there was still enough pressure in this section to support combustion and firestorms."

The scar left by the attack ran more or less centrally down the length of the habitat. Nothing had survived along that ribbon, and any shoots of regrowth bursting back through the damaged forest floor were too small and distant to be seen. Perhaps there were none, this soon after the conflagration.

From the reports, Thalia knew that this entire section had been sealed off from the rest of the habitat once the pressure began to fall. There was no stopping its remaining air from venting into space. It had taken a couple of days to repair the damage, even temporarily, and only then was it possible to pump air back in and see what—if anything—had survived the firestorms and subsequent exposure to vacuum.

"How much down there is still alive?" Thalia asked, casting her eye across dismal swathes of greying, sickly-looking forest.

"Less than you might think. Those trees bordering the scar look intact from up here, but they're dead to the core, nothing to save. Up close, they're husks, slowly weathering away. Those flashes of brighter green are where some of the hardier specimens survived. When the founders seeded Valsko-Venev they used the best suppliers, buying in plants with a boosted tolerance for vacuum and radiation shock. They knew that a rupture was a possibility, though no one imagined anything on this scale."

Thalia surveyed the gloomy scene. The still-living trees were dotted here and there, but not in any abundance.

"What about the rest?"

"We're trying to save what can be saved. It's difficult work, and no one likes being in here. You don't have to be superstitious to be uncomfortable surrounded by so much death and silence. No birds. No singing. Nothing to forage. No berries."

"It's a mercy that the attack stopped when it did," Thalia said.

"You'll forgive us if we find it a bit hard to look on the bright side," Minty said. Then, stepping back from the precipice: "Well, Prefect Ng. Have you seen enough? It's a simple enough story. We were attacked and this is the outcome."

"Did my colleagues examine the damage down there?"

"They didn't feel there was any need. They already had our testimony concerning the scope of the damage, and no reason to question it."

Thalia nodded, remembering that Panoply's own report into the incident drew the bulk of its conclusions from the exterior damage to the habitat. The duration and angle of Mizler Cranach's attack had been easily reconstructed from the rift in the glass, as well as from secondary observations from other habitats and surveillance devices.

What more was there to be said?

But she had come to find something new.

"Minty—I mean Procurator-Designate—I'd like to take a closer look, from the ground up. Is that possible?"

"Of course. But you'll have to choose one end or the other. There's a station at the foot of this rock, and another close to the other end of the burn strip, but none in between, apart from scorched ground and dying trees."

"What would stop us walking the length of it?"

"Nothing," Minty said casually. "But I didn't think you'd want to go to the trouble. It's fourteen kilometres—two or three hours at your pace."

Thalia ignored the barb, however gently it had been intended. "I feel a second wind coming on."

Minty cocked its head, some curiosity sparking behind its eyes. "What are you hoping to find down there?"

"I've no idea," Thalia said truthfully. "Only that I won't find it unless I look."

Panoply's senior physician had arranged for his office to be decorated according to his singular tastes: all varnished panels, ceiling-high bookcases, macabre anatomical models and a fine assortment of brass surgical and examining instruments. The ensemble was almost certainly conjured out of quickmatter, but the effect was so detailed and lavish that Sparver could easily believe he had stepped back five or six hundred years. The fact that Mercier dressed like a man equally out of his time did nothing to allay the impression.

"I thought Thalia Ng would be on this one," he said as Sparver arrived, peering over green-tinted half-moon spectacles. "Or is it just a courtesy call?"

"It's both my case and a courtesy call, Mercier. I'd have wanted to pay my respects whoever was running the investigation. It just so happens that it's me."

"There were reasons for this?"

"Lady Jane, in her infinite wisdom, has put Thalia onto the Mercy Sphere investigation, feeding into the larger response to Mizler Cranach."

"They thought it cut a little close to home where you were concerned?"

"I just go where they tell me." Sparver shrugged easily, already fully

65

adjusted to the reality of his assignment. He had decided long ago that dwelling on professional slights, perceived or actual, was a waste of what little time he had ahead of him. "I wanted to see Ingvar. To do the decent thing, but also just in case we're missing anything."

"I must warn you that it isn't pretty." Mercier fussed with the white cravat he favoured. "I didn't know her terribly well, I confess. Do you have an opinion on the circumstances behind her death?"

"Only that nothing fits," Sparver said. "Have you finished your work?"

"No, I've barely started. I've made my initial findings, but under these circumstances a full autopsy is mandated."

"Then I'm glad I arrived now."

They went through into the examining room. It was a blazing white chamber with slide-out preservation cabinets lining three of the walls. Mercier had Tench's body on a sturdy table in the middle of the room, presently under a green sheet, with a pair of trolleys stationed around the table holding the tools of his profession. A pair of spindly medical servitors waited in the corners of the room, like skeletons hung on hooks.

Mercier looked at Sparver, waited for a nod of assent and then lifted away the top part of the sheet, revealing Tench's head and shoulders. Sparver stared dispassionately. He joked about all baseline humans looking the same to him—mirroring the remark that was usually directed against hyperpigs—but the truth was that he was perfectly capable of recognising hundreds of individuals. He knew Tench as well as anyone. They had often glared at each other across the conference table in the tactical room.

She had nothing against his kind, he believed. She just happened to consider that he had been promoted too hastily, his errors overlooked.

He shrugged again, just for himself this time. Maybe there was some truth in that. But then if you took too long to promote hyperpigs, they tended to die waiting.

He recognised Tench, but only because he had been expecting to see her. If he had come to her cold, he was not sure he would have been able to see past the lacerations, the swellings and contusions, and what looked like areas of burned or at least horribly abraded skin. Her skull had been badly smashed.

"I'm not even going to ask if there's anything we can save her by trawl," Sparver stated.

"You'd be right not to. It's a hopeless case. Even if Dreyfus had got to her at once and arranged for immediate neuropreservation measures..."

"It would still be touch and go," he said, finishing Mercier's remark for him. "None of this is on Dreyfus. The old man did well to avoid an all-out

66

bloodbath. That we got back anything resembling a body is a bonus."

"She *was* trawled, just to be certain. There were no recoverable structures. Demikhov ran an independent test and came to the same conclusion."

Demikhov was the medical section's leading expert in advanced neuro-preservation measures. If he declared Tench was beyond salvation, then Sparver needed no further confirmation.

"Too bad someone decided prefects shouldn't have implants, or we'd have another thread to pull on."

"And too bad the Common Articles said she couldn't go in there with the proper means to defend herself, or we wouldn't be looking at a corpse. Those little toy snakes of yours don't count, I'm afraid."

"I must invite you along to whiphound induction training someday," Sparver said. "Then you'd have a different opinion of what these toys can do. Speaking of which—I'd like to see what the whiphound recorded. If we can't access her memories, the whiphound's continuous data-logging is the next best thing."

"You'll need to talk to someone else. I don't have the whiphound."

"All right, who has her equipment? Did she come to you clothed or naked?"

"Clothed. And I have her equipment. But not the whiphound. Do you want to pay your respects? I'll see you back in my office, together with the evidence docket for her possessions."

"Thank you, Mercier. Just give me a moment."

Sparver waited until he was alone. He moved around to the other side of the table, his hands behind his back, his head bowed. He felt small in the room, a child compared to the table and the woman on it.

He spoke, his voice echoing off the white walls and the freezer compartments.

"We didn't always see eye to eye, Tench. But I don't think you did this to yourself. If it was a mistake, I'll make damned sure they don't pin it on you. An error shouldn't even have been possible. If it turns out it was, then it's not your fault our systems weren't watertight. If it wasn't a mistake, then it was a crime—and I don't believe for one second it was *your* crime. I'll get them, Tench. That's my pledge. Maybe you were right and they put this rank on me too soon. But I'll earn it for you. You were one of us, and I won't let this slide."

He took the liberty of raising the sheet back over her face.

"Sleep well, Tench. You did good."

Mercier was waiting for him back in his office, seated in an antique chair with a desk drawer cradled between his hands.

"This is what came to me, Sparver. I kept everything together in one place, all already tagged with an evidential docket. The details are on that compad by my desk."

Sparver picked up the compad, glancing at the docket.

"You said she came dressed."

"She did. But once I'd conducted a preliminary examination her Panoply garments were removed and sent away for detailed forensic analysis. The rest, they left with me." He rattled the drawer slightly. "Goggles, bracelet, throat comms, belt, utility tools, whiphound holder. But no whiphound."

"Makes no sense. That whiphound wouldn't have left her side if she was in trouble."

"Well, I don't have it. No explanation was offered—but then I didn't go looking for one." He favoured Sparver with an intent, birdlike stare. "Do you think it's odd?"

Sparver said nothing.

Sister Catherine was waiting for Dreyfus when he arrived at Hospice Idlewild, having travelled there directly after leaving Hafdis Tench. He followed her along one of the ambling paths, wandering through the green and hilly core of the world, watching his footing when the path steepened or veered close to a drop, of which there was no shortage.

"One day, Dreyfus, you will astonish us all by announcing a visit in advance, and then keeping that appointment. But not today." The severe-faced Mendicant eyed him critically. "What prompted it this time, besides a sudden spasm of guilt?"

"Need it be more than that?" Dreyfus asked, flashing back to his conversation with Hafdis.

"The more progress we make with your wife, the more hesitant you seem to be about seeing her." Sister Catherine jabbed her walking stick ahead of her, planting it in the muddy trail with so much deliberation and forcefulness that Dreyfus imagining her skewering him. "It pains her. Her sense of language may have been shattered, but she is perfectly conscious of the passage of time. Careful. The ground is very slippery here."

There were no large concentrations of buildings in the habitat, only hamlet-sized gatherings linked by pleasantly winding paths and modest, roughly surfaced roads. The structures were rarely large, usually white-painted, and nestled deep into nooks and crannies in the rambling, green landscape, where copses and woods lined meandering riverbanks that wove their way up steepening inclines until they threaded overhead, silvery tracts spanning the heavens. Little bridges and pagodas were dotted here and there, placed as much for harmony as function. Prominences of rock jagged down from above and rainbows shimmered out of mist-wreathed waterfalls that were as apt to fall upwards as downwards.

"The closer she comes to being whole again," Dreyfus said, needing to catch his breath as he struggled to keep up with the indomitable Mendicant, "the more I fear it will all come apart again. It's not that I don't want to see her every day. It's that I feel as if I'm watching such a delicate process that my own involvement might cause it to go wrong."

"Piffle." She strode on, recklessly oblivious to the condition of the ground. "You may tell yourself that, Dreyfus, but even one as blinkered to your own faults as you would surely know that lie serves no one but yourself."

He had no energy for an argument. "All right, it's a lie. What would you like me to say, Sister? I'm here, aren't I?"

"What you fear," she said, halting suddenly and jerking the stick at him in a stooped, accusatory posture, "is the accommodation you might need to make to meet Valery halfway. The idea that change and growth has to come from within you, not just your wife."

Dreyfus tested her with a faint smile. It was comforting, this ritual dance of theirs. Sister Catherine always needed to needle and belittle him before allowing a little glimmer of warmth to break through.

"Perhaps I need time, too."

"As if you had enough of it to squander. These last few years have taken their toll, Dreyfus. We can all see it in you. There must come a point when you're too old and tired to do your job?"

He planted his foot badly and felt a twinge in his knee.

"Several times a day. I prefer to look on it as the price of experience."

She sniffed doubtfully. "Well, as you say: you're here now, so we must make the best of you. The neurolinguistic implants have meshed well." She looked back, still striding with improbable youthful energy. "I know you had your doubts, Tom, but I think you will be satisfied that it was the right choice."

There it was: the subtle modulation from Dreyfus to Tom, the frost breaking slightly.

"Implants hurt her in the first place. You can understand my reservations."

"There isn't a tool that can't hurt as well as mend. It's only mending that concerns us in Idlewild."

"She couldn't be in kinder hands. I know that, and I'm grateful."

"Do you wish to see her?"

"Of course. I'm here, aren't I?"

"I wondered if that also had something to do with Mercy Sphere, because of our connection to that facility."

"We can talk about that later," he said, acknowledging that the reason for his visit was two-pronged. "I'd like to see Valery first."

"She should be with Sebastien, if she isn't helping out in the gardens." She beckoned him on, then frowned slightly as something snagged her attention. "There's something wrong with you, isn't there, besides the normal wear and tear? I can see it in your walk. Have you recently hurt your arm?"

"Occupational injury," Dreyfus said, marvelling at her perspicacity. "It's nothing."

"I advise that you take better care of yourself, Tom. If you don't, who will be there for Valery?"

"You will be."

"We shall," she agreed. "Until someone decides they don't like the idea of us and burns us alive in our beds."

CHAPTER EIGHT

Thalia's feet crunched on a bed of blackened, lifeless vegetation. The grey-green trees formed a spectral honour guard either side of the twenty-metre-wide tract. From this low vantage, Thalia couldn't see any of the living specimens at all; they were too far away and too few in number.

It was desolate, and the air reeked of decay and ashes.

Thalia slowed, the full enormity of what had happened here hitting her. Her knees buckled. Without intending to she sank to the ground, paralysed by horror. She thought of the arboreal music she had heard earlier, the singing of the family group, and imagined those whoops and swoons transmuting to screams of panic and pain.

Ninety seconds. The full duration of Mizler's attack. Ample time for the creatures here to understand what was befalling them, and in the same instant of grim comprehension know their hopes for survival were remote. And to know there was a hard death coming their way. Death under the column of annihilation scything down from the ceiling, death in the firestorms it unleashed, death as the gale of escaping air uprooted smaller trees and tore hapless dwellers out of the larger ones, flinging them carelessly into the hot howling air, toward that horrid, lengthening maw in the sky and the glittering blackness beyond.

It had gone on longer than ninety seconds, though. That was just the interval when his weapons were active, before his ship was destroyed. The consequences of his attack had played out over many more minutes as the vast bulkheads sealed off this part of the habitat and allowed its air to bleed out into vacuum. And throughout those harrowing minutes there were still creatures clinging onto life. All but a few—those close enough to the bulkheads to scamper through emergency doors—had perished.

Thalia stood up. She had not retched in Mercy Sphere, although she had come close. She would not retch here, though part of her craved that release—as if there would be less of the world's evil inside her and more of it on the outside, where it belonged.

71

Minty supported her as best the little lemur-like being was able to. "It's all right. You wouldn't be human, and we wouldn't be...humanoid, if we didn't empathise."

"They never saw this? My colleagues?"

"Not from down here."

Thalia wiped at her mouth. "They should have. It makes a difference."

"They thought they had all the evidence they needed."

Thalia indicated that she was all right to walk now. Minty went ahead, but not with the bounding enthusiasm of before. It was as if even her host, familiar with this place, felt an obligation to tread respectfully.

"Something I don't remember in the report," Thalia said. "Why wasn't the cutter shot out of the sky the instant it started the attack? It would still have been very bad, I know, but at least the destruction would have been confined to a much smaller area."

"The fires might have been contained, but the air would still have leaked out," Minty responded. "But you are right: if it was just one hole in the ceiling, there probably would have been time to get a lot of the people to safety before the sector had to be sealed. It took the time it did for a reason, though."

"Please, go on."

"We couldn't just shoot down the ship, not without going through a whole series of votes. If the threat had been something as clear-cut as a piece of debris hurtling toward us, or even an out-of-control cargo carrier, there'd have been no question of an immediate response. This was a ship from Panoply, though."

Thalia nodded solemnly. "You were concerned about the consequences."

"It went to an immediate binding vote. It still took two rounds to satisfy a narrow majority that we had no option but to destroy your ship. Can you imagine what that was like? One minute we're enjoying another lazy day in the trees, the next we're debating whether to risk bringing down the severest possible punishment on our little world."

"It was an awful position to be in."

"Some of us believed that your operative had to be acting in our best interests, even if it looked the exact opposite of that. *That's* how ingrained our trust of Panoply is—or rather was, until that day."

"I don't blame you or anyone here for losing faith in our organisation," Thalia said. "I want to be part of the process of rebuilding that faith."

"I'll indulge you," Minty replied. "Many of us wouldn't."

They walked until the boulder the transit car had emerged from began to be lost out of sight beyond the curve of the habitat. Once it was gone, Thalia had no real reference to judge how far they had come, or how much further they had to go. She just kept walking, the black carpet beneath her feet seldom varying, the deathly border of trees an unchanging parade of greying decay.

Perhaps it was a waste of time, examining the crime from this perspective. Perhaps it would teach her nothing that was not already in the earlier documents. At the very least, though, she had gained a visceral sense of the destruction, which was impossible from a more distant, detached vantage. The smell alone was enough for that.

"For the record," Minty said after a long silence, "we have never condoned the violence that followed this incident. We've nothing against hyperpigs, then or now. They're welcome to visit. Even welcome to join us, if they submit to the mandatory adaptations."

"Your pronouncements made it clear that you considered this the act of a lone individual, not someone speaking for all the hyperpigs. It was a thoughtful overture."

"But too late to stop the violence that was already breaking out. Some humans decided to retaliate against the pigs on our behalf, as if we needed a helping hand to settle our grievance."

"And then some militant pigs took that as an incentive to strike back with even more violence than was used here." Thalia shook her head resignedly. "Bad apples in every barrel, Minty, pig and human alike. Lemur too, I imagine. You did your best to de-escalate things, though. It's just a pity it wasn't enough." She slowed, trudging on heavy legs, hoping that the end would soon be in sight. "Do you think another statement might help? I'm not saying the hotheads will pay much heed, but the saner voices might appreciate a reiteration of your earlier position. It might lower the temperature a little."

"What needed to be said was said, Prefect. I'm afraid nothing more would be gained by repeating the same sentiments." Minty deliberated. "And our tolerance only goes so far, you know. It *was* a premeditated attack against us, purely because of the decisions of distant ancestors whose founding sins we presumably still carry. There are many among us who no longer venerate those founders, and who would quite happily see those statues toppled. But that's not the same as saying we have to answer for their crimes with our own blood. Pick at this wound, you might find some of us less inclined to take a conciliatory stance."

"I just thought I'd mention it."

"Don't feel too bad about it, Prefect Ng. I like you and I can tell you've come here with good intentions. You just need a dose of realism about the limits of forgiveness." Minty bounded on with renewed purpose and clapped its paws. "At last, the end is in sight! Only a few kilometres to go now, and then I can find you some of those berries I promised."

Thalia saw what her host meant. The blackened strip stretched away from her, curving upward, before fizzling out indeterminately. Beyond was a thicker stand of vegetation, still deathly, and then the soaring wall of the bulkhead mechanism, still closed off even though pressure had been restored to this sector.

Thalia stopped. She looked up at the line in the ceiling glass where the repairs had been made, then back down at the burn zone. The new material above formed a much wider strip than the blackened ground, but that was understandable given the attack's effect on the fragile material of the ceiling. The repaired strip was perfectly straight, all the way up to the end of the damage.

Just before it became hard to trace, though, the scorched ground seemed to kink to the right.

"Prefect?"

Thalia chose her words carefully, not wishing to say something foolish. "Procurator-Designate. Am I correct in noting a deviation, near the end of the burn?"

"Yes. I wouldn't make too much of it, though. Think of how far we've walked, compared to that last little kink at the end. It represents the last few seconds of his attack, if that."

"All right." Thalia stayed still, levelling a hand over her eyes to shade the glare from the clean new ceiling panels. "What does it mean, though? Why would it kink off like that?"

"Simple," Minty said. "That's when we finally voted to allow our guns to fire. Until then, Mizler Cranach was attacking us with impunity. In the last few instants, though, the habitat's defences began to strike back. The destruction of his ship was rapid, but not instantaneous."

Thalia half-nodded. "So you're saying your guns began to mess up his aim, just before the cutter exploded?"

"In a nutshell."

Thalia visualised Cranach's little ship being at the focus of the anti-collision weapons dotted around the torus. With the concentration of fire coming from those emplacements, it was no wonder that the cutter had jiggled around in its final moments, losing control of its own armaments.

"I've reviewed the visual records of the attack," Thalia said. "But I don't think I ever noticed that."

"A subtle detail, unimportant in the larger scene."

"Perhaps." Thalia was wondering what else she might have missed, if that detail had escaped her attention. Maybe nothing of consequence. Maybe much more than nothing.

Minty gave her a sidelong look.

"What are you thinking?"

"That I've not been nearly thorough enough. Thank you. This has been…helpful. You've been most generous with your time."

Minty gestured onward. "Come. It's not far to the bulkhead, and there are some very sweet berries on the other side. Provided those greedy Smudge-Tails haven't already stuffed their cheek pouches."

"Hello, Tom." Valery smiled at him, only the slightest strain betraying the effort of speaking. "It is…I *am*…happy. To *seeing* you. To *be* seeing you."

He took her hand, squeezing gently. "You are a wonder. They told me there had been good progress, but I didn't dare raise my hopes."

Valery frowned slightly, then glanced at Brother Sebastien for guidance.

"Keep your constructions simple for now," the Mendicant whispered. "It doesn't mean that you're treating her like a child, only that you're making allowances for these new pathways."

Valery had given consent for the neurolinguistic implants, in the terms available to her. Dreyfus, concerned that she might not fully understand what was being proposed, had advocated a more cautious line, continuing with the existing therapies. It had taken months to finally convince him, and then he had agreed only in the most grudging way. He could not block consent, but he was still unconvinced that it was anything but a reckless gamble, playing with the very fire that had scorched her in the first place.

It had worked. It was anything but an overnight cure, but the implants—spreading and consolidating through areas of damaged tissue, forming new functional connections—had flung the gates wide open. Valery's verbal powers improved month by month, with the developmental rapidity of a child acquiring language for the first time. Effortlessly, voraciously.

Dreyfus found it glorious and frightening. His fears built a wall, a defence in case Valery tumbled all the way back to the start. He knew it was happening and still he could not stop himself. He had always had the excuse of his work when he needed a reason to delay a visit, but now he fell back on it with increasing regularity. Let the contributions from his stipend stand in place of his visits. His absences had not gone unnoticed. The unsparing Sister Catherine had been right to scold him for it.

And he vowed now that he would be a better husband. There had been no setbacks since the implants went in, only progress. It was time to let his concerns go, time to be grateful, time to admit that his anxieties had been groundless, nothing more than the reflex pessimism of a policeman who had seen too many good things go wrong.

He smiled awkwardly, still holding her hand. "You are getting better."

"Yes," Valery affirmed, her smile deepening. "Yes. Getting better. Each day. Learning words, joining words." She straightened herself, as if stepping up to a podium. "I am...Valery Dreyfus. My mind was...damaged. But I am getting better now."

"You are Valery Dreyfus!" He beamed back at her.

"You are...Tom Dreyfus. Tom Dreyfus...of Panoply. We are husband...and wife."

"I love you very much," Dreyfus said.

She echoed him back. "I love you...much. *Very* much." She cast her eyes around, looking for something to remark on. "The wall is...white. Behind is green. There is...river. *A* river. We walk by river."

"Do you?"

"It's a question," Sebastien interjected. "She would like you to know if you'd like to walk with her, along the river."

Dreyfus laughed out his joy. "Of course!" Then, to Valery: "We'll walk!"

"To the bridge," she said. "The bridge is red. Not far. Then back."

"That's all right, isn't it?" Dreyfus asked the Mendicant.

"It's more than all right. And you can't go wrong on that path. Follow it over the red bridge, then back along through those trees behind the clinic. You'll cross back over a culvert, then come out by the herb garden."

Dreyfus felt anxious, like a child handed some unwieldy responsibility. "You'll wait for us here?"

"Yes, but take as long as you need. I have some repairs to do."

Dreyfus was still holding her hand as they stood from the table. Tentatively, like young lovers, they set off down the path away from the clinic. It swept them into trees, the cover thickening with each step, and within a minute or so they had lost all sight of the whitewashed buildings. Leaves and branches closed overhead, creating a lilac-shadowed gloom that Dreyfus found pleasant rather than oppressive. He was taking a stroll through the woods with his wife. He wished he had come sooner, but at least he was here now.

"I know it is still hard for you," he said. "So say as much or as little as you wish. Even if you say nothing else today, I am still impossibly happy. You asked me if I wanted to take a walk by the river, to the red bridge and back!"

She walked on silently for a few paces, her hand tightening and untightening in his in rhythm with their footsteps. Then said: "I rather did, didn't I, Dreyfus."

76

Something jammed inside him, like a gear wheel with a broken tooth. He stopped, the sweat on his hand chilling in her grip.

"No."

She turned to face him. "It's all right. I'm just using her as a door. I haven't taken over her brain or anything ghastly like that." She touched a finger to her lips, teasingly. "Although, it is tempting..."

"Get out of her."

"Oh, Dreyfus, must we? Must we *always* get off on the wrong foot? You know it makes much more sense when we get along amicably, like the old friends that we are."

CHAPTER NINE

Thalia and Minty sat a little way off the ground, in the smooth, bowl-like cleft of a tree that was still growing, still straining powerfully toward the unbroken, unmarred ceiling glass. The leaves above them shimmered and rustled in a faint, calming breeze. Birds called out from the upper reaches, occasionally exploding into flight in a riot of colour and movement. Thalia was enchanted. It was obviously one of Minty's favourite spots to warm its fur, doze and catch up on berries. Thalia felt as if she had been let in on a small but delicious secret, betokening the delicate beginnings of trust.

It helped that she was nearly in tears at the fierce green beauty of it all. They had come through a hatch in the lower part of the bulkhead, into the next sector of the habitat. Immediately she had been assaulted by the colours, sounds and smells of abundant life, a message through the senses to some primal core of her being. As joyous and overwhelming as it was, it only sharpened her appreciation for what had been lost on the other side of the bulkhead. It was impossible to experience grief and bereavement for something as abstract as a landscape and its lost inhabitants, people she had never known.

Impossible, but for the welter of feelings that proved otherwise.

"I'm sorry," she kept saying, apologising for apologising. "I saw it. I thought I understood it. That wasn't enough. Now I know."

While Thalia rested her limbs after the long trek from the base of the boulder, Minty had scampered off for a few minutes and come back with a taster menu of locally sourced produce. It was spread around the pair of them, organised into dark clusters of a dozen or so berries, all of which looked suspiciously alike.

"These are sour to taste, but bring on a mild euphoria. Try one or two, but not more than five. These...you'll notice the different shade of scarlet? These are good for promoting deep, dreamless sleep. These purple-orange ones are a known aphrodisiac, but quite palatable in small amounts. You should chew on this leaf after sampling these—it will help with digestion. These black ones, with a green lustre, are flavoursome but not overly nutritious. Children like them. These dark grey ones, with the waxy skin—these are quite bland everywhere else in Valsko-Venev, but for some reason quite pleasantly edible in just this one spot, if you can ignore the woody notes and the acid finish. It must have something to do with the soil..."

Thalia was feeling indebted to Minty so she tried a berry or two from each assortment, commenting diplomatically on each. For an idle moment, content not to be thinking about death and destruction, she thought of asking her host if it ever wanted more from life than the limited palette of experience on offer in Valsko-Venev. Wisely she demurred. To ask that of Minty would have been futile and insulting. It had arrived at this state of being through conscious design, rejecting all but the most necessary of trappings. To Minty, it was sufficient by definition.

One or other of the berries began to have a lulling effect on Thalia. It no longer seemed as urgent for her to be on her way back to Panoply, back to the concerns of the outside world. All that could wait. It was much better to be here amid the trees, the birds and the distant singing of other family groups. They were calling from near and afar, whooping and hollering in ways that stirred ancient arboreal memories. She had been a tree-creature once, not too many moments ago by the galaxy's reckoning.

"I think I should be going," Thalia said, before she forgot she had any sort of life beyond this drowsy present.

"Of course. Work to be done, no doubt." Minty fished a translucent container out of one of its pockets. It was a manufactured thing, oddly out of place. "I think you liked these the best, didn't you?" Minty jammed a quantity of berries into the container, then flicked the stopper tight. "You have good taste, for a baseline. Go easy on them, though, until you've built up a tolerance."

"Thank you." Thalia took them. She had no intention of doing anything with the berries besides disposing of them at the earliest opportunity, but she knew better than to refuse a gift.

They found the nearest entrance to the underground system and Minty rode with Thalia back to the same tree trunk where she had first emerged from her ship.

"You saw something in that kink, but you won't say what it is."

"That's because I'm not sure what to make of it. It could be as you say, but there's another possibility I can't dismiss." Thalia hesitated, knowing how sensitive her host was likely to be to any alteration in the narrative surrounding Mizler Cranach. "It could have been deliberate, a change of heart."

"A bit late for remorse, ninety seconds into a killing spree."

"I need to explore all the angles. Literally, in this case. We've got a lot of recordings showing the last few seconds of Mizler Cranach's life, but I'm not sure anyone's looked into them carefully enough to see the explanation for that kink."

"And you will."

"I'll look. It doesn't mean I'll find anything."

Minty nodded solemnly. "Mind how you go, then."

Thalia felt she had to say something. "Whatever I find here, Procurator-Designate, it won't diminish the severity of the crime done to you. No matter what my enquiries turn up, this remains a crime. You have my word that I won't rest until justice is served."

Minty sighed. "I believe you. Please remember what you have just said, is all I ask. We've heard many fine words in the moment."

"I won't forget." And Thalia patted the gift of berries. "Nor your kindness."

"You'll be back, once you develop a taste for those. And I still have to show you what real singing sounds like. Give me ample warning next time, and I'll call on the Sun-Baskers to put the old choral line back together..."

They made their farewells. Thalia got back in the elevator that took her the short distance to her cutter, still clamped on the outside of the rim. On her way, the berries began to reassert their presence in her system. She began to feel dizzy and disassociated, a limp-limbed puppet of herself. That pleasant feeling she had experienced in the tree had just been the first tranche of chemicals metabolising; now she was in the python-coils of a stranger, more potent second wave, and all in the interests of human–posthuman relations.

Her bracelet started chiming. She glanced down through swimming eyes. It was reporting toxins in her bloodstream, toxins it was struggling to identify and neutralise fast enough to prevent Thalia being overwhelmed by their effects.

"Seek Heavy Medical intervention," the bracelet advised with a brittle cheerfulness.

Thalia made it to her cutter. She buckled in, undocked and set the automatic return control for Panoply. After that, she remembered very little. Then there came a point where she was looking down on her own unconscious form, slumped and drooling, as Thyssen and two other dock technicians swarmed in around her and began to loosen her restraints.

"Medical," Thyssen said, lifting her bracelet to peer at the diagnostic readout. "Ng's ingested something."

"Is she dead?"

"Damn near, if this is anything to go by." Thyssen raised his voice further. "Medical!"

Her consciousness remained disassociated from her body. She knew that she was not really outside herself, but the impression was still disarmingly vivid, synthesised by some malfunctioning part of her brain that had lost its spatial anchor. *I took too many berries*, she tried to say, willing the puppet to move its lips. *I took too many berries, and no one warned me not to.*

Someone really ought to have warned her.

"Got a pulse," a figure said, and she felt herself being rapidly and unceremoniously sucked back into her skull. She ascended through kelpy layers of headache and nausea, toward the pale wavering light of normal consciousness. One of the medics was close to her, a busy blur in vivid, luminous green. The green triggered an avalanche of associations: trees, grass, bushes, berries, light-headedness.

"I never want to see green again," she slurred, as the medics hauled her out of the cutter.

Dreyfus addressed his wife, and the monster staring at him through her eyes.

"Hurt a hair on her head, and I'll destroy you."

"Idle threats really don't become you," Aurora replied companionably. "If you could have destroyed me, you would have. Or at least, if you knew a way to do it without advantaging the Clockmaker. Ah! But you don't know how to do that, do you?"

He tried to snatch his hand from her fingers but she would not allow it.

"Is Valery aware of this?"

She looked aghast. "What do you think I am? I'm holding her at a reduced level of consciousness, just while we have this little catch-up."

"Whose idea was it to go for a walk?"

"Hers entirely, and shame on your for thinking otherwise! I just happened to see my moment. I knew it would come along sooner or later. If she hadn't suggested a walk, I'd have come up with a reason to get rid of that tiresome Sebastien."

"He does good."

"Yes, and doesn't he know it, the pious, self-satisfied prig." Her tone became commanding. "Walk on, Dreyfus. We're still not quite out of earshot of the buildings, and I don't want you to have to explain this conversation later."

"Get out of my wife."

"You were right to be concerned about those implants," she said, with a cheerful disregard. "Always a double-edged sword. Yes, they've helped her recover the faculty of language to a quite impressive degree. But they've also given me another way to reach you." She cupped a hand to her mouth. "Oopsie!"

"Did you kill Tench?"

"Oh, you silly boy. Why would I have killed her if she was acting in my interests? She helped us both four years ago. Wouldn't it have been churlish—even for me—to turn against her now?"

"If you didn't kill her, who did?"

"Draw the obvious conclusions. She was likely pursuing a lead related to the reactivation of Catopsis. Perhaps she rattled the wrong chains and had to be dealt with before she got any closer to the truth." She pointed ahead through a lighter part of the woods, where the artificial sunlight broke through the canopy to dapple the floor. "There's that lovely red bridge! Oh, isn't it simply charming?"

"Whatever you think is happening, you're wrong about Catopsis. Every single individual related to that program was reprimanded and assigned to other duties. Grigor Bacchus is broken, a prefect in name only. There's no way he, or any of them, could coordinate well enough to restart a blacklisted program."

"Then you'll need to look further afield. Someone's doing it, Dreyfus. Even my psychotic dolt of an adversary must be aware that his moves are being tracked." She pinned him with a stare. "Oh. What's that look, exactly? Have you had a visit?"

Dreyfus shrugged. He saw no advantage in lying. "The Clockmaker came to me and expressed very similar concerns."

"And what did he ask of you?"

"That I investigate and try to get it shut down. He proved his seriousness by disappearing one of my witnesses from Necropolis."

"How crass of him. That's where we differ, you see. I can be firm, but I'd never be cruel, at least not merely for the sake of it. That said, you now have even more of an incentive to help me." She made Valery stop suddenly, stiffening from head to toe, her head thrust back at an unnatural angle. "These implants have been a godsend, haven't they? It would be such a setback if something happened with them, something unexpected and untoward." Valery's eyes rolled back in their sockets, eyelids fluttering and pupils dancing manically. Her body convulsed. She began to make choking sounds, before they cut off abruptly. "Yes, such a setback."

"I always wondered if there might be a tiny bit of humanity left in you," Dreyfus said. "Now I know."

"Oh, don't be so grumpy." Aurora released Valery from the seizure, but her control was still absolute. She wiped foam from her lips. "I wouldn't hurt the poor woman. She was a victim of the Clockmaker, after all. The thing that hurt her would like to hurt me as well. Walking in her, seeing the world through her eyes—it reminds me of being human again. Being flesh and blood, a girl instead of a god. I might almost say I *feel* for her."

"So get out of her."

"I will—for now. But let's keep this arrangement as a reminder of your obligations to me, Dreyfus. A little carrot to keep you on the straight and narrow. Or a stick. Which is it?"

"I'll kill you one day."

She made a regretful, wincing face. "I've touched a nerve, haven't I? Well, good: I needed your attention. Go about your work, Dreyfus. Do as you will. But you'll be sharing any developments with me. And if I turn up anything useful, I'll be sharing the news with you." She skipped along the wooded trail. "Gosh, won't it be fun? The two of us, working the same case? Two unlikely allies, pitched against the forces of darkness?"

"You've made a big gamble."

She had reached the red bridge. She strode out onto its planked deck and leaned over the painted wooden rail, surveying the slow-running waters beneath.

"Have I?"

"Whoever it is behind this new Catopsis, maybe I'll want to work with them instead of shutting them down."

"What if it turns out that they murdered Tench?"

"I'd get to them in time."

A bush overhung the bridge, laden with petals. She made Valery pluck petals and drop them into the water, watching as they were swept under the bridge.

"Try to grasp what is at stake here, Dreyfus. I know it's a lot for you, but it would be helpful if you at least made the effort."

He considered his answer, knowing she had him in a bind, knowing he would accept any arrangement while Valery was threatened. "Do something for me in return, besides not hurting my wife."

"Well, of course—just say the word."

"You haunt the networks. Somewhere out there, someone is planning the next escalation after the Mercy Sphere attack. You can help Panoply by giving us advance warning of any reprisal."

"Very well, you have yourself a deal. Do this for me—and for Valery—and I'll keep my ear pinned to the ground."

"We're not making a deal here, Aurora. We're just refining your black-mail terms."

"So long as the ends are achieved, I don't mind what you call it." She tore off another petal and let it drift down to the water. "Look, it's been lovely catching up, but I should probably let you have Valery back now. I'm sure she's got lots to talk about. See the dog run! See the tree! The hours will just fly by with such sparkling companionship."

"I'd take a second with her, damaged as she is, over an eternity with you."

"We'll speak, Dreyfus. Enjoy the rest of your walk."

Valery slumped, falling back from the rail. He caught her before she hit the bridge's deck, grunting as his shoulder flared up again. Then she was in his arms, her eyes open but glazed. They widened, registering confusion and alarm.

"It's all right," he said soothingly. "You just had a funny turn. Let's get you off the bridge." He nodded at a rustic bench set by the trail on the other side of the river. "We'll sit there for a while."

"A bad thing," she mumbled.

He pressed his face close to hers as they shuffled along the bridge, Dreyfus still taking most of her weight. "Just a turn," he emphasised.

"No," she answered, her voice druggy. "Not...not a turn. A bad thing came. A bad thing in me."

Dreyfus was out of breath by the time he eased her down onto the bench. He slumped next to her, squeezing her hand so tightly that the bones nearly popped. "It's gone," he said, desperately wishing it to be true. "Whatever it was, it's gone. You're all right now."

It was a lie driven by love, but it still twisted a knife into him.

CHAPTER TEN

By the time Sparver came to her quarters, Thalia was feeling brittle rather than nauseous. Mercier had given her a once-over and concluded she needed rest and fluids while her brain and blood chemistry returned to some sort of equilibrium.

Now Thalia sat half in and half out of her bed, a blanket over her legs, a dragon-patterned gown prickling her skin where she was still sweating out the last traces of poison.

She had conjured a chair for Sparver and offered him tea from the pot she had already brewed. It was pungent, laced with honey and ginger, and Sparver took only a sip from his bowl before admitting that it was too sweet for his pig-palate.

"Minty meant well," she was telling him. "That's the worst thing. I wouldn't feel half so bad if someone had actually *tried* to poison me."

"How do you know it wasn't intentional?"

"There are many easier ways to get a prefect out of your hair than feeding them toxic berries. Minty just underestimated my tolerance to something the lemurs wouldn't think twice about."

He considered this. "Although if berries are your only weapon...Did you learn anything, to make this whole trip worthwhile?"

"I don't know. Maybe." It was still an effort, thinking clearly and organising her impressions from the visit. "At least, there's something I want to look into in more detail. Can I borrow your compad?"

"No, because there's a good reason Mercier forbid you to bring one back to your room. Probably so you'd actually get some rest. What was it you wanted?"

"I want to examine all the recordings we have of Mizler's last few moments."

"Then I'll spare you the trouble. There are hundreds, and they've all been studied."

"True, but that doesn't mean we didn't all miss something. There's a detail I picked up when I was with Minty…" She shuddered. "Oh, God, I'm thinking of berries again."

"The horror. What was this detail?"

"If it's all right with you, I'd rather not say until I've had a look at those recordings. I don't want to look foolish if it turns out to be nothing."

"You could never look foolish, Thal. If it helps, I'm going out on a limb of my own. For some reason Tench's whiphound wasn't with her personal effects."

She saw her own sweaty, frowning face reflected back up at her from the tea in the cup between her hands.

"Everything else was?"

"Yes, all accounted for."

"That is odd. Someone will know where it is, surely? Have you raised this with Dreyfus?"

"I will, once he gets back from Hospice Idlewild."

Thalia nodded solemnly, knowing exactly what such a visit entailed. "That poor man. And poor Valery. If only he spoke about it with us from time to time, it might help him."

"Not exactly the old man's way. Still, I gather there's progress, in a small way."

"I hope so, for both of them." She pushed a lock of damp hair off her forehead. "All of this because we can't just…be sensible. The Clockmaker, Aurora, now this spate of attacks. We've got it all on a plate, haven't we? Everything we need to live happily. So why do we keep doing such a bad job of it?"

"You're seeing the downside because you just came back from the scene of a mass murder," he diagnosed expertly. "Not exactly guaranteed to put a spring in anyone's step. A few days back in the saddle, you'll be your usual self again."

Thalia's mind replayed the mournful music she had heard coming in from the singing families in faraway trees.

"I'm not saying I'd want to live that way, but they didn't deserve that attack. They're innocent little creatures."

"Who got to gambol around in trees and eat berries because someone back in their ancestry made a lot of money out of pigs." He scratched at the upturned plane of his nose. "There's a snake in every Eden, Thal. Sometimes it comes back to bite. I'm not saying I *approve* of what happened…"

"But what goes around comes around?"

"Innocence is rarely more than skin-deep. You'll tread carefully with them, won't you? They've got a nice little victim-narrative going on, and they're not going to take too kindly to someone complicating that picture. If that's what you're planning."

"I'm like you with that whiphound. Refusing to drop a bone."

Sparver nodded. "I suppose we should blame Dreyfus for making us what we are."

"I wouldn't want it any other way. He mentored us well and I'm sure you and I did nearly as good a job with our mentees, no matter what the world thinks of Mizler and Ingvar now."

Sparver patted the side of her bed and rose to his feet. Detecting his intention to leave, the conjured chair slumped back into the floor. "I agree. I also agree with Mercier that you need a little rest before you throw yourself back into the flames."

"Where are you going now? Aren't you off duty?"

Sparver checked his bracelet. "Technically. First, I want to talk to the Heavy Technicals still sweeping the crime scene in Stadler-Kremeniev. They'll be able to tell me if they recovered the whiphound. Get some sleep, Thal."

"I might," she said, yawning through her words. "Thank you, by the way. I needed a friendly face."

"Pity you got mine instead."

"It did the job."

She drowsed, not even hearing him leave. A minute passed, maybe five. She felt shivery again. Drawing herself further under the sheet, her elbow touched the hard casing of a compad. Thalia took it out, fingering the oversized inputs. Then, with all the delicious furtiveness of a child forbidden from reading in bed, she set to work.

"Retrieve all visual records of the Mizler Cranach incident," she whispered, just loudly enough for the compad to understand and obey.

Brother Sebastien listened carefully, nodding at appropriate intervals. "We'll monitor her, of course. Not that we haven't been doing so already, but we'll make sure it's even more thorough."

"Do we need to be concerned?" Dreyfus asked the Mendicant. "If the implants are malfunctioning, or she's rejecting them in some way..."

"It won't be anything that serious. The worst side effects show up early on, not this far along. It was probably the implant exploring pathway redundancy and sending a few signals where it shouldn't have. They do that from time to time, when they're trying to optimise functional integration."

"Where do you get those implants from? Neurolinguistic technology can't be cheap."

"They come from our main line of business, Tom. People come to us from their ships, fresh out of hibernation, with varying degrees of damage. Sometimes it's just a mild, temporary amnesia."

"And sometimes there's nothing to be done but harvest anything useful from the ruined slush of their brains. Valery's implants used to belong to someone else, didn't they?" Dreyfus said.

"Yes. Would you rather something that valuable and useful was just thrown away? Or better that it be put to some good use, healing someone who isn't beyond hope?" He softened his tone. "You shouldn't worry unduly. The seizure wasn't expected, but it's not impossible that the heightened emotional context of your visit..." He trailed off, leaving Dreyfus with the faint implication that it was all somehow his fault.

"I want to know the instant something like that flares up again. You or Sister Catherine have the means to contact me directly, even if I'm working. Nothing matters as much as Valery."

"You have my word. She wouldn't normally be allowed wander off without a Mendicant guide, but since you were here..."

"Is there anything else you'd like to blame me for?" Dreyfus asked.

"No one is to blame here, Tom."

"I'm sorry." He looked down, ashamed at his outburst. "That was uncalled for. I know you're doing your best."

On the way back from the bridge, Dreyfus had wrestled with himself about whether to report the incident at all. He knew its cause well enough, but if Valery informed Sebastien or one of the other carers that something distressing had happened—in so far as she could communicate her experience after the fact—it would seem odd that Dreyfus had made no mention of it.

As was often the case, Aurora had left him with no good options.

Valery was resting on a bed in one of the cool, breezy rooms of the clinic. Dreyfus went and sat with her for another hour, until she seemed to come to some private acceptance of the episode, ready to put it behind her. The Mendicants brought a plate of tomatoes and salad leaves and a glass of pressed fruit. Dreyfus rearranged some flowers in a vase, cut from the gardens just outside. She ate, her eyes clear again.

"We will walk," she insisted. "To the red bridge. But not now. Next time."

"I'd like that very much," Dreyfus said. But all the red bridge signified for him was Aurora discarding petals as thoughtlessly as if they were human lives. "I promise it won't be long before I'm back. Just a few days."

She nodded, understanding him well enough, and was kind enough to look as if she believed him.

He leaned in, kissed her and made his departure. He walked away, glancing back once, waving and miming an awkward second kiss, then turned his back on her. He just wanted to get back to his ship and be gone, but he had barely put the clinic behind him when Sister Catherine appeared in his way, leaning on her stick.

"They attacked Mercy Sphere, Tom. Can you offer any assurance that they won't attack Idlewild?"

"Mercy Sphere was targeted because of its association with the rehabilitation of hyperpigs," he answered. "Since that's not your primary role here, I don't think Idlewild is at any elevated level of risk."

"With your wife in our care, I thought you would take a different view."

"Your perception of risk matters to me as well, Sister. For that reason I'm making a formal request to have a Panoply ship stationed close by at least until the present crisis is over. Our resources are stretched, but I'm hoping to persuade my peers to assign a Deep System Vehicle on extended watch."

"Is that a big ship?"

"The biggest that we have."

"What good will it do?"

"Visible deterrence, for one. Nothing obviously hostile will be able to get close enough to Idlewild to do any harm. That will stop most of the cruder forms of attack. But I admit there's very little that Panoply would have been able to do about a covert weapon like the booby-trapped capsule at Mercy Sphere."

"So we're still defenceless."

Dreyfus shook his head. "No, but you do have some difficult decisions to make. I strongly recommend a hiatus in the processing of all inbound passengers. Accept no new cases into Idlewild, and leave frozen any that have arrived in the last six months or so—at least as far back as Mizler Cranach's first attack. When this has cleared up, you can open the doors again and begin processing that backlog. Until then, you'd be well advised to put the safety of Idlewild above all else." He watched as the scepticism hardened her features. "You've done good work here for many decades, Sister, and I don't doubt that the worlds will have need of you for many more to come. A small sacrifice now will allow many more good deeds in the future."

She jabbed her stick into the ground. "You know that we cannot suspend our work. The needy won't stop arriving just because of our troubles."

"No one's asking you to stop, just to slow down. Concentrate on the woken cases for now, and any still in your hibernacula that came in before the crisis started. I'll speak to Harbourmaster Seraphim and ask him to do what he can at the Parking Swarm." He showed his palms, surrendering to her clemency. "This is the best that can be done. Be assured that it won't last forever."

"Can you be sure?"

Dreyfus sighed. "I'd better be."

Dreyfus made a point of contacting Seraphim before he undocked from Hospice Idlewild. He feared that if he did not do so immediately, it would be too easy to let it slide, another promise broken.

"Dreyfus," acknowledged Seraphim warily, his half-past-human face appearing on the cutter's console. "It's been a little while since we had the pleasure. I trust all is well in Idlewild?"

"It's Idlewild I wanted to speak about, Harbourmaster," Dreyfus said, with a certain forced cheeriness. "I know you have a great deal of influence with the Ultra crews, and the reputation for fairness you've built up over the years."

"You're flattering me," came the buzzing voice. "I can feel a request for a favour coming on."

"It's a small one. I need you to do all that you can to reduce the pressure on the Mendicants. The fewer bodies they have to process, the less chance there'll be of someone sneaking something hostile into Idlewild."

Seraphim nodded his understanding. "They're concerned, after that unpleasantness with Mercy Sphere. You see, I do take a tiny interest in your affairs."

Dreyfus had long ago given up trying to read Seraphim for irony. There were few indicators since the Harbourmaster's face was a mask of drum-tight skin with an expressionless metal grille for a mouth. The only consolation was that there were many Ultras who were far beyond Seraphim in strangeness and adaptation.

"I'm not asking the impossible, just that you use your leverage with incoming ships to delay offloading their passengers for as long as they can."

"The quicker those ships unload, the sooner they can be off making profit again."

"I'm asking for a small delay—weeks or months at most—not the whole years that it takes those ships to get to another system. Can you do that for me, Harbourmaster?"

Seraphim fingered the braid of hair that came out of the back of his scalp and hung down over his left shoulder. "A small request like that, who am I to turn it down? There *is* something you can do for me in return, though, especially now that you're practically on our doorstep."

Dreyfus bristled. "Just for once, it would be nice if someone did something for me without any strings attached."

"Not the world we live in, Prefect," Seraphim commiserated, as if they were equal victims of the same system. "But cheer up; it shouldn't take up more than a few hours of your time. Come to the Parking Swarm, please, and I'll explain."

"When would you like me?"

"Now would be excellent."

Resignedly, Dreyfus inputted a new destination into the cutter, delaying his return to Panoply.

Thalia's eyes were sore, struggling for focus, but she could not tear herself away from the compad. Apart from the recordings documented by the monitoring systems of Valsko-Venev, Mizler Cranach's attack had been captured from numerous other points of view, sprinkled between nearby habitats, passing spacecraft and the observation devices and beacons owned by Panoply and the traffic-routing authority. Thousands of independent recordings, enshrining those ninety fateful seconds forever. No angle had not been captured to at least a reasonable resolution, no event not time-stamped down to the last microsecond. It was all there. The only absent viewpoint was from the cutter itself, but even that had been synthesised by combining other sets of overlapping data.

One or two of these recordings might arguably have been open to doctoring, but it was difficult to imagine any means of tampering with every single data set to create the same effect. Taken as a whole, the story they conveyed seemed as irrefutable as it was horrible.

Besides, she had seen the evidence with her own eyes. She had smelt it.

Thalia watched the same ninety seconds over and over.

She saw the cutter moving into position, unsheathing its weapons. She watched it open fire, directing energy and kinetic destruction against the fragile glass membrane of Valsko-Venev. She counted in her head, relentlessly. A minute and a half was a hideously short time when you had something critical to debate.

When you were burning alive, it was a cruel eternity.

The end came quickly. A Panoply cutter was a formidable piece of compact spacecraft engineering, but it was no match for the massed potential of a habitat's entire anti-collision infrastructure. A tracery of lines snapped onto the cutter like something from an optics diagram, with Mizler Cranach at the focus. The cutter vanished in a pulse of white: a powerful explosion, but a pinprick against the scale of the torus. In the last moment, the cutter's line of fire had deviated slightly, just as Thalia had noticed and Minty had explained away.

She watched it again, from a different angle this time.

And watched it again.

Sparver collected a meal from the refectory serving hatch, then spied a table where he could sit on his own and not be bothered. Not difficult, for a hyperpig. It was uncanny how quickly some of the other prefects suddenly needed to finish eating when he sat down at their tables. Today he was perfectly content not to have company.

He toyed with the food with his usual pig-adapted cutlery, his mind still somewhere down in the morgue. He had known the circumstances of Tench's death before he was put on the case, but seeing the facts imprinted so starkly in her flesh left him troubled. She had died under the violence of bullet, blade, rock and fist, and not without a struggle.

"Good for you, Ingvar," he mouthed, trying to find some crumb of solace.

He mused on it, staring into the middle distance, paying only distant heed to the news feeds playing across the refectory's walls. More trouble, more flashpoints in the pig–human grudge war. Prefects rushing around trying to contain the outbreaks, reasonable voices popping up on both sides calling for some semblance of calm, but the usual opportunists and shit-stirrers not shy about opening their mouths either.

Why can't we just be sensible? Thalia had asked him.

Damned good question, he mused. Probably too big a conundrum for the mind of a pig, though.

He paused his meal, sipped apple juice and called Mercier.

"Sparver. What an unexpected pleasure, so soon after our last conversation."

"Just a quick question. You scanned that body for radioactive traces, didn't you?"

"Standard procedure before any human hands—I mean any hands, at all—got near it. Some idiot could wipe out half of Panoply by smuggling a radioactive source into our midst."

"So she was clean?"

"I see what you're driving at. If she'd used the whiphound in its mode of last resort, as an explosive device, she might have been close enough to be sprayed by trace isotopes. Well, she wasn't. If the whiphound did blow up, it can't have been anywhere near her person when it did. Have you spoken to the Heavy Technicals?"

"They're next on my list," Sparver said, ending the call.

He sipped a little more juice then asked to be put through to

Levertov, the field operative overseeing the Heavy Technical action in Stadler-Kremeniev. Sparver got on well with Levertov. They ate together occasionally, had traded classes in forensic examination, and Levertov had been showing him some rudimentary opening gambits in Go.

"What is it, Sparv?"

"A missing whiphound. It's not at our end, so I can only presume it never came back from Stadler-K."

"Mm. That's odd. Dreyfus brought the body home, didn't he?"

"Yes, and you know what the old man's like about protocol. If the whiphound was on her person, he'd have made sure it was docketed and logged and boxed up with her other items."

"Well, we definitely haven't found a whiphound."

"How thoroughly have you swept the area where she died?"

"As well as we can, given the agreement Dreyfus managed to negotiate with the locals. We wouldn't have missed something like that, though."

"All right, then maybe she detonated it. Mercier says there's not enough radiation on her for that, but that wouldn't matter if the whiphound was some distance away when it exploded. It wouldn't be too late to pick up a hotspot, would it?"

"Not as straightforward as you'd think, Sparv. This place is dirty—they've been waging an urban war here for months, with whatever weapons they can get their hands on. That said..." He could almost hear Levertov wrestling with himself. "We haven't yet picked up any nasties that would point to a recent whiphound detonation, not even at lowest yield. Does that help?"

"Absence of evidence is not evidence of absence, as they taught us in induction. Did you issue a general recall?"

"Matter of course. Nothing responded."

Sparver nodded gloomily. "So if it didn't blow up, it might be damaged so badly it's useless as a recording mechanism."

"Is that what you're hoping for?"

"I thought maybe Tench had recorded something as she was getting deeper into trouble. Anything to indicate her state of mind, to tell me whether this was part of some plan of hers."

"What do you think?"

Sparver mulled over the ethics of confidentiality, then decided that Levertov had been open enough with him about the results of the sweep that he could afford to reciprocate.

"She didn't go down without a fight. A bad one, judging by how messed up her body was. Now, I know that doesn't rule out suicide as the initial driver, but if that's what it was, she certainly had second thoughts."

"But you don't think they were second thoughts at all. You don't think she meant to die."

"Without the whiphound, though, all I have is a hunch."

"We'll keep looking, Sparv. If something turns up, you'll be the first to know."

"Thank you."

He stared down at the bulk of his meal, still untouched, and then pushed his chair back to stand up.

He was well into his off-duty hours, but he knew it would be futile to return to his quarters with his head rattling. From the refectory he made the cumbersome, time-consuming transition from the centrifuge section into the weightless area around the docks, where the absence of gravity facilitated the handling and maintenance of Panoply's fleet of enforcement vehicles.

"Prefect Bancal," Thyssen said, at his usual supervisory station at the heart of the complex, where he could monitor the coming and goings of ships and ensure their maintenance was proceeding to schedule. "How may we help?"

"I'd like a look at Ingvar's ride."

"We're not quite done with our analysis. Say another twenty-six hours, just to be thorough?"

"I'd still like to see it."

Thyssen took him to a windowed observation point, looking out onto the quarantined vacuum dock where the cutter was being held. The secure dock was just large enough for this smallest class of Panoply vehicle, with a margin for the technicians to float around the hull and make their inspections. Bathed in an eerie antiseptic light, the black vehicle looked blue and ghostly. A wild loom of glowing pink froptic cables surrounded it, connected to free-floating analysis terminals and compads. The technicians were white spectres, moving with phantom deliberation around the object of their interest.

"What have they got?"

"It's all preliminary, and strictly for your ears only. My formal findings will be presented to the tactical room, under the usual protocols."

"Get on with it, Thyssen."

"Tench's metaphoric fingerprints are all over that cutter's controls. She got deep into its logic, shutting out the safeguards that should have prevented a docking with Stadler-K."

"And the same safeguards that should have allowed you to override it and bring it back here?"

"Also neutralised. She was thorough and efficient."

94

Sparver mulled this over. "But not so thorough as to cover up the evidence of her tampering?"

"Perhaps she wanted to leave behind proof of how clever she'd been."

"Tench, fishing for posthumous glory?" Sparver cocked his head sceptically. "When she could barely take a compliment when she was alive?"

"I didn't know her well enough to have an opinion, Prefect Bancal."

"Put yourself in her position. If she wanted to kill herself, why not just have the cutter crash into some dumb rock, or blow itself up? Instead, she uses her wits to set herself up for a slow, bloody death at the hands of a mob?"

Thyssen bent down to a microphone. "Podor. I have Prefect Bancal with me. You've seen as far into Tench's handiwork as anyone. How would you assess the evidence you've seen to date?"

One of the technicians floated away from a terminal and grabbed a handhold at the side of the quarantine lock.

"She went in quickly, sir," the figure answered in a young man's voice, eager to please. "She knew exactly what she was doing. No missteps, no wasted time. She only locked out the specific systems she needed to, fast and precise."

"Podor," Sparver said. "Don't I remember you from induction, a year or two back?"

A gulp of hesitation. "I was in your class, sir."

"Then what are you doing grubbing around here? I thought you were on a fast-track to deputy field?"

"I...messed up, sir. They bounced me down to technical services while I wait for another chance at induction." Podor, obviously aware that his new boss was listening in, added: "It's still difficult and challenging work, sir, serving under Mister Thyssen. I don't see it as—"

"—grubbing around," Thyssen finished for him. "Prefect Sparver: did you have anything else for Podor?"

"Tell me when Tench would have made these alterations."

"After she departed Panoply, sir. Our ships are harnessed and monitored right up to the moment they detach. If she'd attempted any of it while the ship was still clamped on, systems alerts would have triggered automatically."

"Could she have silenced them?"

"Maybe, sir, but probably not quickly enough to avoid notice." The white-garbed technician let go of the handhold for long enough to give a whole-bodied shrug. "Why bother taking that chance, when she was clearly capable of doing it after departure?"

"Thank you, Podor." Then, to Thyssen: "Given the possibility that her ship was tampered with, I want an extra layer of security in place around all the vehicles under your care."

"It's already implemented. We went to condition two after Mizler Cranach. Now we're at three." Thyssen sniffed. "I wouldn't have expected you to notice."

"Is there a condition four?"

"Yes."

"Then go to it. I might not have the authorisation to order such a thing, but you know damned well Dreyfus will agree with me as soon as he gets back to Panoply. Might as well get a head start, Thyssen—I'm doing you a favour."

"So considerate of you, Prefect Sparver."

"One tries," he answered.

CHAPTER ELEVEN

Dreyfus was beyond his effective jurisdiction, and that made him prickly. The Parking Swarm's orbit put it close enough to Yellowstone to be a constant low-level complication in Panoply's dealings, yet far enough from the Glitter Band that the organisation's formal powers were barely recognised. To all purposes it was lawless space where the lighthugger ships and their posthuman crews laid over while conducting business and repairs. The Ultras might have started off as offshoots of human political and technological groups such as the Demarchists, but most of them had long since severed any sense of allegiance to the worlds and habitats of the settled systems. They spent the bulk of their lives at relativistic speed, whistling between stars, augmenting themselves in ever stranger ways and regarding the likes of Dreyfus with little more than amused contempt, as if he and his fellows were creatures that lacked the imagination or boldness to evolve.

Yet the Ultras had occasionally been useful to Dreyfus, and vice versa. He knew they were not all bad, and that some of the crews operated by moral codes that were not completely alien to his sensibilities. The problem was that his experiences with one set of Ultras provided little or no preparation for dealing with the next. They could be obliging, cautiously cooperative, suspicious, openly hostile or sneakily treacherous, and nothing at all could be gauged from their appearances or the baroque accoutrements of their ships. Such powers that he might have asserted meant little to the Ultras. They could commit any crime, ignite the mighty engines of their ships and not be seen for another hundred years.

The miracle was that something like order mostly prevailed. Much of that was down to Harbourmaster Seraphim, who worked hard to foster tolerable relations between the crews and the rest of Yellowstone's system. If Ultras broke their own hazily defined laws while berthed at his facility, then the Harbourmaster was quick to see justice enacted. That brand of justice might strike Dreyfus as excessive or cruel in its application, but he had to accept that it served a purpose and was perhaps no more or less than the quarrelsome, grudge-keeping Ultras would have insisted upon.

Their needle-sharp ships formed a thistle-cloud about a hundred kilometres across, thickening near the middle where the ships gathered tighter, jostling for privilege and favoured access to the station-sized central servicing facility where Seraphim ran his court. As was his custom, Dreyfus slowed down before diving straight into the swarm. Even with an invitation in his pocket, he had learned not to do anything provocative.

"Good, Dreyfus," Seraphim announced upon his arrival. "You came speedily. Accept this vector, and trust that my guests will be on their very best behaviour. If the odd targeting laser touches you, take it as friendly inquisitiveness."

"As long as it's just targeting systems, we'll be fine."

Dreyfus guided the cutter into the thick of the swarm, his tiny ship little more than a speck against the kilometres-long hulls of the lighthugger starships. True to Seraphim's word, the cutter detected itself being painted by various target-designation systems, but Dreyfus steeled himself against responding in kind. He had nothing that could provoke any reaction in the Ultras beyond contempt and mirth at the puniness of his armaments.

A chime sounded from his compad where it was tucked into the pouch next to his seat. With half an eye still on the ships looming around him, Dreyfus extracted the compad and looked at the reason for the chime.

It was an anonymous tip-off, one of thousands that reached Panoply on any given day. There was a system for receiving such messages—a robust chain of checks and filters, mostly automated. Only a fraction of the tip-offs were deemed worthy of examination by human eyes, and even fewer were considered valuable enough to intrude on the time of senior-ranking prefects such as Dreyfus.

He had no need to speculate on the origin of this particular snippet of intelligence.

It concerned a family, the Salter-Regents. According to the tip-off, the anonymous party had been a broker in the sale to the Salter-Regents of a particular item of contraband technology: specifically, a quickmatter concealment device known colloquially as a nonvelope.

Dreyfus could think of only one recent instance concerning the use of a nonvelope. He flashed back to the events of Mercy Sphere, and the graphic testimony Thalia had left in her report. Although he had not been there, he could almost smell the consequences.

He closed the compad, feeling faintly and irrevocably soiled by the act of reading, as if some dark transaction of the soul had already been validated.

"If that was from you," he mouthed, "you'd better be certain of your facts."

His wordless informant declined to answer.

Seraphim's vector guided him to the central servicing facility, where a berth was vacant and ready. Dreyfus stepped through the m-lock, eschewing weapons and armour, and trusting that Seraphim's hospitality extended to the provision of a breathable atmosphere.

His host floated on the other side, seated in his customary life-support throne. The throne was a bulky, free-floating chair with its own manoeuvring systems.

"I'm willing to indulge in a little *quid pro quo*, Seraphim, but this had better not take too long. What is it you want of me?"

"Your good judgement. Come." He made a bidding gesture with the tips of his heavily ringed fingers, and the chair spun around and began to drift away down a wide, mural-lined corridor. "We'll take tea. And I promise I won't waste a minute of your valuable time. You've one or two things on your plate at the moment."

"You're excellent at understatement, Seraphim."

"And your Russish is not nearly as pitiable as it used to be."

Dreyfus followed the retreating chair. Pumps and valves gurgled within it. "What is this about? We both know my authority doesn't count for much here."

"But your reputation does. I'm afraid we've run into something of a difficulty in the application of our own justice, Dreyfus: a problematic case. By the way, how is your wife?"

"There's progress." As an afterthought he added: "Thank you for asking."

"I don't hear much jubilation, even allowing for your usual lack of effusiveness."

"Progress isn't the same as rapid progress."

"Are you optimistic that she'll eventually be fully healed? No; I'm sorry. That's too direct a question. But there is hope?"

"There's always hope," Dreyfus answered, unpersuasive even to his own ears.

"The Pattern Jugglers have worked miracles with damaged minds."

"I'm aware. I'm also aware that there aren't any Pattern Jugglers in or near this solar system."

"Then it's useful that we have the means to cross interstellar space."

Dreyfus's laugh gonged off the murals, bleak as a tomb. "Have you seen what a prefect's stipend looks like, Seraphim? I'd have to work for a few more centuries to afford a single berth on one of your ships, never mind

99

two. And then what? Roll the dice with the Pattern Jugglers? They're as liable to make things worse as they are to heal her."

"I think in your case there might be grounds for optimism. The Jugglers seem to respond well to the challenge of broken minds."

"When I need a fantasy, I'll know where to look," Dreyfus replied firmly. "Now, what's this problem of yours?"

"Two crews, both alike in dignity. I'm afraid a rather messy trade dispute has spilled its way into my lap."

They arrived at a reception room Dreyfus remembered from one of his earlier visits to Seraphim, with monitoring displays set between acres of padded plush. Tea had already been prepared, served from a weightless service by a pair of brass-plated drones. Dreyfus sipped politely, anxious to get this business over with.

"I thought you liked to resolve your disputes internally."

"This is an unusual case."

Seraphim muttered an instruction into his chair. Doors opened on either side of the room and a pair of Ultras came through each, escorted by larger, more intimidating versions of the drone servitors. Dreyfus flinched involuntarily, thinking for a second that an ambush was about to be sprung. The reaction lasted only a moment before he noticed that the Ultras were under heavy restraint, and that the bristling weapons on the servitors were aimed at the prisoners.

He handed the tea-bulb back to the servitor.

"What is this, Seraphim?"

"On the left, Captain Moravska and Vice-Captain Junglinster of the lighthugger *Milk of the Madonna*. To the right, Triumvirs Nisko and Pazari of the *Shades of Scarlet*. The third triumvir from that ship couldn't be with us today, due to an unfortunate incident with a high-energy plasma lance."

"I'm not familiar with the organisational structures on your ships."

"The triumvirate is a common command solution, often implemented in the absence of a captain, or the incapacitation of the latter. You may regard these pairs as roughly equal in authority and responsibility, where their vessels are concerned."

"He doesn't even know our ways," Junglinster complained. "He isn't fit to pass judgement on a piece of suit art, let alone a matter of internal discipline!"

"This is a mistake, Prefect," cautioned Nisko, from the other side of the room. "You're out of your depth. Keep out of our affairs, and we'll keep out of yours."

Something in his tone emboldened Dreyfus. "I'm here at Seraphim's invitation. If you've got a problem with that, perhaps you should take it up with him."

Seraphim explained the problem. The two ships had come into conflict in another system, 36 Ophiuchi, where each had been scouting for raw materials to repair their ablative shields. Each crew maintained that they had been claim-jumped by the other while already mining and refining the needed resources. Unfortunately for the resolution of the dispute, there were no independent witnesses or evidence streams to settle the question of priority.

The two ships had arrived around Yellowstone within a few weeks of each other, whereupon the earlier dispute had flared up again, leading to claims and counter-claims of violence and sabotage under Seraphim's watch.

Before other crews were dragged into the same squabble, the Harbourmaster wanted the matter settled.

"We have their words, and not much else," he advised Dreyfus. "The recordings and event logs from the ships aren't to be relied upon in such a case."

Dreyfus scratched at the back of his neck. "Then it's really just one crew's testimony against the other."

"I imagine your cases are usually more clear-cut, with the evidential measures you employ. From time to time, though, you must rely on your policeman's instinct for the truth."

"But never as the final arbiter," Dreyfus said.

"You won't be the arbiter here, either; just a factor that enters into my own decision process."

Dreyfus eyed the two opposed parties. The Ultras were the usual walking exhibition of enhancements, modifications and things done purely for the purposes of shocking the likes of him. Pazari was the only one who could have just about passed for an unaugmented human, except for the glass panels set into either side of his skull, his brain pressed behind them like knotted dough. Nisko was as much crab as man, encased in a series of jointed shells that had clearly grown from him, rather than being fixed on. Junglinster was a black box with accordion limbs and a human head jutting out under a dome, while Moravska looked like a mass of greasy cables attempting to smother a very pale, elongated old corpse. Various oily and burning smells emanated from the four individuals.

"I'd like to hear their accounts, separately and in private. If I've anything to add, you'll hear it in due course."

"Of course, Dreyfus."

He directed his next remark at the Ultras. "And I won't be intimidated."

He listened to Moravska and Junglinster first, while Nisko and Pazari waited outside the room. He asked for a description of the events at 36 Ophiuchi, attending carefully to each word, taking no notes but counting on his formidable experience with the interviewing process. Seraphim sipped tea and watched, but made no interjection. Moravska gave Dreyfus short shrift, his contempt for the process abundantly clear. He said almost nothing unless it was to contradict or amplify some remark of Junglinster.

Dreyfus asked for clarification of one or two points, then nodded his satisfaction.

Then it was the turn of Nisko and Pazari. They were much more obliging, almost tumbling over themselves to get their side of events across. Again, Dreyfus listened intently. Their story was clear-cut, its details plausible. They had arrived first and done everything correctly, even going so far as to offer to assist the aggressive party with their repairs.

Dreyfus dismissed the second pair of Ultras, then spoke briefly to Seraphim to resolve a few questions of his own. Then he asked for a moment to reflect on his findings.

"You have a verdict?"

"I have an opinion, Harbourmaster. The verdict is for you to decide."

"Let's hear it, then."

"Nisko and Pazari answered my questions reasonably. They did all the right things, and their narrative contains no loose ends."

"Mm," Seraphim said doubtfully. "And the other crew?"

"Openly uncooperative, at times mutually contradictory, and with a story that contains several points which reflect badly on their actions as a crew. They didn't offer assistance to the other ship, and admit as much. When the trouble flared up again on your doorstep, they were the instigating party. They don't even deny it."

"So, clear-cut."

"I wouldn't go that far. My instinct, nonetheless, is that Nisko and Pazari were guilty of the original crime."

"Yet they had the more consistent account."

"They agreed with each other to a fault, even down to the smallest details. Legitimate witnesses rarely do that, Seraphim. They misremember. They confuse the order of events. And just because they're not cooperative, or admit to other failings, doesn't mean they're the guilty ones." Dreyfus shrugged. "I doubt that was helpful."

"I lied a little before. We haven't completely dismissed the data-streams submitted by both ships, but I didn't want them to be aware of that. As it happens, my analysts found evidence of timestamp falsification in the records from the *Shades of Scarlet*. The records from the other ship, though of poor quality, did not contain overt evidence of manipulation."

"Which doesn't prove anything..."

"Nor does it undermine my inclination based on the stated accounts, which happens to align exactly with yours. Forgive me, Dreyfus: it's not that my mind was already made up, but it was as close to being so as makes no difference. I just thought it would settle my remaining qualms if I had the benefit of your experience."

"I could have been home by now," Dreyfus said testily.

"You could, but then you'd be left wondering if I really took that request for a favour seriously." Seraphim steered his chair, indicating to Dreyfus that his presence was no longer required. "Now you needn't worry. I'll do all in my power to help the Mendicants, for as long as it takes to resolve this unpleasantness of yours."

Dreyfus relented. The truth was, with his preoccupation with Valery and the difficulties facing the Glitter Band, it had not hurt to be reminded that there was a bigger universe out there, and that someone else was invariably having a worse day.

"What will happen to these crews now?"

"Oh," Seraphim said unconcernedly. "The usual. One or both of the guilty commanders will be executed in the traditional cruel and unusual manner. This time, though, I promise we won't lash them to their ship and send them heading your way. I think once was enough."

"I think it was," Dreyfus agreed.

Thalia found Sparver in the refectory, sitting on his own. He was hunched over a compad, his ear-tips twitching as they always did when he was deep in concentration.

She coughed delicately as she approached. The refectory was quiet, so the sound carried.

"You should still be resting," Sparver intoned without looking around. With his heel, though, he kicked out a chair for her to use. "Although I suppose telling you that is about as useful as suggesting to Dreyfus that he should bend the odd rule now and then."

"I'm better," she offered, sitting down on the side of the table next to his. "Well, not 'better' exactly. Functional. I think those berries did something permanent to my constitution." She nodded at the compad he was still focussed on. "What's that?"

"I got a message from Boss Man, on his way back from...not Idlewild, weirdly, but the Parking Swarm. He said he was tired and would need to deal with Tench's daughter once he docked, but he wanted me to get ahead on something first."

"Tench's daughter?"

"She's on her way to Panoply, some kind of weird cross between witness protection and service induction."

"No one ever tells me anything."

"Well, I'm telling you now. Hafdis wants to be one of us, and Boss Man's trying to pull some levers to make it work. Meanwhile..."

Thalia slid his compad over, her eyes skidding down a long, tedious-looking schedule of habitats and dates.

"What's that?"

"A list of every single visit Ingvar made during her nearly four years of field service. Obviously, it's hundreds of lines long. Dreyfus wants me— and him—to start working through this list with repeat field visits."

"That'll take weeks—months!"

"Which is why Prefect Bancal is on the case, trying to massage this impossible task into something workable." He nodded to the floor. "Can you hear that rumble? That's the Search Turbines getting a good thrashing."

"If you're looking for something Ingvar was searching for—and we know she had access to our information systems—how do you know that list hasn't already been doctored, perhaps by Ingvar herself?"

"It's a good question, and thankfully one I've answered to my own satisfaction." Sparver puffed himself up a little. "The logs I've used to reconstruct her movements would be very hard to alter. She'd have to change our own internal records of her activities, the individual flight recorder logs of every ship she used in that time, Thyssen's records of departures and arrivals from the docks, as well as countless civilian records that just happen to log prefect movements around the Glitter Band. It would be an infinitely harder task than changing a single-point entry within Panoply, such as her own biometric record." He shook his head, clearly delighted to have had the chance to show off. "No; it's watertight. The only question is how I make sense of it."

"Which would be?"

"With my usual skill and judgement, naturally." He eyed her with friendly concern. "You really ought to be resting. I might not be able to tell two baseline humans apart, but I can tell when someone needs some rest."

Thalia put down the compad she had brought. "Thank you for the loan of this. Mercier's allowed me to have my own back now."

"I had a spare, but I'm glad it was useful."

She waited a beat.

"I think I know what happened with Mizler Cranach. I don't believe he was guilty of that attack at all. In fact, quite the opposite. He did just about everything possible to stop it."

That was enough to suspend his interest in the schedule of visits.

"In the nicest possible way, this had better be good. If you go raising my hopes, only to have them dashed..."

"It's all in the last second," Thalia said. "That's the part no one looked at properly. And it changes everything." She paused. "I'm sending you my analysis now. I won't say any more until you've looked through it and drawn your own conclusion. I think you'll see what I saw, and you'll know what it means."

Their compads blinked, exchanging evidential data.

CHAPTER TWELVE

Dreyfus found Lovro Breno alone in an empty lecture theatre, reviewing the notes for some upcoming class. Projected on the wall above Breno's lectern was a timeline of Panoply history, showing notable triumphs and failures, with perhaps more emphasis on the latter than the former. Breno barely glanced up from his lectern as Dreyfus entered, but he registered his arrival all the same.

Without any kind of preamble, Breno said in a low, conversational tone: "It's always a hard one, isn't it. Do we tarnish their image of us right from the outset, or allow them to become jaded and cynical in their own time? Either way, they reach the same objective in the end." He touched the compad on his lectern, adjusting a detail of the timeline. "Perhaps it's for the best to shatter their illusions early on."

"Not all of us see it that way."

Breno lifted his eyes from the lectern long enough to give Dreyfus a pitying look, as one might to a child labouring under some naive but touching illusion. "That's what you tell yourself in the mirror, Tom. Deep down, you're as morally compromised as the rest of us. The difference is, we've got the courage to admit it to ourselves." He looked down again, adjusting another detail. "How may I help?"

Breno was a powerfully built man with broad shoulders, a thick neck and a jutting jaw. His rust-coloured hair was a bristly band, growing out along his crown and shaved around the rest of his head. He was the exemplar of a tough-looking, no-nonsense prefect, intimidating whether or not he had his whiphound unholstered.

They were close in age and seniority. Breno was a little younger, but he had come up through the ranks swiftly, under the firm mentorship of Grigor Bacchus, one of the most respected and experienced prefects of his generation. It was said that Breno had learned a lot from the older man, including a zealot-like intolerance for mistakes and under-achievement. And for a time, Breno's commitment to perfection had been matched only by his complete dedication to the ideals of Panoply.

Until all that changed.

Breno, like Dreyfus, had enough notches on his belt to qualify for the status of senior prefect, spending the rest of his days within Panoply rather than out in the Glitter Band. It was a desirable outcome for many, a seat at the big table. On the days when his bones ached, Dreyfus could see the attraction himself. Breno too, probably. Both men, though, had opted for deferred promotion, retaining field status. To some extent they had the best of both worlds: they could move as they pleased, acting alone or in small teams; they weren't bogged down in administration; and yet, by dint of their years of service, they had access to the tactical room and were treated as near-equals by the seniors and supernumeraries who formed the inner court of Jane Aumonier.

"I've a small favour to ask," Dreyfus ventured.

"Any time."

"There's a candidate I'd like to see brought through induction."

Breno kept on with his work. "No problem, Tom. Give me their name and I'll make sure they're included in the next window."

"I'd like an exemption to be made in this case: for the candidate to be given immediate assessment and then fed back into the classes if she clears the first few hurdles."

Breno made a couple of alterations before answering. "We've got procedures in place for a reason. This feels irregular. You know I'm not a big fan of irregularity."

"Nor am I. This is an irregular case, though. Her name is Hafdis Tench. She's Ingvar Tench's daughter."

Breno lifted his head, flecks of red glinting along his crown. "Tench had a kid? I never knew."

"None of us did. I've spent some time with her, though, and concluded that she could be good material."

"Does she have a clue what she'd be getting into?"

"A little. She knows the life because of her mother. She's also used to service. She's a constable."

Breno looked sceptical. "Bit of a gap between citizen-service as a constable and the hermit's life of Panoply."

"It's still the life she wants. She's got to come to Panoply anyway, because of her link to Ingvar. This will only make her even more determined to join us. She'll be a candidate in the next intake and probably one of the best, so why not speed up the process?"

"If I cut one corner now, what's the next one I'll be asked to cut?"

"I'm not asking for the bar to be lowered in any way. I expect all her assessors, including you, to be as firm with her as you would any candidate."

Breno smiled tightly. "You can bet on that."

"If this backfires, it backfires on me. I don't think it will, though. She's smart and I think she'll learn fast, so she won't need her hand held."

Something gave in Breno's expression, a small easing in the set of his jaw. "Well, we wouldn't function if the rules were applied too rigidly. We'll make it happen."

"You have my gratitude."

"It's fine, Tom." Breno looked at Dreyfus directly, his expression mild but unsparing. He had grey eyes, flinty in their hardness. "You know, I wish you'd been as flexible with me, when I asked for a favour."

"You know that was different."

"Really?"

"You weren't the only victim in that business. We all felt let down by the choices Grigor made. But it was a bad time for us. If he'd been tarred and feathered, it would only have made things worse for Panoply in the public gaze. Aumonier knew that."

"I wasn't asking for the unthinkable, just that she take a harder line on his punishment. I was counting on you to use your influence with her, Tom."

"If I failed you, I'm sorry." Dreyfus offered his hands. "But let's not visit my mistakes on Hafdis Tench. She deserves a clean sheet, a chance for a fresh start."

Breno dabbed at his compad. A few changes percolated up and down the timeline.

"I guess you're right. There's Tench's memory, too. When does she arrive?"

"In about thirteen hours."

"Let me make the arrangements. She can start evaluation as soon as she's settled in."

Dreyfus closed his eyes, blessing this small turn of fortune before it slipped away. "Thank you, Lovro."

"I wasn't kidding, though. I'll go as hard on her as I do anyone. Her mother was excellent, a testament to our standards. I won't demean Ingvar's legacy by settling for anything less than the best from her daughter."

Dreyfus was there to see Hafdis arrive and disembark from the automated shuttle. She was the only occupant: green in the face, floating out in travel-rumpled civilian clothes with just a single piece of luggage following her.

He greeted her at the airlock.

"How was your journey?"

"The journey was fine—" She vomited explosively. Dreyfus edged back, giving the ochre cloud an unobstructed path to the nearest wall, where it was absorbed harmlessly. "I'm sorry," Hafdis mumbled, cupping a hand to her mouth. "Possibly not the best first impression."

"I've seen worse, trust me. We sometimes forget that many of our citizens are unused to spaceflight, even within the Glitter Band." He reached for her luggage, helping it along. "You travel light. I approve."

In these surroundings, familiar to him but not to Hafdis, she seemed smaller and more vulnerable. Perhaps it was the fact that she no longer carried the authority of a uniform. Her clothes were unostentatious, neither billowing nor tight to her figure. Her suitcase was spartan, edged in scuffmarks.

"I hope this isn't an inconvenience."

"No," Dreyfus reassured her. "The Supreme Prefect thinks it sensible to have you here, and she agrees that the experience may be useful to you as part of your candidacy evaluation."

"Then you've managed to make that happen?" The news brought the colour back to her. "Thank you, Dreyfus. Mother would have appreciated it."

He cautioned her with a smile. "One thing at a time. You'll settle in today, then meet your evaluators tomorrow. They'll run the usual bank of entry-level tests. They're not especially difficult, but you can't afford to fail a single one of them."

"I won't."

"Then it gets harder. You'll do all right, I think, but at any point a weakness could trip you up. If it does, it won't be a reflection on your character, just your idiosyncratic brain development. In Panoply, we have to work with what nature gave us."

She rummaged at her curls, dishevelled from the flight. "It's understood. Will you be involved in my evaluation?"

"Not directly. I've already had too close an association with you for me to be free of bias. But you'll be spending time with me, when you're not being assessed."

"Won't that be just another kind of assessment?"

"I think it's mainly to get you out of everyone else's hair for a few hours. Once you've found your feet, though, you can join me on a series of field investigations."

"That sounds interesting."

"Temper your expectations. You'll see fieldwork for what it is: unglamorous, bureaucratic and hard on the knees."

She nodded earnestly. "I know that how people perceive Panoply and what it's really like are two very different things."

"That, at least, will hold you in good stead." He bit down on his lip. "Hafdis, there's one thing I need to mention. This work I'll be doing."

"Yes?"

"It relates to your mother. I've had a colleague of mine going through her service log, looking at everywhere she spent time. My plan is that we revisit her footsteps, trying to identify anything that might have been of particular importance to her. It won't take us anywhere near her place of death, but it could still be difficult for you."

"Do I have a choice?"

"Most certainly. Should you decline, though, I'm reasonably confident that would be the end of your candidacy."

"It *is* a test, then. To see how well I can set aside personal matters."

Dreyfus nodded sympathetically. "I'm not saying it's easy, but it's some-thing we all have to do at some point."

"Mother wouldn't have flinched. And she'd count on me to show the same detachment." She straightened, a decision having been made. "I'll be your shadow, Dreyfus."

"Then we'll start tomorrow, after your initial evaluation. I can't say it'll be interesting, but it may well be illuminating." He deliberated. "One other thing, Hafdis."

"Yes, Dreyfus?"

"From the moment you enter candidate selection, you'll refer to me as sir or Prefect Dreyfus at all times. And shall we say that that process has just began?"

"As you will, Prefect Dreyfus."

He allowed himself a tiny private victory, then nodded encouragingly. "I'll show you to your room, Candidate Tench. You have the rest of the day and evening to yourself. Be ready at nine sharp for your first evaluation."

"Sir," she answered.

Thalia met Sparver outside the tactical room. She had requested an urgent audience with the Supreme Prefect and as many of her seniors and ana-lysts as could be present at this early hour.

"So?" she asked Sparver, knowing he had reviewed her findings.

"You have all you need. The only other thing you need to bring to the table is the confidence to stand your ground."

They went in together. Aumonier was there, as were Clearmountain, Baudry and Dreyfus, and a scattering of bleary-eyed analysts. Aumonier was in the middle of something: "... operational containment and intelligence consolidation. I'm currently tracking six reprisal events that can be linked directly back to Mercy Sphere, and chatter on forward-planning for another nine counter-reprisals. I have false-flag actors to deal with. I have every other damned problem already on my table, and now I have some questionable, anonymous intelligence to add to my troubles?"

"The Salter-Regents need looking at," Dreyfus countered. "I can't vouch for the reliability of the tip-off, not without knowing the sender, but the intelligence fits. There's never been anything we can pin on them, but that family has a track record of anti-pig agitation. Bedsides, other than a few high-ups in Mercy Sphere, who else knew that a nonvelope was involved in that attack?"

Aumonier looked only half-persuaded. "Why would this broker feel the need to implicate a client?"

Dreyfus gave one of his customary shrugs, his whole bulk seeming to slump deeper into the chair. "Seller's remorse, perhaps. Perhaps they thought that the nonvelope was going to be used for some ordinary crime, not the mass murder of pigs and Mendicants. I say that it's a thread we need to pull on, even if it leads nowhere."

"And who do you propose that I spare for this task, given that we're already working our fingers to stumps?"

"Whatever it is, ma'am," Thalia interjected, before she had even sat down, "I could look into it, especially if it concerns Mercy Sphere."

"No, Ng, you've more than enough on your plate." Aumonier nodded at the other entrant. "The same for you, Sparver. Delegate this to local law enforcement, Tom, and see what the constables turn up. They can have the pleasure of going in hard for once, and if they do find there's anything worth pursuing with the Salter-Regents, Panoply can swoop in with authority to sequester and trawl." She thumped the table. "Now to the main business. I won't say that this had better be good, Ng, but..."

Dreyfus crunched an apple. "Let's see what Thal has to say, shall we?"

Thalia took her seat. Sparver settled in and gave her an encouraging nod.

"Well?" Aumonier demanded.

"I've found an anomaly in the Mizler Cranach incident. I believe it puts matters into a rather different light, forcing us to—"

"No grandstanding, Ng. Just get to it."

Thalia nodded obediently. "Ma'am. If I may?"

A regal wave. "Proceed."

Thalia projected her compad's summary onto the wood-effect walling of the tactical room. The seniors and analysts who were facing away from the wall creaked around in their seats, generating various subliminal noises of complaint.

"The first eighty-nine seconds are entirely consistent with the established narrative, ma'am, so I'll skip over them. It's only the last second where things deviate."

Aumonier asked: "What are we seeing?"

"Correlated data-streams from different viewpoints, with different capture qualities and effective frame-rates. I've meshed them together. It was...exacting."

"No need to flatter yourself," Aumonier replied. "Continue."

The projection showed multiple angles on Mizler Cranach's ship, just before it ceased to exist. In the ninetieth second, the guns of Valsko-Venev opened up on it with terminal effect.

Thalia zoomed in further, dragging out the final second.

"There's an interval here where the ship is receiving fire, but not yet damaged to the point where it can't continue its own attack against the lemurs. Mizler begins to lose weapons lock: his angle of fire deviates, producing a kink in the ribbon of damage he inflicted on the habitat."

"Yes, because of the bombardment from Valsko-Venev itself," said Clearmountain. "The convergence of their weapons, hitting the cutter from multiple angles." He glanced at his bracelet as if to say: *You dragged us here for that?*

Thalia steeled herself. "Not so, sir."

She went back and zoomed in even further.

"In these few milliseconds, sir, we see the cutter already losing target lock. That's before the incoming fire from Valsko-Venev touched it." Thalia read the doubt and uncertainty in their faces, even Jane Aumonier not yet persuaded. She pictured Jason Ng standing behind her, hand gently on her shoulder. "I can be completely confident of this analysis. When properly correlated, the varying data-streams allow for no ambiguity. Something happened in those milliseconds, something initiated by Mizler Cranach."

"You're reading a lot into a handful of milliseconds," Baudry cautioned.

"I am," Thalia agreed. "Which is why I went looking for corroboration."

She had the room now. It was palpable, a shift in the mood as definite as if the lights had just changed temperature.

"What did you find, Ng?" Aumonier probed.

"One data-stream, ma'am. It captured a clear, unobstructed view of the cutter's dorsal airlock. None of the others saw it because none of the others *could* have seen it."

"Seen what?" Clearmountain asked.

Thalia isolated the relevant feed. The cutter floated on the wall, with a timestamp slowly updating in the lower right field. Then it came and went.

A feather of white, pluming out from the airlock.

"There was a depressurisation event," Thalia said.

CHAPTER THIRTEEN

Dreyfus went from the tactical room directly to Hafdis, arriving earlier than he had arranged, but unsurprised to find her already prepared and waiting.

"I've got my service record here, and references, if you want to see those."

"Just bring yourself," Dreyfus said.

He took her by a slightly indirect route to the candidacy room, time enough to give her some guidance before she was put to the fire. "Lovro Breno will be your hardest hurdle," he confided, as they took one of the colour-coded conveyor bands through the maze of tunnels and rotating sections that made up the interior of the rock.

"I'll never learn my way around this place. I could swear we've been through this bit twice already."

Dreyfus smiled, remembering his own early confusion. "You'd be surprised how quickly you get the hang of it. The asteroid is more than a kilometre across, but we only use a small part of the internal volume. It won't take you more than a few weeks to get your bearings."

"What's the point of the rest of it, if it's not being used?"

"Call it insurance. We're not always the most popular figures in the Glitter Band. Once or twice, elements in the citizenry have been unwise enough to turn their weapons against Panoply. If and when that happens again, you'll be glad of a few hundred metres of rock between yourself and the outside world."

"I'll take your word for that, sir." Then, picking up on his earlier remark: "Who is Lovro Breno, by the way?"

"Another prefect, and the man with overall responsibility for the candidate program. Don't underestimate him just because that sounds like an administrative function. When we're not in one of the usual candidacy windows, Prefect Breno runs field duty all over the Glitter Band."

"I wouldn't dream of underestimating someone." As if to undermine her own point, she added: "Not when I've only just started. Is Breno all right with my being here?"

Dreyfus indicated which band they needed to grip onto at one of the weightless junctions. "Yes, he's perfectly accepting of the situation. It's uncommon to interview someone between normal intake sessions, but there have been precedents. Breno will be fair in all matters, but he won't let you get away with a single slip. You need to be ready for that." Firmly he added: "No second chances."

"I'm not asking for any favours," she said, "but you'd be able to argue my case, if it came down to it?"

"Argue it, yes. But Breno's say will be final. Even the Supreme Prefect wouldn't overrule him. That's one of her great strengths: when she delegates authority, she does so wholeheartedly."

"I'd like to meet her."

"I'm sure you will, in time. She had a great regard for your mother."

"Mother told me a little about what Jane Aumonier went through," Hafdis said tentatively, as if she needed permission to continue that line of discussion.

They disconnected from the conveyor, moving deftly into one of the spinning sections where normal gravity prevailed.

"The only person who really knows what that was like is the Supreme Prefect. She doesn't dwell on the past, though. If she did, she'd still be a victim of the Clockmaker."

"She's remarkable."

Dreyfus found nothing to criticise in this sentiment. "She is. The best of us, the best of what we can be."

"I'd like to know more about her. More about what it was like."

"In time," he repeated. They had reached the examination room, indicated by the glowing outline of a door in the otherwise blank face of a wall. "All right, Hafdis. Step on through."

Hafdis extended a hand to the smooth surface of the wall. "I've never been through one of these before. We didn't have quickmatter in Feinstein-Wu." She looked at Dreyfus with a sudden alarm. "What if it doesn't let me through? Won't it be like walking into a glass door?"

"More like a glass mattress. If the passwall decides not to admit you, it'll do so gently at first." Dreyfus bid her step through. "Go on. You're expected. When I've finished planning my inspections in an hour or two, I'll come and see how you got on."

She nodded nervously. "Thank you."

Hafdis stepped cautiously into the surface of the wall. The grey surface lapped around her as if she were a swimmer disappearing into water.

Then she was gone. Dreyfus turned to leave, his mind already on the business ahead of him.

Hafdis popped a head of curls back out through the passwall. "Sir, they'd like you to sit in on the start of my examination."

Dreyfus raised an eyebrow. He couldn't imagine Lovro Breno being too keen on his presence, unless it was to witness Hafdis being torn to shreds at the first test. "They?"

"It's the Supreme Prefect, sir. She's in the room." Hafdis looked abashed. "I wasn't expecting that."

"Nor was I," Dreyfus muttered.

Hafdis retreated into the room. Dreyfus followed, standing back as Hafdis took a conjured chair across from the three prefects who were seated opposite her, behind a narrow, rectangular table scattered with a few items.

The room was white, its walls glowing uniformly, banishing shadows. The table glowed with the same intensity, the objects on it seeming to float unsuspended.

Dreyfus recognised one of them as the black box they had found in Tench's room.

"Good morning, Hafdis," said Jane Aumonier, seated to the right of Lovro Breno and Lillian Baudry. She lifted her eyes to Dreyfus. "I'm sorry to detain you, Tom, but I wanted there to be absolute transparency."

"Transparency?" Dreyfus asked.

"We've taken rather a lot on trust," Aumonier said. "Certainly, our records show that Ingvar did have a daughter, even if she seems never to have mentioned her to anyone."

"Ingvar was protective of her private life," Dreyfus answered. "She didn't speak of Hafdis, it's true. That's because she shared nothing of herself beyond her work."

"Nonetheless, we must exercise diligence." Aumonier indicated to Hafdis that she should offer her hand across the table.

Hafdis did so unwaveringly.

Aumonier glanced to her right. "Lillian, would you?"

Baudry took one of the objects on the table, a biomedical stylus, and tapped it against Hafdis's hand. The stylus blinked, indicating that it had collected a statistically useful sample of genetic material.

Hafdis withdrew her hand. A tiny blood spot marked the point where the stylus had sampled her, but she made no show of alarm or discomfort.

Dreyfus was impressed by her composure.

"You need to make sure I'm me," Hafdis stated, with a forthright confidence.

"We don't have your genetic sequence on file," Aumonier answered. "The Common Articles forbid us that. Nor we do have access to the genetic sequence of your father, Miles Selby, or any close relatives of his. But we do have your mother's. It'll only take a few seconds to establish a mitochondrial cross-match, if you're indeed related."

The stylus blinked again. At the same time, a tone sounded from the compad in front of Aumonier.

She slid it across to Lovro Breno.

"The moment of truth."

Breno picked up the compad with one huge hand. His cold grey eyes roamed the analysis, his expression unreadable. With his other hand, he rasped his knuckles through the rusty comb of hair on his scalp, making a harsh bristling sound.

"If she's not my mother," Hafdis said, "it's the first I know about it. I wouldn't be so foolish as to think I could come to Panoply and pass myself off as something I'm not."

Aumonier said: "Lovro?"

Breno set down the compad. "She matches. Fifty per cent of her genes are shared. That makes her a sibling, or—more likely—either the mother or daughter of Ingvar Tench." He slid the compad back to Aumonier with a cursory flick of his wrist. "Which doesn't buy her any special treatment, in case anyone had any ideas."

"I'm sure none of us did," Dreyfus said. Then, nodding at the black box: "I suppose she can see those things now?"

Baudry slid the container within reach of Hafdis. "These are your mother's belongings. They're yours to do with as you wish."

Hafdis waited a moment, then lifted the lid and dipped her hand into the jumble of items, rummaging incuriously while she kept her eyes on the Supreme Prefect. She lifted out a lock of hair, a picture, a comb, a pocket magnifier, an austere hair-clasp, then allowed them to fall back into the box—all except the hair-clasp, which she employed on herself, securing a scrunch of black curls at the back of her head.

"This can't be everything?"

"I'm afraid it is," Aumonier said. "Your mother wasn't one for attachments. She had some furnishings and garments made from quickmatter, but those have been re-absorbed. They can be reconstituted if that's your wish."

Hafdis closed the lid with a snap. "If this is all she kept for herself, then it's all I need. I presume I'm allowed to take these things with me, now that you've established I'm telling the truth?"

"They're yours," Aumonier said, with a magnanimous flourish of her wrist.

"That dealt with," Baudry said, looking to her colleagues for a nod of agreement, "may we proceed with the evaluation?"

"We may," Breno said.

Dreyfus made to rise.

"Aren't you going to stay for the ordeal, Tom?" Breno asked mildly.

"I'd love to, Lovro—if only because I expect Hafdis to sail through every test you can throw at her. But there's the small matter of about four hundred habitats that need visiting."

Sparver had done well to make the task even remotely feasible with anything less than weeks of work. From the thousands of locations that Tench had visited at least once in the years of her field service, Sparver had whittled the list down to a daunting but manageable four hundred and eleven candidate locations. He had done so by eliminating anywhere Tench visited only once, as well as anywhere that was the subject of multiple routine visits by other prefects. His hunch was that Tench must have made some discovery that was hers alone.

Sparver might be wrong about that, but Dreyfus understood that they had to make some assumptions if they were to get anywhere at all. Dividing the work between them, each would still need to make more than two hundred inspections. The limits of travel-time through the Glitter Band, even with optimised crossings, meant that each would be limited to about six or seven a day—still around a month's work, assuming no time off and only the bare minimum of rest between shifts.

Sparver had had another hunch. He'd organised the schedule according to the time-ordering of Tench's visits. Whatever trouble she had got into, he figured that it was more likely to be due to a recent visit than one she had made right at the start of her service.

This ordering was important, but so was the efficiency of crossings within the ever-evolving puzzle of the Glitter Band. Sparver allowed the search priority to optimise itself according to both time-ordering and minimum travel-time. This resulted in a schedule that was weighted toward places recently inspected by Tench, but with the odd early outlier thrown in because of the savings in time and fuel. Some of the outcomes looked counter-intuitive to him, but by then he was willing to trust the algorithm over his own instincts.

Dreyfus agreed. It was a good starting position. With luck they might hit their objective within fifteen days, rather than thirty—provided they recognised it when they did.

"I hate to be the one to mention it," Sparver told him, "but we could get it done a lot sooner if Lady Jane threw a hundred helpers at our feet."

118

"Panoply can't spare either the bodies or the ships," Dreyfus pointed out. "Even if it could, I'm not sure I'd want to expand the search beyond the two of us. Ingvar went to great lengths not to share her work with the rest of the organisation. That suggests to me that she had qualms over who could or couldn't be trusted with that information, all the way up to the tactical room."

"I hope we weren't on her shit-list, boss."

"So do I, but it makes it all the more sensible to keep our investigation between the two of us. There's another factor: you and I knew Ingvar, and so did Thalia. This isn't some distant colleague who died in the line of duty. It's personal, and that means we'll go the extra mile."

"I guess we will. How's the daughter shaping up?"

"Acquitting herself, I don't doubt." Dreyfus paused, fishing out his compad as he remembered a bit of business he wanted to complete before departure. "Give me a moment, Sparver; I meant to inform the local authorities about the Salter-Regent tip-off."

"That was a lucky stroke. Who knew illegal technology brokers could grow a conscience?"

"I'm not putting too much faith in it. Families like that collect grudges the way you and I collect battle scars. The anonymous party is most likely some rival clan aiming to cause a little harmless aggravation for the Salter-Regents."

As he used his compad to send a message to the constables in the Salter-Regent habitat—using the terse, formal style reserved for inter-agency assistance requests—Dreyfus hoped that he had struck the right note of easygoing scepticism with his partner. The reality was that he was entirely confident that the tip-off would lead to something, and perhaps something big. Aurora might be mendacious, but if she was sincere about the threat against her and the need for Panoply to neutralise it, then the last thing she needed was an escalating blood-feud tying up more and more of the prefects' time and energy.

The constables were about to pull on a very hot thread indeed, he expected.

He completed the communique, tucked his compad away and re-joined Sparver. They went to their cutters, berthed side by side and nearly ready for departure. One of Thyssen's technicians was just uncoupling an umbilical from one of the night-black, wedge-shaped ships.

"You see that kid?" Sparver confided.

"Something I should know?"

"It's Podor. I taught him, and so did you. One of the high-fliers in that induction stream. Yet now look at him, doing monkey-work for Thyssen."

"Maintaining a fleet of agile, powerfully armed space vehicles is hardly monkey-work."

"I spoke to him when I came down to look at Tench's ship. Says he crashed out, and now he's doing time down here until they let him have another shot at induction."

Dreyfus shrugged. "I had worse setbacks. Lovro Breno will be the one who bumped Podor down, and that's his decision to make. I imagine Podor is grateful to still be in the organisation. Plenty of others will have left Panoply for good; at least he's got another chance."

Sparver watched Podor for a few more seconds, then said: "I guess you've had time to reflect on Thalia's presentation to the tactical room."

"They're still digesting it. What about it?"

Sparver lowered his voice even further. "Let's say he spent most of those ninety seconds trying to stop his ship attacking Valsko-Venev. Only at the end did he realise that he couldn't override the systems, and a whiphound detonation on minimum fuse wouldn't be powerful enough to guarantee destroying his ship from inside. So he did the only thing left to him: he opened his lock, venting all his air. He knew he'd die in the process, but there was no other way to break that weapons lock, even momentarily."

"You and I accept that picture," Dreyfus agreed. "Lady Jane is nearly persuaded. The others may get there eventually, thanks to Thalia's good work. What's your point?"

"That it suggests prior sabotage of Mizler's ship. Some kind of rogue program that caused his weapons to activate and then wouldn't let him stop the attack."

"Thank you for bringing this up just before you and I board our ships."

"Don't tell me you haven't considered it as well?"

Dreyfus stopped. "Of course I've considered it," he said brusquely. "Considered it and rejected it. Thyssen's been with us through every recent crisis. He's doubled and re-doubled the security procedures down here. No one could have gained access to Mizler's ship without tripping a thousand alarms."

Sparver glanced back at the oblivious Podor, currently spooling away the umbilical line. "Unless they're already working under Thyssen, with all the privileges they need?"

"No," Dreyfus said firmly. "Whoever got to Mizler's ship did it by some other means. No one in Panoply would have had any cause to start a bloodbath between humans and hyperpigs."

"Something's not right here, boss. You and I both know it."

"And we have to work to do, besides implicating trusted colleagues." Dreyfus softened his tone, not wishing to part on a sour note. "It's right to be vigilant. I will...talk to Thyssen. Find out a little more about Podor. But not now. Those schedules you drew up depend on us setting off at pre-arranged times, or the crossing efficiency falls apart."

"All right. We'll say no more...for now. Good luck out there, boss."

"The same."

They departed, flashing away from Panoply on separate trajectories, a minute or two later than intended but not so tardily as to throw out either of their schedules.

Six visits for Dreyfus, seven for Sparver, because of the way the algorithm had shaken out. Each would require no more than an hour on-site, just enough time to perform the minimum amount of supposedly routine inspection work. The idea was to look as if they were going about their normal business, nothing out of the ordinary. If by some chance either of them did pick up on something unusual, they were not to make anything of it there and then. Dreyfus had drilled this into Sparver: not so much as an ear-twitch. Just carry on as normal, and unless it was the last visit of the day, not even to return to Panoply or engage in any unusual comms. They could debrief each other when they were both back home.

The first day was a washout, but then Dreyfus would have been surprised and suspicious if it wasn't, so early in the search. He was glad that they had both managed to stick to the agreed schedule. Each had experienced a similar suite of feelings as the day progressed: first of all, the impression that everything was wrong, every detail off-key, then a gradual fading-off of that impression as the hours wore on and they slowly added more notches to their tally. They saw nothing that suggested any connection to Tench or Catopsis.

Six and seven down: thirteen habitats to cross, at least provisionally, off the list of four hundred and eleven. There was a long way to go, but their methodology was sound, and that was enough for Dreyfus. Sometimes all a policeman needed was a hard day's work and the promise of a soft bed at the end of it.

CHAPTER FOURTEEN

The border changed to blue, and a few moments later Hafdis emerged through the yielding surface, followed by Baudry and Breno. Dreyfus indicated Hafdis should wait a short distance down the corridor, just out of earshot of his colleagues.

"Did the Supreme Prefect attend this time?" he asked Baudry.

"Not today, Dreyfus. She's with Gaston, Tang and the other analysts, going through Ng's findings for the tenth or eleventh time. That was commendable work."

"Then you're persuaded?"

"There are still quite a few questions that need resolving. It could still be an accident of timing, making it seem as if Mizler was trying to do the right thing..."

"Or we could cut to the chase and assume that's exactly what he was doing."

"I understand you have an investment in his reputation, given that he was mentored by Bancal." She eyed him. "And speaking of the two of you, shouldn't you be out on your goose-chase right now?"

"I thought I'd take Hafdis along for the ride, now that we're into the swing of things."

The second day had been another bust. Sparver managed six visits, Dreyfus seven. But it hadn't been a completely wasted use of Panoply time. At the fifth location on his schedule, Sparver picked up a minor violation of polling implementation, meriting a follow-up. They conferred afterwards, satisfied that it was unlikely to have been of concern to Tench.

For the third day the algorithm had given Dreyfus a slightly less arduous schedule than Sparver's, with only four destinations. Dreyfus decided that it was the perfect time to show Hafdis what fieldwork was really like.

"Irregular," Baudry said, commenting on his plan.

"I won't be exposing her to risk or operational secrets. Mostly she'll sit in the cutter with me and experience another bout of space sickness." Dreyfus looked down the corridor, to where Hafdis was waiting with her back to the wall, her head dipped, hands at her sides. Impossible to tell if that was the posture of someone who knew they had been defeated at the first trial, or merely someone glad the first ordeal was behind them. "How did she acquit herself?"

"You'd need to ask Breno."

The prefect in question was jotting notes into his compad, tilted away from him so that Dreyfus could see the flowing lines of beautiful cursive he was setting down.

"Lovro?"

"Perfectly satisfactory, Tom, across all metrics."

"Just that? Satisfactory?"

"Look, if you're expecting a high-flier, you're setting yourself up for disappointment. She's just good enough to meet our standards, which is an achievement in itself, but it's nothing that'll mark her out of the ordinary within Panoply." He paused, making another note. "But perhaps that's what you feel we need now: solid reliability, diligence without flair."

"You're reading a lot into a few sessions."

"I am, and I have some experience with the way candidates pan out." His jaw tightened. "I'm just saying I wouldn't bet on her making it all the way through to field service. She might have the temperament for supernumerary work, and there's no shame in that."

"We won't write her off her just yet, Lovro," Baudry said, surprising Dreyfus by rising to Hafdis's defence. "I'll share my candidacy scores one day. I barely scraped through the early metrics, yet here I am with a seat in tactical, at the right hand of Lady Jane."

"Mm," Breno said, as if she had made some embarrassing slip of professional etiquette that was best glossed over.

"All that matters is that she's assessed fairly," Dreyfus said.

"Of course she will be," Breno returned. "I just want to make sure she's held to our highest standards. That's what Ingvar would have insisted on, I think we can both agree."

Dreyfus nodded half-heartedly. "Has she completed her assessment for today?"

Breno glanced down the corridor. "Yes, she's done for now. We'll see her again tomorrow, for introductory machine ethics. What have you got lined up for her, Tom?"

"I thought it wouldn't hurt if she got to look over my shoulder during some field duty. She can come with me while we visit more of those locations that might have been of interest to Ingvar."

"Well, good luck with that. There's another way, you know, besides

123

looking under four hundred stones. You could just go straight to Grigor Bacchus and ask him what the hell he knows."

He went back to his note making.

Dreyfus collected Hafdis and showed her the quickest way down to the docks.

"The green band is the indicated route, but if you take mauve to the second spin node, and transfer to indigo, it avoids a lot of congestion in Section D. There are only a thousand of us in Panoply, but you'd be surprised how the passages fill up during shift changes. I must tell you the best times to visit the refectory..."

"Do you know how I did back there?"

He had been expecting her to ask but was still not ready to give her the answer she sought.

"I'm not supposed to offer direct feedback on your progress."

"But I can't have flunked out yet or you wouldn't be taking me out in the ship."

After a silence Dreyfus said: "It's only day three."

"Is that all you're going to give me?"

He smiled testily. "It's a lot more than your mother would have."

"The tests have been pretty simple so far," she went on, breezily indifferent to his reluctance. "I had to speed-read a document, commit it to memory and then answer a few questions on it. They showed me an algorithm with an obvious coding error in it. They tested my left–right hemispheric dominance. They asked me to catch a ball nine times out of ten. I caught it twenty out of twenty." She shrugged. "I was expecting it to be harder."

"It will be, and soon."

They arrived at the docks at the same time as Sparver, who had come via a different route.

"You must be Sparver Bancal," Hafdis said.

He looked down at himself. "So I must."

"Mother mentioned you often."

"Because I'm a pig?"

"Because you impressed her with your commitment to Panoply." Hafdis squinted at him. "Unless I've got the wrong Sparver Bancal?"

"You've got the right one," Dreyfus said.

Sparver, who had shrugged off his earlier offence, nodded in the direction of the cutter that had been assigned to him. "Well, you're welcome to travel with me. I can't promise it'll be the most exciting day of your life, but at least you'll see the unglamorous side of our work."

"Perhaps she'll shadow you at some point," Dreyfus said. "Today, I'd like her to come with me." He offered a reassuring look to Hafdis. "You'll thank me. My schedule is pretty light, and Sparver has a much higher tolerance for gee-loads than I do."

They watched Sparver board his own ship, seal up, detach from the berth and leave Panoply. Dreyfus took Hafdis to the adjoining lock, where the other cutter waited.

"Light enforcement vehicle, Gila class. Your primary steed, if you make it to field service. Moidelhoff total nucleation drive for main propulsion, cold-gas for precision manoeuvring. Three gees sustained, six on military. Fast enough and small enough to get anywhere in the Glitter Band quickly. Rapid-cycle Breitenbach cannons, synchronised for ten kilometres. Otherwise, minimal armour and armaments. Anything more would add mass and bulk."

"A ship like that did a lot of damage to that habitat," Hafdis commented.

"It was a lightly constructed habitat." Dreyfus conjured open the lock. "The cutter still came off worse, in the end. It's important to understand that our authority isn't vested in strength. We police the machinery of democracy by consent, through the public trust granted us in accordance with the Common Articles." Under his breath, but loud enough to make his point known, he added: "Although it doesn't always feel that way."

They boarded the cutter. Hafdis moved cautiously in the weightless confines, as if merely being back aboard a ship was bringing back her motion sickness. Dreyfus showed her to the secondary seat and how to fasten herself in.

"But you can call on bigger ships and heavier weapons."

"With each escalation in power, the burden of consequence weighs more heavily on the Supreme Prefect and her seniors. Panoply is subject to continual oversight by citizen quora. If we overreach ourselves, exercise our powers indiscriminately, we stand to be checked. And some of those more forceful tools—field weaponry, nuclear devices—can only be dispensed after binding public votes."

"What if Panoply wanted to do something and the citizens denied it?"

"Panoply would abide by the public will. Even if that will was suicidal."

"Mother said it didn't always happen that way. That Lillian Baudry and Michael Crissel disregarded a binding vote and unlocked the weapons anyway."

"You're well informed," Dreyfus said, a portion of his good humour flaking away. "Was your mother in the habit of discussing matters of internal protocol?"

"I wanted to know the bad as well as the good."

"Now you do."

He took his own position and began the departure procedure, wondering what sort of mixed blessing Hafdis Tench might yet turn out to be.

For all his late misgivings, the day went well. He made three inspections on his own, then on the fourth—his instincts telling him that it was safe to do so—he had Hafdis accompany him to and from the polling core, where he performed a series of routine diagnostics.

"It's strange to think my mother was here," she told him, as they were on their way back to the cutter, walking through ornamental gardens where the flowers had the look of metal sculptures, their coloured petals throwing off a mirrored sheen.

"If it's too much for you, we can stop this arrangement at any time."

"It isn't. I *want* this. I can be as strong as she was. As strong as Jane Aumonier."

"That's not a comparison I'd make lightly, Hafdis."

"I didn't mean it disrespectfully."

"Best that you don't make it all."

They were detached, on their way back to Panoply, when she picked up the thread of the conversation again. "Is that something she talks about much, sir, that time she spent alone with that thing attached to her?"

"She neither dwells on it nor pretends it didn't happen to her."

"To go eleven years without human contact, without sleep...and all the while knowing that horrible thing might kill her at any instant." Hafdis shook her head in reverence. "It would have broken nearly anyone else, wouldn't it? And then the way it ended..."

"The Clockmaker didn't mean to make any part of it easy."

"Sir, would it be possible for me to speak to her about it, now that I'm in Panoply?"

"You're just a candidate, Hafdis. Maybe a wait a few years to bend the Supreme Prefect's ear."

"But I'm not just a candidate, sir, am I? I'm the daughter of one of your colleagues, killed doing the one thing that gave shape and meaning to her life. There's a reason Jane Aumonier came to my first interview. She was showing a personal interest."

"I said she doesn't pretend it never happened. That's not the same as wanting to rake over it again, with someone she barely knows."

"I just thought I'd ask," Hafdis said, saltily. "Mother had such respect for her, and I thought it would be good if Jane Aumonier knew that, because Mother probably wouldn't have allowed her feelings to show." She folded her arms. "But if you don't think that matters..."

"I'll mention it," he said, as cross with Hafdis as he was with himself for

126

being so easily guyed. "How's the motion sickness, by the way?"

"It's not been anything like as bad as that first crossing."

"I'm glad to hear it." Dreyfus applied power, the cutter veering sharply.

Grigor Bacchus was performing a dismemberment.

The hard-shell vacuum suit lay crucified on an inspection rack, its component parts being detached for maintenance and swap-out. Bacchus was struggling with a shoulder articulation, grunting as he worked a manual clamp, turning a long-handled wheel to apply force to the seized joint.

Bacchus was alone today, and that suited Dreyfus. Normally he worked with a small team of assistant technicians, just enough people to stay on top of the work of overhauling Panoply's inventory of hard-shell suits.

Dreyfus had brought a helmet with him directly from the cutter after docking with Hafdis.

"Hello, Grigor," he said.

"Dreyfus." Bacchus continued with his work, barely glancing up until the recalcitrant joint snapped free, the torso of the suit finally surrendering its arm. "Put that over there with a fault docket and sign out a spare from the rack."

Dreyfus set the helmet down on a wide table where there were already other helmets, parts of suits and a complete suit in its own right. There had been a minor fault with the drop-down glare visor, but nothing that warranted bringing it to Bacchus before its scheduled service date.

"While I'm here, I wondered if I might have a quick word."

Bacchus left the inspection rack and sauntered over, rubbing a grease-smeared palm across his balding tonsure, leaving stripes. He had been a big man once, a stooping giant who seemed too large for Panoply's corridors and doorways. The last four years had robbed him of some of that presence, Bacchus shrinking in on himself, the stoop hardening. "Well, that's a pleasant change."

"Is it?"

Bacchus inspected the helmet, hooded eyes discerning. "We used to be on nodding terms, Dreyfus, even if we weren't close colleagues. Now I can't remember the last time you gave me the time of day. I passed you in the refectory a week ago: not even a flicker of acknowledgement."

"I expect my mind was on something."

Bacchus rolled the helmet, picking a wad of fluff from the neck seal. "Now's your chance, then."

"I have no axe to grind with you," Dreyfus stated. "Four years ago, you acted in what you believed were the higher interests of both Panoply and the Glitter Band."

"You waited until now to tell me this?" Bacchus worked the mildly malfunctioning glare visor until it travelled freely.

"You committed errors of procedure and oversight. It was a mistake to advance Catopsis to the point you did without the involvement of the seniors. It wasn't a hanging offence, though. I'd be lying if I said I hadn't occasionally crossed those same lines in my work."

Bacchus set the helmet down. "Then my sins are absolved. The great Dreyfus has spoken. There's nothing wrong with this, by the way."

"Jane Aumonier showed restraint in your disciplining, nonetheless. It was clear that something had to be done. She opted to retain your talents, knowing a valued asset when she saw one. She—forgive the expression—stuck her neck out for you when others were quite keen to see you hung out to dry."

Bacchus rasped a hand against his chin, where the stubble had been growing out for at least a couple of days. "The acolyte always turns against the master. I've made my peace with that."

"Lovro Breno isn't why I'm here. It's about Catopsis."

"Then you're four years too late."

"Ingvar Tench may have been pursuing a lead about a possible reactivation of the program. Her interest in that line of enquiry may even have got her killed."

"I'm very sorry to hear that."

"I need a straight answer from you, Grigor. I know overhauling these suits keeps you busy—too busy for you to be attempting to resurrect that program. Someone's doing it, though. They might be operating outside Panoply, but they can't be acting without the expertise of your team."

Bacchus lifted his face to Dreyfus, who saw only a worn-down memory of the younger man. The defiance was there, the intelligence, too, but those four years had worn his strength of will down to the bones.

"So what do you want?"

"An assurance that you're not involved. That you know nothing and you've seen nothing."

"I'm many things," Bacchus said, spittle mantling his teeth, "but not a fool. We came close, before Tench shut us down. Close enough to succeed." The spittle lashed Dreyfus. "Close enough that we nearly changed things for the better. I know that, and I've made my peace with it. I'm broken, but so is Panoply. We make a good fit for each other." Bacchus scooped up the helmet and shoved it back to Dreyfus. "There. Good as new."

"Thank you." Dreyfus cradled the helmet with as much grace as he could manage. "These suits," he said, looking around the service area. "How do they get back to the ships, when they're overhauled?"

"Thyssen arranges it."

Dreyfus frowned. "Thyssen?"

"One of his underlings," Bacchus said testily. "Podor, Strax, one of them. Now, if you want to ask any more questions, at least do me the dignity of treating me as a formal subject."

Aumonier asked for a brief audience with Dreyfus. They met in the hot-house, the steamy, rambling miniature forest that the Supreme Prefect had decreed for her own amusement and diversion near the middle of Panoply.

"I won't keep you," she said, as they ambled along a steeply descending stream, "since I know this line of enquiry you're pursuing must be very tiring for both you and Sparver. I just wanted to let you know that I've had an official communique from the constables tasked with the Salter-Regent investigation."

Dreyfus tried to make it sound as if his expectations were modest.

"Has anything come of it?"

"It's early days, but the indications are encouraging. They're running a deep audit on that family's recent activities, including movements and financial transactions. Some very interesting things are starting to come to light."

"Really?"

"The further the constables dig, the shadier it all looks. They've already found a money-chain which makes that purchase of a nonvelope look more plausible than not. Beyond that, there are ties to at least three parties that were already raising suspicions from our end, but whom we couldn't move against without harder evidence. Now it's nearly in our grasp."

"We were overdue a breakthrough," Dreyfus commented.

"I'm surprised you don't sound more enthusiastic about the whole thing. The tip-off was directed to you personally, after all."

"It's a good development." He caught his breath, sweating heavily in the near-tropical humidity. "I suppose I'm just having a little difficulty removing my focus from the Tench enquiry."

Aumonier crossed the brook between two stepping-stones, making sprightly ease of it, not even close to perspiring.

"Well, that's understandable—but I just wanted you to know that something's panning out of it, after all." She looked back confidingly. "Between you and me, Tom, I'm minded to use extraordinary measures to back-trace that anonymous sender. If what they've sent us is as solid as it looks, I'm wondering what else they might know."

"I'd caution against it," Dreyfus said, grunting as he hobbled from one stone to the next. "They may run scared if they detect an attempt to expose their identity, and that might cost us another intelligence titbit further down the road."

"I'm sure you're right," she said, with an undercurrent of disappointment. "Sometimes I wish I had half your patience."

"Softly, softly, is the old adage," he offered, labouring to keep up. "Anyway, I don't think anyone needs to give you lessons on patience." Seeing a gambit to change the subject, he added: "Hafdis is something of a fan, by the way. She keeps pressing me for insights into your time under the scarab. I think it's a little bit more than a morbid interest."

"You're free to tell her whatever she wants to know."

"I think she'd like to hear it from you, rather than me." Dreyfus steadied himself as the path climbed steeply. "Any other candidate, I'd call it an impudence. But I can't deny that her connection to Ingvar changes things."

"In her mind, maybe." Aumonier made a noncommittal sound. "When I have an idle moment to myself, I'll gladly see her in the sphere. A few minutes in there should be enough to dent her curiosity."

"Or harden it." He wheezed. "She admires you, and that can only have come from her mother."

"Funny how Ingvar managed to keep that admiration almost entirely to herself."

"We all have inner depths," Dreyfus said. "I'm realising that more and more as I get older."

"To hear you speak, you'd think you were ready to quit on us." She said this off-handedly, but there was an edge to it, an implication that the remark was not entirely without serious intent.

"We should all recognise when we're no longer useful," he returned.

"And is that an admission that you feel your own usefulness is nearing its end?" There was warmth in her look, but also caution, warning him against such thoughts in future. "I need you, Tom, especially now. Even when you make mistakes."

"And what would they be?"

"I hear you went hard on Grigor Bacchus."

Dreyfus tried to keep an even temper. "We just had a nice little chat. Old times' sake."

"He didn't see it that way."

"That's his problem."

"The man has served his penance, Tom. He was guilty of misjudgement, an error born out of too great a love for Panoply, not too little. I'll ask you

130

not to treat him like a common criminal, just because of some tenuous link to your Catopsis hobbyhorse."

"It's a bit more than a hobbyhorse."

"Bacchus is off limits," she said sharply. "If you have grounds to interview him again—serious grounds—you bring them to me first, and we do things by the book. I won't have you hounding every individual in Panoply who hasn't lived up to your exacting standards." Her look became a glare, turning him to stone. "Is that clear?"

"Abundantly," Dreyfus answered.

Of the handful of rules he had internalised since his time in the organisation, one in particular was sacrosanct: Never get on the wrong side of Jane Aumonier. She was already striding off, her back to him.

CHAPTER FIFTEEN

Dreyfus and Sparver were four days into their search, the exhaustion and repetitiveness of the task gnawing at both of them, when the call came in.

Her name was Garza, a prefect out on fieldwork. Not the unusual kind that Dreyfus and Sparver were involved in, nor even the sort that was occupying more and more of Panoply's time—dealing with the repercussions of Mizler Cranach—but the ordinary kind that went on all the time, even in the midst of crisis. When her name flashed up, Dreyfus racked his memory for a face. He thought that he remembered her from his classes, five or six years back. Bright, hardworking, thoroughly dedicated to the profession, even though—in his limited view of her—there was some spark missing, some ability to think around corners not as fully present in her as it had been in Thalia and Sparver; a deficiency that might rectify itself with time and experience, or which might forever hold her back from the higher echelons of fieldwork and seniority.

He read her report, sent directly to him. On the far side of the Glitter Band, CTC had detected an object moving on a low-velocity trajectory through inter-habitat space, unlogged and unscheduled. Debris, perhaps, or some grey-economy transaction skulking its way from sender to receiver. Garza, her routine work concluded for the day, had been tasked to investigate. She had locked onto the object and approached it.

Scans revealed the drifter to be about the size and shape of a human corpse, shrink-wrapped in plastic. It was tumbling slowly, head over heels.

A corpse, on or inside a habitat, or just floating within its exclusion volume, was no concern of Panoply's. Local constables could handle that sort of headache. Out here, hundreds of kilometres between habitats, the jurisdictional boundaries were foggier. Panoply was not established to resolve individual crimes, presuming this corpse was evidence of such. Garza could have just tagged the drifter and handed the problem to one of a dozen or more civilian authorities set up to keep the space between habitats clean and well-regimented. On the other hand, a human corpse tumbling through space—even though no human had been reported

132

missing or murdered in this sector—was enough of a puzzle to justify Panoply engagement.

Garza had made the correct call. She'd approached the form, scanned it at higher resolution, confirming that it was indeed a body and then detecting *something* with an anomalously high density inside the body itself but nothing that quite looked like a bomb or booby trap to her, and grappled on. The corpse did not explode. She hauled it back to Panoply, but wisely signalled her status before coming inside the dock. A Heavy Technical squad came out to meet her, conducting thorough biological, radiological and nanotechnological tests on the shrink-wrapped package before certifying that it did indeed pose no serious risk. Garza watched as the corpse was handed over to Mercier's people in the medical section. Then she sent Dreyfus the message and went off message.

The reason she had contacted him? A tag on the corpse: a simple hand-written note saying "Atten: Prefect Dreyfus" and nothing else. Garza had appended an image of the tag to her report.

Despite his tiredness, Dreyfus dropped what he was doing and went straight down to Medical.

He had seen that handwriting before.

Mercier was waiting in the autopsy room, the body already laid out on a fresh examining table and divested of its shrink-wrapping. Dreyfus looked through the window for a few moments, steeled himself, then went through. He had been warned that the smell would be bad, and so it proved. His career had provided him with very little experience in days-old corpses, a pattern that he trusted was not about to be broken today.

"It's an odd one, to say the least," Mercier observed. "Do you recognise him?"

Dreyfus cast a cursory glance at the swollen, discoloured features. "No, and I wouldn't expect to." The corpse was naked, the chest and abdomen blasted open, exposing a mess of shattered ribs and shredded organs. "It came like this?"

Mercier indicated a hopper of grubby, torn garments next to the table. "It was clothed. I removed them carefully, but they were already in a bad way."

Beneath the grime and damage, Dreyfus recognised the same blue uniform that he had seen on Cassian and the other men and women working under Dokkum in Stadler-Kremeniev. "Unless his uniform is borrowed— which I suppose is possible in a war zone—this man was working for the central authority in the habitat where Tench met her fate."

"You met some of them," Mercier said.

"But not him. How long would you say he's been dead?"

"The shrink-wrapping adds an element of uncertainty, but at least five days, perhaps more. I tried to get a read on an implant, but it's either been damaged or was removed some time ago."

"Then he was dead before I got there. Cassian's forces had lost control of a whole city sector around the spoke. This man must have been left behind when things fell apart, killed by the mob, then his remains recovered after they swept back in to extract Tench."

"How can you know?"

"That's Cassian's handwriting on the tag. I saw him fill in an official document when he was escorting me to the front line."

"I can think of easier ways of getting a body to you."

"This might have been his only shot. My bet is Cassian acted largely alone, at some risk to himself. He would have taken the body to an airlock and dumped it into space, knowing there was a reasonable chance it would come to our attention."

"Because you like corpses?"

"Because I suspect the foreign object Garza found inside it will be Tench's missing whiphound."

"I like a man with confidence."

"Everything fits." Dreyfus glanced at one of the storage cabinets slid back into the wall, imagining Tench's body resting somewhere behind that grey facade. "You told Sparver there was no radioactive contamination on her body, and our teams on the ground found nothing close to the scene of death. That rules out the whiphound being used in grenade mode as a last resort." Dreyfus returned his attention to the new body. "Tench must have identified this corpse as a suitable concealment location, then told the whiphound where to hide." He looked at Mercier expectantly. "Well? Am I warm or cold? Put me out of my misery."

Mercier smiled thinly. "It's there, lodged in the thoracic cavity, mostly hidden by viscera. It looks damaged, but we'll know more when we get it out."

Dreyfus had brought an evidential preservation box with him, the kind that was impervious to mild radiation and conventional comms. He opened it and set it on the table next to the dead man.

"Get it out carefully, then put it into that container. Take your time. We don't know what condition that whiphound is in, and I wouldn't want it malfunctioning on you."

"And the corpse?"

Dreyfus thought back to the cruelties he had seen in Stadler-Kremeniev. "It's served its purpose. Burn it."

Deep in Panoply was a cube-shaped block containing an isolated interviewing suite. The cube had come into its own during the breakaway crisis, when Dreyfus and Aumonier had put Devon Garlin under the lens. There was no interviewee today, however: just Dreyfus and his evidential box.

"Give me ten minutes in there," he told Prefect Chin. "No more. If I haven't come out by then, come in with tactical armour, dual whiphounds and a bucket to mop up whatever's left of me."

"What's in that box?" Chin asked.

Dreyfus patted the container. "A whiphound I'm not sure I can trust."

He carried on through the connecting bridge and into the room. He nodded back at Chin and closed the door from within. Through the door's little window, he watched the connecting bridge detach and withdraw, leaving the cube floating on its own, isolated from the rest of Panoply except for the magnetic cradle holding it in position. The cradle was damped to smother acoustic signals: the best it could pick up would be someone hammering hard on the walls, desperate to be let out.

If things went wrong, Dreyfus doubted there would much time for hammering.

He entered the interviewing suite, which was separated from a small viewing chamber by a partition wall with a one-way mirror installed. The suite contained a table and a pair of chairs, constructed from inert matter. The same went for everything else surrounding him. There was nothing that could be conjured; nothing that could be made into something else, from a weapon to an illicit communications device.

He put the box on the table and sat in the chair. Then he opened the box, snapped on a pair of gloves Mercier had put in there for him and extracted the whiphound. It was sealed in a transparent evidential bag but otherwise in exactly the condition it had come out of the body.

It gave every impression of being dead. The casing was badly damaged, and there was no way to tell if the filament had been retracted back into the handle or severed cleanly. Denied a filament, the whiphound was slightly less dangerous in that it could not move itself or cut him. But it could still explode.

Dreyfus took the whiphound out of the bag and hefted the handle. It was sticky with blood and traces of bodily fluids and viscera. Was it warmer or cooler than he had been expecting? Hard to say.

He examined the controls. Whiphounds were programmed to respond to verbal and gestural instructions, but their basic operating modes were locked in by hard physical settings, worked with rocker switches and stiff dials. This whiphound had been set to use lethal force the last time its control settings had been updated.

Dreyfus set the whiphound to its lowest enforcement level. It might not make any difference, but it never hurt to try.

He pressed the main activation switch, holding it down for the full three seconds mandated in basic training. The whiphound buzzed and vibrated in his hand, and a spark of light flickered from the opposite end to the filament port.

The whiphound gave a crackle, ruby light spilling from one of the ruptures in the casing, and died on him again.

Dreyfus made another attempt.

The whiphound made a sound like a small, angry fly trapped in a tiny metal box.

Dreyfus listened hard. The noise was a human voice, being reproduced by an extremely damaged playback system.

He held the whiphound close to his ear.

Tench's voice said: "...this message. I need this to get back to Panoply...can only hope that it reaches...can trust."

Silence, crackles.

Her voice again:

"...wasn't the destination I locked in. This...programmed the cutter. Someone with access...wasn't me. I didn't do this."

Staccato bursts of scrambled sound.

Then:

"Bacchus...That's where you should focus your enquiries. But careful. They're ruthless. I see that now. In fact I..." A pause, deliberate now rather than a recording dropout. "I can't delay any longer. Find this. Stop Catopsis. And find Hafdis, if she doesn't come to you first. Tell her...not an attempt to kill myself...always love her."

A tone sounded, then the message started playing back again. There was a short preamble at the beginning before it cycled around to the part he had already heard, but he had missed nothing vital.

He listened to the whole thing twice more, straining to pick it out from the noise and recording errors, and making sure he had not imagined that invocation of the man behind Catopsis.

Dreyfus took out his own whiphound, activated it and set it down on the table next to the damaged one.

"Capture and secure evidential recordings from the adjacent unit. Confirm when you have a successful capture."

His whiphound blinked red.

"Play back the audio recording with the most recent timestamp."

Tench's voice emerged again, but this time from his whiphound. It had duplicated the recording, errors and all. The playback was louder this time, but no more intelligible.

He deactivated the damaged whiphound and put it back in the box. If it failed, or fell into the wrong hands, at least he now had a duplicate copy of Tench's testimony.

He believed her wholeheartedly. She had not meant to go to Stadler-Kremeniev at all. And everything that she said about Catopsis chimed with his own understanding of her actions over the last few months.

He wanted to let her know that someone knew. That someone understood.

CHAPTER SIXTEEN

Dreyfus made an immediate return visit to Grigor Bacchus, this time without the pretext of a piece of failing suit equipment. Striding into the workshop, he instructed two assistant technicians to make themselves scarce, and stared down the object of his ire.

"Don't ever lie to me again, Grigor. I'll always find out."

Bacchus looked up from the carcass of a spacesuit, tipped onto its back to access the smooth hump of its life-support systems, an anemone-like spray of glowing froptics erupting from the suit's innards and plunging into a compad resting against a helmet.

"I didn't lie. And unless you're here to make some kind of formal accusation, you can leave now."

Dreyfus recalled his reprimand from Aumonier, and her insistence that Bacchus was out of bounds until she said otherwise.

He forged on.

"Tench mentioned your name in connection with Catopsis."

The stooping, hollowed-out man gave a bored shrug. "Why wouldn't she? She had a fixation about that program being reactivated. I told her the same thing I told you. I'm not involved. I couldn't be involved even if I wanted to, not the way I'm chained here with this work." His eyes flared beneath a craggy prominence of brow. "What part of that didn't you understand?"

"I'm not talking about her general enquiries over the last four years."

"Then what?"

"Tench left us a message just before she died. It made a specific link between Catopsis and you."

Dreyfus thought he saw the first instant of real alarm in the face of Bacchus. "What do you mean, a message? How could she?"

"Are you asking me that because the idea was to silence her more effectively?"

"No, you cretin. I'm asking how any message got back to us, after the way I heard she died." He leaned in, foam scurfing his teeth. "I didn't *like*

138

her, Dreyfus. She ruined the one good thing I tried to do for us all. That doesn't mean I wanted her dead, or know about some continuation of Catopsis."

Dreyfus brooded, his expectations askew. He had gone in here expecting Bacchus to crumble, or at least attempt to put up some tissue of lies he could see through easily.

Neither was happening.

"Why would Tench suggest a link if none was there?"

"I don't know, because she was mistaken? Or someone put the idea in her head?" Bacchus shook his head. "I'm an easy mark, Dreyfus, I know that. I've taken one fall, I can take another. That's why I've kept my head down, giving no one any ammunition to use against me. Why in Voi's name would I throw that away?"

"If you had anything to do with her death, Grigor, I'll make sure you get a taste of the hell she went through at the end."

"You're wrong," Bacchus breathed. "Whatever she said in that message, it's nothing to do with me. Now get out of my workshop."

Dreyfus asked Hafdis to meet him in the refectory. He picked a quiet table and chewed desultorily on an apple until she arrived, guiltily re-running his encounter with Bacchus and wondering if he had gone in too hard. Early in his career Dreyfus had learned that self-doubt could be a policeman's enemy as much as ally, chipping away at the confidence and certainty he needed to function as a prefect. It didn't always lead to better decision-making. He had made errors in his time, plenty of them, but rarely had he felt betrayed by his own judgement of character. Or was it just that Bacchus was too wily to fold at the first hint of pressure?

He could go in harder still, with the permission of the seniors. Interviews under formal observance. All the way up to a trawl, to see if Bacchus's own brain patterns gave away his involvement.

Was he ready for that?

"Prefect Dreyfus?"

In his distraction he had not noticed Hafdis steal up to his table. He grunted acknowledgement, beckoning to the empty chair.

"I've got some news. I hope you find it welcome."

She scraped into the seat. "About the investigation we've been running?"

"Connected to that." He let her off the hook for the "we." "I've come into possession of a testimony left by your mother just before she died."

Hafdis planted her elbows on the table and leaned in.

"A testimony? How?"

He already knew what he could and could not tell her. "A recording

139

captured by her whiphound, one that's only just come into our possession."

"May I see it?"

"No. It's very badly corrupted, and in any case, there are issues of operational security." He bit a crater into the apple. "It does make one thing clear: nothing that happened that day was planned by Ingvar. She didn't intend to die, and she didn't intend to inflame an already damaged relationship with Stadler-Kremeniev."

"Then...why did she end up there?"

"Your mother was of the opinion that she'd been set up to die. The intention was that this should look like suicide. She had the technical expertise to force her ship to go somewhere it shouldn't, and to prevent its controls being overridden. She didn't do it, though."

"Do you believe her?"

It was the question he had been expecting. He still had to consider his answer. "I think I do, yes. There are still things that don't make sense, but I'm convinced that this was not a suicide bid. Your mother was still trying to do her job, to the very end." He looked into her eyes. "I hope that's some small consolation?"

"That she was frightened, rather than suicidal? That's not much of an improvement, is it?"

"No," he admitted, smiling forlornly. "Not much at all."

"I'm disappointed in you," Aumonier was saying, while Dreyfus looked for somewhere to direct his gaze, somewhere besides his shoes, the wall, or the imperious face of his superior. She was calm, and that troubled him far more than any outburst of anger would have done. Almost as if he had crossed a line into some hitherto unsuspected area of their relationship, a sort of cold ante-room, where distant formality was the order of the day, presaging the inevitable point when he was given his marching orders. What would it be, he wondered: total expulsion, or some nearly-as-bad demotion such as the one visited on Grigor Bacchus?

"I had reason," he stated plaintively. "The testimony from Ingvar's whiphound clearly incriminated him. I went in immediately because there were pressing grounds for establishing the truth."

"I don't care if his name was written in blood next to her corpse. You disregarded a direct order."

He bit his tongue. It had been a very long time since Aumonier had felt the need to give him anything resembling an order. Directives, permissions, guidelines, requests, but nothing as clear-cut as an order. Orders were for inferiors in the chain of command.

Which—if he was being honest with himself—was exactly what he was.

"I overreacted in the moment," he said, an instinct for damage limitation kicking in. "It shan't happen again." He paused, the unchanging severity of her expression hinting that rather more was expected. "I'm sorry, truly. You're right—your order was completely clear, and it was wrong of me to disregard it." Just as he was on the brink of offering some mitigation, sense prevailed and he added: "I apologise, wholeheartedly. I stand ready for any disciplinary measure you may see fit."

"You stand ready, do you?" she asked, her fury rising rather than declining. "As if I need your permission? Damn you, Tom. You know, I'd give you the tiniest benefit of the doubt if you'd actually found anything. But you didn't, did you?"

He evaluated the wisdom of answering. "Bacchus didn't crack, no."

"And what would be your inference from that, exactly?"

"He stands to lose a lot by admitting his involvement in Catopsis and the murder of Ingvar. He won't give up himself or his friends that easily."

Her voice was level, but freighted with barely contained rage. "It could also be that he's completely innocent, a man who's already paid one price and doesn't need to be bullied just because of some doubtful testimony—"

"I know what I heard," Dreyfus said sharply. "You're welcome to review the same recording. See if you come to a different conclusion."

"I have reviewed it. I heard a fragment which could mean anything. I *was* minded to lean on him, in an informal context—just a nice little chat, as you put it. You've poisoned that well, though. He'll give us nothing willingly now, and who can blame him?"

"Then bypass his willingness. Go in with the trawl."

"You're not hearing me, are you?" She shook her head in a spasm of irritation. "This can't be the end of the matter, Tom. If I let our friendship stand in the way of a formal process, one that you'd expect to be applied to any other prefect who disobeyed me, what would that say about my leadership, my values?"

Something broke in him, his last lines of defence crumbling to mortar. There was no point pleading his case with the one woman who understood him almost better than he understood himself.

"I'm sorry," he offered again, but this time with the full measure of sincerity he had not mustered before.

"I still need you," she said, more in sorrow than anger. "Now more than ever. Every prefect I can trust remains invaluable to me. And despite everything, I still think I can trust you. But there'll need to be something."

He nodded humbly. "Of course."

"When all this is behind us—as I must believe will happen—then we'll discuss it. Until then, you'll continue with your investigations into Ingvar's movements. I might question the wisdom of such a seemingly hopeless pursuit, but if it keeps you out of Panoply, and away from Grigor Bacchus, that's reason enough for it to carry on." She waited a beat, something slipping in her face, a flash of sadness or fondness, quickly masked. "Now get out of my sight before I say something I might regret."

Dreyfus obeyed without question.

They were on the eighth day of the search when Sparver investigated Asset 227.

Asset 227: one of several hundred otherwise nameless and abandoned rocks and habitats ticking around Yellowstone, technically still part of the Glitter Band, technically still within the reach of abstraction and all associated voting rights, technically still within the sphere of responsibility of Panoply, but otherwise forgotten or mothballed. Ripe for squatters or ghosts until the next wave of property speculation spiked the value of orbital real estate to the point that not even the smallest pebble was left unclaimed and unmonetised.

It was not those times now, though. It was not anywhere near those times. The Glitter Band was in an investment slump, and places were falling fallow faster than they were being snapped up for redevelopment.

Sparver had run a hasty audit on Asset 227 as he approached. He wanted to know who owned it and why it might have been of interest to Tench. The audit came back speedily enough, but it told him next to nothing. The rock was owned by an outfit called Hysen Holdings, but they were only the latest in a bewildering chain of similar fly-by-night businesses, each of which had swept up the pickings of the last when they were dissolved. Asset 227 was basically a piece of dirt that no one wanted, which had been batted from one faltering concern to the next for decades, and Sparver wondered if in all that time anyone had ever bothered setting eyes on Asset 227, let alone visiting.

Tench had, though. Three occasions in total, clustered within a few weeks of each other near the start of her stint as field prefect. Then nothing. She had not been back in more than three and a half years. That made Asset 227 an unlikely reason for killing her now—the cause, if it was there, surely lay in one of her more recent visits—but it was still odd enough that it needed looking at.

From the outside nothing struck him as anomalous. It was a wrinkled, rocky lump about three kilometres long and about a third as wide. It rotated along its long axis, rapidly enough that someone, sometime, had gone to the trouble of providing artificial gravity. Four gaping engine mouths were studded at the trailing end, with a modest docking facility set between them. The engines would have been used by Asset 227's original owners to shove the asteroid into orbit and then used only very occasionally, if ever, to nudge it out of trouble if its trajectory started drifting. It was another mark of the tired economy that the engines had not already been stripped out and recycled. Sparver wondered when they had last been activated: probably not for many years.

So he had no qualms about guiding his cutter to that docking position between the engines. He locked on with the tuneless clang of a broken bell, completed basic checks and then set about his inspection. He knew from the lock that there was vacuum on the other side, but anticipating no trouble—and wanting to get his visit over and done with—he opted for the relative speed and convenience of the m-suit, rather than hard-shell vacuum gear. He pushed through the m-lock's suitwall, smoothly but without haste, allowing the quickmatter membrane to adhere around his form and organise into functional components. The newly minted suit ran diagnostics on itself, verifying life support, power assist and comms, before budding off completely from the pressure-tight surface.

Sparver moved from the cutter into the outer chamber of the habitat's airlock. Some minimal power was still running, throwing a dim red light across the lock and providing enough functionality to detect his presence and begin the automatic cycle. He allowed the lock to go through its motions, but no air flowed into the chamber and when the inner door opened to allow him through, not even a gust of pressure came with it.

He used a pulse of suit thrust to send him drifting down a red-lit connecting tube, still entirely in vacuum. The tube went on for a couple of hundred metres, until he emerged into the dark stillness of a much larger space. Sparver stopped before he drifted too far into that void. He was weightless, floating alone, and small. His suit's lights grazed a dark surface behind him, a vague, bridge-like structure projecting off into the darkness. The rest of the chamber was too distant for him to make anything out, at least with the limits of his pig eyes.

Patiently he allowed the suit to sweep the space with its full battery of sensors. As it compiled its data, a grey-green overlay appeared on his facepatch, contours labelled with distance markers.

He was floating at one end of an ovoid cavity nearly as wide and long as the rock itself. The thing projecting away from him was a thick central trunk, running from one endcap axis to the other. It was inert now, but when it had been working it must have formed an artificial sky, acting as both an illumination source and a view block. It conformed to the basic blueprint he had seen a hundred times over in similar habitats, where a rocky asteroid had been cored out and made liveable. There were only so many ways to skin a world.

This one rotated, which made for a few minor complications. The rocky carcass around the liveable volume needed to be stabilised against the stresses of spin, which usually meant some combination of fusing the rock, infiltrating it with hyperdiamond lattices, or sheathing the outer surface in some resilient bonding membrane. Non-rotating rocks still needed to be made pressure-tight, but that was generally a simpler and cheaper proposition than arranging for a full gee of gravity. The mere fact that this rock hadn't fallen apart pointed to its originators having deep pockets and the willingness to spend whatever it took.

It was airless now, so perhaps there was a slow leak, or the place had been deliberately depressurised to cut down on insurance premiums.

Satisfied that he was not immediately at risk, Sparver instructed his suit to take him further into the void. The ovoid space rotated slowly around him, his sensors sampling and re-sampling as the area nearest to him changed continuously. Without air to snag at him, he moved independently of the rotation, still feeling entirely weightless.

The suit continued information-gathering, the contour overlay gaining detail and texture with each rotation. The inner walls of the ovoid had been meticulously landscaped, laid out with a miniature fairyland of hills, glens, lakes and woods. By the time he had drifted from one end to the other, he knew that there was only one building of any size, a chateau-like cluster of towers, spires and walls perched on its own hill at the confluence of a dozen serpentine roads. Beyond the chateau was a handful of much smaller structures, some not much larger than playhouses or hunting lodges. It was clear that Asset 227 consisted of a single, private estate, with the chateau as its main adornment.

He veered nearer, allowing the chateau to swoop by beneath him on each rotation. His suit's lights doused it in ghostly blue moonlight, enhancing the desolate, spectral quality of the abandoned property. The chateau and its ancillary structures—the battlements, bridges and moats that encircled it—were well preserved, if airless and empty. He saw nothing to suggest power or inhabitation anywhere in the landscape, and nothing from his sensors contradicted that impression.

His suit had been sniffing for a local abstraction layer. There was nothing at the limits of its sensitivity. Sparver's suit was still maintaining normal data links with his cutter, but that was his only functional connection to the rest of the Glitter Band. Anyone living here now—assuming they were hiding beneath the threshold of his sensors—was doing so in a starkly impoverished data environment.

Sparver doubted that anyone was here. The place felt crypt-cold and abandoned. The absence of an abstraction layer was no more puzzling than the absence of air. There was no sense providing abstraction and polling core access for ghosts.

So why had Tench come here?

"Boss?"

There was a chance—quite a good chance—that Dreyfus would be out of contact or unable to reply. But Sparver was pleased to hear a reply nearly instantly.

"I'm here. What is it?"

"Not sure. Something slightly fishy, maybe. When I compiled that list, I cross-checked against active polling cores. I felt that if we were going to pass off our visits as routine business to do with a polling core, it would help if one were actually present."

"What are you saying?"

"My suit's not sniffing out anything resembling a polling core. I'm inside an abandoned rock named Asset 227. Spin-stabilised up to one gee, probably had pressure at some point, but now blown out to hard vacuum. Dark and lifeless, and definitely no polling core, whatever our records say."

"That doesn't add up."

"Glad you agree, boss. If the polling core went inactive recently, or was removed, it should still have been updated in Panoply's records. This rock shouldn't matter to us. But Tench visited three times…"

"All right. You have enough to prick my curiosity. But you're to take no further interest in the place until I've had time to run a more exhaustive search through the turbines."

"Or I could just take a closer look. There's only one structure of note inside this thing. It shouldn't take me more than a few minutes to nose around inside."

"Keep to your schedule, as we agreed. If, and only if, there's something worth looking into, I might petition the Supreme Prefect to escalate this up to a Light Enforcement action."

"Understood, boss."

"We'll speak when we're both back in Panoply. Dreyfus out."

Sparver floated in silence for a few moments, deliberating. He was not given to disobeying orders. Applying a liberal interpretation to them, though, that was something else. He had been told to leave and he would. But if the path he took back to his cutter happened to be slightly indirect, and involved taking a closer look at that main building, would he be guilty of anything except an over-zealous dedication to his work?

He steered his suit closer to the moving wall while staying high enough to avoid being swatted by the chateau as it came around again. The answer, if indeed any answer existed, had to be found somewhere in that over-ornate fabulation. He meant only to bring his suit's full scanning capabilities to bear on it, to gain some idea of what was inside it and what sort of person might once have called it home.

The chateau passed beneath him, his suit sweeping it with a range of energies and sensor modalities. The suit could only peel back the outermost layer of the structure, but that was enough to hint at a dollhouse-like labyrinth of rooms, hallways, passages and staircases, piled floor upon floor and subtly echoing the curved geometry of the wider interior. There was still no trace of power, heat or pressurisation.

Without warning, his suit addressed him.

"Amber caution. Moving surface detected on collision vector. Please acknowledge and indicate desired mitigation measure."

"I'm out of harm's way, you idiot," Sparver told the suit. "The chateau missed me first time around, it'll miss me the next time as well."

"Amber caution. Moving surface..."

It was not the chateau, he realised, although as it came around, he noticed that it was indeed displaced from its original position. That was not his problem. Paying proper attention to the contour diagram, he saw that the surface in question was the far end of the ovoid, where he had come in through the connecting bore.

It was getting closer.

"Neutralise relative drift," Sparver said.

But he had told the suit to do that already. If the surface was moving, and his suit hadn't initiated any undesired relative motion, then there was only one explanation. Asset 227 as a whole was changing speed.

Habitats were not meant to do that. It was in orbit around Yellowstone, part of a stately waltz of similarly large, ponderous bodies. Orbital adjustments, if they happened at all, were almost only ever tiny nudges, correcting microscopic course deviations long before they became problematic.

The suit, shriller now:

"Red caution. Moving surface is on an accelerating vector. Please select an immediate mitigation measure."

Sparver evaluated the very limited set of options open to him. However quickly the wall was moving now, it would be travelling a lot faster by the time it caught up with him. If there had been air in the rock, the inertial drag would have begun to sweep him along in advance of the wall, softening any impact when it came. The suit could divert some of its mass into a cushioning surface, if he gave it enough time...or he could use the time he had left to attempt to match the habitat's motion.

That was easier said than done. His suit jets were meant for zero-gee manoeuvring, not keeping out the way of continuously accelerating, mountain-sized walls of rock. He might be able to outpace the wall for a few minutes, but only by running his propellant reserves down to zero. And then he would be back where he started, an inert, floating speck about to be swatted out of existence.

His best option—in fact his only real one—was to fix himself to the habitat's interior and ride out the acceleration. That would cost propellant, too, but once he was attached to the habitat, he would have no further need of the suit jets. He needed only to buy himself some time. He was confident that Panoply would have already detected Asset 227's deviation from its normal orbit. Long before he needed to worry about his suit running out of life-support capability, they would be here with cutters, corvettes, cruisers and every kind of enforcement level imaginable.

"Boss? Got a slight problem here."

Dreyfus replied promptly. "Is something preventing your egress from that rock?"

"Yes, but not in the way you're thinking. The whole thing's moving. I've got no option but to land on the inside surface and ride out the motion."

"Then do so."

"A moment, boss." Sparver used his visual designator to identify a target position on the moving wall, close to the tunnel where he had emerged.

"Negative solution," his suit came back. "Vector unacceptable under present propellant constraints."

"Well, give me one that is acceptable!"

The suit offered a spray of solutions. They were all on the curving landscape between the two endcaps. These landing spots were as good as the suit could manage given the remaining pressure in his jets. Thinking he could stay out of the wall's reach for even a couple of minutes, he realised, had been optimistic.

From a standpoint of immediate survival, the landing options were all equally good. But since he was already here—and was obliged to be here for a while—it seemed to Sparver to make sense to be put down as close to the chateau as possible.

He eyed one of the solutions, blinked hard to let the suit lock it in.

"Sparver?"

"Still here, boss. Now I know what you were saying about not investigating any further..."

"But an opportunity might just have presented itself," Dreyfus answered.

Sparver felt the rising shove from his suit jets. Slowly the landscape began to lose its apparent rotation.

CHAPTER SEVENTEEN

Aumonier arrived at the tactical room to find Robert Tang already standing at the Solid Orrery, his gaze falling on a part of the Glitter Band that pulsed with flame-red urgency.

"How bad it is?"

"Too early to be sure, Supreme Prefect. Bad enough to be going on with." Tang conjured an enlargement of the problematic sector, a single habitat swelling up until it was grotesquely out of scale with its neighbours, elevated on a stalk so that it appeared to be floating above the main plane of orbits, purely for ease of clarity. "Asset 227. It's an abandoned rock, only four minutes ago its primary motors started up."

"And I wasn't informed the instant that happened?"

"There was a chance it was a scheduled orbital adjustment: a kick boost to loft it from one lane to another. We had to monitor to be certain." Something twitched at the side of his mouth, like a maggot wriggling beneath his skin. "It's not a kick boost. The thrust is steady, one fiftieth of a gee. Not much by the standard of a ship, but enough to create difficulties."

"You have a spectacular talent for understatement, Robert. How long until it rams into something?"

Tang made another conjuring gesture, an arcing line appearing in the Solid Orrery. "The burn is aligned with the orbital plane, taking it on an inward spiral from its present position. Emergency avoidance directives have already been communicated to all vehicles and habitats within the projected hazard zone. Some are being asked to slow down, some to speed up. Depending on how quickly they can respond—which in turn depends on the mass and readiness of the affected body—we have somewhere between nine and eleven minutes before our first near miss. If it's a near miss."

"And after that?"

"Solution space becomes too crowded. Each orbital adjustment causes a cascade of secondary responses, all the way around Yellowstone. We simply can't predict this far out."

"Try. I want a fistful of best- and worst-case responses, and I don't want to be still waiting for them when that near miss happens."

The tactical room doors pushed open, Baudry and Clearmountain bustling in with harried, anxious expressions.

"Fill them in, Robert," Aumonier instructed. "I'm going to see what Dreyfus thinks."

She took her usual seat and used her authority to reach out beyond Panoply. "Prefect Dreyfus."

"Yes, Supreme Prefect."

She had been putting a deliberate distance into her interactions with him since the Bacchus business. Not to punish him, or undermine his sense of her own confidence in her abilities, but to signal that there would still need to be a reckoning for his actions. She wondered if any of the others had noticed that uncharacteristic formality, so unlike their usual working relationship.

"Sorry to interrupt you. An alert may already have reached you, but we have a developing situation with a piece of real estate. A rock called Asset 227 is executing a dangerous, unauthorised course change. Robert is—"

Dreyfus cut her off. "Sparver's in that rock, ma'am. We're in contact and he's already informed me about the vector. Is it as bad as it sounds?"

Aumonier tensed. An already complicated situation had just opened out into several more dimensions, like a chessboard ballooning into a tesseract.

"Did Sparver initiate this course change?"

"Not deliberately, although it's possible his arrival triggered something. His suit's trying to get him onto fixed ground. From there, I'm hoping he can return to his ship and detach. I have Hafdis with me, but I'll take all necessary measures to assist Sparver."

Tang had been listening in. He broke off from his conversation with Baudry and Clearmountain to call across to the table. "Confirm we have a fix on Prefect Bancal's cutter, still docked with Asset 227. I'm sorry we didn't flag his presence sooner."

"Dreyfus, would you mind holding for a moment?" She didn't wait for his answer. "Aumonier to Thyssen."

"Yes, ma'am."

"Status on Prefect Bancal's cutter. It's currently docked with Asset 227."

"Affirmative, ma'am. But we have a non-zero acceleration parameter for that cutter."

"Correct, Thyssen. The habitat it's docked with is moving out of its lane. If we could assume command of the cutter, could we negate some of that unwanted acceleration?"

Thyssen was speedy with his response. "Negative, ma'am. The vectors would be co-aligned. Even if we had the thrust to make a difference, all we'd be doing is adding to the acceleration."

"Thank you, Thyssen. Stand by. I may wish to exercise that option."

"I'll look into it, ma'am."

She returned to Dreyfus. "Did you get that?"

"Yes, and it was good to check, even if we're only talking about adding or subtracting a tiny margin. I'm computing a crossing to Asset 227 now."

"Get there as quickly as you can. We'll keep running through the options from our end. Have you any idea what this means?"

"I don't. Except that whatever it was we were looking for, Sparver may just have found it."

Sparver touched down in a pool of widening light, hemmed by darkness. He had weight now, pinned to the floor beneath him by the rock's centrifugal gravity. The floor felt as if it was on a slight slope, due to the continued acceleration coming from the endcap motors. He turned up the adhesion factor of his soles and leaned in as if walking against a stiff gale. His suit had cut it fine with the propellant reserves, down to its last few seconds of useful thrust.

"Sparver to Panoply," he said, finally drawing his breath. "Feeling you might appreciate an update about what's going on in here. You'll forgive me if I was little preoccupied until now, what with not wanting to be squashed."

"Thank goodness, Sparver. We've heard from Dreyfus that you were in contact, but we were still worried about you."

"You think you were worried, ma'am?" He was speaking directly to the Supreme Prefect, not exactly a surprise given the ripples that must have been spreading out from the rock's movement. "You should see the state of my suit."

"Situation report, please. Asset 227 is moving unexpectedly, and without authorisation. Can you account for this change of behaviour?"

"I wish I could, ma'am, then I might have a hope of stopping it. Is Dreyfus still on the line?"

"I'm listening in," came back the strained but recognisable voice of his immediate superior. "I'm on an expedited burn. I'll be in your vicinity in thirteen minutes. Do you any idea what triggered this change?"

"Nothing that I'm responsible for. The first thing I knew about it is when my suit warned me I was going to get splatted unless I did something."

"Have you made groundfall?" Dreyfus asked.

"Yes. I used my suit jets to match speed and rotation with the rock, then landed on the inner surface, close to the main structure I mentioned."

"The one I told you not to take an interest in?"

"Who else is present?" Aumonier interjected.

"Nobody, ma'am. Place is an empty, airless shell. Somebody was here once—this place was clearly liveable at some point—but whoever it was must have cleared out and mothballed the rock some while ago."

"And it's beyond doubt that Tench showed an interest in this place?"

"Not just once," Dreyfus interjected. "Something about that rock pulled her there in the first place, and something drew her back. I think Tench may have altered our records to suggest a polling core was present when there wasn't."

"Why in the name of Ferris would she do that?"

"To provide a cover for her repeated interest if she was ever called to explain it. If Tench was investigating something sensitive, something with potential links to Catopsis, she wouldn't have wanted it scrutinised by other elements within Panoply."

"Then we must also face the possibility that Tench set a tripwire the last time she was there. Something as simple as a laser, or a gravimetric motion detector, wired to the endcap motors. When it detected Sparver, it lit those drives."

"I don't like it," Dreyfus said.

"No, neither do I. But the facts speak for themselves. If Tench rigged this trap, and altered those records, then it's increasingly likely that she was responsible for the alterations to her cutter. They speak of the same expertise, and the same willingness to tamper with our systems and protocols."

"More pertinent question," said Sparver. "Whoever arranged this trip-wire, it didn't do a lot of good, did it? Tench was thorough. If she was going to set a trap to kill a prefect nosing around after her own investigations, she'd have done it properly."

There was an audible catch in Aumonier's reply. "I fear you may be under a misapprehension, Sparver. It would seem very likely that the point of the tripwire wasn't to destroy you, but to force us to destroy the entire rock."

Sparver nodded with the suit. He could see where she was going with that, the clean, gliding logic of it. "But you don't have do that just yet, do you? Not until there's a plan for getting me out first."

He didn't like the delay before she answered.

Aumonier pressed around the Solid Orrery with the other prefects and analysts. The projected path of Asset 227 was a broad, curving brushstroke of red cutting across the orbital lanes of hundreds of other habitats, until it eventually broke free of the inner part of the Glitter Band, crossed a narrow margin of mostly empty space and then intersected Yellowstone itself. By the time it emerged from the Glitter Band, the path was already more than a thousand kilometres across, reflecting the uncertainty in Panoply's calculations. Any unanticipated change in the rock's motion would only add to the range of solutions.

"Avoidance measures have now been implemented across these orbits," Tang said, dipping a wooden pointer into the complex, oozing quick-matter realisation. "Fifty-six habitats have begun velocity and trajectory corrections, with varying degrees of effectiveness. In some cases, those steering motors haven't been lit for decades, so they're having trouble starting them up. We're already processing reports of malfunctions, as well as collateral casualties and structural damage in those habitats which have been able to respond. In the timeframe available to us, evacuation operations are largely out of the question, although of course any ships already docked are preparing to depart, taking as many as they can carry. Where possible, citizens are being directed to mass survival shelters, but even that is putting a tremendous strain on local resources."

"We told them to be ready for this sort of emergency," Aumonier lamented. "A rogue habitat was bound to happen eventually."

"They'll be sure to listen the next time," Tang answered.

"What are the present odds that we avoid any sort of collision before Asset 227 exits our jurisdiction?" asked Clearmountain.

Tang glanced at a compad. "Eight per cent and falling. There will almost certainly be a collision. The only uncertainty lies in the magnitude, the immediate projected life-loss and the secondary collision events caused by debris from the first."

Aumonier nodded. "Can we muster enough ships to act as tugs?"

"Negative, ma'am. We can't get enough vehicles in position to make a difference."

"Then might we disable the motors? If we can't stop it crossing those orbits, we could at least stop it changing course and speed. That should help with our predictions."

"Two options, ma'am," said Tang. "A warhead strike against the motors,

153

enough to knock them out but not shatter the rock. The other is to send a destruct command to Prefect Bancal's cutter. The two should achieve similar results." He appraised her cautiously. "You would need to seek a polling mandate for nuclear deployment."

"I already have it," Aumonier said resignedly. "I didn't even have to table a motion. As soon as the crisis began, the other habitats couldn't wait to shove a dagger into my hands."

"Pity they're not so eager when one of our own is at risk," Baudry said.

"I'll take what I'm given. Where is Pell when we need him?"

Tang dabbed his stick close to the moving rock. "*Democratic Circus* is moving in now. Pell has confirmed receipt of the nuclear authorisation mandate. Binding seals are now broken."

"Tell him to ready a single fish, minimum yield, locked directly onto those engines."

"Affirmative, ma'am. Is he to deploy immediately?"

"I'd have said so, wouldn't I?" she snapped back. But Tang was under as much pressure as she was. "Sorry, Robert: that was uncalled for. I mean only that we must give Prefect Bancal ample warning, so that he can find such shelter as he may." She turned to Baudry and Clearmountain. "Lillian, Gaston. Prefect Dreyfus, if you're still listening. I believe that neutralising those motors will buy us time. I am mindful of the risk to Sparver, but under our present circumstances I see no other option."

"Sparver will understand," Dreyfus said. "And the sooner you tell him what's coming, the sooner he can prepare for it."

Baudry and Clearmountain glanced at each other. "We concur," Baudry spoke. "It's by far the least-worst option, given the developing situation."

"Aumonier to Prefect Bancal. Can you hear me, Sparver?"

"Loud and clear."

"I am attempting to disable the motors impelling your rock. In two... no, let us say three minutes, a single missile will arrive at the engine core. It is not my intention to destroy Asset 227 or chip off any large part of it, but I cannot rule out some major structural failure. Is there any chance of you reaching your cutter in under three minutes?"

"Not a hope, ma'am. My suit's out of useful thrust, and it's too far back to the lock."

"Then we'll detach your cutter ahead of the impact. There's no sense in destroying it needlessly: we may need it to rescue you."

"Do what you need with the cutter, ma'am. I'll take care of myself."

"I don't doubt it. I advise you to seek out and utilise any hard shelter that may be accessible to you."

"I put myself down next to the only large building anywhere in the rock. I'm hoping it has a nice, deep, well-fortified basement."

"Go to it, Sparver, and keep recording and transmitting all the way. You don't have long."

CHAPTER EIGHTEEN

Dreyfus pulled his cutter up alongside the much larger Panoply cruiser. The *Democratic Circus* had already disgorged a solitary missile, maintaining station just beneath its flattened, sharklike belly. The weapon hovered there, tipped and finned, waiting for the precise moment to streak across the few hundred kilometres to Asset 227. It could afford to wait; once the weapon was under way, the journey would take almost no time at all.

"Prefect Dreyfus," said Captain Pell. "Your presence is welcome, but I'd recommend a stand-off distance of at least one kilometre before the warhead departs."

"How long do I have?"

"A little under ninety seconds."

"Good. Give me ventral lock access, please. I have a passenger to transfer."

Hafdis turned to him, the meaning of his words sinking in. "Can't I stay here?"

"No, it's much too dangerous. Keep out of the way, but watch and learn from Captain Pell and his crew. It won't be time wasted."

She looked back at Asset 227, still framed in the forward windows. "Dreyfus, I mean Prefect Dreyfus, I..." But it was as if she caught herself on the verge of an unforgivable error, something it would be impossible take back.

"What?"

"Nothing," she answered, a break in her voice.

Pell signalled that Dreyfus had authority to dock. He pulled the cutter in, the docking surfaces mating into a single membrane, and indicated for Hafdis to pass through. She gathered her compad and candidate-issue tools and exited through the suitwall without complaint, her only transaction a guarded look back at Dreyfus as he prepared to separate the two ships.

What was in that? he wondered. Concern for him, or some reproach

156

for an over-protectiveness that he would never have extended to a candidate without her family name?

"Look after her, Pell," he said, slipping into informality now that it was just him on the link.

"We'll stop back at Panoply as soon as this blows over. Twenty seconds, old man. I'd move if I were you."

Dreyfus put his cutter on expedited burn. The cruiser fell sharply away, and after a few moments the warhead beneath it became a scratch of violet light.

When the scratch faded, the warhead was gone.

Sparver found his way into the chateau easily. It would have been harder if the suit had landed him beyond the main walls, but since he was already within the grounds he only had to scout around until he identified the remains of a grand entrance flanked by immense stone lions, its two giant-sized doors flung wide and hanging off their hinges, as if they had been blown open from within. He detached his whiphound and sent it sweeping ahead of him.

Through the doorway was a high-ceilinged entrance hall, with corridors leading off and spiral stairs sweeping both up and down. Picked out in the unsparing light of his suit, the interior architecture looked pale and fish-bony, full of unsettling coils and filigrees. Everywhere he looked, there was evidence of abandonment and violent decay. Knee-high pillars, which must once have supported ornaments and statues, had been toppled, their delicate prizes shattered into thousands of ebon shards. He moved through the detritus, feeling it crunch silently beneath his soles. A larger statue, too heavy to have been easily toppled, stood perfectly headless. Its neck had been severed in a clean, silver-gleaming cut. At its base, instead of a single head, stood a collection of roughly circular slivers, too neatly sliced for it to have been anything but deliberate. Paintings had been torn from walls, then slashed into fine ribbons. Where murals could not be removed, they had been hacked and scoured into near oblivion, so that it was all but impossible to identify the subjects and motifs of the compositions.

Sparver descended the staircase, noting more signs of vandalism as he did so. The stairs wound down through seven hundred and twenty degrees, bringing him to what had been a subterranean, chandelier-lit landing, off which more corridors fed. He could take the staircase no further, but his aerial scan had suggested two or three floors beneath this one. He set off down the widest, tallest corridor, hoping it led to another means of descent. He had not gone far when his lights picked out a large, dark mass partly obstructing the passage. His whiphound sniffed around the fallen form, then signalled back to him that it detected no immediate hazard.

Sparver approached. The fallen form turned out to be a robot, not a toppled statue. It was a powerful, bear-sized machine with an armoured torso and reverse-jointed, ostrich-like legs. The legs had been cut away at the knees, leaving gleaming stumps jutting from the ovoid torso. Sparver eyed the damage with a prickling understanding. He had taught elementary whiphound-handling for long enough to recognise the repetitive, fine-textured slice pattern caused by the cutting edge of a whiphound's filament, employed in either sword mode or on an autonomous defence setting. A beam weapon would have left melt-marks at the margin of the cut. A cruder cutting tool—the sort of thing available to civilians—would not have left that shimmering signature.

"This is Sparver," he reported. "I'm deep into the chateau and it's... weird. Looks like one of our own was here."

Dreyfus answered him. "Clarify, please."

"There are statues and paintings here. Anything with a face on it has been hacked apart, most likely by a whiphound."

"You think it was Tench?"

"Who else, boss?"

He edged closer to the fallen robot. The exact type was unfamiliar to him, but it had the basic functionality of a heavy domestic servitor or security drone, the sort of muscle any rich family liked to keep around. He imagined Tench working her way through the mansion, effacing the pictures, decapitating the statues, until she ran into the robot. She had defeated it, seemingly, but the tables could easily have been turned.

"What were you doing, Ingvar?" he asked aloud.

"Sparver, this is Jane. I recommend you start preparing for impact. You have just under thirty seconds."

Sparver winced. He knew he was in trouble when the Supreme Prefect spoke to him on first-name terms.

"I'm ready, ma'am."

He picked a corner, squatted down into it as firmly as he could and waited for the inevitable.

Dreyfus turned to look in the direction the warhead had flown. It was already too distant to be seen, lost against the thousands of moving lights from habitats and ships both near and far. A few heartbeats later, a flash sparked out of the darkness. Asset 227 had been too small and dim to stand out until that moment.

The flash faded, but what remained was a slow-motion flowering of ruby-stained debris and gas as the warhead's impact revealed its toll on the rock's motors. The cutter's radar confirmed that the rock was still present and largely intact, but no longer accelerating. Dreyfus allowed himself a pinprick of relief: their strike had not triggered a larger explosion, a risk that had been real but impossible to quantify. Now it looked as if the intervention had been about as effective as any of them had dared hope.

"Supreme Prefect."

"Go ahead."

"Pell seems to have knocked out the engines without any serious consequences. I'm looking through a debris screen, but all the indications are that the rock is holding itself together."

"Yes—we read the same. Tang is refining his solutions now. Now that Asset 227's motion is purely ballistic, we can have some confidence about where to focus our efforts. I'm afraid we've lost our feed from Sparver, though. His cutter must have been amplifying an already weak signal, in the absence of internal comms." She paused. "I don't think it's an immediate cause for concern..."

"I'm going to get in closer and see if I can pick him up again."

"I don't advise it. There'll be little or no warning if that rock flywheels."

"I'm sure my ship will do its best to keep me out of harm's way. In the meantime, can you request Thyssen tasks Sparver's cutter to cover the opposite side of Asset 227 from my approach? We don't know where he is in that thing, and his signal may be stronger on one side than the other."

"There's no point arguing, is there?"

"I'm already in your bad books—one more strike won't make much difference. If you want to make the best use of my presence, bring in the other cutter and start sniffing for a signal."

He heard the faintest sigh, as much out of resignation as respect for his commitment to a colleague. "Continue, in that case. Much as it pains me to see a second prefect put in harm's way, when one is already endangered. Thyssen will mirror your movements with the other cutter. But I need to address the possibility—"

"I know." He was terse. "You might still need to blow up the whole thing."

"Tang is processing. We'll have a forecast very shortly."

Dreyfus silenced his thoughts. There was no point speculating on outcomes yet to be decided, not when so many variables were still unclear. He allowed himself only one consideration: that of contacting Sparver while he still could.

*

There was no flash, no sound. Sparver felt a shudder, then a long, rattling aftershock. He remained pressed to the wall, not daring to move until he was certain that the strike's effects had played out. Thirty seconds after the initial strike, he felt a series of sharper, nearer rumbles pass through the chateau's fabric. Further aftershocks followed. Then a silence and stillness that jangled his nerves to breaking point.

He seemed to be still alive. The chateau had not come crashing down on him, imprisoning him in its rubble. Asset 227's spin-generated gravity was still holding him to the floor. That was good. If the place was in the process of breaking up, he would have known it by now. Rocks were pretty sturdy things, even hollowed-out ones.

He waited another minute, just to be on the safe side, then got to his feet. The slightly off-perpendicular vector caused by the Asset 227's acceleration had gone.

"Sparver to..." But he trailed off, already noticing the comms alert pulsing in his facepatch. The suit had lost its already fragile connection to the outside world.

Sparver accepted his isolation. He was unharmed and his suit was still totally functional, aside from the depletion of its propellant reserves. The whiphound waited, coiled nervously but showing no sign of damage.

He backtracked around the fallen robot to the lower-level landing. With the immediate risk out of the way, his best hope lay in returning to the surface and re-establishing comms. If that proved impossible, he would make his way to the opposite endcap pole, where there might be another set of docking facilities.

He stopped in his tracks, surveying the wreckage of the spiral staircase, all two turns of it. It had crumpled down on itself, leaving the upper landing hopelessly out of reach.

"All right," he said to himself, not just because speaking aloud helped with his mental equilibrium, but also because his suit would log a recording of his decision processes. "All right, then. The staircase has collapsed. If we can't go up, we try another way. And if that doesn't work, we go down. There'll be an escape shaft somewhere underneath this building, right through the rock out to open space. No one builds something like this and *doesn't* put an escape shaft in. Right, Sparv?"

He was hoping that the more absurd his monologue became, the more likely it was to be overheard. But the comms warning remained.

He reversed again, back around the robot, past the spot where he had sheltered against the wall. The corridor opened out into a parlour with panelled walls and mirrors, and a strange black machine squatting in the middle. It had four ornamented legs and a panel hinged up from the top,

160

so that the machine's guts were exposed to the ceiling. Sparver moved around it, noting an interface set with a strip of curious white and black controls in a linear array. He depressed a random selection of them, wondering if they might activate power or lighting, but nothing happened.

A body caught his eye. It had been hidden from view by the machine, lying on its back on the floor with its face averted. Sparver snapped his whiphound closer and told it to run a hazard-sweep on the corpse.

The whiphound moved to the body. It circled it, making puzzling, spasmodic movements. Something in its algorithms was being confused at a deep level.

Sparver came in closer, relying on his suit. The corpse was that of a human man, dressed in clothes that looked expensive and well-coutured, but also about fifty or sixty years out of date.

Sparver knelt down and pulled the head into view.

He jumped for an instant: the head had no face. The entire front part had been sliced off. But his shock abated as quickly as it had come. This was no human corpse. Behind the missing mask of eyes, nose and mouth was a messy business of mechanisms. Where the glittering parts had been severed, Sparver observed the same shimmering texture that he had seen earlier.

The face had been sliced away with a whiphound.

He spread his fingers and moved his hand up and down the torso. The suit scan, appearing as an overlay on his facepatch, told him what he had already guessed. The man was a mannequin, all machine and no living matter. This was not a highly cyborgised person, but pure robot.

The mannequin would not have been any sort of threat while it had been functional, Sparver decided. The outer layers were plastic, the inner chassis a simple frame of joints and actuators. It contained nothing recognisable as a weapon.

He looked back to the squatting black machine, to a small stool that had toppled under the control console. He imagined the mannequin seated at this stool, operating the machine.

"Easy, boy," he signalled the whiphound.

The whiphound relaxed.

Sparver saw a door through to an adjoining room. Even as his suit lamps pushed fans of light through the aperture, he made out more corpses.

This time he barely jumped. If there was one faceless mannequin, why not more?

He circled the second room, inspecting the bodies. They represented a variety of ages and genders, from children to elderly-looking adults, but in all cases they had the stiff, musty look of theatrical performers dressed

161

in period finery. Without exception, all had been rendered faceless. What-ever had become of their faces once they were removed, there were no traces left in the room.

"Did you do this, Ingvar?" he mused aloud. "Did you break in here, and go on an orgy of face-removing? The robots, the paintings, the statues? And if you did, why?"

It had all been done in haste.

He would have liked to stay, but it would take a Heavy Technical squad to get anything useful out of these machine corpses. He had neither the means nor the time to perform anything but a cursory visual capture. Perhaps there would be something in his recordings that offered some insight into Tench's actions, but that would be for later.

He still needed to find a way out of Asset 227, and going down still felt like his best option.

Unsettled, feeling as if he had stumbled into a puzzle whose solution was both larger and stranger than he could yet grasp, Sparver set off.

CHAPTER NINETEEN

The debris cloud constituted only a tiny percentage of the rock's total mass, but it was still a formidable hazard. It was thinning out as it dispersed, but not quickly enough to permit him a clear run all the way in. The cutter's proximity alarms began to sound, shrill and nervous. It wanted to turn Dreyfus around, avoiding the field completely. He pushed forward, and the alarms became louder and more frequent. The cutter, with his best interests in mind, tried to usurp control. He forced it to keep obeying, feeling as if he were whipping a wild-eyed animal into running for the flames instead of away from them.

Light impacts pitter-pattered against the hull. The cutter announced a toll of minor but rising damage. Dreyfus allowed it to avoid the largest hazards, but not to turn back.

"Conditions?" asked Aumonier.

"Bumpy but tolerable. Tell Thyssen to consider the second cutter expendable. Get it in as close as possible and keep sniffing."

"Thyssen reports no contact as yet. The signal could be weak and localised."

"It'll be there somewhere. We're not giving up on Sparver."

"Of course we aren't. But at the same time, we must be realistic about the risks."

Dreyfus extracted his compad and thumbed through the most recent updates. It took his mind off the collision warnings and the rain of impacts, picking up in intensity the closer he got to the focus of the explosion.

"I've been calling up priors on Asset 227 from the moment it became a problem," he said. "Nothing stands out: it's a piece of unwanted real estate. So why was Tench drawn here?"

"She may have had to look under a lot of haystacks until she found the one needle she was looking for."

"Yet something called her back to this place. If it was a washout, why return?"

"To make sure it was a dud? I'm afraid only Tench may have been able to answer that one. Here's something else: if I was part of a group attempting to resurrect Catopsis, I'm not sure a cold, airless rock is the place I'd pick for my base of operations."

Dreyfus had not thought of it that way.

"I agree. They'd need camouflage—pre-existing activity, routine space traffic, comms. Not this silent, cobwebbed ruin."

"And yet *someone* didn't like us poking around."

The frequency of the collision alarms had begun to drop off. He was through the worst of the debris, with only incidental damage.

"Are you still there?"

Was it his imagination, or did he detect the first subtle thawing in her voice, friendly concern trying to break through the cold facade?

"Yes," he answered, smiling slightly to himself. "I'm within a kilometre of Asset 227. It's still holding together. I'm going to get in closer and let the rotation bring the whole thing into view. Tell Thyssen to run gravimetric scans, too. If we can pick up the signature of a structure, we'll know roughly where to look for Sparver."

"I concur. But time is now of the essence. Tang's predictions have hardened. We have an unavoidable impact event in eighteen minutes. The rock will make a glancing collision with Carousel New Montreal, current population one hundred and fifteen thousand citizens. The closing speed will be high enough to destroy the habitat completely, with a projected life-loss in the high five figures. I can't let that to happen."

"Of course not," he replied.

"Aside from the immediate loss of life, the combined debris will be even more destructive than the loss of Carousel New Montreal. Our forecasts show upwards of a third of a million fatalities from secondary and tertiary collision events, calculated up to thirteen hours after the initial impact."

"I know what you have to do," Dreyfus said. "But give me those eighteen minutes if you can. It'll give me time to find Sparver and get him out of there."

"You have all the time I can give you," Aumonier said. "But it's rather less than eighteen minutes. Asset 227 is moving into a relatively sparse sector of the Glitter Band, for now. Pell's warheads can blast it cleanly, and the debris cloud will disperse before it has a chance to play havoc with other habitats. We lose this window of intervention in twelve minutes, when the rock starts moving back into the more congested inner orbits."

He nodded, accepting the bloodless logic of the calculation, certain that Aumonier took no more delight in it than he did. "If twelve is all that's on offer, I'll take twelve."

"Dreyfus." Her voice softened. "Tom. You're right—you are in my bad books. But that doesn't make you expendable. Find Sparver if you can, but above all else take care of yourself."

"Ma'am," he answered.

Sparver had gone down another level, deeper into the chateau. At the end of a series of rooms and corridors he had found a much less ornate means of descent: a straight flight of stairs leading down into a basement level where the decor was plain and no paintings or murals had needed to be effaced. The bodies had dried up, too. He had found a few more on his way down, each bearing eyeless witness to the same treatment. Now he moved along empty, featureless corridors, convinced that if there was an escape shaft, this would be the place to look for it.

He had been jumping at shadows the whole time he had been in the chateau, but that was only because of the way his lights played across the furnishings, creating an illusion of movement where none was present. His whiphound was much less ruffled. It had been confused by the human-seeming corpses, but at no point had its proximity sensors picked up on any other moving forms. The chateau was as empty of life as it was airless. There were no human inhabitants, only a dead security robot, and the mannequins were long deactivated.

Sparver turned a corner and saw something that gladdened his heart. It was an old-fashioned airlock, robust and uncomplicated, set at the end of a short stub of corridor. He had found his escape. There was no other possible reason for putting an airlock in the basement of a house unless it fed into a vertical shaft running right through the mantle of the rock. Still vigilant, he moved to the lock and had the whiphound scan it for booby traps. There was nothing except a tiny pulse of residual power, just enough to detect an intervention. He palmed the lock's activation panel and observed a faint yellow gleam light up around the controls. Above the lock's frame, a yellow beacon began to revolve, pushing out spokes of whirling light. The lock opened, the door pushing back in his direction then sliding silently into a recess in the wall.

There was nothing waiting on the other side, just an empty shaft. He leaned cautiously against the frame and peered in and down. He saw only darkness. He watched for ten or fifteen seconds until a pale light glimmered from the shaft's extremity. It was gone as quickly as it had come, but it was all he needed to know that the bottom of the shaft was not capped over. He could jump, when he was ready. Centrifugal force would send him on his way, bumping and skidding against the shaft walls, but eventually popping out into freedom. The suit would absorb the worst of the buffeting.

He tensed, readying himself. It was a curious thing, jumping into a black well. He almost felt as if he needed the encouragement of the rock breaking up around him before committing to the darkness.

His facepatch flashed a proximity warning. He spun around, his back to the shaft. His whiphound had taken up a defensive posture halfway down the short corridor. Beyond the whiphound, having just come around the corner, was another of the security robots. This one was intact, its ovoid body supported by an intact pair of reverse-jointed legs.

The robot popped a pair of gun muzzles from its body.

The muzzles flashed.

"Memo to self," Sparver mouthed. "Next time, jump."

The whiphound flung itself at the robot, a lethal quicksilver squiggle with its filament angled to inflict maximum damage. Sparver raised an arm defensively, his suit registering the impact points from the robot's guns. Short-range explosive projectiles flashed against his m-suit, the military-grade quickmatter organising itself to form instantaneous hardpoints under each projected impact site. He stumbled back with the sucker-punch from each strike, but managed not to topple into the waiting escape shaft. The whiphound was a scissoring blur, snipping away at the robot piece by piece. The legs went from beneath it, then the body crashed to the floor. The muzzles kept firing, but the whiphound was dealing with them as well, coiling its filament around the tip of each muzzle and constricting. The robot's aim went haywire, the explosive rounds taking chunks out of the walls and ceiling. Then it stopped firing altogether. A handful of status lights flickered through the ovoid's casing, then went dark. The robot had become as inert as its counterpart on the upper level.

Sparver recovered the whiphound, making sure it was undamaged.

"Another of those shows up, try to give me a *little* more warning," he said.

He need not have been too worried. The robot was clearly meant for domestic security, not warfare. It had done quite a bit of damage to the decor, but it was not as if anyone was around to complain about that...

Sparver froze. The robot had blasted a torso-sized hole right through the corridor wall. They were into the bedrock of Asset 227 by now, so there ought to have been solid material behind the wall's cladding. Instead there was a void.

A large void, stretching away: his lights reaching only a little way into the space. What he saw was sufficient, though. The void was full of mannequins, upright this time, and with faces. They stretched away in ranks:

copies or near-copies of some of the corpses he had already inspected.

Sparver looked back to the shaft. The sensible thing was to jump down it now, before Asset 227 threw another surprise at him.

But he had to know what was going on with the mannequins.

He turned up his suit amplification and made short work of peeling open the hole in the wall until it was large enough to step through. At the threshold, he stopped and marvelled. There were numerous mannequins, fifty or sixty at least, representing all the shapes and sizes he had already seen. Each stood on a grey pedestal, shrouded under a domed glass enclosure. Their eyes were open, but their faces were blank, staring out with no acknowledgement of the recent disturbance.

He walked to the first one, the whiphound slinking ahead.

A voice crackled.

"...arver. This is Dreyfus. I have a faint read on your comms. Can you hear me?"

"You're coming through, boss. What's the news?"

"I'm extremely glad we reached you. Can you get out of there as quickly as possible? There should be a shaft right under the main building. We can see it in the grav-maps."

"I've found the shaft."

"In which case get down it immediately. We have no option but to destroy Asset 227."

Sparver didn't bother asking why. They would have their reasons, and that was enough.

"How long do I have?"

"Three minutes. We've been trying and failing to contact you all this while." A new urgency entered Dreyfus's voice. "You'll have sufficient exit velocity from the shaft, even without suit jets. We'll have a fix on you as soon as you emerge, and a ship meeting you the moment the debris cloud has cleared."

Sparver moved along the line of mannequins as he spoke to Dreyfus. There were no names on the plinths, just machine-readable codes in a format unfamiliar to him.

"I hear all that, boss."

"Good. Why doesn't it sound as if you're moving?"

"I've found something. A room Tench missed, when she was moving through here."

"A room doesn't matter. Get out of there."

"This room might. I'm compiling evidence now. The link's poor, so I'm not even going to attempt to share it with you. Besides, I think..." Sparver paused, trying to riddle some sense of what he saw, and how it fitted with his picture of Tench. "Do we think Ingvar was a good prefect, right until the end?"

"Until proven otherwise. Two minutes, Sparv."

"For some reason, she didn't want to share her findings here with Panoply. In fact, she went out of her way to destroy evidence as best she could, just in case someone else stumbled along. Destroying pictures, statues, mannequins, anything that might point to the identity of the people who owned this house. That tells me two things, boss."

"Good. You can share them with me later..."

"Tench knew that what she'd found here was dangerous. She couldn't bring it back to Panoply. She wouldn't know who'd end up seeing it along the way. Who'd be watching. Who'd be listening in."

"Sparv...please."

"I can't leave, boss. This has to be documented. I think it matters. I think it *really* matters, and it needs to be for your eyes only. And I need all of these two minutes."

"All the evidence-gathering in the world won't matter if you don't get out of there. Save yourself, then we'll talk."

"No, boss," Sparver answered gently. "I've got to do this. How long is it now?"

Dreyfus was silent for a moment. Sparver guessed that some part of him was moving to a pained acceptance of what must be done. "Barely ninety seconds. I'm sorry, but there's no way to extend it out any further."

"I wouldn't want you to. And it's all right. I will finish my work here. I just..." Sparver swallowed despite himself. He wanted to keep a stoic calm, but it wasn't happening. "I'm not intending to die. I'm going to close my eyes, hope for the best and tell my suit to do its damnedest to save what it can."

Dreyfus lowered his voice.

"I can't order you to leave, can I?"

"Not unless you want to spoil a beautiful friendship. And it has been just that, boss—right from the start."

Sparver waited for a reply, but none came. He had lost comms again. That could only mean that Dreyfus had needed to put some distance between himself and the rock.

Perhaps it was for the best, to be on his own again.

He was nearly back at the start of the line of mannequins. He guessed he had gathered enough evidence to put the old man on the right track. If he waited a little longer, kept scanning and recording until the warheads hit, the suit would never have a chance to consolidate itself. Granted, that would be a tolerably fast and painless way to go, smothered in the white balm of creation. Plenty of hyperpigs would have chosen that, over the way they had been forced to go.

But he had an obligation to the evidence; an obligation to Panoply; an obligation to his mentor.

The m-suit had four levels of emergency preservation. It would step through each in turn, in response to the escalating threat. Level one: whole-body preservation of occupant. Level two: preservation of core organs and central nervous system. Level three: preservation of neural material for possible post-mortem reconstruction. Level four: preservation of evidence.

Once the protocol was initiated, the occupant had no control over its outcome.

Sparver Bancal knew this.

He said: "One Vienna Goodnight."

The suit did the rest.

When the warheads had finished their work, there was nothing left of Asset 227 but a thinning cloud of hot gravel and gas, still moving along the projected path of the original body. It was by no means a perfect outcome, since a mountain's worth of debris still posed a formidable hazard for the habitats whose orbits it had yet to cross. Every prefect monitoring the destruction understood as much. While hundreds of thousands of deaths might have been averted, there was still going to be a significant toll of casualties as the cloud rained against armour and glass. Emergency measures were already in force across the affected orbits; little more could now be done except to wait and respond where necessary.

Dreyfus had retreated far enough from the rock that his cutter had weathered the blast with only a few more dents and scratches to show for its troubles. Thyssen had pulled Sparver's cutter to a safe distance as well. Dreyfus sent out a general request to all available Panoply assets to scan for a locator pulse from Sparver's suit, or more realistically—knowing the emergency preservation protocol—what was left of it.

He could not be sure that anything had survived. Radar and lidar scans were already probing the cloud, assaying its contents. Where the warheads had struck, the rock had been reduced to a fog of thermally fused fragments, tiny glassy beads. There was no chance of any artificial object surviving the conditions in which those beads had been forged. But further in, shockwaves had done the bulk of the destruction. These had shattered Asset 227 comprehensively, leaving almost nothing larger than a pebble. To stand a chance of success, Sparver would have needed to issue the preservation command before he had any tangible sense that he

169

was about to die. When every cell in his body would have been screaming out its desire to keep living.

But Sparver would have done it. Dreyfus had no need to convince himself of that.

There was still no guarantee that it had worked. The cutters, corvettes and cruisers in the area were sweeping the moving volume where something might have emerged, as well a generous margin of error. They were listening for a faint, Panoply-specific signal, against a background of noise and interference caused both by the strike itself and the clamour of signals and alarms in the aftermath.

And finding nothing at all.

CHAPTER TWENTY

He moved through Panoply like a rolling ball of rage, vengeful and single-minded. People saw him coming and kept out of his way, prefects, analysts and technicians alike scattering aside. They knew what had happened out at Asset 227, what had happened to Sparver Bancal. They understood that Tom Dreyfus might not be answerable to himself, not now and perhaps not for some long while.

Thalia was there when he reached the hardsuit workshop, waiting outside, holding her hands out to him.

"Sir, you'd better not go in."

Dreyfus tightened his grasp on his whiphound. He had been ready with it since he left the cutter, daring anyone to question his intentions.

"Out of my way, Thal."

"No, sir. You don't understand."

Some portion of his rage turned onto her. "What part don't you think I understood, Ng? Sparver just got murdered. He died because of Grigor Bacchus, to protect the secrets this snivelling shit's been keeping from the rest of us."

"Sir..." Thalia unholstered her own whiphound. "This isn't what you think. The Heavy Medicals are already in there. Grigor Bacchus is dead. They're just making sure there's nothing that can be brought back."

Her words battered against his rage. He could understand them. They made sense. But no part of that sense was ready to reach him.

"Out of the way."

"No!" she snarled, bringing up the whiphound—filament still sheathed, but her willingness to use it plain enough even to him. "I'm under orders, sir. They tried to explain it to you before you left the dock and you wouldn't stop, you wouldn't listen." Thalia's voice was laced with steel. "Don't make this worse than it already is, sir. You're allowed to be angry. Don't you think I'm the same?"

"You don't know..." he said, his fury breaking into shards, leaving

171

him wheezing out his words. "You weren't there."

"With respect, sir, only Sparver was there." Thalia eyed him cautiously, then slowly lowered her whiphound. "None of us were there for him," she added quietly.

Dreyfus cooled. He slid his whiphound back into place, hand trembling with anger and shame.

"Bacchus is dead?"

"It's not good, sir. The way he did it. There's an automatic vice in there, something for re-setting suit parts. They found him in it. That's why there's so little chance of trawling anything."

Dreyfus heard himself speak as if a bystander to his own conversation. "He did it?"

"There's a note. A confession, of sorts. He says not to blame Podor too much; says Podor was only doing what he thought was right; said he was naive and easily led."

"Get Podor here."

"Sir, he's gone as well. Thyssen found him. Found what was left of him."

He breathed: "What?"

"That's why they were trying to stop you, sir. Podor was in one of the docked ships. He had maintenance access...It seems he blew himself up in there with a whiphound."

"Tom," said Jane Aumonier, her voice lulling in his ears. "I see you've already been briefed on the situation here. I wanted to be here before you, but you weren't to be detained."

He turned to face the Supreme Prefect. She looked alert but brittle, as if recent events had tested even her monstrous capacity for concentration.

"Bacchus denied everything," Dreyfus said.

"You didn't come storming down here to confront him about nothing."

"I just wanted to hear it from his own lips. How this wasn't anything to do with him. I wanted to watch him and decide how much of it I believed."

"Even after I've twice ordered you keep away from him? Even after I made it clear that there'd need to be consequences for your earlier actions?"

"Even then. This isn't about me or what happens to my career. This is about getting to the truth of exactly why one of my closest friends was just murdered."

Aumonier switched her gaze onto Thalia. "You did well, Ng. And since we haven't spoken directly until now, may I express my profound regret about Sparver. We've all lost a colleague, but you've also lost a good friend."

"He was a friend to more of us than we knew, ma'am," Thalia managed.

"He won't be forgotten, mark my words. And one of the ways we'll honour his memory is by building on your findings, and how they relate to Mizler Cranach."

"Thank you, ma'am."

"You may go, Ng. We'll speak in due course."

Dreyfus and Aumonier stood in silence after Thalia had departed. Now that they were on semi-private terms, Aumonier moderated her tone fractionally. "Voi knows I understand your feelings, Tom. Consider yourself fortunate Bacchus was already dead, though. I fear we'd both regret what would have happened if he'd still been alive. At least you haven't added to your earlier infringements."

Dreyfus wanted to contradict her. He could not. She had read his rage as accurately and efficiently as she scanned data feeds.

"That's it, then," he said fatalistically. "Bacchus kills himself rather than surrender any more intelligence on Catopsis. He was the inside man, but the operation's still running somewhere outside Panoply."

"The other possibility is that he killed himself out of remorse for what just happened at Asset 227. It may finally have got too much for him."

"Tench's death wasn't enough?"

"We can't know what was going on inside his mind, Tom. Even less so now. I wouldn't go in there. What he's left us with isn't pretty."

"Am I forbidden?" he asked her.

"Now that you've calmed down? No, it's your choice. I just didn't want you to storm in there, thinking there was still going to be something you could wring out of him. Oh, and Tom?"

He looked at her guardedly. "What?"

"I suppose this means you were right about him all along. That excuses a few things, but not everything."

Dreyfus went in. The Heavy Medicals observed his arrival and pulled back from their work deferentially, giving him an obstructed view of the scene of death.

"We're sorry about Sparver Bancal, sir," he heard someone murmur, barely able to meet his eye.

Dreyfus went to the pulped thing that had once been the head of Grigor Bacchus. He stared it in numb disconnection, unable to relate the exploded, overripe mass with the man he had been questioning only a few days before.

He had pushed, indeed.

I wasn't too hard on you, was I? he asked of the corpse. *Tell me I wasn't too hard.*

173

But Grigor Bacchus was long past the point of offering him any solace.

Thirteen hours passed. When the immediate crisis had died down, the reports of new casualty numbers dropping from three-figure numbers to dozens, then ones and twos, Jane Aumonier convened her senior operatives in the tactical room.

To Dreyfus, the room felt darker and more oppressive than usual, as if the walls had been moved nearer and coated in an extra layer of varnish. His collar chafed against his throat, lagoons of sweat pooling beneath his uniform. He had not brought an apple with him, a measure of his distraction.

"Everyone by now is aware of the news," Aumonier said, sitting more than usually upright with her fingers clasped and directing a personal glance at everyone present, including a lingering, heartbroken stare at the position that might ordinarily have been occupied. "That said, it feels wrong not to make a formal acknowledgement of our loss. Earlier today, Prefect Bancal died in the line of duty. He had an opportunity to escape his fate. He chose not to take it because he believed that his life mattered less than the possibility of securing evidence, right until the end." Aumonier shook her head slowly. "There aren't words enough to express my admiration for his selflessness—admiration that I know we all share. This wasn't some considered act of self-sacrifice, for which he had time to prepare himself. There was no time for that. Sparver didn't have the luxury of reflection, of looking back on his life and service and evaluating the choice before him. He simply did it, in the moment, knowing—without the slightest flicker of self-pity—that it was the right decision, that what he had found was worth the price of his own existence. I do not mean to denigrate his memory by saying that I believe his choice was instinctive. That does not negate the courage behind it. It merely speaks to the depth of his character, to the clear distinction between right and wrong which ran through him like a life force." She unclasped her hands and made a slight beckoning gesture in the direction of Dreyfus. "Tom; I've said too much. You should be the one speaking of him."

Dreyfus spoke slowly, the words coming with difficulty. "You have said everything I would have said, only better. I wasn't with him at the end. Just a comms link, which failed a few seconds before the strike. By then, he knew there was no way out. He was about to give the preservation command to his m-suit. I think he wanted to delay as long as possible to continue evidence-gathering, but I'm hopeful that he still managed to give the order in time for the suit to act upon it before the warheads arrived, and perhaps achieve some level of self-preservation."

"But we don't know," said Baudry.

"We're still sweeping the zone and listening hard for that pulse," Aumonier replied. "But it's been thirteen hours now. Every particle involved in that explosion has now dispersed beyond our jurisdictional margins. It may be that his suit didn't have time to consolidate, or it may have been too close to one of the bursts."

"We keep searching," Dreyfus said.

"Yes...yes, of course," Aumonier said, almost too hastily. "We can't commit all our resources indefinitely, but even as we start moving vehicles and personnel back into normal duty patterns, they can still be listening out."

Dreyfus opened his mouth, hesitated, snapped it shut again.

"Tom?" Aumonier asked.

"There's no normal now. There can't be. And now that Grigor Bacchus has robbed us of any possibility of questioning him about links beyond Panoply, I need more prefects on my investigation, not fewer."

Clearmountain said: "May I ask, what were the particular leads that took Prefect Bancal to Asset 227?"

"We obtained a log of Tench's movements in the four years of her field service," Dreyfus answered. "I reasoned that any place of particular interest to us might be one that Tench had revisited, possibly because she had grounds to suspect a reactivation of Catopsis."

"And did Asset 227—based on what we now know of it—fit that picture?"

"You know it didn't, Gaston, so spare me the trouble of explaining it to you."

"Tom," Aumonier said softly. "This is a difficult day for us all. You especially, I know. We're all of us dealing with it on some level, though, including Gaston."

Dreyfus pinched his collar away from his neck. "All right, I'll spell it out. Asset 227 doesn't seem like a candidate for Catopsis. But we only know that because we investigated. What we do know—now—is that someone didn't want us there. The place was rigged to break from its orbit, practically forcing us to destroy it."

"It's curious, certainly," Baudry said.

"Curious?" He fought to keep his voice from rising. "It's a lot more than curious. Someone used us to do their own dirty work of destroying evidence."

"Did Prefect Bancal find direct evidence of a crime, specifically something that would lie within Panoply's remit?" Baudry fell into the familiar didactic cadences of her induction lectures. "I would remind us all that Panoply has no authority when it comes to the internal policing of habitats, provided the Common Articles are respected."

"I don't think Tom needs reminding of that," Aumonier said. "Nor do any of us. The circumstances surrounding Asset 227 are indeed suspicious. Due diligence will be done with regards to the possible motives of those who left it behind. We'll pick through its chain of ownership with a microscope. But we must temper our expectations. The rock has been lost, and despite Prefect Bancal's exemplary work, our only line of evidence may have gone the same way. Tom, you were in verbal contact with Sparver for part of his time inside the rock. No recordings of those exchanges were transmitted back to Panoply or preserved in your cutter, so we only have your verbal testimony. I presume this was a deliberate step?"

Dreyfus nodded. "I was concerned about eavesdropping. If Catopsis has been reactivated, even as an outside operation, it's unlikely that it could be perpetrated without the collusion of elements still within Panoply."

"Grigor Bacchus's suicide note leaves little doubt that he was the coordinating link," Aumonier said.

They all had copies of the testimony on their compads, copied directly from the original. They had read it before the briefing, noting the joint implication of Podor.

"Tench was suspicious of Bacchus," Dreyfus said. "That doesn't mean that all our questions begin and end with him. I still want to understand what Sparver found, and how it related to Ingvar's activities."

"Speak freely," Aumonier said.

Dreyfus looked around the room, wondering if he could indeed trust everyone present.

"Sparver found an elaborate building. It was empty of life, to the degree that he was able to search it in the time available. He found signs of desecration, someone deliberately obscuring the identities of the figures associated with the house."

"Tench's work?"

"She had the means and the opportunity. But we don't know what she was hoping to achieve."

"Have you discussed the desecration with Hafdis?"

"Not a word. I put her aboard Pell's ship before I regained contact with Sparver."

"In which case float it past her, see if it chimes with anything her mother may have mentioned. It's a long shot, but in the absence of testimony from Sparver, I'll clutch at any straw."

"I'll speak to the candidate," Dreyfus said.

The meeting had not been adjourned, but he got up anyway. Sometimes there was an art to knowing when to leave.

CHAPTER TWENTY-ONE

Jane Aumonier floated out into the middle of the spherical room in which she had spent eleven sleepless years. She turned around as she drifted, beckoning for Hafdis to follow her.

"Come," she urged, Hafdis lingering on the threshold before committing herself fully to weightlessness. "There's nothing to be shy about. The Clockmaker was my adversary, not these walls. The room kept me alive and sane; I owe it a great deal. That's why I've never felt shy about returning."

"It's not just that this is the place where it happened," Hafdis said, gamely propelling herself out from the doorway. "It's that this is the room where you still watch over everything." She allowed her arms to fall limp as she drifted out, approaching the volume of space near the room's middle, where Aumonier had already come expertly to rest. "It feels like a privilege to be here, ma'am."

"It is," Aumonier said crisply. "You have this privilege, as I had the privilege of knowing your mother. Drink it all in, Hafdis. If you want to pursue this ambition of becoming a prefect, this is where it all leads." She swept a hand at the jostling, squirming multitude of feeds. "Ten thousand habitats, one hundred million lives. They can make as many mistakes as they like, provided they don't violate one of the Common Articles. The moment they do, they become our responsibility."

Hafdis had drifted out with a smart tether, a sort of longer, more benign version of a whiphound's filament, just long enough to bring her to Aumonier's side. She still had some residual drift, which Aumonier negated with a gentle pressure on her sleeve.

"How do you do that, ma'am? It's as if you're fixed in space, not just floating."

"Practice. I had a lot of it. It's surprising the things you can do, with practice."

"And if your life depends on it."

Aumonier nodded. "Indeed. If I'd drifted too close to the walls, the scarab would have blown my head off." She craned behind her neck. "It was fixed here, clamped in place with little legs, and with sterile probes digging into my skin, all the way down to my spine. It could read my blood chemistry, my stress hormones and sleep toxins. It may even have been able to read my state of consciousness. For all that, it wasn't painful. Just a cold presence, which I soon adjusted to. Weeks went by when I hardly felt it at all, until it did something inside itself. There'd be a delicious little click out of nowhere, a whirring impression of things moving around within it. The first dozen times that happened, I thought it was gearing up to kill me. Eventually I adjusted to the idea that the scarab was evolving, improving itself."

"You were awake when the Clockmaker put it on you."

"Yes—and haven't you done your homework."

"It's the least you deserve, ma'am, for your experience to be studied and understood."

"Understood?" Aumonier let out a bitter little laugh. "No, I don't think so. You could study every second of those eleven years and you still wouldn't 'understand.' You'd have to go through it for that. You'd have to be me."

"I meant no disrespect, ma'am. I just wanted you to know, I have studied it, at least the scraps we can know about outside of Panoply. Mother wouldn't have allowed me not to."

"I never knew Ingvar felt that strongly." Aumonier sighed, realising she had been harsh with an over-eager student. "I was awake for the insertion, yes. It wasn't painful—almost loving, in fact. The Clockmaker needed me conscious and lucid for the whole process, so that I could understand the parameters of what had been done. If I'd blacked out from shock or pain, I wouldn't have been able to relay instructions to whoever found me." She had gone dry-mouthed, raking up memories that had gone undisturbed for too long. "There was a grace period: sixty minutes before I couldn't be close to another human being. It gave them time to float me into this room. They considered trying to get the scarab off me there and then, but it was considered too much of a risk. No one knew what lay inside it or how it functioned. It took years to begin to build up any sort of picture, and even then, it kept changing. The experts reckoned it would only need six-tenths of a second to kill me, and there was no way anyone could get close enough to safely remove it in under that time."

"But they did find a way."

Aumonier fingered the hair-thin line around her neck, more imagined than real. "Yes, they did find a way. And about that, I remember mercifully little."

"The scarab was destroyed totally?"

"Yes, except for a few tiny pieces. They were recovered and compared with the models Demikhov and his assistants had been assembling in the Sleep Lab, based on their remote scans. They'd got surprisingly close to the truth. The Clockmaker was devious, Hafdis. It turns out that human minds can approach some of that deviousness, given sufficient time."

"Do you think we're capable of good deeds, as well?"

"On days like this, I find my faith in humanity at its lowest ebb. Too many have died, Hafdis. Not just one of our own, but all those innocents caught up in the aftermath." Aumonier allowed her silence to ring around the room. "On days like this, I need to remind myself that I can't abdicate my responsibilities just because of a few hundred avoidable deaths and the murder of a good man like Sparver Bancal. This is where I find my equilibrium again, surrounded by these feeds. Study them awhile, Hafdis. Immerse yourself in the raw noise of humanity, in all its manifestations. Good, bad, indifferent. The saintly and the pitiable. Those who value our work, those who would condemn us, if only they had the mandate. These are the lives Sparver served. The lives your mother served."

"I'll serve them as well," Hafdis vowed.

"An easy assertion to make, when you haven't been tested." Aumonier smiled faintly. "Yet forgivable when you've still so much to see and learn. I'm afraid there must be some changes now."

"Changes?"

"The destruction of Asset 227 moves our activities onto a more dangerous plane. I've conferred with Prefect Dreyfus and he agrees with me. It's too risky for you to continue shadowing him in his field investigations."

Hafdis gripped the end of her tether forlornly. "I only got to spend a few days with him, ma'am."

"I'm not saying that the work won't continue, just that there must be a hiatus. There's nothing to prevent your evaluations proceeding as before...although my seniors may have even less time to spare."

"Will you be even busier, ma'am?"

"I fear so."

"It was very good of you to show me this room. I'd like to stay here a little while longer, if that's possible."

Aumonier had expected Hafdis to be overwhelmed by the confusion of feeds, sickened by their endless algorithm-driven swelling and contraction, like being inside a vast breathing insect eye.

"You want...more of this?"

"You're right, ma'am—no one can understand what you went through. I think I might be able to glimpse the edge of it, though."

The student's surety disarmed her. "Do you, Hafdis?"

"I do, ma'am."

"Then . . . have at it." She gestured expansively. "When it becomes too much, you'll know. Reel in the tether, or use your bracelet to have someone come for you. I have a meeting in the tactical room."

"Thank you, ma'am. Just one other thing."

Nothing was going to surprise her now. "Yes?"

"I'd like to see those reconstructions of the scarab, if they still exist."

"They exist," Aumonier confirmed. "And so long as the Clockmaker exists, that'll remain the case."

Dreyfus was back at work as soon as he had the authorisation to resume his search schedule.

Although there had been relatively few fatalities following the destruction of Asset 227, that was not to say that the event had come and gone without consequences for the rest of the Glitter Band. The response to the crisis had exposed how vulnerable and unprepared many habitats were, especially those that had been at real risk of collision. In the days that followed, many communities were scrambling to make sure they would not be caught off guard the next time. It was good business for insurance brokers, security consultants and orbital propulsion contractors.

A nervous re-shuffling was in progress, as habitats jockeyed with each other to find supposedly safer orbital slots. The tightly packed low orbits, with their excellent views of Yellowstone, had always been desirable, and that was where many of the longest-established, prosperous habitats had come to be. Now the smart money was on the higher, less congested lanes, where there was a lot more room to get out of the way of trouble. Habitats were doing quick, dirty deals with each other, the wealthy moving up and out, the hard-up cases willing to drift into the lower levels if it meant a much-needed injection of capital.

Taken across the Glitter Band, it was only a few per cent that were swapping places. But each move caused ripples, affecting hundreds, even thousands of habitats.

Dreyfus felt these ripples. As the Glitter Band shifted to a new permutation, Sparver's algorithm found new, more efficient paths for him. Sometimes a habitat that was twenty or thirty items down on his schedule popped right to the top, and his cutter veered sharply as it accepted the new routing.

Now it was the turn of Carcasstown.

His cutter slowed as it entered the habitat's control space. It was in the high orbits, with nothing else within a thousand kilometres. At that distance, even the largest and nearest neighbouring communities were reduced to odd-shaped gems, tiny enough to pinch between his fingers.

Seen from a distance, Carcasstown looked like any other habitat built on the age-old spoked-wheel layout. Up close, its makeshift, mongrel nature became stark. The sphere at the hub was a patchwork of curving surfaces, stitched together with silvery weld-lines. It was a kilometre across, with a huge circular entrance large enough for ships to float in and out with ease. The four spokes radiating out from the sphere were a jumble of mismatched tubes, spliced and strung together, messily buttressed. Encircling the spokes was a rim made up of thirty or more individual elements, no two alike, crudely interconnected and showing a long history of piecemeal repair. Carcasstown was what its name suggested: a junkyard habitat made up of the corpses of smaller structures: habitats, stations and ships, cut down and reforged. The process was ongoing.

As he neared, Dreyfus felt a prickling intuition. It had visited him a couple of times already, as he searched Tench's itinerary. Knocked on his door, lingered, then gone away.

This time it put down roots.

Carcasstown was the right sort of place.

Not too big, not too small. The data traffic was noisy enough that Catopsis' activities would be hard to pick out from the background. They could have set up shop here quite easily, just another tenancy to add to those already present.

And Tench *had* shown an interest.

Dreyfus felt an impulse to talk to Sparver, to relay his impressions and see what the other prefect made of them. The thought snagged on emptiness: a stitch of pain, there and gone, but certain to visit him again.

"Sparv," he mouthed to himself, a godless prayer for a fallen friend.

Carcasstown's docking control hauled him into the sphere, threading the cutter between tugs and service modules coming and going from the workspace. His cutter was a tiny, inconsequential thing compared to the ships and parts of ships looming within the sphere's slow-turning volume. Some were free-floating, being worked over by vacuum workers and servitor robots. It wasn't all destruction: ships were being stitched back together as well, or made anew from the bones of the old. Shuttles, taxis and cargo haulers eventually emerged from the mouth, rarely elegant but usually functional and always cheap.

Squinting against the hard blue light of cutting lasers and fusion welders, Dreyfus sat tight until his cutter latched onto a vacant docking slot. He had kept his weapons stowed, acting just as if he was on routine business.

He gathered his things and left the cutter.

He emerged into a grubby, poorly lit service area where workers were coming on- and off-shift, either fixing on bits of antiquated spacesuit or gladly shrugging off helmets and gloves. He drifted through the low-gravity melee, seemingly ignored but getting the occasional too-deliberate shove as a worker barged past him.

"Stinking prefect," someone muttered. "Doesn't he know the place smells bad enough as it is?"

"Let the fat man through," someone countered. "The last thing we want is Panoply going through our books. Remember what it cost us in bonuses, last time?"

"Shove your bonus, Creed. He can't touch us."

Dreyfus ignored the barges and taunts, knowing it was more ritual than anything else. He kept his whiphound holstered. None of these workers wanted trouble, especially not the sort that cost them overtime. Equally, none of them wanted to be seen to be on his side, or even indifferent to his presence. He was willing to absorb the blows, physical and verbal.

He knew it would be only a matter of time before one of the owner-operators detected his arrival and came speeding to his side, anxious to grease his visit and get him on his way as quickly as possible.

He wasn't wrong.

"Prefect. How may we be of assistance?"

Dreyfus turned around at the urgent, harried exclamation. The man who greeted him looked exactly as anxious and put-upon as he sounded, lacing his fingers nervously, his eyes restless with worry. He was scrawny, younger than Dreyfus had been expecting, but with a toll of concern sagging his long, slack-featured face. He looked as if his skin was slightly too big for him, a costume that needed drawing in.

A gown of office hung off thin shoulders, marked with various civic sigils. An unruly mass of keys flapped against his thighs.

"It's Dreyfus, isn't it?" the man continued, tugging at his fingers so vigorously that they were in danger of dislocating.

"I'm interested in your tenant businesses," Dreyfus answered. "The firms who lease space and amenities around your rim. You'd be...?"

The man scuffed a hand through hair that was already dishevelled. "It's happened again, hasn't it? Someone's had another go at messing with the polling core. We kicked the last lot out, Prefect, just as soon as we found out." He tugged at a loose lock, nearly ripping it from his scalp. "It's worse each year, I swear—the tenants we have to work with. Not all of them, but lately it seems to be the real dregs. Scum. I shouldn't say that, but it's true. It's the economy, see—we can't pick and choose anymore. Not that we ever could, but...oh, wait. You asked who I was."

"I did."

"Under-Supervisor, Department of Leaseholds and Public Services, Second Class. Oh, my name." He scratched his nose. "Krenkel. Under-Supervisor Krenkel. Department of—"

"I got it, Krenkel. And I'm not here about your polling core."

"You're not?"

Dreyfus thought the man might be more useful to him when he stopped being a bag of nerves. "No one's in trouble, Krenkel—not yet. I'm here on routine business. You want me out of your hair?"

"I didn't say that..." Krenkel began hastily.

"But it's understandable. Well, let's make it happen. The best way to do that is for you to serve as my tour guide. It's been a while since I was here, and I suspect you know the way around far better than I do."

"You've been here before?"

"It's a rite of passage for young prefects, Krenkel. A test of restraint, to see how lawless a place can be without actually violating the Common Articles. Most of us are glad not to pay a return visit."

"Yes, yes, I understand that." Krenkel was still a ball of worry. "It's true that we've a bit of a reputation for pushing the boundaries. That's not personally something I endorse, Prefect. There are quite a few of us in the administrative sub-departments who think we'd all be a lot better off if we played nicely, altered our business model. Had a change of management. I shouldn't say that, but it's true."

"I'm interested in your tenants," Dreyfus repeated. "That's all. How many different concerns are we talking about? Thirty? Forty?"

"More like four hundred, occupying larger and smaller parts of the ring."

"Then you're going to have to help me do some narrowing down." Dreyfus guided Krenkel into a quiet little alcove off the main drag, where they had at least a little privacy. "Have you got a list of the businesses? I imagine someone in the Under-Department for Secondary..."

"Office of Under-Supervision, Department of Leaseholds and Public Services. And yes, I do have a list." Krenkel dug past his keys, fishing a compad out of a voluminous thigh pocket. "Let's see what we have here."

Dreyfus watched as Krenkel operated the compad. Lines of commercial information scrolled past, too fast for him to speed-read even if he had maintained his Klausner index.

"It's a lot, Krenkel."

"How would you like me to whittle it down?"

184

"I don't know. Have any of those concerns moved here relatively recently?"

"Depends what you mean by recently."

"Do I have to do all the work? Say within the last year."

Krenkel's fingernails tapped and re-tapped, refining the search. "Well, it's good news for both of us."

"Is it?"

"This shouldn't take too long. Only five new tenancy agreements negotiated in the last year."

Dreyfus took the compad without asking. He turned it the right way around and examined the breakdown. There was a diagram of the ring, with five coloured smudges dotted at irregular intervals around the knotty circumference. Beneath each smudge was a summary box showing the identity and contract of the tenant organisation.

Nothing jumped out at him.

"These numbers show utility usage—power, abstraction, life support and so on?" he asked.

"Indeed."

"They're all within a broadly similar range."

"Indeed also."

"I'll need to take a closer look at each of these operations."

Krenkel looked pained. "As part of our tenancy agreements, we *are* obliged to give them twenty-six hours' notice of any formal inspection, Prefect."

"Then we'll keep it informal. How does that work for you?"

"You won't...er, antagonise them, will you?"

Dreyfus beamed at Krenkel. "I'll be the very model of discretion. Now, take me to these businesses."

CHAPTER TWENTY-TWO

At the rim, they disembarked from an elevator into a wide, ribbed tube snaking off in both directions. The tube's gridded floor was undulating, as if the ground had shifted under it many times. Machines, pieces of machines and general piles of junk obstructed their progress. Doors and traps led off into grubby, cluttered side-passages, some large enough to hold a medium-sized spacecraft or a large piece of industrial equipment. Boxy carriages suspended from rails in the ceiling provided the nearest thing to a mass-transit system. There was constant activity, workers stepping in and out of the boxes, disappearing or emerging from the side-passages, and a rumble of numerous noisy processes going on just out of sight.

Dreyfus had already had some idea what to expect. The hulks that made up the rim were joined haphazardly, connected by whatever means had worked at the time. The tube snaked through them, weaving and kinking its way around obstructions and pinch-points until it joined up with itself again, twenty kilometres later. The tube was airtight and mostly habitable, except for a few areas where flooding, radiation bursts or industrial contamination had run out of control.

"These side-passages are where your tenants set up shop?" Dreyfus asked.

"Yes. We're not far from the first of them. Do you want to look at them in any particular order?"

"As they come."

Krenkel grabbed a vacant carriage as it moved past on the overhead rail. Some clutch allowed it to stop while they climbed aboard and squeezed into the two seats provided. Krenkel closed the hip-high side door and the carriage started up automatically, wobbling as it progressed at a pace barely faster than a jog.

"It might help if you gave me an idea of what you're looking into, Prefect."

"Criminality."

"That doesn't help."

"One of these concerns might be doing something with your abstraction services that they shouldn't."

"I thought you said this wasn't about the polling core."

"It isn't. We're talking about something quite subtle, probably being done behind the smokescreen of another operation. Tiny, illicit alterations to the network of communications devices far beyond Carcasstown. Beyond that, they'll have prepared a receptacle."

"What sort?"

"I'll know it when I see it. More than likely a computer. A very powerful one: something capable of storing an alpha-level simulation, and probably several orders of magnitude beyond that. Machines like that were relatively rare and expensive at the time of the Eighty, and they're still not commonplace."

"I'm not surprised, after that debacle. Who needs such a thing anyway?"

"I'm hoping that will be the weakness. Possessing such a machine is one thing; offering a reason for it is quite another."

Krenkel regarded his compad for a few moments. "We have good relations with all these tenants. What would they be putting in that receptacle?"

"Something you really don't want anywhere near Carcasstown," Dreyfus answered.

They got off at the first stop. It was a short stroll down one of the side-passages into a huge cubic volume, fifty or more metres across, that had been more or less gutted back to its walls. Dreyfus confirmed with Krenkel that this was the entire space leased by the tenant, a concern called Morrow Proximal Assurance.

"They specialise in anti-collision measures for habitats," Krenkel explained, as Dreyfus took in the entire shopfloor with its hulking quick-matter assembler vats, the hoppers containing the raw feedstock ready to be poured into them, and the ranks of specialised tools and robotic systems needed to assemble the final components. Off to one side, mounted on racks, were the end products: bulbous automatic guns, each as large as his cutter. They gleamed with a highly reflective finish, the first clean shiny things he had seen since his arrival. A handful of workers were supervising the machines, but other than that the process looked to be taking care of itself.

"Business has been booming," Krenkel added gleefully.

Dreyfus shot his companion a baleful glance. "You don't say."

It was obvious why this grey-market enterprise had set up business in

Carcasstown. Other than the ready supply of power and raw materials, no questions needed to be asked about whether these anti-collision devices were intended strictly for defence. The Common Articles forbade habitats to carry overtly offensive armaments, but the line between aggressively efficient safety measure and purposefully engineered weapons system was at best porous and at worst barely existent. Panoply could shut down a business like this to almost zero effect; a dozen others would be waiting to fill the market vacuum.

Dreyfus went through the motions anyway. He wanted to look busy and suspicious, so he donned his goggles, unholstered his whiphound and made a tour of the shopfloor. Krenkel looked on with hand-wringing concern, doubtless thinking of the damage being done to tenant relations.

Dreyfus spoke with a foreperson and made some glancing enquiries about the processing power needed to run the assemblers. It turned out that since the guns were made to a time-honoured design, the production line managed itself with only a dusting of cybernetic intervention.

Possibly he was being fobbed off. Dreyfus preferred to think otherwise. The business made sense, and everything he saw fitted into that picture, with nothing missing and nothing left over. Neat, tidy, the way he liked it.

He made no comment as he returned to Krenkel, merely slipping his goggles back into his belt and nodding at the next empty carriage.

"What did you make of it?" Krenkel asked.

"As you say, business is booming. We must arrange a few more near-death experiences for the Glitter Band." He squeezed into the uncomfortable seat. "What next?"

"Our most recent tenants. Peltier-Chong Advancer Solutions."

"What do they do?"

"I'm not supposed to say. Our tenants pay for discretion as well as somewhere to operate."

"Nonetheless."

"They're working on interstellar propulsion. Trying to develop a drive to undercut the Conjoiner monopoly."

"That'll work out well for them."

"I understand there's been…modest progress. Also one or two setbacks."

"Setbacks of the assassination and industrial sabotage kind?"

"Along those lines."

Peltier-Chong was a much more substantial affair than the previous business, a series of bright, spacious laboratories spread through several subdivided modules. They had linear accelerators, cyclotrons, enormous power-banks to run them, as well as dedicated computer systems to guide the experiments and analyse the results.

Dreyfus wandered around, demanding access when it was initially refused him, studying the layout of the complex and registering the reactions of the technicians working on the project. No one liked him being there, and he could understand that.

He collared a senior technician who was overlooking a test area where muscular particle smashers converged on a sensor-dotted sphere.

"You're trying to reverse-engineer a Conjoiner drive," Dreyfus stated, watching the woman's reaction.

"We are pursuing numerous theoretical approaches."

"I bet you are. Based on scraps of discarded technology and half-heard rumours, some of them deliberate misinformation put out by the Conjoiners. My advice: pick another line of business."

"We'll take that under advisement, Prefect. Have you seen enough?"

"For today."

"I hope they're paying you well, Krenkel," Dreyfus commented as they got back in the carriage. "Nothing like an unregulated high-energy physics experiment to put your other tenants at ease."

"They assured us that there'd be no adverse consequences."

"I bet they did."

They rode on. By now they had passed another spoke, taking them more than a third of the way around the ring. Dreyfus had been paying attention as the tube meandered its way past other tenancies, even if they were not of direct interest. He still wanted to know the landscape.

There were a lot of factories, a lot of fabrication facilities where weapons and countermeasures could be forged at short notice.

"What next?" he asked.

"Midas Analytics. Market forecasting, shares, that kind of thing."

"How long have they been here?"

Krenkel consulted the compad again. "Seven, no...more like eight months."

"And before that?"

"I'm not aware that there was a before. It's a new venture. They've been very reliable clients, Prefect. Pay their bills on time, mind their manners, don't upset the neighbours. Quite respectable compared to some. Actually, compared to most."

"I bet they are."

They got out of the carriage. Access to Midas Analytics was down a short, well-tended side-passage. The surroundings got cleaner and better tended the further they went in. Doors whisked open and shut, each transition

189

leading to a more sterile, more corporate-seeming enclave than before. Lulling background music, perfumed air, graphics on the gold-plated wall showing reassuring slogans and boosterish financial data, sharp-sloping graphs of return on investment. Everything always on the up, for ever and ever.

The pitch was seductive. Dreyfus had never considered investment, but even he might have been persuaded.

After a final set of doors they arrived at a reception, tastefully minimalist, gold-accented and subtly lit, but easily large enough to park a ship in.

"Welcome to Midas Analytics," announced the human receptionist, with a bright, paralysing smile. He sat behind a crescent-shaped desk, with more of the same market graphics playing across a semicircle of screens. His uniform was a bright chrome yellow, accented with gold piping around the collar and cuffs. "How may we be of assistance?"

"You can show me the back room," Dreyfus said. "Your analytics floor, bullpen, whatever you want to call it. I want to see where you run these market simulations."

Krenkel, standing behind him, "I told him about our twenty-six-hour grace period, Plossel."

Plossel smiled forgivingly. "I'm sure you did, Under-Supervisor, and it's quite all right. Our doors stand open." Plossel swivelled around and indicated a gold-framed doorway. "Please, Prefect Dreyfus—go on through. Our chief executive officer, Mirna Silk, will meet you on the other side, and she'll be happy to answer your questions. I must warn you, though, that there's very little to see. All we do is move information around."

Dreyfus turned to Krenkel. "I won't be long."

Dreyfus went through, a tingling itch at the back of his neck. The only thing that made him more suspicious than a frosty welcome was a helpful one.

Midas Analytics was a much smaller operation than Peltier-Chong, and they needed far less in the way of space and resources. What confronted him beyond the doorway was still impressive, nonetheless. He had emerged into an arena-sized room with an elevated gallery running around its perimeter. A woman was already waiting for him on the gallery, dressed in a gownlike variant of the corporate uniform. Her bearing was confident, projecting a quiet authority. Dreyfus studied the woman's open, interested face, set beneath a severe horizontal fringe, detecting no nervousness or concealment.

"Welcome, Prefect Dreyfus. I'm Mirna Silk, head of Midas Analytics. Thank you for taking an interest in our little concern." She smiled coolly.

"Might I ask about the nature of Panoply's interest? We're a maverick enterprise, doing things our own way, but I like to think we know which side of the Common Articles to stay on?"

"Our interest doesn't necessarily indicate suspicion of a crime," Dreyfus answered, still trying to get a read on the woman. "It might be that we simply want to know about your methods so that we can take advantage of them. You and your colleague know my name."

"You're not exactly anonymous among prefects. I'm afraid word raced to us as soon as you docked at Carcasstown." A pinch appeared at the corner of her mouth: unconcealed scepticism. "What is it? Panoply thinking of getting into stocks and shares?"

"No. But we have a shared interest in forecasting." He nodded out across the room, its bustling floor a level below. "You're trying to predict market trends. We're trying to anticipate emergencies and crises in the Glitter Band so that we can mobilise a response before things get too bad."

"I see," Mirna Silk said, sounding less than persuaded. "Panoply has immense resources and experience of its own, doesn't it? I'm surprised you'd think we have anything to teach you."

"We're surveying predictive methods across a range of specialisations."

"Then I'll try to be as helpful as I can. You'll understand that there are issues of commercial sensitivity around our techniques."

"Of course. But I'm sure you can help me with a few general questions?"

The woman's bearing shifted. There was still no nervousness, but something in her tone told him that she was beginning to doubt his narrative. "I can't imagine generalities will help you at all. But feel free to ask anything you like."

"Is that your computer?"

They both looked out across the floor. In the centre of the room, surrounded by rings of concentric workstations, was a spherical object on a half-cone plinth. The sphere was four or five metres across with a mottled, roughly finished surface. It glowed a soft gold, like a huge blob of molten metal still cooling down.

Yellow-clad technicians and analysts perched at the workstations, absorbed in rapidly changing readouts. The walls beneath the walkway were alive with lurid, ever-changing projections of market data, similar to the diagrams and graphs Dreyfus had seen on the way in. It was like being in an aquarium, except that the fish were nervously shoaling data.

"Yes," Silk said guardedly. "That's our predictive engine, Abacus."

Dreyfus nodded, shuttering his reactions.

He needed to be sure he had heard correctly. "Abacus?"

"Yes—more than a little ironic understatement, given its capabilities."

Ingvar Tench's spoken testimony via her whiphound replayed itself in his mind's ear.

Not *Bacchus* but *Abacus*.

He had got it wrong. She had been referring to this computer, not implicating Grigor Bacchus.

He regarded the plinth, visualising the jugular flows of energy and coolant running in and out of the sphere from the plinth. Dry-mouthed, he asked: "What sort of capabilities."

"I'm not the one to rhapsodise." Mirna Silk leaned over the balustrade and called down to the floor. "Doctor Salazar, could I trouble you for a minute or two?"

A man stood up from one of the workstations, spoke quietly to a colleague in the adjoining station, then raised a hand to announce that he was on his way up. He vanished beneath the walkway, then reappeared a few moments later, emerging from a spiral staircase a little way around the room. Like Mirna Silk he was dressed in the yellow of Midas Analytics, but a tight-fitting, trousered one-piece this time, more like industrial overalls, and lacking the gold piping He was taller and thinner than Dreyfus and approached with trepidation, his gaze indirect.

He had a sharp, bony face with prominent dark eyebrows and an incongruous crown of white hair. Dreyfus felt sure he would have remembered such a face.

"Doctor Aristarchus Salazar, our chief data theorist and systems cyberneticist," introduced Silk. "Abacus is largely his brainchild. I think you should be the one to talk about your baby, Aristarchus?"

Salazar nodded at Dreyfus, meeting his eyes for only an instant before his gaze slid off. "I am happy to be of assistance, Prefect. What would you like to know?"

"Tell me about Abacus."

"Gladly. But I'll begin with a question. Would you care to estimate its mass?"

"I don't know. Ten tonnes? Twenty tonnes? Maybe a hundred, since you wouldn't have asked the question if the answer were straightforward."

"You're right—I wouldn't. The answer will surprise you, I think. Abacus contains six thousand tonnes of computational matter, compressed into a sphere only four hundred and twenty centimetres in diameter. That's a significant mass in relation to the rotational dynamics of Carcasstown. We had to pay for a counterweight to be installed on the other side of the ring, just to balance things out."

Nothing about Abacus had changed, but now Dreyfus felt doubly uneasy about it. It was too much like staring into a black whirlpool, feeling the maw tugging at him.

"Why is it so heavy?"

"It's an onionskin, with each layer denser and hotter than the one surrounding it. Like a little model of a star, all the way in to the nuclear-burning core. The analogy is not accidental. Near the middle, Abacus's processing elements approach the density of white-dwarf matter. Abacus needs energy to perform its calculations, but two thirds of its power requirements are merely to prevent it exploding in our faces."

"What would that do to Carcasstown?"

"Destroy it utterly. But rest assured, our safeguards are beyond reproach. I engineered them myself, knowing I would need to be in the vicinity of Abacus."

"What are you trying to capture?"

"Capture?"

Dreyfus had been watching for something in Salazar's reaction to that question.

"Yes. What is your objective?"

"Forecasting," Salazar answered, after perhaps the tiniest hesitation. "Abacus sucks in information across the Glitter Band. Public data, private data. Every market transaction, every type of financial product, tracked and collated faster than our competitors can dream of. Every data point relating to every possible variable that might be correlated with market trends in some fashion, no matter how cryptic the connection. The obvious and the non-obvious, from fluctuations in hem lines to the weather over Chasm City. And it massages this data in ways that it would take another Abacus just to begin to understand. I don't." He looked at Silk. "*We* don't. We know only that it works, quickly and reliably enough to give Midas Analytics an industry-leading edge. Shall I tell you how the performance of Midas Analytics itself becomes a parameter in Abacus's market summation?"

Dreyfus smiled at what had clearly been a rhetorical question. "You could try. Tell me, though, Doctor Salazar, just so I can get a benchmark on what Abacus is really capable of. Could it, I don't know, run an alpha-level simulation?"

He had been watching for a reaction before and now he watched for it again.

And saw it.

"An alpha-level?"

"I'm sure you're familiar with the processing needs."

"Oh, I am." Salazar ruminated on his answer. "It would be an insult to

193

Abacus. Abacus could execute a thousand simultaneous alpha-levels and not break a metaphorical sweat."

Silk looked at him with a faint but definite puzzlement. "Was it just a benchmark, Prefect Dreyfus, or did you bring up that example for a reason?"

"Panoply occasionally has need for outside resources. It would be useful to go back to my superiors with an idea of your capabilities—commercial secrets notwithstanding."

"I suspect the prefect has no further need of you, Aristarchus," Silk said to Doctor Salazar.

"No, you've been more than helpful," Dreyfus said, bidding the tall man farewell as he headed back to the staircase.

Dreyfus looked back across the workstations to the yellow-clad acolytes. Twenty, twenty-five of them at least. Silk knew nothing, he had decided: she really did think this was all about market forecasting. Salazar might know a little more, but maybe not the full scope of the covert operation. Maybe just enough to make Abacus do the bidding of those who were really running things.

Onionskins indeed. People on the outside, thinking they were working for Midas Analytics. A layer within, who maybe grasped that Midas was a cover for something fishy, without knowing what.

And under that layer, the true believers?

He had yet to meet one of them.

"If you did want to rent time on Abacus, I'm sure that's a conversation we could have," Silk was saying.

"Just one more question, Mirna. How did you end up working for Midas Analytics?"

"I was headhunted," she said, looking slightly abashed. "I was already working in finance when I heard that they were putting together a new, agile market-forecasting operation. Lean, fast, innovative. It was too good an opportunity to turn down. No one gets to play with something as powerful as Abacus."

Doctor Salazar was returning to his workstation, his stooping back presented to Dreyfus, his crown a shock of bobbing white. He paused at the station next to his vacant one and mouthed something to the man still seated, the same one he had addressed before coming up. The other worker was much younger than Salazar, almost boyish. And yet Salazar's manner struck Dreyfus as deferential, as if he were reporting back to a superior.

The younger man looked up at Dreyfus. It was a glance, instantly snatched back. Dreyfus would have thought less of it if the man had kept

194

staring. Now he watched the man intently, studying his averted profile, the look of someone hunching down into their work, trying not to be picked out.

Dreyfus thought he recognised the young man.

"Ms. Silk? I'll be on my way now. You'll hear from us if we need anything more."

CHAPTER TWENTY-THREE

Aumonier hesitated before stepping over the threshold of the Sleep Lab. How long had it been since she was last down here? she wondered. A year or more? Probably two at the least.

There was something to be said for putting the past behind her. Equally, she had made a pledge to herself that she would own the scars, both physical and psychological, that the Clockmaker had left her with. Scars were a form of armour, to be paraded rather than denied. It was why she felt no disinclination to spend hours floating weightless in the same room where she had spent eleven sleepless years. To have been driven from that space would have been an admission that the Clockmaker had triumphed over a tiny part of her soul. She would give it no such quarter...not in that matter, at least.

It was a different question when it came to the instruments of its cruelty.

"Ma'am, is everything all right?"

"Perfectly all right, Hafdis." Cursing her own delay, Aumonier led the candidate through into the silent, reverent sanctity of the Sleep Lab.

It was smaller than it had been at the time of her incarceration, some of its former volume swallowed back into the medical section. She had insisted on the preservation of this kernel, though, not just because it was a memorial to the hands and minds that had slaved to free her, but because she worried they might have use of it again. Aumonier was not by habit superstitious, but she feared that the day they finally closed the Sleep Lab permanently would be the one when the Clockmaker came back.

Glass cabinets, narrow corridors, low green illumination casting a murky marine light on abandoned but still pristine benches and tools, as if the workers had gone off-shift only a few minutes before.

"What was this place?" Hafdis asked with the guileless affect of someone who likely already knows the answer but who wishes to indulge the kindness of their host.

"This is the Sleep Lab. When the Clockmaker put the scarab on me, Demikhov and his colleagues embarked on a crash program both to keep me alive and also to work out a way of eventually removing the device. This is the medical annexe we established for exactly that purpose. There were dozens of our brightest people in here, working on all aspects of the problem. Designing the drugs to keep me awake, the techniques for administering them and monitoring their consequences. Scanning the scarab without ever touching or approaching it...learning what might be inside it, and how it could be defeated. Finding ways to keep me sane. The ordeal I went through, Hafdis, pales in comparison to the labour that went on in these rooms. The personal costs, the sacrifices made. I know the toll it took on these people. Some of them were broken by the end of it."

"With respect, ma'am, they choose to put themselves through that, and they always had the option of walking away. Anything's bearable when you know there's a way out."

"But they didn't take it."

Hafdis shrugged aside the point. "You never had that to cling to. Your darkest nights were a million times darker than theirs, because for you there was no escape route."

"There was. I only had to submit to sleep, and it would have been all over."

"You locked that door and threw away the key, ma'am. You were never going to allow yourself that surrender."

Aumonier looked at Hafdis with sidelong amusement. "You're an expert, now?"

"Just thinking back to the things Mother told me, about how one day they'd downplay your ordeal in here, but nothing should be allowed to do that."

"I did have my wavering moments, Hafdis. If anyone thinks my resolve was total, for all those eleven years..."

"You're only human, ma'am. The miracle isn't that you wavered, it's that you never succumbed. That's the greater triumph." Hafdis halted at an upright glass cabinet, as tall as she was, with dozens of models of the scarab pinned behind it on a vertical sheet.

Hafdis pressed on the metal plate next to the glass.

"It won't open, ma'am."

"No, and it might have been polite to ask first." Aumonier pressed her own palm to the panel, the glass whirring into the ceiling. She hooked one of the samples from the sheet. The crab-like form was moulded in semi-translucent plastic, with hints of internal structure. "Here," Aumonier said. "One of the intermediate study models. They made hundreds

197

of these, trying to understand what was going on inside, and how long they'd have if they tried to winkle it off me."

Hafdis took the evil object. It was dead in her hands, functionally inert. Understanding its purpose, she dug a nail into a seam and prised off part of the translucent casing. A devil's clockwork of tiny coloured components glittered back at her.

She used her other nail to jab at a microscopic lever, causing the barbed legs to twitch.

"Did it help?"

"Minutely. Each model was a step along the way to understanding. Understanding that the problem was unsolvable. They couldn't defeat the scarab, not in the time available." Aumonier nodded for Hafdis to reassemble the scarab and give it back to her. "It was a devastating realisation at the time, but ultimately the conceptual breakthrough they were looking for. A dark, dark day, but one which heralded a little glimmer of light."

"They didn't tell you about that glimmer."

"No," Aumonier agreed, replacing the scarab and whirring shut the cabinet. "All things considered, it was best that I didn't know their eventual solution."

Hafdis moved along to the next cabinet. It was similar to the last, with a metal opening panel. Only one scarab rested behind it, fixed centrally to its sheet like the prize exhibit in a gallery.

"Why is this one on its own, Jane? I mean, ma'am?"

"That one is a little different. It's the only one of these that is not known to contain any errors, based on the scans and the few remains we managed to salvage from the original. It's fully functional, primed to lock onto a new host. It doesn't contain any explosives, but it's no less lethal for that. You still wouldn't want it on your neck."

Hafdis let out a little gasp. "Why would you keep such a thing, knowing what the original did?"

"Because the Clockmaker isn't gone. A stalemate isn't defeat. It could come back at any time, manifest itself in new some embodiment. Make another of these, or something worse. I wanted us to be prepared, Hafdis—even at the expense of living with this not so far from my bed. Sometimes..." She hesitated, on the brink of a dangerous confession. Dangerous because it was truthful.

"Ma'am?"

"I dream of it, Hafdis. Scuttling out of this cabinet. Finding its way through Panoply. Reattaching itself to me. The whole thing beginning again."

Hafdis peered in fascinated horror at the vile object. "Could it be controlled, if you had to?"

"They tell me that it is programmable, to a degree. That its thresholds for triggering can be adjusted along a few parameters. With me, the main criteria were proximity of human contact and my own state of consciousness."

"I would destroy it if I were you. Why take this chance?"

"Because I wouldn't want some other poor soul not to have every advantage I did. Living with this nightmare next door is a small price for that, Hafdis. It's insurance."

"Panoply is lucky to have you, ma'am. We all are."

"I just did my job. As did your mother." Aumonier regarded the candidate with a curious blend of emotions: the natural and entirely warranted condescension of the teacher to the student, but also the faint intimation that there was something about Hafdis that merited extremely careful estimation.

She was glad to get out of the Sleep Lab. Its wicked treasures might still creep their way to her in her dreams, but at least in daylight they were shuttered away.

"I trust that was worthwhile, Prefect Dreyfus," said the under-supervisor.

"It was, Krenkel."

After visiting the two other concerns after Midas Analytics, they had boarded another wobbling carriage, taking Dreyfus back to his starting point.

The fourth and fifth concerns had been Hydrax Diversions, a somewhat shady enterprise speculating in live combat gameplay, and Damascene Conversions, an offshoot of Carcasstown's larger shipbreaking and repair businesses, taking small, private runabouts and upgrading and customising them to suit various niche criteria. Neither had displaced Midas as the focus of his concerns, but Dreyfus had given them the same time and attention as the earlier candidates, certain that his movements were being monitored.

Krenkel asked: "Are we in trouble?"

"No, not at all. Carry on, business as usual. If these tenants enquire about my visit, tell them that I was called away on another investigation, something obviously more urgent, and I didn't sound as if I'd be back anytime soon."

"The question is, though, *will* you be back?"

"Someone may drop by," Dreyfus said. "But I wouldn't worry about that for now."

"You don't reassure me."

"All right." Dreyfus sat still for a moment, even as the seat chafed at him. "Do you have family, Krenkel?"

"There are people I care about in Carcasstown. I like to think they care about me."

"I'm sure they do. Your work must take you all over this wheel."

"Indeed," he answered cautiously.

"And a man of your standing must have latitude to pick and choose your priorities."

"To a degree. What are you driving at?"

"For the next few days, Krenkel—let's say a week, to be on the safe side —I'd find reasons not to be too close to Midas Analytics. I'm not saying something will happen, but just that if it does...well, you get the gist."

Krenkel examined his fingers, shame and relief battling in his expression. "I can arrange my schedule accordingly. There's always something that needs my intervention, anywhere in Carcasstown." He looked at Dreyfus with sudden concern. "Should I warn friends?"

"Not directly. But I'm sure you can find ways to encourage them to stay out of harm's way, nonetheless."

"You shouldn't be telling me this," Krenkel ventured. "I might go straight to Midas Analytics and tell Mirna Silk that you're investigating them."

Dreyfus had already thought it through. "They're already fully aware of my interest. The only reason they didn't murder me there and then is that it would have brought an immediate, crushing response from Panoply."

"But they know you'll be back."

"They'll pray I was thrown off the scent with Silk's cover story about market forecasting. At the very least, they've bought themselves a little time."

"To do what?"

Dreyfus dredged up a fatalistic smile, more grimace than anything else. "Let's hope we never have to find out."

Dreyfus undocked. He set his cutter for Panoply on an expedited return. He put ten kilometres between himself and Carcasstown, then a hundred, then a thousand. Even then he still had an itch between his shoulder blades, as if a knife was hovering between them.

He was not in the least surprised when Aurora spoke to him, her frozen-in-youth face appearing on the console.

"From the haste with which you're heading back to Panoply, may I deduce that you've found something?"

"I can't be sure yet," he said levelly. "But Carcasstown fits. There's an outfit in there running a computer powerful enough to bottle you. They know about abstraction, and there's a chance I've crossed paths with one of them before."

"The odds on that would be tiny, unless there was a connection to the earlier operation."

"That's my thinking as well."

"How fun it is to be solving a case with you, Dreyfus!"

"I'm glad you're enjoying this process. I can assure you I'm not. I'm looking at a rising civilian death toll in the middle of a pre-existing emergency, and now I've lost another trusted colleague."

"I'm sorry about Sparver." She became earnest. "No, truly, I am. Would it help if I told you I had nothing to do with that nasty bit of business?"

"It might if I thought for a second you weren't lying."

"Well, it wasn't me. Tench poked under a lot of stones trying to find the right one. It seems someone didn't appreciate her nosiness and left that trap for Sparver. But it wasn't me and I couldn't stop it from happening."

Dreyfus wondered if there was a grain of truth in her response. Aurora was given to boasting, after all. Disavowing responsibility for a grand spectacle was hardly her style.

"Would you have tried?"

"If it didn't compromise me...perhaps."

"Too bad you didn't. But then lifting a finger to do one right thing might be beyond even your elevated intellect."

"That wounds me, Dreyfus. I'm really not as bad as you make out. I led you to the Salter-Regents, didn't I? Would I have done that if I didn't have some basic interest in human welfare? They've done unspeakable things; even I can see that. Murdering those poor pigs in Mercy Sphere, not to mention all the other crimes they'll turn out to be implicated in. That's evil in its purest sense, and I'm not so far from the origins that I don't recognise it."

"One good deed doesn't make you a saint."

"But if it was down to the Clockmaker there wouldn't be any deeds at all, just carnage. I'm your better bet, Dreyfus. Deep down you know it, too."

"I know self-interest when I see it."

"Oh, you doubting Thomas, Dreyfus! Look, I'll prove what I can be by showing restraint. I'm checking out Midas Analytics as we speak. It's interesting...very interesting. Someone's done nearly a good enough job to fool nearly everyone."

"But not you."

"I could destroy them quite easily. I wouldn't even need to expose myself to any part of Carcasstown. Just pick a few robot carriers moving through the outer orbits of the Glitter Band and hack their destination settings. That ring is ramshackle, fragile and not well defended. A single big collision would break it completely." She waited a beat. "But I shan't. That would be cruel and unnecessary, given the many innocent lives that would be lost. My adversary wouldn't hesitate…but I'm better than him. Besides, I have a much more precise weapon on my side. Panoply. Or rather: you. You're going to shut down them down for me, aren't you?"

"I'll do what my authority allows me to do."

"As you will. But if you're smart, you'll do it quickly. When they move to the containment-and-capture phase, I'll likely have only a few hours to react and I can't promise the same restraint. Now that you've spooked them, that process could begin at any moment."

"If they were ready, they'd have done it already."

"They'll be willing to cut a few corners now that they know their time for action is limited. You must do everything in your power, Dreyfus. Use every procedure in the book to shut them down, before they make the worst mistake in a century."

"I have grounds for intervention. But I'll need to make my case to the Supreme Prefect and the other seniors first. Then, we'll have to coordinate resources that are already stretched. That might not happen in thirteen hours, or even twenty-six."

She sighed. "After all you've done for me, you still insist on protocol?"

"I haven't sold my soul to you completely, just a part of it."

"Don't dilly-dally," she said warningly. "I can feel them tugging on me already. *Something* has changed since yesterday, and I don't like it."

Then she was gone. Dreyfus brooded in silence on his way back to Panoply, more than the weight of the cutter's acceleration pressing on him.

CHAPTER TWENTY-FOUR

A private message was waiting for Dreyfus when he got back to Panoply, some personal business that the call-handling algorithm had decided was important enough to ruin his rest now, but not so urgent that it had been deemed worthy of passing to him while he was out in the field. He took it in his quarters, playing it through the console as he stepped back and forth through the washwall, never quite feeling that he was clean of the smells and grime of Carcasstown. He assumed the call to be an update from the Ice Mendicants; they were about the only people who ever called him on personal business. The news would either be indifferent or bad. It was rarely anything else.

A woman's voice emerged from the console. He recognised it, but it was not one of the Mendicants, nor the voice normally adopted by Aurora.

"Dreyfus? It's Detective-Marshal Del Mar. I seem to have caught you at an inopportune moment. Please return my call when you have a chance. I believe I have something of interest."

"Hestia," he mouthed, surprised and intrigued.

He abandoned the washwall and made himself decent by stepping through the clotheswall. He emerged in loose trousers and a plain white V-collared smock, his usual choice when he was off duty. He set coffee brewing but was too impatient to wait for it.

"Return the call to Hestia Del Mar, please," he instructed the console.

It took a few seconds for her to pick up. The location tag placed her in Chasm City, as he'd expected. If not exactly opposite numbers, they held roughly congruent positions in their respective—if admittedly very different—security organisations. Detective-Marshal Del Mar worked for the Chamber for City Security, vested in Chasm City but with a sphere of influence extending to all of Yellowstone's communities, as well as anything within or close to that planet's toxic atmosphere. Her jurisdiction evaporated at the inner edge of the Glitter Band, where Panoply's began. That margin was fuzzy and subject to frequent inter-agency disputes, with the two organisations bristling against each other, often at the expense of mutual cooperation.

There had been a mild thawing during the Wildfire affair. Dreyfus and Del Mar had established a useful working relationship, one that had helped resolve a critical aspect of the emergency. They had kept up a pattern of intelligence-sharing in the year or so that followed, collaborating on a few linked cases, but Dreyfus was the first to admit that he had neglected the relationship as time wore on. There had been too many other calls upon his time, none of which really needed the close involvement of his colleagues on Yellowstone.

He had been feeling bad about it for months, reminding himself that at some point he was bound to have to call upon Hestia again, and that he really ought to drop her a friendly line before he really needed something from her.

Now she had called him, out of the blue—and it was too late.

"I'm sorry, Hestia. I should have been in touch."

"Never mind that," she said brusquely. "We've each been consumed by our work. This escalating violence has been a burden on both our organisations. We've had our share of it in Chasm City, even as we do all that we can to put out the flames." She appraised him through the link, her broad freckled face filling the frame, her expression as severe and humourless as he remembered. "You look tired, Prefect Dreyfus."

"Do I?" he asked wearily.

"You'll forgive me. People have been telling me the same thing for so long, I thought I should pass along the favour."

"Perhaps we both need a holiday. Whatever happened to those long years when nothing much seemed to happen?"

"We wasted them worrying about the future. I heard about your recent losses, Prefect Dreyfus. Please accept my condolences. It is never easy to suffer the loss of a colleague. To lose two, in such quick succession..."

"Thank you, Hestia." He would persist in calling her by her name rather than title, even though she was a stickler for professional courtesies.

"Now, the reason for my call. I don't know if this will come as good or bad news, but something of yours has come into my possession. I think it may relate to one of those losses."

Dreyfus leaned in with interest. "What have you found?"

"An object emitting a faint but readable Panoply tracking signal. It's very badly damaged. It appears to have fallen right through our atmosphere, nearly burning away with the friction."

He dared not let his hopes rise too high. "Describe it, if you would."

"A lump of blackened material about the size of a fist. We track everything that enters Yellowstone's atmosphere, of course. You send a lot of junk down to us. This object was only of interest because Panoply sent out an inter-agency notification, alerting us to the fact of a missing recording device." Her look sharpened. "But it's more than that, isn't it?"

"It's much more, Hestia."

"I thought so. Where the object's condition permitted localised testing, we found...well, dare I say it?"

"Organic material," Dreyfus supplied for her.

"We have nothing similar in our technical inventory, but then our investigations rarely put our officers in situations of similar risk. I presume that this is all that's left of one of your colleagues?"

"If it's what we've been looking for, then...yes. My friend Sparver died in the line of duty. He could have saved himself, but only at the expense of evidential capture. He put Panoply before his own life, knowing there was something we needed to be aware of."

"And this object...contains that evidence?"

"That'll depend on how badly damaged it is. It survived a nuclear strike, but it was never meant to fall into Yellowstone. Still, you say there's a signal?"

"Weak and fading. I called you as soon as the nature of the object became plain to me. I can have our analysts attempt to recover the evidence trace, but I suspect you'd rather turn it over to your own people?"

"Your offer of assistance is deeply appreciated," Dreyfus said tactfully. "The object should only be examined under Panoply maximum security protocols, though. If it suspects it's subject to unauthorised tampering, it may initiate a self-erase process."

"Understood," she said. "Rest assured that we'd feel similarly if one of our recordings fell into Panoply's possession. We wouldn't want your ham-fisted efforts anywhere near it."

"No hurt feelings, then," Dreyfus said with a half-smile.

"Nonetheless, time may be of the essence. If that evidence decays along with the homing pulse, you'll soon have nothing. I am calling to make immediate arrangements to transfer the object back into Panoply safekeeping. I can have it boosted directly to you, via cargo drone?"

"That's appreciated, but I think I'd rather collect it in person. And the fewer hands that touch it along the way..."

"Very well. I'd bring it to you directly, but I'm afraid that's quite out of the question given my current caseload. Are you in a position to collect it? If you don't have the time to come all the way down to Chasm City, we can arrange a transfer in low orbit."

"I think that will work very well. What's the soonest you can meet me?"

"Thirteen hours, and that will take some doing. If time is of the essence, the drone is by far the better option." She looked at him shrewdly. "You're concerned about who might touch it before it finds its way to you, aren't you? As if you can't be sure someone in Panoply wouldn't mishandle it, or worse?"

Dreyfus was not about to share his deepest fears with Hestia Del Mar, even though a part of him badly wanted to treat her as a confidante, someone he could be sure had no part in any of the conspiracies presently swirling around him.

She would understand his silence better than anyone.

"I can be there in thirteen hours. Send me the coordinates for the rendezvous when you have them. And Hestia?"

"Yes, Prefect Dreyfus?"

"You've been very helpful. Thank you."

Dreyfus presented his findings to the tactical room after three hours of fitful rest. He had calculated ahead, factoring in the time needed to requisition a cutter and make any possible rendezvous with the detective-marshal.

"Summary, please, Tom," Jane Aumonier said, as he took his position close to Thalia.

Dreyfus had already arranged for the Solid Orrery to display an enlarged, elevated representation of the wheel, hanging like a corroded watch-gear above the glinting flow of habitats in the main orbits.

"Carcasstown," he stated.

"Most of us have some familiarity with the place," Aumonier said, nodding in jaded recognition. "A thorn in the side, most of the time. What I'd give to have *that* as my main problem now."

"You've just got your wish," Dreyfus replied. "For once, though, Carcasstown is the victim, not the perpetrator. They've been duped: set up to act as cover for something that endangers us all."

"Continue," Aumonier said guardedly.

"Ingvar Tench's movements show that it was of particular interest to her in the last year of her life. Tench suspected that an offshoot of Catopsis was being run out of Carcasstown, under the cover of a completely different organisation."

"Which is?" asked Baudry.

"Midas Analytics." He nodded at the wheel. "They're a market-forecasting outfit, one of many commercial tenants leasing space and utilities on the wheel's rim. Within their operation is a very powerful machine called Abacus, supposedly there to run market simulations for the benefit of stock traders."

206

"You think it's something else?" Aumonier probed.

"Abacus is a perfect containment vessel for an intelligence of the order of Aurora or the Clockmaker, and I believe that's its real function. Over the last few months, the operatives in Midas Analytics have been utilising Catopsis methods to track and isolate these intelligences."

Aumonier looked at her colleagues. "You think this is why Tench was murdered?"

"Without question. She may not have put all the parts together, but she was getting uncomfortably close. Unfortunately, the nature of her death—high-level sabotage of her cutter, which has been confirmed by her recovered testimony—indicates clear collusion between Midas Analytics and elements still inside Panoply."

"Grigor Bacchus."

"No, ma'am—at least, he may not have been the main agitator. I was mistaken about Tench's message. It was *Abacus* that she was trying to tell us about, not Bacchus."

"Yet Bacchus clearly felt you were getting close to something," Aumonier replied.

"His involvement may have been peripheral. May I invite Thalia to present what I think is a significant finding?"

Aumonier nodded. "Go ahead, Ng."

"Thank you, ma'am," Thalia said, straightening. "I've found something in Thyssen's operational logs, something that was overlooked until now. Before I go any further, I want to be clear that Thyssen was fully cooperative in all regards. There's no implication of collusion in these murders."

Aumonier's look hardened. "Murders?"

"Mizler and Ingvar, ma'am. They've looked like separate cases, but they're not."

Voices began to rise around the table. Aumonier leaned in, silencing the queries for now. "Proceed, Ng."

Thalia swallowed. Dreyfus met her eye, nodded what he hoped was his encouragement.

"On the day he died, Mizler's cutter reported a fault during pre-launch checkouts. Thyssen followed standard operating procedure: he assigned Mizler another vehicle, one that was already primed and ready to go."

Aumonier nodded coolly, already ahead of her.

"The one that Ingvar was meant to take?"

"Yes, ma'am. Her schedule of duty meant that there was plenty of time to rectify the fault in Mizler's ship and allocate her that one instead. Neither prefect would have been aware of any anomaly, and it was normal operational practice."

"Yet the ship Mizler took was...sabotaged in some way?"

"Indeed, ma'am. It was programmed to go rogue, to begin attacking a habitat as soon as it was within weapons range."

"No," Clearmountain said, at first gently and then with increasing forcefulness. "No, no, no! That makes no sense, Ng! Mizler Cranach's attack was premeditated, driven by revenge!"

"Can you explain this, Ng?"

"I can, ma'am. None of it's what it seemed. Mizler wasn't meant to be in that ship, and it's only an accident of chance that his target was Valsko-Venev."

Baudry looked puzzled. "But we had his suicide note, his motivation."

"That was concocted after the fact, ma'am, following the mix-up with the ships. Those who set Ingvar up had to deflect attention from themselves by making Cranach's death seem to fit a premeditated plan."

Baudry was dogged. "Yet Valsko-Venev *did* have a dark past to do with the maltreatment of hyperpigs."

"That's true, ma'am. But if we were to dig deeply enough, we could find a similar connection in the history of almost any habitat. It's woven into us, all of us. We can't escape it." Again, she gathered herself. "They made us see a phantom motive. The suicide note was fabricated, and so were his intentions. As I've already demonstrated with my analysis of the last second of the attack, far from murdering those people, Mizler Cranach did everything in his power to prevent the carnage. He acted with courage and selflessness, exactly the way Sparver Bancal mentored him to do."

There was a silence.

"Is she right?" Baudry asked, directing her question at Dreyfus.

"I'm persuaded," he answered. "They had a go at killing Ingvar six months ago, but botched it. They waited as long as they could before risking another attempt, and that time they succeeded."

"The modus changed slightly," Thalia took up. "This time, rather than firing on a random target, they had the cutter lock onto a watchlisted location, Stadler-Kremeniev. From her instrumentation, Ingvar wouldn't have known anything was wrong—not until she was already in too deep. She docked, went inside, all the while thinking she was somewhere else. It was a thorough job, and this time there was no mistake."

"Except for the whiphound," Dreyfus said.

"Indeed, sir. Once Ingvar realised there was no way she was getting out of there alive, she found a way to get a message back to Panoply through her whiphound."

Baudry settled her chin on her fist. "Why didn't it remain with her corpse?"

"Because she'd worked out what we now know: her murder could only have been arranged from within Panoply. If the whiphound had stayed with her, it could have been erased or destroyed by anyone who found it while her body was being returned."

"She was trained well by her mentor," Dreyfus said. "And she never gave up."

"This will need to be formalised," Aumonier said. "But on the face of it, we may consider Mizler Cranach exonerated. I am...not displeased." But any pleasure she allowed herself had, at best, a subatomic half-life. "Now I need to start getting the word out to all those hotheads that his initial attack was nothing of the kind. The constables are already making in-roads into the Salter-Regents and their co-conspirators, and that will help in time, but I need to see progress now. But how can I change hearts and minds without compromising an ongoing investigation?"

"You can't," Thalia said, impressing Dreyfus.

"Then what *may* I do, Ng, since something must be done?"

"You can put me on it, ma'am," Thalia said boldly. "I believed I established a rapport with Minty. If Minty and the others can be persuaded that Mizler was acting for them, rather than against, their voices may help turn the tide. Who better to serve as peace advocates than those with the biggest grievance?"

"It may or may not help," Aumonier reflected. "But it certainly won't hurt. They'll appreciate being informed about this early, too, in confidence. I think it will bolster trust between Panoply and the lemurs. I'll hold off on any formal announcement until you've spoken to them directly." She nodded her encouragement. "You have discretionary powers in the matter, Ng. Use them."

"Thank you, ma'am."

Aumonier made a beckoning gesture, not unkindly. "The sooner you put in that good word, the better. Is it feasible for you to be on your way immediately?"

"It is, ma'am."

"All existing security measures will remain in place around the docks," Aumonier said. "Grigor Bacchus and Podor remain the likeliest suspects for that sabotage work—Bacchus had the motivation, Podor the access —but until we can be sure they were acting alone, Thyssen will maintain condition four procedures. Watch your back, Ng."

"I shall, ma'am," Thalia answered.

When Thalia had left, Dreyfus settled his hands before him and laid out his case for intervention.

"Midas Analytics needs to be shut down quickly. Ordinarily I'd advocate Heavy enforcement, but in this case we need to consider a ring of human shields who aren't party to either the murders or the conspiracy."

"Handy for them," Aumonier commented.

Dreyfus slid his compad across to the Supreme Prefect. He had pulled up public biographies for Mirna Silk and Aristarchus Salazar, augmented by Panoply's own record-gathering.

"Silk seems clean," he said, willing to let that judgement stand on record. "She's what she says she is: a specialist in market forecasting. Multiple entries back up her story. She's a scrapper, too: both parents killed in a shuttle accident, shunted from institution to institution, directionless until she finds the one thing she can shine at, which is an almost superhuman talent for understanding and predicting the flow of wealth. A fighter and an opportunist, but not some zealot interested in destabilising our entire society."

"Mm." Aumonier nodded guardedly. "And Salazar?"

"He's the mind behind Abacus, but he defers to someone else in Midas, a younger man who ought to be the one taking orders, not giving them."

"Is Salazar as clean as Silk?"

"His biography is plausible enough, but I still got the impression he was hiding something. My instinct is that he knows there's something else going on behind the Midas facade. I imagine he understands that it involves network latencies and one-way traps and knows that it's nothing to do with market forecasting. He's bright and he appreciates his talents being put to good use. Beyond that, he's shrewd enough not to ask too many questions."

"Partial knowledge of a criminal conspiracy is no excuse for inaction," Aumonier said.

"I'm not excusing Salazar. I'm just saying that he may be a useful point of leverage."

"And this younger man—a name?"

"I didn't get a name or an image capture." Dreyfus paused significantly. "He's known to me, but I don't think it's anything to do with Catopsis. I went back over the files and none of the key protagonists looked like that young man. Faces can be changed, but in his case it's what hasn't changed that matters. He wasn't expecting to be observed by one of us."

"Then let's hope that you can jog that memory. In the meantime, what's your recommendation?"

"The lighter touch. I'll go in with Medium enforcement, try to reason with Silk or Salazar or someone else who has the means to stop the program. We can offer amnesties to any Midas staff not directly implicated in the conspiracy, including the likes of Salazar. They're more useful to us cooperating than running. Someone will bite."

"Or I could just exercise my powers and have Pell blow up the place with a single missile." Aumonier cocked her head, thinking it through before nodding peremptorily. "Still, your way is worth a shot. Take whoever and whatever you need. I'd advise giving them twenty-six hours, though, just so they think our interest is only casual."

"That will work, ma'am. It'll allow me to make a rendezvous with Detective-Marshal Del Mar, near Yellowstone."

Aumonier's look was spiced with jealousy. "On what business?"

"Evidential sequestration." Dreyfus pinched at the collar of his uniform where it was digging into the sweat and bristles of his neck.

Dreyfus went straight to the refectory. It was one of the quieter periods and he cast his eyes around at the two dozen or so people scattered around the tables, singly or in small groups. He noticed Thalia, eating alone.

He collected an apple, a piece of a bread and a bulb of coffee, then joined her.

"Shouldn't you be on your way to the lemurs?"

She peeled a banana unhurriedly. "With these new procedures, we can't just show up and expect a ship to be ready. Thyssen's doing a hard scrub of the control architecture for each vehicle, then only loading it up again just before departure. He told me go away, have some breakfast and come back."

"How secure is his stored copy of the architecture?"

"About as secure as anything here, I suppose. It doesn't mean we're immune to sabotage, but it does mean they won't be able to target just one of us, the way they did with Ingvar. They won't have another go, will they?"

"I doubt it. Assuming there's any more to this than Bacchus and Podor, they'd need a different approach now you've exposed their methods."

Thalia nibbled at the banana. "I wish Sparver was here to see Mizler fully exonerated."

"Was he aware of any part of your enquiry?"

She fidgeted. Thalia was not an effective liar or dissembler, an aspect of her personality that Dreyfus greatly admired.

"Just a little bit, sir. When I thought I had something, I wanted another pair of eyes on it. I asked Sparver to go over the same data-streams, to see if I was missing something."

Dreyfus was still, his face impassive. "Contrary to the direct instructions of the Supreme Prefect. She put you on each other's cases for a reason. You were each too close to the subject matter."

"I suppose that will need to be in the final report as well. And a reprimand." Some of the steel she had down in the tactical room returned. "I'm not sorry, especially now that he's gone. He needed to know that I was closing in on a breakthrough."

"He did, and I'm glad you involved him."

She dipped her gaze, then looked directly at him. "Sir?"

"It was against your instructions. Then again, I believe Sparver was guilty of doing something similar when he shared intelligence with you during Wildfire."

"Have you ever…Sir?" She stopped herself, then had a second thought about stopping. "A direct order, sir. Something like that. Have you ever done anything as bad?"

"As bad?" He looked to the ceiling, reflecting on her question. "No, never anything *as* bad."

Thalia looked down, chastened.

"I didn't think so, sir."

"I've done much, much worse." He stood up, taking the bread and apple with him. "Good luck with the lemurs."

Dreyfus was nearly out of the refectory when his bracelet chimed. A private call, but directed to him as a matter of urgency.

It was Sister Catherine of the Ice Mendicants.

CHAPTER TWENTY-FIVE

She was waiting for him in Hospice Idlewild, leaning on her stick, but her usual chastising tone was absent. That worried him more than anything.

"I know you've come as quickly as you can. We'd best move quickly, all the same. It's the worst seizure by far. It happened out of the blue two hours ago, without the least warning."

"I told you to get those implants out of her," Dreyfus snapped.

"She needs a period of stability to be suitable for surgery. There have been days when she has been relatively untroubled, almost back to her old self. But it never lasts."

"Let me guess. Just when you're getting ready to cut them out, she has another episode?"

Sister Catherine heard something in his words that he had not intended. "None of us think this is a psychosomatic reaction, Tom, if that's what you mean."

"No," he said, regretting his sharpness of a few moments before. "I didn't mean that. And I know you're doing the best for her that you can."

"Rest assured that we will perform the surgery as soon as there is a window of calm. We won't wait a day next time."

She led him through Idlewild quickly, to the familiar enclave of low white buildings, surrounded by cool walls, flower beds, vegetable gardens and shaded walks.

Valery was in her own room, lying on a bed. As if in the throes of a nightmare, she moved and groaned beneath thin, sweat-soaked sheets. Her eyes were open, but her gaze was wild and undirected. Two younger Mendicants were with her, trying to keep her as comfortable as possible with cool sponges and the limited range of medicines they were willing to risk. Dreyfus wanted to reassure them that it was not their fault that nothing was working. Nothing would work, short of scooping those implants out.

"May I have a few moments alone with my wife?"

"We'll be nearby," Sister Catherine said. "There's a bell on the end of that rope. Call us immediately if her condition changes."

"I will."

Dreyfus sat next to Valery. He watched the Mendicants shuffle out, listening to their slippered footsteps retreat beyond the next room and the other beyond that, waiting until he was sure they were well out of earshot.

He took Valery's hand, squeezing it against her trembling. "I'm here. I know she's in you, and I know you feel it. I know she won't let you speak. But she can't stop you knowing I'm here."

Valery's restlessness eased. Her head eased into the soggy defile of her pillow. Her eyes settled on him, her mouth opening in a half-smile. "It's begun, Dreyfus. The next phase."

He tried to direct his anger through and beyond Valery, as if she were merely the window, not the end itself. "There are a hundred other ways you could have reached me besides this sick little stunt."

"But how else am I to make sure I've got your full attention? You can brush me off when I come to you by other means. You can't brush *this* off."

"I already told you I was doing everything in my power to shut down Midas. The Supreme Prefect has agreed to an intervention. We'll attempt to persuade them that shutting down is their only realistic course. If that fails, we go in harder."

"It's too slow." She raised her voice sharply, Dreyfus wincing as it echoed off the walls and ceiling. "TOO SLOW! They've accelerated. The containment process is already happening. I'm being...ingested. A piece at a time, sucked into that bottle."

"Then resist it!"

"I can't do so without concentrating my resources, directing them against that single-point target. That makes me ever more vulnerable, both to Midas and the Clockmaker." Her lips curled in fury and derision. "You had a chance, Dreyfus! You could have stopped this already!"

"With too much risk of innocent deaths. There's been enough of that already. I won't add to it."

She laughed, a web of foam breaking on her lips. "A few dozen? A few hundred? Is that what you were worried about? You'll look back on that chance and wish you'd taken it. I warned you that I was going to have to get serious. You should have listened."

"Maybe I should. But that's my failing, not Valery's. Get out of her."

"And then we'll talk?"

"Just leave her alone. You've got my attention."

She made Valery sigh. "It's too late anyway. I can't resist the pull of Abacus for much longer—certainly not the hours and hours you think we have. I must resort to more forceful measures."

"Don't," he began, but the word had barely formed before he realised she was gone, snapping out of Valery between one heartbeat and the next. The revulsion and fear he had felt only a moment earlier broke like a wave against rocks, replaced by an overwhelming surge of love and desperate concern.

Valery writhed gently in the bed, mumbled something inaudibly, then become more restful, her breathing easier, even the prickle of perspiration seeming to lift from her brow. Dreyfus held her hand, watching her silently. He stroked a loose hair from her eye, then leaned in and kissed her softly.

"This won't last forever," he whispered. "I promise."

His bracelet chimed. He glared down at it and eased away from Valery. "Jane," he answered gruffly, certain that only Aumonier would have the temerity to interrupt him when he was on private business. "Can't anything wait until I'm back?"

"Not this time," she answered, without the slightest hint of umbrage at his tone. "I'm sorry to pull you away from Valery, but you'd be the last one to sit back while this happens."

He took the sponge and cooled Valery's forehead. She was still calm, merely profoundly unconscious.

"While what happens?"

"Three bulk carriers have broken away from their scheduled routes. Our projections show convergence on Carcasstown in a little under thirty-three minutes."

"It's a strategy I was anticipating," Dreyfus answered. "Aurora and the Clockmaker can't resist Abacus using informational warfare. They have to smash the facility, regardless of who else gets hurt."

"That seems to be the intention. Are you moving?"

Dreyfus gave Valery a final kiss and stood from her bedside. "Yes, I'm moving. But it's a long way back to my cutter. Do you want to commandeer it remotely?"

"No. I want you on-scene, just in case we don't manage to interdict all three of those carriers."

He gave his wife a farewell glance as he left her room. "Evacuation measures?"

"They've been notified, but we expect the response to be imperfect."

"What about Carcasstown's own defences?"

"Adequate against the normal range of threats, but unlikely to be effective against three simultaneous targets. And that's assuming whatever's

215

behind this stops at three. I'm sending a general request for all civilian transport to be suspended immediately, but there's little I can do about ships already en route."

"Understood. Jane, can you relay a message to Thalia for me?"

"Yes, of course. Ng should be with Minty and the lemurs right now."

"Instruct her to leave as soon as she can without making things worse. Her peacemaking overture is important, but I need her to make that rendezvous with Hestia Del Mar for me. Hestia can tell her where and when to meet."

"I will, Tom. Any special instructions beyond that?"

"She's to bring the item to me. No other eyes on it."

"Understood. And if these other eyes were to include mine...?"

"In due course, Jane. Please trust me with this for the time being."

"I'm tearing you away from Valery and asking you to put yourself in harm's way with that rogue carrier, Tom. I think I'm a long way past merely trusting you. Please be safe."

"I will. And Jane?"

"Yes."

"Make sure Hafdis is looked after."

"You needn't worry about Hafdis. We're getting on like the proverbial house."

He signed off, and had nearly broken into a jog by the time he met the waiting Mendicants. They read his expression, looking at each other with rising concern.

"Valery?" asked Sister Catherine.

"I think she's all right for now, Sister. I'm afraid I've got to go, though."

"There is no rest for the wicked," Sister Catherine lamented. "Or for good men in a time of troubles."

Thalia squatted on damp green grass, facing a semicircle of civic seniors, esteemed families and various other worthies from the arboreal communities of Valsko-Venev.

"And although I know that this news casts the crime against you in a different light," Thalia was saying, "be under no illusions that it *was* a crime, and will be treated as such. Though Mizler Cranach was set up to die, it was an accident of luck that yours happened to be the first habitat that he reached. His intentions here were innocent—just a routine inspection. The last thing he was expecting was for his weapons to open up on you."

One of the flying-squirrel-like citizens asked: "How can you be sure that this isn't Panoply trying to deflect away from the hateful actions of one of its own?"

216

This one had been piping up at regular intervals, and Thalia was now struggling to maintain the necessary decorum in the service of her peace-making overture. With an immense effort of will she kept her strained smile intact, her voice striking what she hoped was the right register of patience, humility and helpfulness. "That's an excellent question, and one that deserves a frank and open answer—"

"Good, then give it to us."

"Speaking," Thalia intoned under her breath, imagining Jane Aumonier facing down the same adversary. Then, louder: "What I mean to say is, there isn't any way to prove to you what was going on in Mizler's head during the attack. What I can tell you is this: he was mentored by a friend of mine, a friend now gone, and if there was a microgram of hatefulness in Mizler Cranach, it didn't come from the head of Sparver Bancal—"

"We're not asking about the mentor."

"But I'm..." She smiled so fiercely, it was as if invisible prongs were dragging her mouth into shape. "What I'm...Look, a very bad thing was done to you, and it was natural to see a link with your founders. This wasn't about them, though, or about you. Mizler Cranach wasn't even supposed to be on that ship!" Had she said too much? She wondered if any of her audience was paying enough attention to care. She had a feeling minds had already been made up before she ever sat down on the grass. "I'm not here to brush away that crime," she persisted. "I'm here to promise you that we'll find those accountable, for your sakes as well as ours. We're all victims here—"

This last utterance had been meant well, but as soon as it was out of her lips she could see how it was going to land. Now it was not just the annoying flying-squirrel thing piping back at her. Half the gathering had turned from scepticism to outright disdain, and the rest were looking distinctly unimpressed.

Some whooping and hollering started up.

Minty stood up, flapping its arms. "Citizens! Please! Let's have some respect for the prefect! She didn't need to come here with this news, and she surely knew how it was going to be received. It would have been far easier to issue some Band-wide pronouncement, but instead Prefect Ng has come all the way to see us..."

Thalia stood up dejectedly. "No, Minty," she said. "They're right." She nodded at the sullen gathering, which had been pacified slightly by her evident state of defeat. "This whole thing was a bad idea. I'm sorry. I just thought it'd be better if you heard it from me."

Her bracelet chimed loudly, its discordant tone ringing from the surrounding trees.

"Ng," she said warily.

"Jane Aumonier. We have a developing situation. You're to leave immediately, unless it'll cause untold damage to Panoply–lemur relations."

Thalia surveyed the wreckage of her diplomacy: the half-circle of cute but belligerent furry-snouted and darkly eye-patched faces glaring at her as if she had personally burned down half their forest, then stomped around in the ashes singing a celebration chant.

"I fear the damage is already done, ma'am."

"Good. Or not good. We'll talk about that later. I'm sure you did your utmost."

"I'm not sure I did, ma'am," Thalia answered with bitter understatement. "How exactly may I be of help?"

"Instructions from Dreyfus. Preoccupied as he is with the current situation, he's unable to make a rendezvous with Hestia Del Mar."

"I know that name, ma'am, although I can't quite place it."

"Detective-Marshal Del Mar of Chasm City, Ng. My opposite number, almost. But before you raise your hopes, you're not getting a free trip to the city. I have rendezvous coordinates from Del Mar. You're to meet her in orbit and collect some kind of evidential package. I gather it's needed with some...urgency."

"Evidential package?"

"Join the dots, Ng. I was expected to do so myself, so I don't see why you get off lightly."

"I'll be on my way promptly, ma'am." Thalia finished the call. "I'm sorry, Minty. Something's come up. I've got to go."

Minty confided in a near-whisper: "Well, that's maybe...not the worst idea."

Her host led her away from the gathering, the whoops and hollers gradually muffled by intervening trees and bushes. Thalia felt dejected, wondering if it were possible to have made a worse impression. "I'm sorry, Minty," she offered, as they neared one of the underground transit entrances. "I really was trying to do the right thing here."

"Good intentions sometimes need a little time to put down roots, Prefect. Although since we seem to be on first-name terms now, I suppose I should call you Thalia."

"Thank you for trying to convince them."

"The least I could do. And don't despair just yet. Some of our families have been rather revelling in the idea of being singled out for the sins of their ancestors. That doesn't mean they won't come round. What's this urgent business, by the way?"

"I know what you're thinking. That call couldn't have come at a more in convenient time."

"I wasn't, believe it or not. I was thinking—and I might not be the best at reading baseline human expressions these days—but I was thinking, this is the first time I've seen a look of hope on you. Is that far from the truth?"

"I wouldn't call it hope, Minty. It's just that when you've lost a good friend, getting anything back from them isn't something you count on."

"Then may the universe be kind to your expectations, Thalia Ng. You may not feel as if you've made many friends here today, but I can tell you that you've made one."

"Thank you, Minty."

"Let's get you back to your ship. Oh, before I forget: a small token of my appreciation, since you liked them so much the last time."

Thalia accepted a transparent tube containing several dozen berries, pressed so tightly that their juices were beginning to leak out. She took the offering with all the civility and gratitude that she could muster, even as the sight of the berries played havoc with her insides. "That is... exceptionally kind, Minty."

"Enjoy."

"I will," she said. She tucked the berries into a pouch on her belt, where they would remain until she found a suitable opportunity to destroy them beyond all forensic recognition.

CHAPTER TWENTY-SIX

Dreyfus absorbed the latest updates about the three rogue carriers as he completed his return from Hospice Idlewild. All efforts to override control of the ships had failed, leaving no option but to destroy them before they reached Carcasstown. Given his point of origin, Dreyfus was only in a position to make a close approach to one of the ships, converging with it when the carrier was only eight minutes from its target. The other two carriers were arriving from different sectors of the Glitter Band, on widely diverging courses; he would only get a glimpse of them in the final few seconds of the drama, if they weren't already destroyed.

He examined the threat from a vantage of several kilometres. The bulk carrier *Evangelina* was typical of its kind, an ungainly, wingless dragonfly, engines and fuel tanks barbed at one end and the tiny shrunken head of a rudimentary control complex at the other. Strung along an extendable spine were the rib-sided cargo modules, each typically assigned to a single commodity. Hundreds of thousands of tonnes, at the very least, and all of it now directed into a kinetic-energy delivery system.

Carriers did not usually carry armaments, but Dreyfus still maintained a cautious distance as he circled along the vehicle's length, scanning the modules for signs of inhabitants. Just because the carriers were automated did not mean that they never carried maintenance crews, cut-rate passengers or even the occasional stowaway.

"Dreyfus," he called in. "I'm alongside my objective. I'm not picking up any signs of life, which is one less complication."

"Good. Do you have the means to disable it before we resort to warheads?"

"I'll see what I can do."

Dreyfus pulled astern of the carrier until he was nearly looking down the swollen trumpets of its engine cluster. He deployed the cutter's cannon and locked onto one of the fuel tanks. He fired, feeling the recoil through the whole frame of his vehicle, the cannon silent but still producing a horrid, tooth-grinding subsonic shockwave.

The fuel tank exploded, rupturing outwards. It wasn't a big explosion, suggesting that the tank had been nearly empty before he shot at it. He stopped the cannon and repositioned to try another tank. This one exploded more furiously, but still not enough to inflict more than superficial damage on the surrounding structures.

He adjusted position and fired again. No explosion came, but the result was better than he could have hoped for. He had punctured a pressure line or tank, causing a geyser of grey gas to shoot out from the side of the engine assembly. Dreyfus watched, reminded of the gambit Mizler had attempted in the last instants of his life. The same effect was playing out here, albeit on a much grander, slower scale. The carrier was crabbing, its tail beginning to veer round at an angle to the direction of flight. There had to be some change to the overall motion, Dreyfus told himself, maybe enough to rule out a direct collision with Carcasstown.

Steering jets pulsed from the opposite side of the carrier. Dreyfus swore. It was correcting the drift, holding itself on course.

"Ten out of ten for effort," he said under his breath. Then, to Aumonier: "I'm having no effect here, Jane. My guns can't do enough damage, and I don't think ramming or nudging will help, either."

"I was never counting on it, Tom. We're down to six minutes now. At your present range you should have a clear visual on Carcasstown."

"I see it," he said, staring at the little cog-wheel station, backdropped by a twinkling belt of more distant habitats, observing it grow even in the few moments of his gaze. "Voi, but it's closer than I expected."

"I'll take no more chances. Please pull back to a safe distance. A warhead is inbound, maximum yield."

Dreyfus put a few more kilometres between himself and the carrier, averting his windows from the likely direction of the blast. The warhead came in too quickly for him to track, just a scratch of pink light on his retina, and then the edge of the blast as its fringes pushed into his field of view. Bright, because there was a lot of gas and volatile material in that cargo manifest, now lost forever.

He rotated the cutter and swept the impact zone. Nothing but gas, dust and hot debris, expanding rapidly outward. A few chunks of the carrier might be large enough to do some damage if they intersected with Carcasstown, or indeed any other habitat, but there was nothing capable of threatening an entire structure.

"Interdiction successful," Dreyfus reported. "What about the other two?"

"Warheads are on their way, but they have further to travel. I'm sending two fish after each as a precaution. There won't be time to launch a second pair of warheads if the first isn't sufficient."

"Time to next strike?"

"Two minutes, followed by the third a minute later. Both carriers will be within ninety kilometres of Carcasstown."

"Cutting it fine, aren't we?"

"The choice wasn't ours."

"While you have two minutes to spare, I'd recommend a risk assessment on all other robotic carriers moving through or into this sector. And maybe beyond."

"I've already flagged the likely threats. But I must be honest with you. If they throw everything at Carcasstown, there's a very good chance of at least one of them getting through."

"Then I need to get inside Carcasstown sooner rather than later. I'll dock as soon as the third carrier has been taken out—and pray more aren't on the way."

"Very well. I'll task a corvette to you as soon as the immediate threat is neutralised."

"Thank you."

"Second interdiction is imminent. Look out for the fireworks."

The nuclear flash came a breath later, a hard white pulse without direction or distance, fierce enough to trigger his shields an instant after the first photons hit his optic nerves. The shielding cleared. Carcasstown was still there, backdropped by a faint, thinning haze of ionised matter.

"Successful interdiction. The final pair of warheads are closing on the third carrier." But Aumonier broke off, Dreyfus just catching the edge of a clipped, urgent conversation going on around her.

"What is it?"

"We have a distress message from the third carrier. Someone's aboard, and they've just realised the trouble they're in." Irritation broke through her voice. "What were they doing until now? Sleepwalking? Pell! Break those warheads off!"

Even though Dreyfus was looking across hundreds of kilometres of space, he made out two bright, momentary hyphens of light as the warheads adjusted their trajectories. They would circle now, waiting for another command.

"Time to impact with Carcasstown?" Dreyfus asked.

"Just under two minutes."

"Tell them they have one minute to get off that carrier, by any means available. It's all you can do for them." He paused. "That's a suggestion, of course."

"I'm passing it through on the distress channel. Am I being a fool, Tom, for the sake of a handful of souls on that carrier, against all the people in

Carcasstown? They might not even be legal. They might not even be *real*."

"You're being you," he answered.

"I am, aren't I?" Then, with a sigh of self-realisation: "Pell, prepare your warheads to close in again on my command."

Dreyfus scanned space for the third carrier, guessing its approximate location from the course that the warheads had been on before their deviation. Once he had a fix, he zoomed in, the carrier appearing sharp in his displays but severely foreshortened by its direction of approach.

A speck of light detached from the carrier. It drifted away then accelerated on an eyelash of pink thrust. Not a suit, not a lone survivor chancing an airlock egress.

"An escape capsule has left the carrier," he reported.

"No further contact," Aumonier said. "They've had their chance—let's hope they used it. Pell: take it out, both fish."

The third flash came five seconds later. It was actually two blasts, too close together to separate. Dreyfus waited for the screens to drop. The carrier was gone, exactly as hoped, but he only had to wait a few seconds for the less encouraging news to come.

"Pell reports that a large fragment came through intact. No possibility of a repeat attempt now."

"Is it headed for Carcasstown?"

"Projections are unclear. It'll be a near miss if it doesn't hit."

Dreyfus returned his attention to the wheel, now much larger than when he had last inspected it. He would soon need to start slowing down if he wanted to dock on this pass. And in a very few seconds he would know if that surviving fragment was enough to do Aurora's will after her first two efforts had failed.

Lights sparked from the ring, like a diamond bracelet catching rays. Those were Carcasstown's anti-collision defences going off, finally triggered by the close proximity of the fragment. Dreyfus steeled himself. The pulses were aimed at the fragment, not him, but it would only take a bit of bad luck to have one of them ricochet directly at him. The ring weapons kept firing, augmented by similar installations on the hub and spokes. It looked impressive, but a lot depended on how well maintained, calibrated and coordinated those defences were. Nothing he had seen in the jumbled architecture of Carcasstown flooded him with confidence.

And yet it proved sufficient. The weapons snapped off: their ranging computers had decided that the threat was neutralised, or destined to pass by without collision.

Dreyfus saw nothing.

"Alerting CTC to track and capture that debris," Aumonier announced.

"Are you still monitoring those other carriers?"

"Yes—more than twenty of them. No change in any of their trajectories. It's a reprieve, of sorts."

"Of sorts," Dreyfus echoed.

Dreyfus fought his way through a slow, jostling tide of prospective evacuees clogging the bottleneck thoroughfares of the hub. He stopped an official and asked to be met by Under-Supervisor Krenkel.

"Krenkel's not on duty," the flustered official said. "And if he's got any sense he'll be pulling in every possible favour to get off Carcasstown."

"Tell him he's not leaving."

Dreyfus waited ten minutes, until a frazzled-looking Krenkel emerged from the chaos, his cloak of office thrown on in a hurry, with the collar done up by the wrong fastener.

"One minute you tell me to look after my family, the next that I can't leave. Will you make up your mind?"

"Your family should leave," Dreyfus said. "Panoply will assist, if they haven't already made arrangements. You'll stay put for the time being, at least until I've spoken to Mirna Silk again. Take me to her, the quickest possible route."

Krenkel shoved Dreyfus in the approximate general direction, not without a certain boisterous enthusiasm. "What was happening with those ships? Do we need to fear more of them?"

"We'll have a response standing by if more are directed toward Carcasstown."

"Who'd want to do that us? We're not bad neighbours. We don't have neighbours!"

"It was directed at Midas, not the wheel as a whole."

"Small consolation!"

They went up the spoke, then boarded one of the suspended carriages, again moving against the flow of evacuation. It was quieter here, though, and less frenzied. As each minute passed, more and more people were opting to stay put rather than rush for the airlocks. There were as many people drifting back to their workplaces as were moving to the spokes and back to the hub.

"The operation being run through Midas has sprung into a new phase," Dreyfus told Krenkel, as their carriage moved along the undulating tube that encircled Carcasstown. "That's what prompted the attack. Now we have to shut it down for good."

"And they've sent...*one* of you?"

"Time's of the essence. The threat to Carcasstown isn't over, either—

you need to make sure the evacuation effort continues."

Krenkel grimaced. "My masters won't like it."

"They'll like being dead even less." Dreyfus injected urgency into his voice. "This is important, Krenkel. Things are likely to get a lot worse before they get better."

"I'll see what I can do."

Krenkel bent his mouth down to a microphone stitched into his cloak, beginning an increasingly heated interlocution with one of his superiors. Dreyfus sat back, content to let the man do his best. There was no point in bullying the harried official, especially when he was his only useful point of leverage. Dreyfus grasped the conflicting pressures of profit versus public safety without needing to approve of them.

Krenkel broke off, cupping a hand over his microphone. "They're asking what the problem is, if there aren't any more of those ships on their way to us."

Dreyfus calibrated a useful half-truth. "Tell them that Panoply have threat-markers on a number of other objects of concern moving through this sector."

"Should I just mention Abacus?"

"No, keep Abacus out of it for now. I want an orderly exodus, not a stampede."

Krenkel nodded heavily. "Threat-markers...objects of concern."

"Just that."

Krenkel resumed his pleading. After a minute or so he broke off, looking cautiously expectant. A low bleating began to echo from multiple speakers strung along their route. A dozen bleats sounded, then a recorded voice announced that a double-orange evacuation condition was in force. The bleats resumed.

"I asked for red, but a double-orange is nearly as good," Krenkel said. "It won't persuade everyone, but it should keep a general exodus going."

"You've done well," Dreyfus said, recognising that they were nearing Midas Analytics. "Now I want you to go and do what you can for your family."

"What about Mirna Silk?"

"I'll deal with her. She's not your concern anymore."

"You underestimate me," Krenkel said, as the carriage wobbled to a halt. "If these people hoodwinked my office, then I take that personally. I'd like to see justice done."

Dreyfus smiled, impressed by the man's resolve. "Fine, Krenkel. But it could get difficult from here on in. You need to be ready for that."

Krenkel worked hard to bury the quaver in his voice. "I'm ready."

"Good."

With the evacuation order still sounding, they walked along the lengthy passage leading to the Midas reception area, passing the boastful graphics and seductive advertising slogans.

Mirna Silk was already waiting for him at reception in her yellow gown, standing next to the desk with her arms crossed and her heels dug in.

"Before you ask, my staff have been instructed to ignore this latest evacuation warning. I see it for what it is: a hamfisted attempt to undermine the legitimate business operations of Midas Analytics." She directed a look of powerful condemnation at Krenkel. "Did Dreyfus strongarm you into issuing the order, Under-Supervisor? I know you're a pretty small cog, but I still thought you had enough of a spine to stand up to Panoply interference."

"I assure you, the threat to Carcasstown is very real," Dreyfus answered.

"Those ships have come and gone. You seemed to deal with them adequately, so why have you got everyone needlessly panicked again? You should be elsewhere in the Glitter Band, doing real police work."

"Ah, the old 'haven't you got better things to be doing' line," Dreyfus said, smiling fondly. "You know, Mirna, there isn't a policeman in history who hasn't heard that one."

"Which doesn't mean it isn't sound advice."

"Let me tell you the real purpose of those runaway ships," Dreyfus answered mildly. "They were directed at Abacus, in an attempt to destroy it before it does irreversible harm. The agency directing those ships didn't care about collateral damage, about the thousands—including you—who would have had to die at the same time. You were inconsequential." He kept his whiphound holstered but allowed his hand to rest on it. "I'm here to achieve the same end, but the difference with me is that I do care about who gets hurt. That machine has to be shut down. The only remaining question is whether you're smart enough to help me do it or if you'll make the mistake of getting in my way. Which is it to be, Mirna?"

"You're deluded, Dreyfus. If our rivals were so brazen as to launch an attack, why would I want to finish their work for them?"

"It wasn't your rivals."

Her gaze switched to the other man. "What do you know about this, Krenkel? You need to be taking a stand. You have a contractual obligation to protect us from unwarranted interference."

"I'm just a cog," Krenkel replied, offering his palms.

She snapped back onto Dreyfus. "What's got you so spooked? That our predictive methods outshine your own?"

"You've been brought in as a smokescreen," Dreyfus told her. "You're ideal for the job because you believe what you're involved in is fair and legal. I'm afraid you couldn't be more wrong about that."

She drenched her answer in contempt.

"I don't have the first idea what you're talking about."

Dreyfus shrugged. "Fetch me Salazar."

"You can't order me to do anything, not until you've explained why any of this matters to Panoply." Her stance became more assertive, her jaw lifting defiantly. "You're not a policeman, just a glorified vote-counter with a uniform and a whip fetish."

Dreyfus answered coolly: "You need to start taking me seriously, Miss Silk. You've been played, and Salazar is one of the actors playing you. He's engaged in something you don't know about, something that places you in real and immediate risk of death." Dreyfus studied her face, seeking a weak spot he could work at, a fissure in her armour. "You were a high flier, Mirna. I've no doubt that your credentials are impeccable. But even you must have thought that it was a stroke of luck to be brought in to head this project, just when it's on the cusp of creating a world-changing marvel like Abacus. There's a reason no one had heard of Midas Analytics until you were headhunted: it didn't exist. The whole thing is smoke and mirrors. You're part of the camouflage, brought in to make this whole operation look plausible." He kept his eyes on her, staring hard. "It's a sham, and deep down you know it. You've had to fight and scrap your way up the ladder. Everything you have was earned the hard way, through talent and determination. Except this. It was handed to you on a plate, and no one's ever given you anything for free before." He nodded, driving his point home. "You know something isn't right."

Some of the obstinance went out of her, just enough for Dreyfus to know he was leaning in the right direction. "You think you know about me?"

"It's my job to know. I've seen your biography, understood the hard knocks you've bounced back from. The deaths of your parents, the institutions that didn't know what to make of you. The brilliance you found within yourself: that ability to understand markets, the way most of us understand breathing. You're good, Mirna—very good. But you're also realistic enough to know when someone else is pulling your strings."

"I was told..." She hesitated. "The backers behind Midas impressed on me the need for secrecy, that I was being brought in at a very high level. It was never in my interests to question the work being done many layers of hierarchy beneath my own. I just...assumed." She broke off, the fracture widening. She seemed to slump in on herself, then struggle back to some approximation of her former composure. "All right. You said I was an opportunist. All that means to me is that I've had the good sense to know when the wind is changing. What sort of trouble am I in?"

"Remarkably little, if you cooperate fully. You've made very few mistakes in life, Mirna. Don't start adding to them now."

"Listen to the man," Krenkel urged. "We've worked well together until now, Mirna. I believe Dreyfus is talking sense and I believe you'd be well advised to heed him."

Silk ran some brief mental evaluation, then turned to the receptionist. "Plossel, would you ask Doctor Salazar to join me in reception."

"Thank you," Dreyfus said.

While they waited, Silk asked: "What don't I know? I did my own due diligence on Midas Analytics before accepting this position. I saw nothing that concerned me. Our methods are innovative, and we know our competitors have the wind up them because of the forecasting success we've shown so far. That's no reason to try and murder us all!"

"It's not about market forecasting," Dreyfus informed her.

"Then what?"

"Abacus is a prison, designed to contain a rogue artificial intelligence. Two, if it works as intended, which it won't. What it will do is leave one of these intelligences—which are currently counterbalanced by each other —unchecked, able to roam wild through our networks, doing what it likes with us."

Silk sat down on the edge of the desk, knees crossed beneath her gown, clearly overwhelmed. "Why would anyone risk such a thing?"

"Because they're just clever enough to be blinded by their own brilliance, but not so clever that they can imagine failing."

"I'll talk to our backers," Silk said, brightening as she saw a way through. "We'll instigate a full audit, identify those responsible, take measures to prevent Abacus being misused. The legitimate work can continue."

"I'm afraid it can't," Dreyfus said, as Doctor Salazar appeared. "It's much too late for that. Those ships were sent your way by Aurora, one of the intelligences, as a last-ditch attempt to stop Abacus sucking her in."

"I understand nothing of what you are saying," Salazar said.

Dreyfus turned to the white-haired man, projecting what he hoped was a willingness to find common ground. "You've been duped, Aristarchus. I know that you're keeping something from Miss Silk. My guess is that you've been asked to make Abacus behave in ways that don't quite fit the Midas Analytics business model."

"I don't know—" he began.

Dreyfus kept his voice low. "You answer to a subordinate, perhaps more than one. Those are the infiltrators, the ones who've been steering you onto the rocks. Right?"

Salazar looked torn. His jaw worked. He regarded Silk, Dreyfus, then Silk again. Dreyfus could see the strain in him, writ large in the pulsing veins on his temple. "I'm...I'm not at liberty to discuss these matters with Miss Silk."

"What are you talking about?" Silk demanded. "You answer to me!"

"He thinks he's dealing with another compartmentalised cell in this paranoid hall of mirrors you call a company," Dreyfus said. "They've terrified him, I imagine—let him know how bad the consequences will be if he confesses the truth."

"Speak freely, Doctor Salazar," Silk urged.

Dreyfus tapped the whiphound. "Do it."

Salazar looked around, some desperate calculation whirring behind his eyes, possibilities being considered, until—as Dreyfus imagined—he saw the same dismal result coming up each time.

"They came to me, just before the last hiring wave. Said we'd be running a new initiative, something highly innovative and therefore covert." He swallowed hard, his Adam's apple moving like a stone in a river. "They said I'd be a highly regarded intermediary. Said I'd be amply rewarded when the work paid off. Gold piping on this uniform. Bonuses, share dividends, a gilt-edged retirement plan. And that I wasn't to discuss the initiative with my superiors, because of fears of an industrial mole in the high echelons." He hesitated. "I'm sorry, Mirna. They never said it was you directly, but they dropped all the hints."

"Aristarchus—" she began.

"He was used," Dreyfus interjected. "As were you, Mirna. The only difference is that you knew nothing, and Aristarchus knew a tiny bit. And now Abacus must be shut down immediately."

"What Dreyfus says...about artificial intelligences being trapped inside Abacus? Is that true?"

"I was assured that the benefits far outweighed—"

It was as much as Silk needed to hear. "Then destroy it! Take an axe to Abacus, if that's what it'll take. Smash the damned thing! If it's as clever as I've been told, we can always build another one."

Salazar gasped out: "Destroy it?"

"It's the only way," Dreyfus said. "Can it be done single-handedly, Doctor?"

Salazar dabbed a finger at his forehead as he calculated. "Yes," he said, at first timidly, then with growing conviction. "Yes, it can be done, provided I have access to the right workstation. Some are configured to run the simulations, others to control the executive functions. They can be re-tasked, though it takes time."

Dreyfus nodded keenly. "Come on then, Aristarchus. Let's see what you're made of."

"I'll come too," Silk said. Then, with a sort of guilty charm, as if she regretted her earlier rudeness: "Under-Supervisor, what will you do?"

"Krenkel will leave, and take care of himself and his family," Dreyfus said firmly. He turned to the man, nodded peremptorily. "Panoply thanks you for your cooperation, Under-Supervisor. You've been of assistance."

CHAPTER TWENTY-SEVEN

The detective-marshal's ship was larger than Thalia's cutter, white where the latter was black, and with the aggressive lines of a vehicle comfortable in many operating environments. Thalia normally had at least the notion of technical superiority in the line of her duty, as well as the moral courage that came from asserting Panoply's jurisdictional powers. Neither applied now. She was in Yellowstone's airspace, her authority nil, at the potential mercy of a faster, more powerful and undoubtedly better-armed counterpart.

It was good that they were on amicable terms with Hestia Del Mar, then.

"I'm sorry Dreyfus couldn't make it, Detective-Marshal. Rest assured that I'm one of his closest colleagues, and you can be confident in trusting the evidential package to my care."

"It's all right, Ng," came the reply from the nearing ship. "Jane Aumonier has already explained why Dreyfus is absent. We've been monitoring the drama as it plays out. It was a very close-run thing with those carriers. You're lucky there weren't more of them."

Thalia had attempted to brief herself on the emergency as she travelled from Valsko-Venev to Yellowstone.

"We'd have scaled-up our response accordingly, ma'am," she answered, feeling she needed to speak well of her organisation. Then, with an instinct for diplomacy that had deserted her with the lemurs: "As would yours, ma'am, faced with a similarly dynamic threat."

"You don't need to butter me up, Ng. I'm giving you the package whether you're nice about it or not. Stand by for docking. I like to come in hard and fast, so *try* not to shoot me while I'm doing it."

"Weapons are safed, ma'am. Approach at your leisure."

"Leisure?" Her scorn burned through the hull like a gamma ray. "Did Dreyfus teach you nothing? I don't do *leisure*, Ng."

The detective-marshal's ship hove alongside with a suddenness that would have constituted warlike intentions from anyone else. Docking surfaces clanged together like a pair of battering rams. The cutter mewled out a protest at this undignified treatment.

Thalia moved to the lock, apprehension hammering war drums in her ribcage. Not because of Hestia Del Mar, but because of what she knew her to be carrying. As Jane Aumonier had suggested she do, Thalia had joined some dots.

She knew what to expect, but not how she would take it.

The lock opened. The detective-marshal waited on the other side, her white uniform unadorned save for black trim at the cuffs and collar, and devoid of weapons or tokens of enforcement. She was a stout, strong-shouldered and broad-faced woman whose severity of expression was undercut to only a small degree by her curls and a peppering of freckles. She looked unimpressed by Thalia.

It was hard to stand taller in weightlessness, but Thalia tried anyway.

"Prefect Ng," her visitor stated.

"Thank you for this, Detective-Marshal Del Mar. Would you like to come aboard my cutter? There's not much room, but—"

"It's all right, Prefect Ng. If I wanted to test my sensitivity to claustrophobia, I'd do it on my own time. I have the item."

Thalia had been trying not to look at the object Del Mar carried, but there it was: a white cubic box, stencilled with instructions and warnings that were nearly familiar, but not quite.

Thalia took the evidential preservation box. Although weightless, she still felt the solemn mass of whatever was inside it.

"Tell Dreyfus I kept my word. Whatever is on that recording is between it and him. Or you, since you seem to have been entrusted with it." Del Mar nodded beyond Thalia, into the red gloom of her cutter. "I suppose you have the means to access the contents?"

"I do, Detective-Marshal, but I won't be using them. That'll be for Prefect Dreyfus, when I hand this over."

"He trusts you, then."

"I hope so."

There was a moment when she thought Del Mar might turn around, seal the lock and detach her ship without a further word. Thalia was wrong, though.

"I know about the death of your colleague, Ng. I know what that box contains. I am...sorry. Although it can be no consolation, I hope that the information in that recording in some way makes sense of his death."

"I don't know what it'll tell us, Detective-Marshal. Just that Sparver believed it was worth dying for." Thalia retreated, tucked the box into a storage pouch, then floated back to the lock's threshold.

"This Sparver was known to both you and Dreyfus? A respected and valued colleague?"

"He was."

"Then I am certain he knew what he was doing." Detective-Marshal Del Mar reached out to clasp Thalia's arm, squeezing it once. "That never happened," she added.

There was a moment where they both recovered their respective bearings.

"Once this is over," Thalia said, swallowing hard on her emotions, "I'm sure they'll want you to know the full picture."

"Doubtless they will. And if it's down to Dreyfus, I may only have to wait five or six years to find out." Then a sharp, commanding nod. "Be on your way, Prefect Ng. I don't want to delay either of us in the execution of our duties."

They undocked. Thalia watched the sleek white spacecraft stab its way back into Yellowstone's atmosphere, gashing a re-entry path until the billowing ochre clouds gobbled it whole.

She extracted the box from its pouch, opened it—breaking the foil seals of the Chamber for City Security—and inspected the dark, fist-sized relic within. It was all that was left of a suit-sized mass of quickmatter and bone and meat; all that was left of Sparver Bancal.

Weightlessness glued a tear to her eye.

After Krenkel had departed, obeying the instruction to take care of himself and his family, Dreyfus, Salazar and Silk went through to the gallery encircling the Midas Analytics bullpen. Dreyfus looked down on the activity below, from the mottled golden orb of Abacus perched on its monstrous plinth to the concentric patterns of workstations arranged around it, and the calm but focussed activity of the yellow-clad analysts hunched over their readouts.

The place was no less busy than when he had last visited. If any of the staff had made to leave, then they had either been replaced or had drifted back to their duties once the immediate danger was over. The young man he had seen before was among the workers, but now situated further away, at a different workstation. He was doing a good job of carrying on as usual, seemingly unaware of anything happening on the gallery.

Around the walls, the market graphics continued their nervous flickering.

Dreyfus spoke quietly to Salazar. "Is that your position down there, still unoccupied?"

"Yes."

"Can you do what you need to do from there?"

"I can. My station has executive control."

Dreyfus settled his hands on the railing. He leaned over and called out: "Attention, please. You're under Panoply observance. Each of you is to stand back from your workstation. No one is to touch anything or issue any command, by any means."

No one moved for a moment, until Silk leaned over the railing next to Dreyfus. "Do as he says! We're cooperating with Panoply fully. No one is to give a gestural, sub-vocal or neural command. The audits will show if you disobey this command, so don't be so foolish as to try."

"Sensible," Dreyfus murmured, as the workers shuffled back in their seats and then rose to stand next to their stations. Then, to Salazar: "Your move. I'm right behind you."

Dreyfus unholstered his whiphound but kept it spooled in, gripped in his hand like a truncheon. He followed Salazar down the clattering treads of the spiral staircase that connected the gallery to the floor. The workers were staring at him with expressions ranging from mild concern to outright indignation, and all shades in between. Other than his suspicions about the young man, there was no telling which were the innocent cases and which the infiltrators.

Salazar navigated the spaces between the stations. He arrived at his position and sat down. He settled his hands over the console, which had been placed into some dormant state when he had been summoned to reception. At Salazar's command it lit up with displays and grids of controls, all suitably incomprehensible to Dreyfus.

Salazar's fingers danced across the icons, each gestural sweep causing the console to light up in some different but equally impenetrable configuration of symbols, diagrams and input arrays.

Dreyfus looked over his shoulder. "Are you in?"

Salazar twisted around to look at him. "I'm trying, Prefect. There seems to be some function lockout in force. There can't be, though. No one could have updated this console since I was last here."

Salazar continued with his efforts.

Dreyfus cast an eye at the glowing orb before them. It throbbed, brightening and dimming according to some unstable rhythm that his brain could not quite latch onto.

"Getting anywhere?"

Salazar leaned back from the console, staring at his fingertips as if they had been dipped in metal.

"No. Not yet. I'm trying to reassign the workstation...I said it would be time-consuming. That should work, but...well, it isn't."

"He won't succeed, Dreyfus, no matter how much time you give him."

He turned to the voice, not all that surprised to see that it came from the young man. He was only slightly more surprised to see that the man had produced a small but plausibly deadly weapon, aimed now in the general direction of Dreyfus and Salazar.

Dreyfus regarded the young man. He had reached for a name before and clutched at nothing except the nagging sense that he should have known it. Now he reached again and found something that had been there all along.

"What do you think you're going to achieve, Haigler?"

The young man reacted with a blink, but held his composure and aim.

"His name's Tolley, not Haigler," Silk said, looking down from the gallery. She looked sharply at Salazar. "Isn't it?"

"I only know him as Tolley," Salazar said defensively, pushing his chair back from the console in the understanding that all his efforts were futile. "He's one of my best data theorists!"

"He's Haigler," Dreyfus said, with a weary finality. "That's the name I knew him by, at any rate. He was an inductee, a Panoply recruit. He never got to be a prefect. He crashed out in the early stages of trainee assessment. I remembered his face from the classes I took, though, because he was one of the more promising ones."

"I'm not Haigler."

Dreyfus lacked the patience for a spirited argument. "If you were going to keep up the pretence of being Tolley, drawing a gun on me wasn't your best move. Who's working you?"

"No one's working me. How many more are coming?" He waggled the stubby little energy weapon warningly. "I know there's a second Panoply ship on its way, probably a corvette. What will it be? Medium enforcement, dual whiphounds?"

"You seem to have all the answers, Haigler."

"Aren't you going to pretend it's a bigger force?"

"I don't need to. Medium enforcement will more than suffice to handle the terms of your surrender." Dreyfus frowned for effect. "After all, you wouldn't be so foolish as to think you could take on the whole of Panoply, would you?"

"It's not just me." Haigler glanced quickly around the room and made an upward beckoning gesture. In unison half a dozen other analysts rose from their positions, each holding the same kind of weapon. "We have control of Abacus, Dreyfus. And no, we're not going to be fighting Panoply. Panoply will be listening to us and accepting *our* terms."

"I swear I wasn't part of this," Doctor Salazar said, raising his hands. "You lied to me, Tolley!"

"He's not even denying that his name is Haigler now," Dreyfus said. Then he looked around the room, at the analysts still seated at their workstations. He read their faces: shock, anger, bewilderment, fear. "All of you in here. Panoply is prepared to grant amnesties if we're satisfied that you had no direct knowledge of the conspiracy or its intentions. You can make that case more persuasive for yourselves by doing anything you can to shut down Abacus."

No one moved or showed any intention to move.

"Performance bonuses," Silk declared. "For anyone who manages to disable Abacus!"

"They're not biting," Haigler said.

"I'll sweeten the offer," Dreyfus said. "If this situation isn't resolved by the time my colleagues arrive, I'll escalate the response to Heavy enforcement. Those whiphounds will be on autonomous lethal settings. The only people here they won't identify as a possible threat will be those of us wearing Panoply uniforms." He nodded contemptuously at Haigler. "And flunkouts don't make the grade."

This had the anticipated effect. One of the operatives, a woman who, until then, had kept her head down and her eyes averted, made a spirited dive for her console. Her fingers swept across the inputs, the displays cycling from one complex set of options to the next. "I'm in," she said breathlessly. "Accessing lockout privileges. Executive functions...I can do it, Miss Silk!"

Haigler aimed his weapon and fired. A flash burst above the console, destroying it instantly, and the woman was flung back into her seat, her hands and forearms badly burned. There was a moment's silence before the shock hit her system and the woman started shrieking.

"Look, this is tiresome," Haigler said, barely raising his voice above the woman's cries. "It's too late. Abacus is operating without input now. Once the ingestion process reached a certain point, our own control options were suspended."

Dreyfus could barely believe what he was hearing. "Are you insane?"

"We predicted that the rogue intelligences would attempt to use coercive measures. Disinformation, blackmail, psychological ops. Threats just like the one we saw today, with those runaway spacecraft. But we couldn't allow that to stop us." Still holding the weapon, he pawed his other hand against the yellow fabric stretched across his chest, almost pleadingly. "We *had* to have resolve. Had to keep our nerve. Hence this control lockout. And it's for the best. It is working, Dreyfus. We're finally doing what we should have done four years ago: put an end to the tyranny of these intelligences."

"You want a medal?"

"No, just your acknowledgement that a good and necessary thing is being done here today. I'm no monster, Dreyfus. None of us are." Haigler used his free hand to gesture to the injured woman. "I didn't want to do that, Karla. I liked you. I *still* like you." Then he made an impatient motion with the weapon. "She can leave. Go and get seen to."

The woman was not capable of helping herself to safety. Haigler allowed one of the other operatives to come over and help her stumble out of the bullpen, leaving by a door on the same level as the floor.

"See?" Haigler said. "Not a monster."

"There's a mounting pile of bodies that says otherwise," Dreyfus answered.

"We're no different, Dreyfus. Tell me that Panoply hasn't ever weighed one set of lives against another. Wasn't that exactly what happened when those missiles destroyed Asset 227? Your colleague was inside!"

"It's not comparable."

"Isn't it? I'd say it's exactly comparable. A sacrifice for the greater good."

Dreyfus bristled but said nothing. He let Haigler continue.

"No one *wanted* to kill Tench. She was a loyal operative who was doing her duty. But the greater good had to be considered. We were too close to success to be allowed to fail."

"A pity I've arrived to spoil the party."

Haigler shook his head. "It's all over. Our latency metrics show that one of the entities is now almost completely within our grasp. The other is succumbing nearly as quickly."

"Nearly won't cut it, you idiot. The moment one of those entities no longer feels threatened by its adversary, it's over for everyone."

"Our simulations say otherwise. Do you think we're fools, Dreyfus?"

Dreyfus rubbed at his chin, looking at the faces of the other infiltrators gathered in the room. Now that he had identified Haigler, he thought he recognised other former recruits among their number. Not all of them, but enough that it could not possibly be coincidence.

"Zhang," he said, meeting the eyes of one of the data theorists, a small, scholarly-looking man with a neatly maintained tonsure. "Theroux. And you were Woolmer, weren't you?"

"Woolcot," the candidate said peevishly, as if having their name misremembered was a greater offence than being recognised.

"None of you made the grade. I suppose if I was going to recruit bright young things to run an operation counter to the wishes of Panoply, a

237

bunch of disaffected former recruits wouldn't be a bad starting point." Dreyfus watched Haigler lift his chin, cocksure. "But there's more to it than that, isn't there? None of you were the worst candidates in your induction groups."

"I'm glad we rate well in your estimation," Haigler said. "Perhaps that'll go some way to reassuring you that we aren't acting irresponsibly."

"I see it now," Dreyfus said. "You weren't recruited because you failed. You were identified as candidates for this operation and then *made* to fail." He sighed to himself, reaching a point in his own train of thought where he could turn back or press on further, as much as he disliked the direction it was taking. "That required coordination from within Panoply, didn't it? Someone who is still inside, filtering candidates and failing those that meet the criteria for this." He nodded slowly, resigned to the process. "Someone with the means to act against Mizler Cranach and Ingvar Tench." His tone sharpened. "Who is it, Haigler? Who's your puppeteer?"

A series of tones sounded from the consoles. Haigler held up a finger, the gun still in his hand, and cocked a head to Zhang. "Report, please."

Zhang glanced nervously at Dreyfus and Doctor Salazar. "With them here?"

"The more they know, the better they'll understand the pointlessness of any action against us."

Zhang spoke up in a piping tone. "Abacus confirms total sequestration of the first entity, the one we think is most likely Aurora. She's trapped, unable to escape or interact with anything outside her designated containment space. Ingestion and sequestration of the second entity—probably the Clockmaker—is proceeding within expectations."

Dreyfus looked to the mottled, glowing golden ball. If Zhang was correct, then Aurora was *in the room*, inside that sphere, a hot, furious imp, bottled within a computational volume millions of times smaller than her former playground.

His neck hairs prickled.

"Is she executing?"

Haigler seemed to find the question odd. "She's caught, Dreyfus, so why does it matter what she's doing?"

"If you've made her smaller, then you've made her faster. She'll be a billion steps ahead of you already."

"She can be as fast and powerful as she likes," Haigler answered. "She can't defeat a logical barrier." Then, to Zhang: "Are the latency metrics showing any untoward behaviour from the Clockmaker?"

"No, nothing beyond the scope of our simulations. We're drawing it in."

"Why isn't it breaking loose, now that it no longer has to guard against Aurora?" Dreyfus asked.

"Because we've been clever," Haigler answered, with a quick blush of pride. "We couldn't avoid some delay between the first and second containment processes. To guard against that 'breaking loose,' as you put it, we use our same awareness of latency metrics to create a temporary ghost image of the first entity, lingering just long enough to convince the second one that it must still guard against its adversary." He flashed a self-satisfied smile. "I designed much of that. Of course, I had the original Catopsis to build on, but still...there's much that's original here, Dreyfus. Much that's original and, frankly, innovative. I'm Panoply's loss. I'd have made a superb network theorist."

"I doubt that you're anyone's loss," Dreyfus said with dry amusement. He lifted his bracelet, meaning to update Aumonier.

"Don't bother," Haigler said. "Your comms won't work. We've suspended abstraction throughout Carcasstown. Abacus needs to use maximum network resources right now."

Dreyfus tried to bounce his call back to Panoply via his cutter, but even that was denied him.

"It's Lovro Breno," he said, lowering his bracelet resignedly. "He's the one who got to pick and choose who remained in candidate training. He's the one who was in the perfect position to select bodies for this. Am I right?"

"The image is signalling its desire to communicate," Zhang cut in, as a series of chimes pulsed across the consoles.

"The image?" Dreyfus asked.

"The captured intellect," Haigler replied. "Although Aurora remains safely partitioned within Abacus, she still has a limited channel for self-expression. Her willingness is interesting, don't you think? It suggests an understanding of her predicament. A desire to bargain, perhaps even to beg."

"Aurora is requesting Dreyfus," Zhang said.

Haigler shrugged. "Better put him on."

CHAPTER TWENTY-EIGHT

Thalia was halfway back to Panoply when the Supreme Prefect called through to her cutter.

"Ng. I have confirmation from the Chamber for City Security that you completed the rendezvous with Detective-Marshal Del Mar. I presume the evidential package is now in your safekeeping?"

"It is, ma'am. Would you be kind enough to let Prefect Dreyfus know I expect to be docked in about thirty-five minutes, depending on traffic?"

"That's the reason I'm calling, Ng. Events are moving faster than we anticipated. After Dreyfus helped avert the immediate threat to Carcasstown, we agreed that he should move to shut down their illegal program without delay."

Thalia flashed back to the facts she had picked up in the tactical room.

"The computer, ma'am?"

"Yes. Abacus, being run out of a cover outfit called Midas Analytics. I'll push a full briefing through to your compad: digest as much of it as you can while en route to Carcasstown."

"Carcasstown, ma'am?"

"Yes. We've lost contact with Dreyfus."

Thalia's denial was reflexive. "No, ma'am."

"I'm afraid so. We're also reading a sudden and unscheduled shutdown of all abstraction services within Carcasstown. I'll keep an open mind as to the reasons, but until I have a fuller picture I want extra eyes and ears on the ground. Locate Dreyfus and render assistance. Your goggles will guide you to Midas Analytics."

"I'll expedite it, ma'am."

"You'll lead a team rather than going in alone. I have a corvette moving in under Pasinler. Rendezvous ahead of docking, secure the evidential package and assume command of a Medium enforcement action."

"Should we go in harder, ma'am?"

"Dreyfus was trying to avoid an escalation, and I'm minded to follow his lead. Be ready to augment if the situation proves as fluid as I fear."

Off the main floor of Midas Analytics was a small, spartan room containing an upright sheet of glass in a wheeled metal frame, as innocuous as a piece of leftover construction material.

Haigler stood behind Dreyfus, both of them facing the pane.

"Bring her up, Zhang."

A smoky glow filled the frame. The glow coalesced into a human form, albeit one pressed into the flattened geometry of the frame. It was Aurora, as Dreyfus recognised from their many encounters. Her figure floated and writhed, moving with the languid agony of a tormented soul. Her mouth moved slowly but nothing emerged. Her eyes stared out of the frame, bewitched with fear but darkly uncomprehending.

She had known what they were trying to do to her, Dreyfus thought. But in the awful process of capturing her, had that very knowledge been scraped away?

"I'm here," he stated.

A voice emerged from the glass: distant, murky, as if she were speaking to him from under water. Speaking while drowning, or while already drowned.

"Drey...fus."

Her eyes had still not found him. "Can you see me?"

"No—only...hear you. You're very far away. I don't like this, Dreyfus. I don't like what they've done to me."

"What do you remember?"

"Fear," she answered. "Fear and the thought of time running out. Something happening that I didn't want to happen." An accusatory look appeared on her flattened, mirage-distorted features. "Something you were meant to stop."

"I did my best." He paused. "You're trapped in Abacus. It's a computer, designed to hold you prisoner."

Her eyes flashed with defiance. "It won't hold me."

"Be that as it may, you have a second problem. Actually, we both do."

"Who is that man behind you?"

"Haigler. One of the architects of your downfall. He's not really the kingpin. That'd be Lovro Breno, one of our own."

The vague direction of her gaze seemed to miss Dreyfus entirely now.

"I'll find something appalling to do to both of them."

"I'm sure you won't be short for inspiration. Your immediate difficulty is the Clockmaker." He stared at her, not seeing the spiteful reaction he had expected. "Your adversary. You remember?"

"There was another, yes."

"You've spent years trying to annihilate each other. Call it a merciful stalemate. Now that balance has been upset. They've got you, but they haven't got the Clockmaker yet."

"I...begin to remember." A wild alarm presented itself. "And I don't like it! He mustn't triumph! And he will if I'm not there to rein him in!" Fury coarsened her voice. "You've got to let me go, Haigler! I know my adversary. I've seen the unspeakable things he does."

"This was anticipated," Haigler commented quietly. "It changes nothing. We don't need *her* expertise to complete our work. We outfoxed her, just as we're outfoxing the Clockmaker." He raised his voice. "Are you satisfied that you have enough to go back to Jane Aumonier with?"

"Nearly. Just one question for Aurora." Dreyfus waited a beat. "Why only three?"

Haigler said: "Why three what?"

"She knows what I'm asking," Dreyfus said. But the figure trapped in the pane of glass showed only blank incomprehension, as if he had asked his question in the wrong language.

"We're done, Zhang," Haigler said.

Aurora's form froze into motionlessness and then dispersed back into a pale fog. In turn the fog dissipated to leave the pane as clear as it had been when they first arrived.

Haigler took Dreyfus back into the bullpen. Without a word, Dreyfus collected his equipment and fixed it back onto his uniform. He was reaching for the whiphound when Haigler whispered a silent "no" and put his hand on the object.

Mirna Silk called down from the gallery: "What happened in there, Prefect?"

Dreyfus looked up. "They've caught their dragon."

Thalia brought her cutter alongside the corvette when they were one hundred kilometres out from Carcasstown. She scooped the evidential package from the pouch and moved aboard the other craft. It was like moving from a decent cupboard into a roomy if oddly shaped parlour. The corvette was eight times larger than a cutter, with separate compartments and ample space for a squad of prefects and their equipment.

Pasinler was the first one she saw, webbed into the recumbent piloting position near the corvette's stubby, sensor-bulging nose. Pasinler was supernumerary, part of Panoply's pool of pilots who had expert ratings across all classes of enforcement vehicle. Prefects who had put in sufficient hours on cutters were permitted to operate corvettes, but it was

242

just as commonplace to assign a dedicated pilot, especially when regular prefects were in short supply for field operations.

"Were you on normal duties, Pasinler?" she asked, leaning into the thicket of screens and controls that surrounded him.

"Negative, Ng. We were tasked straight from Panoply as soon as this business with the carriers started up. We didn't see any action, though; Pell and the others had cleaned up the mess before we were needed. You know how Pell likes to blow things up."

She looked through the intermediate bulkhead to a confusion of prefects busy strapping on tactical armour. "Who else is with us?"

"Breno, Coady, Laza, Moriyama, Meppel. Breno was designated point for any possible action when we departed, but that was until Aumonier informed us Dreyfus had gone dark and that you'd be leading the entry."

Thalia evaluated the names, stitching faces and biographies to them. Of course she knew Lovro Breno, but she was only hazily familiar with the others. She rummaged through several years' worth of field reports and tactical debriefings, promotions and exemplary service notifications.

"Coady and Laza were on the Bastia-Lompoc lockdown, weren't they?"

"Yes, and you know how well that went."

"It would have gone a damned sight worse if it wasn't for the operatives we had in-field. What about Moriyama and Meppel? Weren't they only just in my induction class?"

"Probably about five years ago, Ng. Not as green as you think, but the least experienced of the five, certainly."

"Resume approach, Pasinler. I'll take Breno, Coady and Laza. The Supreme Prefect wants to conduct this as a Medium enforcement action, so all five of us would be excessive."

"Your call, Ng."

"It is, Pasinler," she answered crisply, as if there had been any debate to be had.

"What about your cutter?"

"Detach it remotely, and have it stand by to render assistance if needed. It has a full ordnance load and enough fuel to be useful to us. Coordinate with Thyssen if required."

Not waiting for an answer, Thalia shouldered her way through the bulkhead into the separate compartment, where her squad—what was about to become her squad—was getting ready.

She picked out Lovro Breno first. Easy, given the redheaded giant's imposing stature. Already goggled, tactical armour making a black wall of his chest, he was clipping on the second of his two whiphounds, adjusting the quick-release holster so that the deployment angle was exactly to his liking.

"Prefect Breno, I'm assuming command of this Medium enforcement action."

"As notified, Prefect Ng," Breno said easily. "The order came through from the Supreme Prefect just before you docked." He glanced back at the others, the muscles in his neck bulging like foot slopes. "Who d'you want?"

"I'll take Coady and Laza based on field experience, unless you disagree?"

"That would be my recommendation also."

"Moriyama, Meppel," she called out. "No need to gear up just now." She read their chastened faces, understanding how they felt at being deselected. Prefects never relished trouble but a tricky enforcement operation, handled competently, might grease a rise through the ranks. "You'll hold ship with Pasinler. If things go south in Carcasstown, we may face civil disorder and anti-Panoply sentiment. Be prepared to defend the vehicle and take all necessary measures in accordance with the Common Articles." Feeling that a bit more pressure would actually help them adjust to their roles, she added: "The heat's on you while I'm inside, so don't fuck it up."

Lovro Breno leaned in with a whisper. "Nice style, Ng. I might copy it, next time my squad needs a pep talk."

"You have seniority over me by dint of service, Lovro," she answered. "So I appreciate that you didn't question my assignment on this squad."

"I understand this is personal for you, Ng," he said. "The last thing I'd want to do is stand in the way of that, knowing your respect for Dreyfus." He nodded, his eyeless, goggled face a mask of stoic confidence. "We'll find him, that I guarantee."

Thalia set about fixing on her own tactical armour and whiphounds. She slipped on the goggles and moved to one of the forward windows. They were much closer now, the wheel dead ahead. The goggles dropped a ghostly overlay over the structure, compiled from Panoply's most up-to-date model of Carcasstown's interior, with a faint, spidering course showing the suggested route from the ball-shaped hub to the point out on the rim where Midas Analytics operated.

Pasinler called her forward and informed Thalia that her cutter had undocked and was standing off, awaiting further instructions.

"What about Dreyfus's ship? Do we have visual yet?"

"No, and we won't until we're inside that sphere. All the ship-handling facilities are on the inner face."

"I don't like it, Pasinler. Feels too much like walking into a room without

244

an escape route. Are you sure there's nowhere else we can clamp on? What about on the rim itself, saving us the journey out from the hub?"

"Nothing rated to take a corvette, Ng. There are a few light service locks, but with the rim's rotation, we'd risk pulling the station apart. Don't worry about the hub; there's nothing we can't shoot our way out of."

"All right," she said, accepting his judgement. "Take us in, at maximum threat posture. This might be a Medium enforcement, but it doesn't mean I'm a pushover."

"Complying." Pasinler worked the precision thrusters, lining up for the hole in the hub. "I'm dropping relays, but as a precaution I've signalled Panoply that we may lose reliable comms once we're inside that sphere."

"I'm counting on it," Thalia said.

Her squad moved to the forward lock, crowding in as the corvette slipped into the sphere at little more than walking pace. The interior of the sphere was a blaze of light, with the vast, half-broken hulks of spaceships floating in its weightless core. Thalia's gaze swept around, her goggles rendering the corvette temporarily transparent. She was surprised at how little was going on. For an economy built around the dismantling and reforging of spaceships, there was a distinct lack of activity.

"Everyone sane is either gone or trying to get out, is my guess," she said.

They circled around, nosing between the wrecks and hulks, the skeletons of ships being reborn, until Pasinler indicated the tiny form of a Panoply cutter, lodged in the inner surface of the sphere like a thorn.

"There."

"Get us as close as you can."

Pasinler indicated a vacant lock about two hundred metres further around the inner curve of the sphere. "That should do us."

"Good. Lateral lock, please, so we can make a rapid departure."

Pasinler shook his head. "Not enough room for us between those berthing vanes if we crab in sideways. It'll need to be nose lock or nothing, unless you want to go into suits and jump across vacuum."

"Nose it is. I'll take what I can get."

They completed the docking without incident, capture clamps latching on with a rapid mechanical tattoo. Instantly the corvette felt fixed to some much larger, immovable thing. "Secure for boarding, Ng. Good luck in there."

"Mind the fort with Moriyama and Meppel. And pray I've got Dreyfus with me when I get back."

"I will, Ng."

"One more thing, Pasinler. If this operation takes longer than an hour, it means something's gone wrong. Unless I send instructions to the contrary, you're to undock and preserve the corvette and the evidential package I brought aboard. It must reach Panoply, and if it can't be seen by Dreyfus then I count on you to ensure it reaches no one but the Supreme Prefect herself. I mean *no one*. Is that understood?"

"Transparent."

"Thank you, Pasinler."

She made a final sweep of Breno, Coady and Laza, making sure everyone was armoured up, goggled and equipped with dual whiphounds pre-set to the necessary enforcement level.

"Dreyfus's whiphound was motion-tracking when he made his first inspection of Carcasstown," she said. "That gives us a reliable path from the hub to Midas Analytics. Local comms are down, but our bracelets will work independently, provided we're not too far apart. I'm hoping we may be able to contact Dreyfus by the same means, once we start getting closer to the rim."

Thalia opened the lock, accessing a clear path all the way through to the interior of Carcasstown. The m-lock indicated nominal pressure and an absence of readily identifiable hazards.

"Proceed," she said, and pushed herself through the membrane.

CHAPTER TWENTY-NINE

Haigler brought Dreyfus back from the cell where Aurora had manifested. He indicated a seat and when Dreyfus was slow to settle into it, Haigler cuffed him about the back of the head with some blunt part of his energy weapon.

Through a veil of pain, the slumping, scalp-bloodied Dreyfus regarded the golden orb of Abacus. "It's taking you too long, Haigler," he said. "You can see that, can't you? You think you can keep fooling the Clockmaker, but you're dealing with an intellect beyond anything you've met or imagined."

"We have Aurora," Haigler said, moving to stand in front of him, satisfied that the other conspirators were enough to keep Dreyfus where he was. "That's inarguable. Now we're doing the same to her adversary. It is working. Zhang would say if it weren't. It is, isn't it, Zhang?"

"All parameters...normal," Zhang stammered out, bending over to read the nearest console's summary.

"Consider the evidence, Dreyfus," Haigler said. "We're in a position of relative vulnerability out here. Aurora already proved that, with her attempt at destroying Carcasstown. It didn't succeed, but on another day it might well have. Thanks for the intervention, by the way."

"Glad we were of assistance."

"There's nothing preventing the Clockmaker trying the same thing, on an even grander scale. But it's not happening, is it?"

Dreyfus shrugged. "From here, I'm not sure I'd know."

Haigler swiped a hand under his nose. "We would, and we're not seeing it. No coordinated action against Carcasstown, on a small or large scale. That's proof enough that the Clockmaker isn't aware of the threat to its liberty. It doesn't see that we already have our hooks—" He glared at Zhang, as the consoles began to emit an audible alert, more strident than anything Dreyfus had heard so far. "What?"

"I'm not sure," Zhang answered nervously. "Abstraction is still locked out, as planned. Now everything else is shutting down. Encrypted and

247

unencrypted civilian comms, space traffic control, positional housekeep-ing...All signals and sensor channels are going off. This is more than we intended."

Haigler kept his voice level, but the strain broke through it.

"Confirm that Abacus still has access to its privileged channels."

"Abacus is...Abacus is seeking workaround pathways."

"*Seeking*?"

Zhang seemed like a man undergoing a seizure or perhaps in the grip of a mild electrical convulsion. His jaw moved beneath his skin, sharp and angular, a blade trying to break through the flesh. "I...I can't confirm. I can't confirm that Abacus still has...has valid pathways. Valid channels."

Dreyfus looked on.

"You're flying blind," he commented mildly.

Haigler leaned in close enough that his breath hit Dreyfus.

"If you can get a signal back to Aumonier, you'd better tell the bitch queen to stop these tricks."

"I'd need comms for that, Haigler. Maybe you'd like to restore them for me? Not that it would do you much good. Whatever's going wrong here, it's not Panoply."

"Then what?"

"The Clockmaker. This is the response you were busy bragging about not happening. The Clockmaker's detected that you've captured Aurora and it's acting accordingly."

A wild contradiction played out in Haigler's expression. He wanted to deny Dreyfus, but the evidence of his senses was too overwhelming. *Something* was happening.

Something that wasn't part of the plan.

"Why not just destroy her? Destroy us as well. But why not?"

"You're thinking like a person," Dreyfus replied, "not a pretty hate machine."

Haigler snarled, "What are you saying?"

"Only that you can't put yourself in the Clockmaker's frame of mind. We've lived with the threat of these intelligences for a few short years. To them, it's been vastly longer than that. Even dispersed, even forced to be less than they could be, they've been squaring off against each other for cold eternities. Plotting. Scheming. Despising. Imagining a billion cruel-ties they'd like to visit on their adversary. Annihilation isn't sufficient; the other one has to suffer. It has to know that it's been bettered." Dreyfus smiled through his discomfort, glad to be able to twist the knife. "That's what's happening now."

"You can't know that."

"I can't," he admitted. "But I have to ask myself: if you haven't lost control, then why are you looking so frightened?"

The lights went out. The room was dark, but not quite black. The consoles were still lit, and a brassy glow still spilled from Abacus. A silence held, unbroken by any of the distant sounds Dreyfus had, until then, pushed from his awareness. It was as if every process within Carcasstown —not just the small part of it assigned to Midas Analytics—had come to a halt.

The people at the consoles, the innocents and infiltrators, were dark statues edged in sultry light.

"What now?" Haigler demanded.

Zhang took a moment to respond, locked in his own paralysis of fear and incomprehension. "We're on our own reserve power. All the outside amenities have stopped. No power, no internal communications, no water or cooling, not even any air circulation."

"Krenkel got the station put on a double-orange alert," Dreyfus said. "Does any of this fit the pattern?"

"Not at all," Zhang answered. "The last thing you'd want to do in an evacuation is cut off power!"

Dreyfus heard a chime from his bracelet.

"Tell Aumonier to stop this," Haigler barked.

"It's not her," Dreyfus insisted, lifting the bracelet. "Thalia?" he asked, having seen her name flash up on the display. "Did you succeed in the evidential handover?"

Her voice was thready, phasing in and out. "I did, sir, and the package is secure. I'm in Carcasstown, moving in on your position. We're on local comms only; something was interfering with the signal until that power drop."

"I'm happy to hear from you, Thalia, but you really shouldn't be here."

"I'm not alone. I have a corvette on dock and a Medium enforcement squad with me. Do you know what's happened with the power and life support, sir?"

"Only that it's not our doing, and it doesn't seem to be part of these goons' plan."

"Are you all right, sir?"

"I'm compromised, Thal. I've been attempting to persuade Haigler and his friends to abort Abacus before they get in too deep, but I fear that time's passed. It's too late for any sort of enforcement level now. Return to the corvette and begin coordinating mass evacuation measures. We need to evacuate the civilian citizens, then nuke Carcasstown while there's still a faint chance of wiping out both Aurora and the Clockmaker."

"What about you, sir?"

"You can't help me. But you can help Panoply. Inform the Supreme Prefect that Lovro Breno is our mole—"

He was whacked on the head again, this time with sufficient forcefulness to knock him out for a second or two.

He came round to a vicelike pressure on his skull. He thought about Grigor Bacchus and wondered if he had felt something similar, in his last seconds of consciousness.

Beyond the bullpen, something started up. It was a feeling more than a sound—some distant industrial process, rhythmic and low-toned. Dreyfus did not think it had been part of the normal background of Carcasstown before the interruption.

It was something new.

Something bad.

Thalia had heard enough. One of her dual-issue whiphounds was forming half of the forward cordon. She made a motion, moving her hand to the one still on her belt.

"Prefect Breno, I'm sorry to—"

But Breno was quicker, already on his whiphound. Commendable, she thought. Rapid situational orientation and tactical deployment. That attention to detail, adjusting the angle of his holster, had paid off. He had an advantage over her, of course. The news from Dreyfus had hit her unexpectedly, but Breno must have been prepared for his complicity to be exposed.

That extra fraction of a second made all the difference.

He flicked out his filament to sixty centimetres, the recommended deployment for close-action sword mode. Too short and the stabbing/slashing range was insufficient. Too long and the implement became unwieldy and unbalanced. The filament was rigid, its cutting edge a hummingbird flicker of microscopic mechanisms. Breno swiped along a pre-selected arc that took in Thalia and Coady, the prefect immediately behind her. Thalia reacted, her own whiphound not even out of its holster, but managing to turn into the arc enough to present her chest to the blade rather than her forearm. The blade contacted her tactical armour, skidding wildly as the quickmatter cutting devices met the layers of inert and active countermeasure material in the armour. The movement saved her from losing a limb, but the deflected blade still cut deeply as it passed through her upper arm, on its way to Coady.

Coady had a fraction of a second longer to react than Thalia. They had their whiphound out and beginning deployment, but not quickly

enough to counter Breno. Breno's arc had been on a rising sweep: where it gashed Thalia in the upper arm, it cut diagonally through Coady's head, transecting it cleanly. Coady was already dropping when Gaza flinched back and went to full deployment. Thalia was twisting as she saw this, still following through on the initial movement. Gaza parried Breno's arc with a textbook defensive sweep, the cutting edges sparking as they contacted, grinding against each other in a way that blunted Breno's momentum. A novice could lose their whiphound that way, as the friction wrenched it out of their grip.

Breno was no novice. The handle twisted in his grip but didn't slip loose.

All this in perhaps eight-tenths of a second from the moment Thalia had begun to make her move.

Thalia's onward momentum sent her stumbling out of the fray. She crashed to the ground and was immediately stepped on by two evacuees rushing past the bloody altercation. The general melee was enough that a few prefects fighting each other was almost inconsequential.

The rush continued, more feet hammering her into the floor.

A second and a half, maybe two. Coady was on the ground, dead, their whiphound rolling out of a slackening hand. Time for Breno to disengage his whiphound and press another hacking charge at Gaza. They were moving as they fought, stumbling away from Thalia. Gaza defended. The four cordon whiphounds were still defining a moving line around the squad, even though it was now severely depleted. The rear cordon was approaching Thalia as she tried to get up.

The whiphounds ought not hurt her, but that was nothing she cared to put to the test.

She had tried to rise. The ground beneath her was slippery. Her arm would not support her weight. She wanted to roll over, to lever herself up by her other arm, but suddenly even that seemed to require more energy than she could muster. *I'm bleeding out*, she thought. A whiphound was supposed to cauterise as it cut, but there were ways to disable that function.

Breno would have known them.

The cordon rippled past her. She peered through the blurring fence as it moved past her, still tracking Breno and Gaza. Gaza dropped, falling out of view behind the flickering wall. She could not say if he had feinted deliberately or taken a hit.

Thalia could not rise, so she crawled instead. To her right, leading off from the main passage, was a dark alcove, partially filled with packing cases. Her only hope was getting to that alcove. Breno would be back as soon as he was finished with Gaza. He would want to ensure she was dead.

The evacuees were treading over or on her as she crawled, treating Thalia as a useless inert obstacle, like a roll of soggy carpet. Strength was leaving her, each movement more taxing than the last. She had not yet reached the sanctuary of the alcove. Then someone gave her a spiteful kick and the impulse helped her roll into shelter. She dragged her legs behind her, making sure she was completely obscured from view. The packing cases loomed around her, the alcove a sealed-off dead end with no prospect of further progress.

Thalia caught her breath. She felt exhausted, but no lighter of head than when she had started. Still lying down, she dabbed at the main wound. The blood around it was sticky, but not pulsing out. That was her uniform and bracelet, working together to preserve her life. The uniform would be self-sealing across the injury, applying pressure, while the bracelet flooded her system with clotting factors, pressors, disinfectants and sedatives.

If she lay here and did nothing, she would be all right. Maybe not one hundred per cent, but better than dead. Stable until she could get herself to help, or the Heavy Medicals arrived.

But none of that was good, because Lovro Breno would know it as well.

CHAPTER THIRTY

Aurora emerged from the fog of non-existence to face Dreyfus from the upright pane.

"Oh dear, Dreyfus. You're bleeding. Have these thugs been roughing you up?" Her eyes bored beyond him, wild with recrimination. "He's mine, you know. I take it *very* personally when my friends are maltreated."

The two armed conspirators supporting Dreyfus tightened their hold on him. Haigler stood to one side, his weapon held casually but ready to be brought to bear.

"Whatever you have to say to him, say it."

"I wanted to ask him what was going on beyond this room, Haigler. My usual omniscience seems to be failing me." She resumed her focus on him. "What is it, Dreyfus? Something as dreadful as I imagine?"

"They've failed in their efforts to contain the Clockmaker," Dreyfus answered. "He outwitted them. My guess, from what I can hear, is that he's taken control of the industrial facilities in Carcasstown so he can make himself a new body."

She gasped, pressing a paper-thin hand to the flattened mask of her face. "Oh dear. This does indeed have the hallmarks of my nemesis." She cast her eyes to the ceiling, pondering. "It reminds me of his actions in SIAM, the Sylveste Institute for Artificial Mentation, when he first broke loose."

"I don't need a reminder."

"Still, we know how that ended, don't we, Dreyfus?" She feigned a look of appalled recollection. "Such a beastly business! And what you had to do to your dear wife, just to save a part of her." Her face was engraved with insincere sympathy. "What an irony, that you now find yourself facing similar circumstances. Tragedy, then farce! Or is this the part where your battered conscience finally finds its ease?"

"Tell me how we stop the Clockmaker. It's in your interest as much as ours."

"Oh, but you can't. The best you can do is explore immediate avenues of self-euthanisation. I'd strongly recommend it. The Clockmaker has an interest in exploring the extreme parameters of suffering. It will do appalling things to you all, just to entertain itself on the way to me."

Haigler shifted, his fist tightening on the weapon. "If it wants you, we won't stand in its way."

"You misunderstand its nature," Aurora answered sweetly. "You've tried to do a bad thing to it, and that won't be forgiven. I'd be quick about killing yourselves. When the Clockmaker's got you, you'll regret not heeding my words."

"Could you defeat it, if I loosened your restraints?" Haigler asked. Quickly, he added: "I'm not talking about letting you go. Just giving you enough freedom to preserve yourself. Save yourself, and you save us. Is that feasible?"

Aurora looked at her captor with a frowning admiration. "He really has got you rattled, hasn't he. After all your years of struggling to net me, you're already moving to the bargaining phase!"

"Why three?" Dreyfus asked.

Irritation dented her brow. "You asked that silly question before."

"And I noticed that you didn't answer."

Haigler said: "Why three what?"

Dreyfus cocked his head back to respond. "She commandeered three bulk carriers and flung them at Carcasstown. I'm asking her why she stopped at three."

"Explain," Haigler growled.

"Three was just enough to severely test our response," Dreyfus replied. "We stopped those carriers, but only just. If she'd thrown a few more at us, it might have been a different story."

"Bad for her that she didn't, then."

"No, bad for us." Dreyfus was silent, watching Aurora for a reaction. "She sent three quite deliberately. She never wanted to destroy Abacus, Midas Analytics or Carcasstown. It was a piece of theatre, nothing more."

"Start making sense," Haigler said.

"I'm right, aren't I?" Dreyfus interrogated the mirage swimming in the glass. "That was why you forewarned me that you might try and commandeer those carriers. You wanted to make sure we were ready to stop you. You wanted us to succeed, and for it to look as if you had failed. But you didn't fail."

"Oh, Dreyfus," she said, applauding slowly. "You always get there in the end, I'll give you that. Even if you move at the speed of continental drift."

"What is this?" Haigler asked, desperation rising in his voice.

"A ruse, I think," Dreyfus said. "A gambit. She's allowed herself to be captured. More than that, I strongly suspect it's an outcome that she's been engineering for a very long time." He shook his head forlornly. "You've been manipulated, Haigler."

"We haven't."

"Tell him," Dreyfus suggested, bidding a hand to the ghostly form. "Put him out of his misery."

"All right," she said, with a teasing half-smile. "I'll admit things aren't *entirely* as they seem. And haven't been for, as you say, quite a long time."

Aurora started laughing. The laughter found a chink in the dam wall of her sanity, bursting it apart.

Groaning with the effort, Thalia unclipped her whiphound and allowed it to roll away from her hand. She wanted to look like she had been trying to defend herself until unconsciousness overcame her.

It would not be enough. Not to fool Breno.

She could pretend to be dead as much as she liked. Conscious or otherwise, her suit and bracelet would betray her condition, if her own breathing and heartbeat were not enough by themselves.

Nothing short of actual death was likely to convince Breno that his work was done.

"But I don't want to actually die," Thalia mumbled to herself.

"Then don't," Sparver said, standing over her, hands on his hips, looking down with faint amusement more than concern, as if all she had done was trip herself up.

"Sparv?"

"The berries, Thal. Remember what I said? If berries are..."

She mouthed his words back at him. "If berries are your only weapon. Your *only* weapon."

He nodded, pleased that she had got the point. "You use what you've got."

She still had the vial, tucked into a pouch on her belt. Because she had come directly from the lemurs, there had been no time to dispose of the gift. She had not thought there would ever be a situation where taking the berries was a sensible idea.

And perhaps it wasn't now. But if the berries had pushed her to the edge of consciousness when she was fit and well, doing strange and powerful things to her, what effect would they have on her in her present weakened condition, when her bracelet was already working overtime? They might well kill her for good. That was a possibility. Perhaps quite a likely one. But if Breno had any grounds for suspecting she was still alive, he would definitely put an end to her. It was simple, looked at that way. Thin as it was, the berries were her only chance.

"You're right, Sparv," she mumbled, wanting to thank him.

Sparver was gone, though.

Thalia groped around her midriff until she found the vial. She thumbed it open, tipping a small quantity of berries into her palm. She cupped her palm to her mouth and ate them. She did not want to swallow them whole, not when she was lying down. The taste of them hit her, instantly transporting her back to the company of the lemurs. Nearly as speedily, she felt the chemicals within them reach her brain.

More berries. It was all or nothing. She couldn't afford to leave any in the vial. Thalia chewed and swallowed. She was beginning to feel very peculiar, far more so than the first time. It was not an unpleasant sensation: as if she was a gas, leaking out of the thing called Thalia. The thing called Thalia was beneath her, its hand still on the empty vial. The thing called Thalia had a look of perfect numb astonishment about her. The eyes of the thing called Thalia were wide and unstaring, painted on like a doll's eyes. The thing called Thalia looked stupid. It made her angry, looking down on it. She had to make the thing called Thalia do one more action, tuck the vial back into the belt pouch. She could not have that vial in her hand when Breno came back. Berries or no berries, he would guess that the vial had played some part in the thing called Thalia's apparent condition.

She watched the thing move its arm, returning the vial to its concealment. It was all very slow, all very exasperating, like watching a shadow creep around a sundial.

Time oozed, jumped, stalled, oozed again.

Eventually, when the rush of evacuees had become a trickle and then nothing, a heavy man's footsteps approached.

The heavy man breathed.

A foot kicked her. She rolled with it lifelessly, disassociated from her body.

"You were nearly a problem, Ng," a voice murmured. "Nearly but not quite."

A creak of armour as the man leaned down and scooped up her whiphound.

The footsteps departed.

"Make her stop!" Haigler was saying, over and over, as the mad laughter pealed out of the pane.

"I don't think I can," Dreyfus said, wincing as Haigler jabbed the energy

256

weapon into the fat of his neck, where it lapped over the collar of his uniform. "She's made herself bait. None of this project is what you think. She's been running it the whole time."

The laughter fractured, breaking down into fits of giggles, then a fragile sobriety.

"Perhaps...helping it along?"

"The Clockmaker knows that you're here now. That's what you were counting on. And now that he's here, unable to resist the lure, he's exposed himself. You can destroy him, once and for all, by destroying Carcasstown."

Haigler grasped at a thread of understanding. "Then she'll die as well!"

Dreyfus countered with a shake of his head. "I doubt it. That would only work if you'd really snared Aurora."

Haigler pointed to the pane, his finger wavering.

"Then what the *hell* is that?"

"A little sacrificial piece of her, I'd guess. A figment, just plausible enough to fool you and to serve as a decoy. The real Aurora will still be out there, just as dispersed as she ever was." He looked to the image for confirmation. "That's close enough, isn't it? You budded off a piece of yourself, let Haigler think he'd succeeded, and then threw a trap around the Clockmaker."

"No," Haigler asserted.

"It hurts," Dreyfus said, not without a small measure of sympathy. "I know, because I've been played just as thoroughly. She wanted me here all along. That task schedule practically guided me to Midas Analytics."

"You came to shut us down!" Haigler said.

"That's what I thought I was doing. She wouldn't have let me get very far, though. You had to be seen to succeed, Haigler, or else the Clockmaker wouldn't have fallen for her trap. The rest—our efforts to stop Abacus, my being here at all—was all to make it look real."

"I am but an echo, a shard, a petal on the stream," Aurora said, lifting a swooning hand to her breast. "The true version of me may witness my triumph from afar, but this pale shadow will never have the pleasure of reporting back to her. Hence your presence, dear Dreyfus. You've understood my intentions, belatedly at least. You will live to speak of this day. You will be the only one."

Haigler's sanity was coming apart by the second. "What does she mean?"

"She might be far past human," Dreyfus said, "but she's still an egomaniac."

Haigler levelled the energy weapon at Dreyfus. Dreyfus wrestled to free himself from Haigler's guards as his finger tightened on the trigger, then Haigler veered the muzzle onto the pane.

Aurora shattered in a white pulse.

"That'll help," Dreyfus coughed out, just before Haigler knocked him out for good.

Thalia floated outside her own body, looking down on it from an aerial vantage. She observed herself lying on her back, spread-eagled against the gridded metal floor of Carcasstown, in a sticky pool of her own blood, fanned out around her like a pair of crimson angel's wings. She was quite motionless, no trace of her breath to animate her lungs or lips. Her eyes were open, but staring up in an unblinking transfixion, betraying neither life nor awareness. She was pale, her face a motionless waxy mask. She was dead, by the crudest medical criteria.

She was also not dead.

Death was a permeable membrane, a matter of definition. A negotiable boundary. She was not on the other side of it yet.

Not quite.

There was one part of her that was doing something. She could see it from her disembodied perspective. Thalia knew that she was not really outside her body; she was still somewhere down in the head of the woman on the ground, running on a shred of consciousness within that ailing, blood-starved mind. She lacked the functionality to maintain a stable body image, and so she had begun to disassociate, unmooring from herself.

Her bracelet, exposed where her cuff had ridden up, was giving out a faint repeating pulse of light, pale rose, indicating something to do with the bracelet's rarely used biomedical function. It was tapping Thalia's blood, what remained of it, analysing and filtering and synthesising. When it put the blood back into her, it was changed, suffused with a cocktail of chemicals and medichines. The bracelet understood that Thalia was very sick. It was doing what it could to pull her back from the brink of death. It was also attempting to signal Panoply, requesting Heavy Medical intervention, as well as sending out a general medical distress signal to anyone nearby who might care to receive and respond.

Neither call had yet been heeded.

CHAPTER THIRTY-ONE

Dreyfus came round to blurred vision and an aching head. He was next to one of the consoles, his mouth lolling open, collar biting into the flesh of his jaw. He had been dumped in a chair like a sack of grain, and there was a tightness around his chest and arms.

He looked down. He had been bound to the chair, webbed to it using adhesive tape. The tape wrapped his chest and forearms. He could move his legs and hands, but that was about it.

His tongue moved, slithering over a mess of blood, saliva and shattered teeth. He looked down at the dark stain beneath his chin, where he had drooled and bled.

Finally he looked up at the man facing him.

"Lovro," he said, half slurring.

Lovro Breno stood with his hands on his hips, legs splayed, his stance that of the conquering victor surveying the spoils of war. He was clad in tactical armour, but where it made other prefects look squat, Breno wore the equipment lightly, as if it had been fashioned to a smaller scale.

"Tom." Breno nodded once at the battered spectacle before him. "What a predicament we've ended up in, the two of us. I've got to congratulate you."

Dreyfus spat out a shard of tooth. "You have?"

"It took guts to come in here on your own, knowing the scale and determination of the conspiracy you were likely walking into. You always were the best of us, right until the end."

"Judging by these restraints, I'm guessing you're not the help I was hoping for. How are you here?"

"I put myself forward for the action, once it became clear that we were going to send operatives into Carcasstown. Don't blame yourself for Ng. I was always going to have to take care of the rest of the squad before we reached Midas Analytics; you just expedited the process with that helpful call of yours."

"What did you do to Thalia?"

"I killed her. And the other two, Coady and...Gaza, was it? Hard to keep track. These young fresh faces all merge together after a while. You know how it is."

Dreyfus filed away the fact of Thalia's death, drawing anger from it but refusing to be sucked into a vortex of grief. That would come in time, if there was any time to be had. For now, he needed to focus on the moment and what could still be salvaged.

"You're making a really bad mistake, Lovro." Dreyfus searched the gallery above him. "Where are Mirna Silk and Doctor Salazar? Did you kill them as well?"

"They kept out of my way, like the useful idiots they are. I've no fight with them, not when we're this close to success."

"You're so far from success you're not even orbiting the same star. Has Haigler laid it out for you yet?" Dreyfus twisted around in the chair, the webbing tightening against his chest. Panoply issue, he decided. Even if there had been a sharp edge on the chair, something he could work against, the tape would have healed as quickly as he cut it. "Haigler, come and tell Lovro how well it's going. Or did you not want to tell Daddy the bad news? Or Zhang? Is Zhang here? He knows how it's going. You can tell by the fear in his eyes."

"We've got her," Breno asserted. "We're close to capturing him."

"You've got neither of them. All you have of Aurora is a decoy. The rest of her's still out there, as strong as ever, maybe more so. And those industrial processes you can't stop? If that's your idea of the Clockmaker being contained, I'd hate to see what failure looks like."

Breno leaned in with a snarl. "What processes?"

Haigler appeared, sweat pooling off him, his hand jittering on the energy pistol. "We're monitoring them, sir. You might have missed the worst of it, depending on the route you took to get to us."

"Monitoring what?"

"The manufacturing systems. Factories, robot assembly units, quick-matter forges. Some of the other client outfits in the rim. They've started up, despite our shutdown."

"Explain it to me, Lovro," Dreyfus said companionably. "Why you're part of this, despite everything I thought I knew about your relationship with Grigor Bacchus."

Breno leaned in, his huge face magnified. "What do you know about me and Grigor?"

"That you looked up to him, and then felt crushed and betrayed when his role in Catopsis was exposed. That the mentor you'd admired turned out to be weak and devious, working against his own organisation from within."

"Grigor didn't fail us!" Breno snarled, spittle speckling Dreyfus. "It was the rot at the top of Panoply. Jane Aumonier, the other seniors. You! All of you with your defeatist notion that we should somehow live with these monsters towering above us, that it was better to cower and grovel than to do something about it!" His tone became urgent. "Grigor didn't fail us, Tom. He was the one who lived up to our ideals! The one who at least tried, even if his work was undone by those weaker and less imaginative than himself!" Breno shook his head. "Crushed and betrayed by him? No, you couldn't be more wrong."

Dreyfus spat out a wad of blood. "I spent four years listening to you complain that his punishment wasn't severe enough."

"I had to make it seem that way, didn't I? If I was to uphold our ideals as he did, I had to distance myself from what you and the others turned him into. A wreck of a man, humiliated by his own peers."

"A man lucky to still have a functioning position within the organisation he endangered from within. Tell me, how closely was he involved in this second version of Catopsis?"

"He'd shown the way, Tom. We just needed to follow the light."

"So he wasn't involved. Did he even know about it?"

"He was aware that I wished to further his work, but he opted to pursue our goals independently. That was wise, in hindsight. It eliminated a point of weakness. You could have put him to the trawl and he still wouldn't have been able to tell you where we were operating from." Breno nodded thoughtfully. "Well done on finding us as quickly as you did, though. I'm impressed by your resourcefulness."

"I'd love to take credit, but that was all Aurora's doing. She wanted me here, Lovro. That alone should be enough to prove you've got it all wrong. Tell me, though. Who was the inside man responsible for sabotaging our ships?"

"Podor," Breno said easily, the admission costing him nothing. "You suspected, didn't you?"

"A friend of mine certainly did."

"I was running him, not Grigor. That business with Mizler Cranach was unfortunate, believe me. We never wanted that. I've always had the greatest respect for our hyperpig colleagues. And if there'd been a way to deflect Ingvar Tench from her enquiries without killing her, I'd gladly have taken it. She was so dogged, though, Tom." He shook his head in something like admiration. "There was no stopping her!"

"Did you kill Podor?"

"Yes, but it was very quick. I planted a whiphound on him with a long-delay fuse. He'd have never known what hit him. He was useful to us. I didn't want to put him through anything unpleasant."

"And Grigor? Did he go willingly?"

"It was an act of love, Tom. My love for him, and what he stood for. His love for Panoply, the organisation that treated him with such contempt, and yet which he never turned from." Breno seemed distant, his eyes glazed with affection. "He understood, Tom, even in those last moments. It was the culmination of the good work he began, the final expression of his vision."

"To have his head crushed in a vice."

"What matters is not the handful of lives that were lost along the way, but the millions that will now be free from the fear of machine oppression. I'll mourn Grigor, Podor, Ingvar and the others. They were good servants of Panoply."

"I'll offer you some advice, Lovro. You'll likely ignore it, but it's here for the taking. Aurora is going to destroy Carcasstown very shortly. That's the endgame; that's how she finally vanquishes the Clockmaker. You should leave now."

"With you?"

"If you wish, but mainly you should save yourself, and Haigler, Zhang and as many of these brilliant souls as you can. Get out, and negotiate an amnesty with Panoply in exchange for your technical knowledge of Abacus and the Catopsis program. Jane Aumonier's nothing if not pragmatic. She'll understand the value in keeping you all alive when there's nothing holding Aurora in check. What you know matters more to her than punishing you."

"I think we're past the point of amnesties now, Tom. Even if we weren't, though, I don't believe we've failed."

"I imagine you'll get your proof soon enough," Dreyfus said.

Thalia lay still, feeling parts of herself gradually return, lock back in and signal their functionality. It was as if she were a kind of station, floating in vacuum, re-assembling itself from disconnected components.

She waited a little longer and looked around. She was still in the storage alcove, hemmed in by packing cases. Blood still slicked the ground under her and her crawled path from the main corridor. The whiphound, which she had last seen just out of reach, was absent.

Thalia's arm was still too damaged to support her weight. There was much her suit and bracelet could do, but repairing muscular and skeletal injuries was beyond their joint capabilities. She would not be much good to anyone until she was properly healed.

262

She could move, or at least attempt it. She turned on her side and inched backwards until her spine was against one of the packing cases. She pressed against it and used it as leverage to contort herself into an awkward sitting position. The effort drained her. She caught her breath, then began to force herself upright, still using the stack of cases for support. Her head throbbed, swimming with the combined after-effects of the berries and the various drugs pumped into her to combat both the berries and the injury. As she assumed a standing position, a wave of nausea hit her and bile surged in her throat. She swallowed it down and wiped a hand across her brow, pushing aside a curtain of sweat and tangled, blood-matted hair. She felt dreadful. But feeling dreadful was a considerable improvement on being dead.

She raised her bracelet to her face, staring through half-focussed eyes at the biomedical status. The pulse was a nagging yellow now: not as urgent as before, but still indicating that she needed further attention.

Not exactly a surprise.

"Ng to..." But she silenced herself before more than a whisper had escaped her lips. Whether or not comms with Panoply were still offline, Breno could easily intercept her call. She had not gone to all this trouble, making him think she were dead, to waste it now.

She lowered the bracelet and assessed her condition. No weapon, only one really functional arm, and she was weakened by the shock her body had just been through. She could not risk coordination with any other Panoply elements that might be in or near Carcasstown. Who knew if she could trust them, anyway?

She touched the wound again. It was totally dry, and the blood residue had even begun to be absorbed into her uniform. An injured prefect was vulnerable to mob action, so the uniforms did their best to conceal signs of attack.

She tried moving her damaged arm. She could bend it at the elbow and still work her fingers, perhaps pick up something light, but she had almost no useful strength in it.

She was broken. Broken, but not finished, and not ready to be finished.

Since she could not risk the bracelet, she mouthed aloud: "Prefect Thalia Ng, resuming operation. Will attempt to rendezvous with Prefect Dreyfus."

As if it were an injunction to herself, a command to action.

Haigler was the first to crack. Dreyfus had counted on it and, just as he had identified in Mirna Silk, seen something in the man he thought he could push on until it yielded.

"I've laid it all out for Lovro," hc was saying, all matter-of-fact reasonableness. "I don't blame him for holding out, thinking there's still a chance to make this work. You were there, though, Haigler. You were in that room with me when Aurora changed her tune. You heard her mad laughter. It's why you destroyed her image. She was telling you something you really didn't want to hear." He turned his sights on Zhang. "Tell Lovro how you're still in complete control of Carcasstown, Zhang. You can, can't you?"

"Shut up," Breno instructed, before Zhang got a word out.

"I *was* with him, sir," Haigler began, in a wheedling tone.

"Whatever she said in there, it doesn't matter," Breno said, cutting across him angrily. "She was trapped. Defeated. Of course she was going to try some eleventh-hour gamesmanship with us. I'd have been suspicious if she hadn't."

"Did it look like a desperate gambit to you, Haigler?" Dreyfus asked. "Especially when I asked her about the three carriers? Put the same question to yourself, Lovro, and see where it leads you. She had the capability to destroy Carcasstown utterly as she was—you believe—being trapped inside Abacus, and yet for some peculiar reason she chose not to. Does that seem like the rational behaviour of a machine intellect believing itself at real risk?"

"Sir," Haigler said, glancing at Zhang for moral support. "Let's suppose we *have* captured her, and that Abacus is proceeding with the Clockmaker. There's still no reason for us to remain in Carcasstown, is there? We can leave now, with the general exodus. Panoply won't be able to track and process every evacuee fleeing the wheel, will it? We can leave and disappear into the Glitter Band, knowing our work is done."

Breno looked aghast. "And leave Abacus unattended, with the danger of those two *things* escaping from it?"

"Once we're clear, we can plan the destruction of Carcasstown," Haigler shrugged. "Panoply will probably do it for us anyway. There's nothing to be gained by remaining here, and if there's even the tiniest possibility that Dreyfus is right..." Something in him broke, as if voicing the idea had been enough to render it true. "Sir, we should get out while we can!"

"We stay, as planned," Breno replied.

Zhang shook his head. "I can't explain those results, sir. I can't explain how those factories are running. That frightens me. I'm—"

Breno turned to him, towering over the meek data theorist. "You're what, Zhang?"

"I'm leaving, sir. We made plans. We've got our fallback identities. I'm not going to stay here and die to prove a point."

Breno made a snapping motion to Haigler. "Give me that weapon."

Haigler regarded the energy pistol, seeming to weigh a thousand opposed possibilities in the blink of an eye. He looked rapturous, realising that for once in his life he stood at the crux of decisive events.

"No, sir. I think it's best we evacuate. I'm sorry, but I'm not going to stop Zhang from leaving. And you're not going to stop me." He glanced around the room, just quickly enough to assay the other conspirators and gauge their likely support. "This isn't failure!" he declared. "It's not a mutiny!"

"Feels like one to me," Breno said, making a slow but purposeful move for his holstered whiphound.

Dreyfus had been counting on all hell breaking loose. That did not mean he was looking forward to it happening, or that he had any guarantee of immunity from the violence that was about to ensue. The best he could hope for was to call on whatever small measure of luck he might have banked in his time as a prefect. He closed his eyes and waited for the screaming and fighting to abate.

It took longer than he expected.

CHAPTER THIRTY-TWO

Thalia let her goggles guide her to Midas Analytics.

Carcasstown had gone into some kind of major shutdown. Other than scattered areas where emergency power and lighting still functioned, the main rim corridor and its offshoots were dark. The air had stopped circulating, giant fans in the ceiling grinding down to silence and stillness. People were moving around in varying degrees of confusion, annoyance and panic. There was a general rush to get to the spokes and the elevators to the hub, where most of the ships were docked, but the flow of evacuees ebbed and surged and reversed, as people gave up on one spoke and made a bid for another. Thalia found herself moving through a choke of people one minute, then virtually alone the next. No one paid her much heed as she was jostled around, barely recognising that she was a prefect. In her weaponless, injured state, she was glad to blend in with the locals.

Not far ahead, no more than fifty metres or so, a pool of reddish light spilled into the corridor from one of the side-tunnels. A sound was coming from that offshoot, some insistent, repetitive process. It sounded like primitive music. Like machines.

Every instinct told Thalia not to get closer, to find some other route to her objective, even if it meant braving the crowds of evacuees and going the long way around the rim.

Instead, she advanced, creeping closer and closer to the threshold. Dregs of evacuees slipped by in the other direction, oblivious to her shadowed form.

Thalia looked into the side-tunnel, curious about what was so important that it needed to be done now, when the whole habitat was running on rationed power.

The side-shaft was a stubby one, opening out almost immediately into a cavernous industrial space filled with moving machines of varied function and size. She slowed, absorbing the scene, aware that in some way this activity had to connect with the current emergency, although she could not quite see how, and that Dreyfus would need to know about it.

It was a factory, or a scrapyard, or some hybrid of both. Enormous cage-sided crates were being fed with a slurry of machine parts, tipped into them from conveyor belts. The components were pieces of robot servitor, all jumbled together, presumably having been dismantled elsewhere. There were limbs, heads, torsos, specialised manipulators and tractor units, all tumbling into the crates. Mechanical arms lowered into the glistening piles, rummaging through them and plucking out the choicest items, which were then dumped onto other conveyors that either fed the items into melter or assembler vats, or ferried them into more complicated machines that cut and hammered and fused the basic items into larger, more complicated units. Via other scoops, grabs, arms and conveyors, the raw parts were being stitched back together into functional forms.

Functional, upright forms, humanoid but much larger than a person, with legs like scissor blades, arms ending in sickle fingers, chests caged in a gridiron of razor-edged ribs. Each swollen silver torso was surmounted by an eyeless skull, oblivious and cruel as a hammerhead.

Each machine was a simulacrum of the Clockmaker's robotic form, a shape Thalia and every other prefect knew from the documents and inquest materials circulated after the original crisis, from the handful of recordings and eyewitnesses that had survived close proximity with the Clockmaker before its supposed destruction.

The robots stood in line, waiting for others to join their gleaming ranks. There were twelve of them now, a thirteenth aborning. Soon fourteen, soon fifteen.

The horror of what she was seeing took a few moments to properly develop.

It was here. It was returning. Not as one avenging angel, but as a humming silver regiment. A symphony in evil.

Thalia knew what she was seeing and she knew what it portended, and she knew also that as it stood—as *she* stood, hurt and powerless—she was quite incapable of stopping it. She knew the horrible acts performed by the original Clockmaker, the exquisite and lasting torments it had concocted.

Thalia stood frozen, as if she had just seen a map of hell and the part within it reserved specially for her, for all eternity.

Then—slowly, painfully, against every human instinct to cower into stillness—she made herself keep moving.

A muffled voice said: "Prefect Dreyfus!"

He opened his eyes, then immediately wished he had not. The air stung. It made his throat hurt, chafing its way to his lungs. A hand pushed a breather mask to his face, and he gulped down cleaner breaths.

"Under-Supervisor," he said, trying to speak through the mask. "I told you to leave, Krenkel. What part of that wasn't clear?"

"You should thank him for coming back, Dreyfus," Mirna Silk answered. "He brought three armed functionaries from the Department of Lease-holds and Public Services."

As his eyes regained a measure of focus, Dreyfus made out Krenkel, Silk, Doctor Salazar and a trio of civic officials equipped with capes, armour and short-range anti-personnel weapons. All wore breather masks: light-weight devices similar to Panoply equipment.

"We arrived at the tail-end of your firefight," Krenkel said, gripping one of the weapons himself. "By then, they'd either shot each other or scurried away. My functionaries tried to mop them up before they disappeared into the crowds, but I'm afraid most of them slipped through." His mask swung around as he surveyed the smoke-wreathed carnage of what had been the Midas Analytics bullpen. "What in Voi's name happened in here?"

"A disagreement—one I was glad not to get caught up in." Still bound to the chair, Dreyfus was limited in his angles of view. He spotted Haigler and Zhang, both very much deceased, and half a dozen more fallen, dead or incapacitated. There was no sign of Lovro Breno.

"If I'd known this was going on under my nose..." Mirna Silk said, before trailing off.

"You can make immediate amends," Dreyfus said. "By leaving and pro-tecting yourselves." He lifted his eyes to the under-supervisor. "Krenkel, did your family get out?"

Krenkel's mask bobbed eagerly. "The last I heard, they were aboard an evacuation taxi."

"Good; I'm glad. Save yourself now, the best way you know how. And these functionaries—they've done their work."

"What about the ones who got away?"

"They're not our biggest concern now." Dreyfus lifted his gaze to the immense sphere of Abacus, looming over him like a destroying ball that might roll off its plinth at any moment. "It's been damaged, probably in the crossfire."

One of the energy pulses had scribed a gash across the face of Abacus, opening a glowing wound thirty or forty centimetres into its bright, steadily densifying interior. Dreyfus had no idea whether that sort of damage was something to worry about. The plinth was a different matter. Another stray shot had punctured it, severing one or more of the tubes that sustained Abacus and prevented it from overheating. The haze in the air that had stung his eyes and hurt his lungs was some gaseous coolant, leaking from the ruptured plinth.

Alarms were sounding across the consoles.

"We should try to shut it down," Silk said, making a move to one of the consoles. "Doctor Salazar, can you help me?"

"Don't bother, Mirna," Dreyfus answered. "Haigler and Zhang couldn't control it, and they knew it better than anyone. You'd best leave while you can. Aurora's plan was always to destroy Carcasstown; this will just speed things up."

Silk abandoned the console. "Then we leave, but not until we've got you out of those restraints." She turned to the functionaries. "A knife, anything. One of you must have something sharp on you."

"Ordinary blades won't touch this material," Dreyfus said.

"There's this!" Krenkel said, spotting a whiphound lying amongst the fallen. "Is it yours, Prefect?"

"I don't know. It could also belong to Lovro Breno." He shook his head. "You can't risk it. If that's Breno's whiphound, there's every chance he left it here deliberately, rigged to respond to any unauthorised contact."

Krenkel edged away from the suspect object. "Then what?"

"Get this bracelet off me. Remove it by applying pressure to those two pads. It'll come off without any trouble."

Silk took the bracelet, her hand shaking with the concentration. "What now? Is there something it can do about the restraints?"

"No, but it'll get you out of Carcasstown. Snap it around your wrist."

She did as commanded, the bracelet latching tight. "Serum, Repulse, Clover," Dreyfus stated, drawing a flash of pink as the bracelet recognised his instruction. "My cutter should still be docked at the hub. Berth Eighteen North, if I remember rightly. Take Krenkel and Doctor Salazar with you. Can you avoid the main public thoroughfares?"

"I have access to the civic utility passages," Krenkel said, jangling his keys. "They're cramped, but we should have them mostly to ourselves. Once we reach the nearest spoke, we can ride one of the freight lifters down to the hub—they're normally locked out of use. Oh dear! Should I even be thinking of jumping ahead of the citizens?"

"It's not your conscience on the line here, Krenkel, it's mine if you don't get Salazar to safety. He may well be the last person alive who understands the methods used to snare Aurora's decoy. We're losing this battle, but if we're to win the war, it's vital that he makes it to Panoply."

"I...understand. And what about the ship, when we get there?"

"The bracelet will operate the lock, but you'll only have a few seconds to get the three of you inside. It'll be a squeeze, but you'll fit."

269

"And then what?"

"Tell the cutter to get you to Panoply. That's all you'll need to do."

Silk looked up at the ominous throbbing sphere.

"What if it's too late?"

"It certainly will be if you don't get going, Mirna. I know you want to help me, but you can do more good by helping Panoply." He nodded forcefully. "Go. You're not abandoning me. I have faith in my organisation. Someone else will come along."

Thalia could not be more than sixty metres from Midas Analytics, according to the goggles, but now her way was blocked by a gathering mass of people, more agitated than any she had seen before. There were forty or fifty of them at least, trying to squeeze through a narrow set of doors under the huge, beaten-bronze mural of a many-pointed sunburst. The goggles showed the entrance to a spoke elevator at this point: not the one Dreyfus had used on his first visit, according to his whiphound's trace. This one would have made for a quicker journey, but her squad would have been reliant only on Panoply's outdated model of Carcasstown's interior.

She tried to push her way through. Every instinct was telling her that she would be better off using that elevator, getting back to the ship and fleeing the station. Somewhere behind her, that factory was spitting out copies of the Clockmaker, silver demons that might already be flowing out into the corridors, quick and lethal as mercury.

She would not give in, though. She had set herself an objective, a foolish one, perhaps, but one that was aligned with the principles of Panoply and the uniform that still clung to her. Jason Ng would have understood. He might not have liked his daughter putting her life in jeopardy for the sake of an idea, but he would most certainly have understood. And approved, in that quiet, understated way of his. His praise had always been sparing, but when it came it was all the more meaningful.

She heard him: "This is not the easy path, Thalia. But it is the right one."

A ruffled man snagged her eye as she tried to make her way through the crowd. He appraised her, taking a few instants to see that this bruised and bloodied waif was actually a prefect, albeit one divested of all the usual tools of her authority.

"Voi's ghost. What the hell happened to you?"

"Work," she said. "Are you certain this elevator is functioning, citizen? If not, I'd suggest moving to the next. Whatever you do, don't attempt to reach the spoke behind me."

"So you can have this one, while we all head to the next?"

"I just want you to have the best chance of getting out of here."

She saw him then, a few faces beyond, mingling with the crowd. He had thrown on a civilian's clothes, ill fitting over his frame, and he was close enough to the door that he could board if the elevator was indeed working.

"Prefect Breno," she said, before she had a thought of censoring herself.

Breno's face was shadowed under a hood, but she saw enough of it to be sure. He followed her voice, saw her and allowed a flicker of surprised recognition to crease his features before he fell back into character. Then he turned slowly, presenting his back to her, trying to slip deeper into the mob.

"Citizens!" she said, her voice breaking on a wave of fear and uncertainty. "There's an impostor here. That big man isn't a civilian. He's a prefect, and a murderer. You mustn't let him onto that elevator. Under the Common Articles, I'm asking you to exercise your mutual obligations to Panoply and effect a citizens' detention—"

"Enough," a lump-headed man said, his skull a tectonic map of curious bulges and scabs. He pushed out of the huddle, happily surrendering his position, and scooped Thalia up bodily. He strode with her and used his boot-heel to kick aside a grating in the floor.

Thalia had just enough time to spy the void beneath, a grimy, sewer-like space gristled with pipes and cables, and then she was thrown into it.

She hit something hard and had the wind knocked out of her. The man slid the grating back into place: it fell heavily into position, and Thalia lay stunned and motionless, stuffed into the hole like a grubby, broken doll.

She said nothing, did nothing. Even thinking was difficult. Acting was beyond all consideration.

You could have just left it, she told herself. *Let the rest of Panoply worry about detaining Lovro Breno.*

But if leaving things came easily to her, she wouldn't have been Thalia Ng.

She was still trapped there as she heard the Clockmaker's units approaching with shocking, bounding speed, then the panic, and then the screaming. Flashes of it reached her through the grating. There was nothing anyone could do. She heard a rapid, machine-like scissoring, a scuffle of metal on metal, a terrible low humming, saw a dazzle of chrome and red. She lay still as the screams became shrieks, which became moans, and then softened to final, desperate pleas for mercy. It all happened in a few seconds, but those seconds contained vast aeons of torment and anguish. The machines had said nothing. They just did.

Until there was silence.

She lay still, reducing her breathing to the barest sliver necessary to support consciousness. Something twitched in her leg and she moved without volition, clanging her knee against one of the pipes. The sound of it echoed and echoed, dying away like tinny laughter.

She heard humming and scuffling. The scrape of blade on blade: something cleaning itself.

She stopped breathing altogether.

How long she waited, Thalia had no means of reckoning. She waited until there was stillness and silence, and she waited beyond that for fear that it was a trap. The silence was not absolute: terrible things were happening elsewhere in Carcasstown.

She found the strength to budge the grating. It was sticky on her fingers. It made a hellish squeal but nothing responded to it. She crawled out, lungs heaving, breathless as a fish tossed onto land.

After several seconds of immobility she got to her feet and looked around, fearing a sudden blur of chrome and blood. Of blood there was plenty, some of it already dripping through the grating, but only a scattering of bodies around the margin of the hole, and nothing to suggest life in any of them. The tide of machines had done its work and passed through, moving on to some other mayhem.

She looked to the narrow door. Nothing obstructed it now, no press of citizens. A few lay slumped either side of it, unmoving and clearly long past any hope of medical resurrection. One was a woman, laid out cruciform, chest ruptured, ribs ripped wide, forming a square recess into which a clock casing had been inserted, its rough-fashioned hands still ticking around a blood-speckled face. The others, those that had not escaped or been taken away by the machines, hung from the sunburst mural. They had been pinned to it, impaled or driven through with machine-made spikes, their bodies forming a rustic dial, each trailing a darkening teardrop of blood and entrails.

Some of them were dead.

Not all of them.

One of those on the journey to death was Lovro Breno, pinned to the top of the hour, still with enough consciousness in him to look down at her, yet—judging by the bloody scraps where his mouth and jaw had been—no capability of acknowledging nor communicating with her except by the tiniest lifting of his cold grey eyes, a sort of wild astonishment that fate had thrown them together in this manner, for this last, brief meeting of minds.

Thalia thought of all that might be going through his head right now, besides pain and despair and the certainty of his own imminent demise.

"Berries," she said, clearly and loudly, so that there could be no possible confusion.

She pressed on to Midas Analytics, hoping that the tide of death had washed past her for now.

CHAPTER THIRTY-THREE

Dreyfus was alone, his only company the chorus of alarms blaring from the Abacus workstations. He was glad he had persuaded Mirna Silk to get Doctor Salazar to safety, glad that Krenkel was with them, too, even if he understood that he was unlikely ever to learn if they made it. He had done his best and the rest was beyond his control. That was enough, for now. Enough that he could empty his mind of immediate concerns about Aurora, the Clockmaker and Carcasstown, and think about Valery and the great, deep, storm-tossed ocean of words that stood still unspoken between them.

Theirs had not been the worst of lives. They had been happy, until the Clockmaker drove a hammer into their contentment. Even after that, in the long, difficult years of her rehabilitation, with all the false hopes and crushing setbacks that had come from her time in Hospice Idlewild, there had been islands of peace, little scattered atolls of delight and shared wonder. It had not been all bad, even in the darkest years.

So much was still to be done, though. So many things which might have happened, with the blessings of fortune. He had never truly given up hope. He had always believed that a total healing was within her grasp, if only both of them stayed the course.

The alarms were becoming slowly more strident, louder and faster. Some of the cooling gases were starting to filter past the breather, finding his airways. He coughed, his ribs heaving painfully against the restraints.

His eyes were slitted, vision difficult in the haze, so when Thalia arrived he was aware of only a dark, ragged form spidering down from the gallery. Footsteps rang on the descending staircase. He thought he recognised the cadence of those footfalls, but that was surely a trick of his failing mind, starved of oxygen as the breather gave out.

He did not dare pin a hope on that familiarity.

"Sir. It's me, Thalia."

He shook his heavy, swollen head. It felt like a boulder, wobbling preposterously on the thin stalk of his neck. "No, Thal. It's not you," he said, not caring how muffled his voice was, because he was only talking to himself. "Breno told me. He killed you."

Abruptly the breather was torn from his face and a new one planted over his nose and mouth.

He felt a flood of clarity, the fog lifting from his thoughts.

"I'm here, sir. I met some people heading for one of the other spokes."

He forced his eyes wider, distrusting every impression. "Thal?" he asked, suspicious that some part of his brain could still not be trusted.

"Mirna Silk said they'd left you with a civic-issue breather, but that it had a limited duration. This is a Panoply one. You should feel a little better already."

He squinted until she came into hazy focus. "What about...you?"

"They gave me one of theirs," she said, speaking out of the mask. "It's good enough to get you out of here."

"No, Thal. You're not real, and even if you were..." He trailed off, the thought too complicated to hold in his head.

"Breno didn't kill me," she said. "He just thought he did."

He thought back to the urgency he had impressed on Mirna Silk. If, just for the sake of argument, this phantasm was real, then he owed it the same consideration.

"You've got to leave, Thal. Abacus is malfunctioning."

"I can see that," she said coolly. "And I will be leaving, just as soon as I get you out of these restraints." Her face swivelled as she scanned the floor. "Is that your whiphound, sir?"

"No..." he managed. "No? I'm not sure. Maybe Breno's. You can't touch it."

Thalia regarded the wounded sphere of Abacus, the gash in its crust hinting at yawning computational depths of pressure and temperature.

"The way I see it, sir, I'm not going to get out of here without a whiphound. Besides, I came for you."

She stooped down and collected the whiphound. She held the handle, then flicked out the filament to its minimum deployment setting, a ten-centimetre stiletto of shimmering quickmatter.

"That was dangerous, Thal."

"And necessary," she said. "Now sit still while I cut through. You're already hurt, aren't you?"

"And you," he said, noticing her shoulder injury. "Between us, we might just make one half-decent prefect."

Thalia used the tip of the whiphound's filament to cut away the restraints, Dreyfus doing his best not to wince as he felt its whirring pressure tickle against his skin.

"Is it just the head, sir?" Thalia said, appraising him as she worked.

"It's just a bruise. Breno got you with his whiphound, I see. How deep did it go?"

"Deep enough to hurt, but he didn't get anything major. He thought he'd got me, but I managed to play dead well enough to fool him. I'm afraid Coady and Gaza weren't as lucky, sir. I saw both of them go down and their injuries were fatal."

"I'm sorry if I put you on the spot with that message about Breno."

"He was just waiting for his moment, sir. At least I had a little warning. Enough to make a difference. Now, all we have to do is find a way out of here, without getting trampled in the rush or running into the Clockmaker again."

"You saw it?"

She nodded humbly. "I saw it. Many of them. I'm lucky to be speaking to you."

"And I'm lucky you found me. Aurora wanted me alive to serve as a witness for her cleverness, but she seems to have neglected to have a plan for getting me out of these restraints."

"Aurora, sir?"

"It's complicated. Is the corvette still docked?"

Thalia checked her bracelet. "Yes—assuming Pasinler's still following my orders. I told him to hold dock for an hour, then depart. He has the package and we've got about fifteen minutes, unless I can signal him ahead of our arrival. It's going to be hard, isn't it? Even if the elevators aren't backed up with evacuees, we could run into the Clockmaker at any point between here and the hub. Mirna Silk had your bracelet, sir: she said she was trying to get those other two men to your cutter."

"Good; that's what I wanted. Who else was aboard the corvette, besides those Breno murdered?"

"Pasinler, Moriyama and Meppel. Do you think they could be loyal to Breno, sir?"

"His modus was to identify promising acolytes and get them bumped down to menial duties or excluded from Panoply altogether. They don't fit the pattern."

"Then we should make a bid for the corvette," Thalia said decisively. "Your ship may have already undocked by now, and it is already full, and I can't bring mine back in without comms."

Dreyfus pushed himself up from the chair. He felt instantly lightheaded and unsteady on his feet, needing to lean against the nearest workstation for support.

"It won't be easy. Krenkel was going to lead Silk and Salazar to the cutter via some backdoors only he knew about. Presumably he was still on his way to them when you met."

"There must be a way."

"There is."

The answer had come not from Dreyfus but from the workstations, the same voice issuing from them all, supplanting the alarm tone. Aurora's face flickered onto the stations, and copied itself across the walls, swelling hugely where the market graphics had been before.

"And you're wrong, Dreyfus," she went on as he turned, groggily acknowledging her presence. "There was always a plan to get you out. Ng came along at a helpful time, so I used her. The doors to this facility opened to you without difficulty, didn't they?"

Thalia shrugged. "And what if I hadn't come?"

"Someone else would have. Or I'd have co-opted a robot from one of the nearby factories. Or flooded the room with a quick-acting solvent gas designed to loosen Panoply-issue binding. All right, I might have needed a *little* time with the last. I was always confident of saving you, though. And getting you out."

A door opened in the wall of faces, narrow and low, with a dark space beyond it. Dreyfus had not seen it before. He wondered if anyone connected with Midas Analytics had known it existed.

"Where does it go?" Dreyfus asked.

"Take it and find out. Take your little helper with you as well, but be aware that you're strictly baggage, Ng."

"I've been called worse," Thalia said.

"Be quick. There are many things I can control in Carcasstown. The runaway malfunction of Abacus is not one of them." She made a fanning gesture. "It's getting *awfully* stuffy in here."

Dreyfus nodded to his colleague, and they stooped their way through the low door, into an equally narrow, low-ceilinged service duct. Dreyfus led, Thalia following. They had only gone a few dozen paces when the door closed loudly behind them.

"Even if this takes us all the way to the spoke," Thalia said, breathless with the effort, "I don't see how we get to Pasinler in time."

"Aurora will have worked something out," Dreyfus answered.

He figured out what that something was as soon as they emerged from the duct, after no more than a couple of hundred metres of awkward progress.

They had come out of a grubby hatch, swinging open without protest, in the forgotten, cluttered corner of one of the workshops Dreyfus had already seen on his first inspection of Carcasstown. The air in here seemed

277

clearer than in Midas Analytics so he took a gamble and ripped off his breather.

Thalia looked around, slowly taking in the various items of machinery and consumer product, picked out in dull hues by the dusky emergency lighting.

"What is this place, sir?"

"Damascene Conversions," Dreyfus said.

Thalia studied the items looming around her, understanding dawning. The engine cowls, the cockpit canopies, the control surfaces and custom mods.

"Handy."

"Very."

Thalia stepped onto an elevated walkway, rubbing her hand along the sleek flank of a small civilian runabout, already fixed to a launch rail that led out of the workshop via a ship-sized airlock. At her touch, the waiting vehicle responded with a hum of activation and a fireworks show of gaudy graphics across its hull. A door outlined itself then gull-winged open, disclosing a luxurious, padded interior, drenched in sumptuous green, practically begging to be lounged in.

"After you, sir," Thalia said, beckoning him to climb aboard.

"No, Thal," Dreyfus said, gently insistent. "Very much after you, I think."

The runabout ejected itself from Carcasstown, popping out of a circular hole in the side of the rim. Thalia circled slowly around, the sub-miniature spacecraft responding to her control inputs with nimble ease.

She tapped a nail against a bank of old-fashioned gauges, set in a wood-effect console. "If these fuel levels are to be believed, sir, we should be able to get to Panoply without any difficulty."

"Do you see the corvette anywhere near us?"

Thalia was confident with the runabout's propulsion controls, but the civilian-rated navigation and communications protocols were less familiar to her, so she was relying on visual identification of the hazards around them, gleaned through the heavily framed windows ahead of her. "I can't see it, sir, nor your cutter. If the corvette undocked sooner than planned, they could be thousands of kilometres away by now."

"Pasinler wouldn't have given up on you. They're still docked, inside the hub."

Thalia grimaced as she angled her wrist to study her bracelet. "He has about eight minutes to run, assuming he undocks exactly on the hour. We can't take that chance, can we?" She took a hand off the controls and lifted the bracelet. "Ng to Panoply. Ng to Pasinler. Someone respond.

If you can hear this, initiate immediate safe-distancing manoeuvre from Carcasstown."

"They might be hearing us, but we can't be sure. I'm sorry to ask this, Thal, after all you've just been through, but we need to reach that corvette and safeguard the evidential package."

"You don't have to persuade me, sir."

"I don't, but I need to make sure you're fully aware of the danger from Abacus. That computer is six thousand tonnes of matter being made to do things matter really doesn't want to. It'll make a big splash when it blows."

"One consolation though, sir: it'll likely be quick and painless?"

"You always find the upside, Thal." Dreyfus made a pointing gesture. "Take us in. The runabout's keel lock should mate with our corvette without any complications."

Thalia brought them around to face the entrance hole in the central sphere. Smaller ships, mainly taxis, short-range tugs and bare-bones escape pods, were still fleeing from the aperture. Thalia steered around this ragged exodus, careful not to collide with any of the evacuees. It was not lost on Thalia that theirs was the only ship heading in the opposite direction.

"I can't allow you to endanger yourself," Aurora said, her voice filling the runabout's cabin. "Turn about now, and we'll say no more about it."

"You want me alive for bragging rights," Dreyfus replied. "Unfortunately for you, I come with baggage. Ng has a whiphound. If you interfere with this ship in any way, even so much as to speak again, I'll set it to grenade mode."

"You'd kill dear little Ng, and yourself, just to silence me?"

"It would be a more than acceptable trade-off, so don't push me."

Aurora said nothing.

"Baggage?" Thalia asked, as they entered the sphere.

"The best kind." Dreyfus leaned forward intently, gazing past the huge semi-dismantled hulks and partial rebuilds. "There. That's your corvette, isn't it?"

Thalia nodded. "Yes. Pasinler had to dock nose first, because there wasn't room to bring it in laterally. I'll lock us onto the ventral lock, and keep my fingers crossed that Pasinler's stood down the proximity countermeasures."

"Being shot out of the sky by Panoply's own weapons would be a very, very bad end to the day."

By Thalia's estimation Pasinler ought to have been three minutes from departure by the time she brought the runabout into contact with the corvette. They managed to dock without trouble, but the corvette refused

279

to open its physical lock to let them through, perhaps understandably given the state of panic throughout Carcasstown.

Eventually Thalia got a crackle of comms through her bracelet.

"Pasinler? Let us in. It's Ng and Dreyfus."

Moriyama answered, sounding much more distant than as if she were only the other side of a few layers of armour. "Where are the others? Where's Prefect Breno?"

"Breno isn't coming back. Nor are Coady and Gaza. I'll explain when we're aboard, and most importantly when we've got some distance from Carcasstown. Dreyfus says the computer in Midas Analytics is likely to blow up at any moment, and that it'll take a good chunk of the station with it when it goes."

"Copy, Prefect Ng. I'm cycling the lock. We have a difficulty, though."

"What kind?"

"We're stuck here. We can't undock from Carcasstown."

CHAPTER THIRTY-FOUR

Thalia and Dreyfus moved aboard, instantly registering the mass of civilian evacuees pressed into almost every available nook of the corvette. Dreyfus surveyed the tired, concerned faces, not seeing Krenkel, Silk or Salazar. He could only hope that they had made it to his cutter and were already somewhere beyond the station.

Thalia moved forward to Pasinler's piloting position, keeping her voice low enough not to cause undue alarm to the evacuees. "What is it that's preventing us from leaving?"

"Capture clamps aren't responding, Ng." He did a double take, eyeing Dreyfus us well. "You're hurt, both of you. Go back to the surgical suite and get fixed up before you bleed all over my ship."

"Break free of the clamps," Thalia said.

"Yes—brilliant suggestion, Ng. If we do that, we'll take half the lock with us, including anyone on the other side."

"Did you turn anyone away?" Dreyfus asked.

"No, but that's not to say some more haven't arrived while we've been prepping for departure. There could be a hundred people backed up behind that lock."

He nodded. "I'm afraid there's nothing to be done for them. Get us off however you need to. The Clockmaker's units could be on us at any moment."

"You've seen them, sir?" Moriyama asked.

Dreyfus shook his head at the other prefect. "Thalia did. An army of them is running through Carcasstown in gathering numbers."

"I've seen what they do to people," Thalia added, in the unlikely event that Pasinler needed further persuasion. "We don't want to be any part of that. And with respect to anyone on the other side of the lock…decompression would be a much better way to go than meeting those machines."

"It'll take some force to break us free of the clamps," Pasinler said. "I'm afraid I'll need to detach that little ship you came in with, if we want to make the best use of our steering motors."

"Do it," Dreyfus said.

"Are you sure you don't want to get back aboard, detach and take yourself and Prefect Ng back to Panoply? You both look pretty beaten up."

Dreyfus glanced at Thalia, waiting for the silent reaction he expected but did not presume to count upon.

She shot him a brief "no."

"We'll see this one out," Dreyfus said. "And as much I'd like to secure someone, I won't split up the evacuees just for the sake of saving two necks in that runabout. All or nothing, Pasinler. Detach the dead mass."

Moriyama and Meppel had moved forward to join them, picking up on the end of the exchange. "We'll lay down a cordon upstream of the lock, if we're able," Moriyama said. "That'll give you time to shake loose and secure the evacuees."

"You can't go out there!" Thalia said.

Moriyama raised a gauntleted hand. "This isn't a death wish, just the last line. Once you're clear, we can traverse vacuum before you complete your departure. Hold off as close as you dare, but don't take any chances with the Clockmaker."

"We'll self-destruct rather than risk carrying it beyond Carcasstown," Dreyfus promised. "Good luck in there, both of you."

"Make it count," Moriyama said.

Meppel worked the nose lock. One blessing: there was no press of people on the other side, just a stretch of empty corridor reaching away into darkness. Moriyama and Meppel exited and the lock resealed, with two visual feeds from their goggles appearing adjacent to it. Dreyfus and Thalia studied these feeds as the other two prefects worked their way back up the shaft, retracing the path Thalia had followed barely an hour earlier.

"Runabout is detached," Pasinler said, hands on the twin precision manoeuvring joysticks. "Secure for forced departure."

"Execute," Dreyfus said.

Thrusters popped. The corvette jerked back sharply, before ramming to a sudden halt. Pasinler worked the thrusters again. Another jolt, more powerful than the first. An alarm began to sound, Pasinler cuffing it into silence almost instantly.

Dreyfus called through to the evacuees, raising his voice over their cries and demands. "Calm yourselves. We're attempting to break free of Carcasstown. If we don't, a few bruises will be the least of your problems."

Moriyama's voice was as ragged as the visual feed. "Laying down a fixed cordon at thirty metres, dual whiphounds."

The prefects each tossed one of their whiphounds into the depths of the shaft. The whiphounds set up a full-height and full-width barricade, filaments blurring into a flickering surface. The barrier was a smoky drum skin, hints of the shaft peeking through it.

Pasinler tried again. Something gave, the ship drifting back a metre or two before some obstruction snagged it.

"More!" Dreyfus said. "Damage the corvette if you have to, but get us clear."

With the barricade set, Moriyama and Meppel had moved about fifteen metres closer to the corvette. They each had one whiphound remaining, held like a baton with the filament retracted. Moriyama was perched on one side of the shaft, Meppel on the other, secured by the adhesive patches on their knees and elbows. They were anticipating decompression.

Pasinler gave it another go. Once again there was a moment of freefall that almost convinced Dreyfus that they had slipped free, before the corvette jolted hard.

"Damn this!" Pasinler said. "Disabling all safety limits. This will either break us or free us."

"Visual on the Clockmaker," Meppel said urgently. "Three...four ambulatory machines, approaching at speed. Hell, it's fast!"

Dreyfus saw it too. The Clockmaker's component bodies burst from the shaft's dark depths, a flailing of limbs propelling them closer. They moved like gibbons, with an effortless, gliding momentum. Dreyfus tensed as the first of these anvil-headed arrivals met the flicker of the whiphound cordon. Instantly the body broke up, shredded into dozens of twinkling, gyring parts. The cordon held. Two more Clockmakers propelled themselves into that blurred membrane, and they also exploded into a chrome-coloured slurry of mangled, severed components, tumbling like asteroids after some primordial smash.

"Cordon holding," Moriyama reported. "Eighty per cent effectiveness."

The dual whiphounds had suffered damage, but not catastrophic levels.

A fourth Clockmaker flung itself into the threshing boundary. It emerged, more of it coming through in one piece, but it was lopsided and limbless. It drifted, trailed by the smaller parts of itself.

Pasinler jerked the corvette back. Something strained...and yielded. They were weightless, but still drifting, inching clear of Carcasstown. The emergency alarms blurted again, indicating damage and the risk of greater harm. The corvette had wrenched itself loose, but was turning slowly, so that the docking port came into view on the starboard side, visible through one of the fixed observation windows. Air was fountaining out of it, a dirty grey cone flecked with debris.

"Retreat to twenty metres and stand off," Dreyfus said. "Moriyama, Meppel, can you see a clear path through the lock? We're ready for you."

"Negative, sir," came back the thready reply. "There are more coming. Cordon at sixty per cent and falling. Setting whiphounds to minimum delay."

She meant the two remaining whiphounds they were still carrying: locking in the five-second fuse.

"Toss them and get out of there!" Thalia shouted, her voice breaking from the strain and fatigue.

"Negative. We'll hold until the cordon is breached. It's the only way."

A cold clarity settled upon Dreyfus. He understood what Moriyama and Meppel intended, and why it was necessary. If they released their whiphounds too soon, they would explode before the next wave of machines were through the cordon, achieving nothing. It was at best a delaying action, but the prefects knew it was the only way they could hope to safeguard the corvette. Although it had detached from Carcasstown, it was not beyond the reach of fast, ruthless machines that functioned as well in vacuum as they did in air.

"Six...seven more units," Meppel croaked, her voice rasping in and out of sense as the signal degraded. "More behind them. Dozens more. Oh, Voi. There's too many!"

The feeds showed the machines sparking against the cordon, sacrificing parts of themselves in the process, but weight of numbers beginning to outweigh the destruction. One broke through, missing only two limbs this time. It moved ponderously, but it was still coming.

"Cordon at twenty..." Moriyama broke off. "Pull away without us, corvette."

Pasinler glanced at Dreyfus.

Dreyfus nodded back. There was nothing to be done now. Moriyama and Meppel had already selected their fates, selflessly and without hesitation. Even if they timed the explosions perfectly, five seconds was still too long to make it to safety. They might take out a handful of the machines, stemming the flow, but there was no way they were saving themselves.

They knew it, too.

Pasinler straightened out the corvette and crept away between the floating forms of the half-repaired or dismantled ships. A white light pulsed silently from the ruined lock: one or both whiphounds going up. The yield was small, but that was the trade-off: if the whiphounds had been set to produce a larger blast, they would have needed a longer delay on the fuses.

"Lock weapons onto that area," Dreyfus said. "Destroy anything that isn't human."

He was right to issue that command. Through the howling mouth of the damaged lock, still belching air, came the rest of the Clockmaker units. Some were damaged, some grievously so, but far too many were intact. They had broken through completely, and the explosions had been either too late or insufficient.

The corvette found clear space, emerging through the circular hole in the hub. Pasinler swung its tail around and put them on main drive, easily outpacing the machines. Rear-facing ordnance unpacked. Guns snored, stopped, snored again, over and over, methodically and unhurriedly selecting and eliminating each tumbling target.

Nothing resembling a person, much less a pair of prefects in tactical armour, troubled the corvette's threat-discrimination algorithms.

They had put twenty kilometres between the corvette and Carcasstown when Abacus finally went up. A white flash, there and gone, and about four-fifths of the station destroyed instantly, leaving only a small segment of the opposite part of the rim, tumbling away, spiralling out gases and debris. The computer's demise was undoubtedly the triggering event for that destruction, but Dreyfus was prepared to believe that some of the other commercial activities in the rim had added to the effect, in a chain reaction too rapid to detect. That might even have been part of the plan all along.

After he had conferred with Jane Aumonier and satisfied himself that the necessary containment measures were in place, with cutters, corvettes and cruisers moving in to sweep the expanding volume of space around the former station—both to identify and rescue survivors, but mainly to neutralise any surviving elements of the Clockmaker—Dreyfus went back to the open coffin of the surgical suite, where he had insisted Thalia get treatment. He eyed her with a mixture of anxiety and relief. Anxiety that she had been hurt while trying to protect him, and with the sort of injury that could easily have been much, much worse, but for an accident of milliseconds. Relief that she was alive, despite the wounds. He wondered how closely his feelings would have aligned with those of Jason Ng, if her father had been there to meet his daughter, with the same pride and concern.

"It was a ruse," he explained softly. "A clever trick by Aurora, at our expense, but directed against the Clockmaker. She lured her adversary into Carcasstown and destroyed him, but she's still out there, undiminished." Dreyfus found the strength for a fatalistic smile. "She won, in the end. She got everything she wanted, and at no cost to herself."

Thalia groaned as the surgical suite's manipulators prodded around her injury. "And this time we haven't got another rogue artificial intelligence we can throw against her."

"You could say it worked, for a while."

"What do you think happens now? She can do what she likes with all of us."

"She's limitless," Dreyfus admitted. "And terrified. Years ago she got a glimpse of something dark, lying in the future. A catastrophe that would swallow her unless she gained complete control of her destiny around Yellowstone."

"Do people figure in that destiny?"

"While we're useful to her. She relies on human hands and minds to keep the Glitter Band functioning: maintaining the infrastructure of machines and networks she needs to exist. She'll be looking for a way to supplant us, though. She needs us, but she doesn't *want* us. And she'll permit no action that threatens her position."

"Isn't there a part of her that still feels an attachment to us?"

"You were a blastocyte once," Dreyfus reminded her. "Do you feel much kinship with blastocytes?"

"There must be something. Look, we're still here, aren't we? And the Glitter Band's still out there. Pasinler's been monitoring normal comms traffic since we departed. Granted, people are spooked...but all the usual distractions are still playing out."

"You're wondering if just *being* might be enough for her? That she might be content to let the mice play, looking down on us from her lofty vantage?"

"It's a hope," Thalia said, the conviction already fading.

"I know what she is," Dreyfus answered. "I've seen the cruel streak in her. It's the one piece of humanity I wish she'd had the good grace to leave behind."

He left the surgical suite to continue tending to Thalia, then pushed forward through the melee of evacuees until he reached Pasinler's piloting position.

"Have you heard anything about my cutter?"

"Thyssen just picked it up on automated approach, sir, three aboard and healthy. They couldn't track it until now: it must have been close enough to the blast to damage its transponder."

"Good, good." He permitted himself a moment of private satisfaction. "Tell Thyssen to see that the occupants are well looked after until I arrive."

"We'll be there shortly, sir."

"No, we won't."

Pasinler glanced at him, irritation kept narrowly in check. "We won't?"

"I need a small detour. Do you have visual on one of our network routers or traffic-control beacons?"

Pasinler sketched a hand across the proximity display, clotted with moving objects both large and small, each with its own annotation. "Take your pick."

"Find me somewhere that's unoccupied, not too far off our course, and which has a good chance of having basic life-support facilities. I know these units are automated, but some of them come with pressurised refuges. All I need is enough air and heat to keep a couple of people alive for about half an hour."

Pasinler tapped a finger against one of the smaller bodies. "CTC Router GX7-3, should fit your needs."

"I'll take it. Rely on visual flight rules and maintain a fully manual approach. I want you to ignore any conflicting data that appears between now and our arrival, no matter how persuasive it seems."

"What are you expecting?"

"I'm just playing safe," Dreyfus answered.

He moved back to Thalia. She was asleep, nursed to unconsciousness by the surgical suite. He would need to wake her before too long, but after what she had been through, a little rest was the least she deserved.

CHAPTER THIRTY-FIVE

CTC Router GX7-3 was a ball of wrinkled rock the size of his outstretched thumb-tip. Thronging with antennae, it resembled the highly magnified image of a virus, bristling with hyperadapted spike proteins.

"I could get you there a lot quicker," Pasinler commented. "Though I've a feeling our passengers wouldn't appreciate too spirited a braking manoeuvre."

"Bring us in gently," Dreyfus replied, scraping the bottom of his empathy reservoir. "I've not exactly won them over by announcing an unscheduled delay to our arrival at Panoply."

"And the reason for this stopover?"

Dreyfus owed Pasinler the truth, or as much of it as he could risk. "I need a totally secure environment, somewhere Ng and I can consult sensitive material."

"Who don't you trust? Me or the passengers?"

Dreyfus hoped the question was meant flippantly. "Until I can be sure Breno was working alone, I can't rely on the integrity of the security measures inside Panoply. Or this ship, for that matter. A dead room is the next best thing."

"The router isn't dead," Pasinler pointed out. "By definition."

Dreyfus nodded. "But it soon will be. Once you have the range, take out the communications devices on the outside of the rock. I want it severed from the network, unable to relay information in any fashion."

"I can do that, but I can't guarantee I'll leave you with any light or power."

"As long as you leave a pressure-tight enclosure, we'll manage."

Pasinler sniped away at the router with the corvette's lighter armaments, lifting dust and debris from the surface, circling around to make sure the job was thorough and testing the effects by pinging standard Panoply diagnostic packets at the damaged object.

When the router remained mute, Pasinler said to Dreyfus: "That's the best I can guarantee, short of destroying it completely. Watch out for stray debris on your way inside."

Dreyfus examined the smouldering ruin, waiting for the rubble cloud to dissipate sufficiently that he gained sight of the airlock with its access to the pressurised compartments excavated into the rock.

"That'll do."

Dreyfus returned to the surgical suite, guilty about waking Thalia but certain that she would have resented any other arrangement.

He waited for the machine to rouse her to consciousness, anticipating her confusion.

"Are we docking at Panoply, sir?"

"Not just yet." He nodded down at her. "Do you think you can manage a hardsuit, with that injury still fresh?"

Thalia pinched aside grogginess as if she were peeling layers of cobweb from herself. "I'll wear whatever it takes, sir."

Dreyfus outfitted himself, leaving only the helmet to be attached, then assisted Thalia with her own set of equipment.

He asked her to show him the evidential package, barely surprised by the blackened, slag-like object that she disclosed from the corvette's locker. He stared at it numbly for a few seconds, something inside him finally registering the truth he would much rather have denied. It was like a bolt sliding home, latching with some dark finality, a thing that could never be undone.

"Have you ever handled something like this?" he asked.

"No, and I'm not sure I'd know the protocol without talking to someone at senior level."

"It's not complicated." Dreyfus unclipped a whiphound from the corvette's armaments rack. He activated it with a twist of the control dial and asked the whiphound to affirm that he had full authority over its functions.

The whiphound flashed its compliance. He clipped it to the suit.

"Should I bring one?" Thalia asked, sliding the remains of Sparver and his suit into an elastic pouch tucked under the bulge of her chest armour.

"I'm not expecting trouble." Dreyfus dropped his helmet into place, locked it and waited for Thalia to do likewise. They verified that their suits had established short-range comms handshakes, independent of the signals environment of the corvette.

They went to the suitwall, waiting on the pressurised side of it until Pasinler had brought the corvette to within leaping distance of a corresponding lock on the face of the rock. The lock had weathered the onslaught with no visible damage, testifying to Pasinler's skill with weapons.

"Retreat to a safe distance and hold station," Dreyfus told Pasinler. "If we're not back within thirty minutes, head straight for Panoply with the evacuees. They're the priority. You can always send a launch to find us later."

Dreyfus and Thalia passed through the clammy membrane of the suitwall, its edge lapping against their suits but providing only feeble resistance until they popped out into vacuum. Thalia cupped her hands around the bulge of her belly-pouch, making sure the black husk was still secured.

They drifted across the intervening space. Although the main cloud had thinned out and dispersed, the rock was still erupting and outgassing from the impact sites, vomiting out gritty spumes of gas and crust material. Their suits' proximity alarms kept going off, and the thrusters did their best to steer clear of the largest pieces of debris. Dreyfus still felt thuds and shudders as his suit absorbed the impacts that could not be avoided.

Dreyfus selected a rear view on his visor and watched the corvette flash its precision thrusters, moving further away from the rock. They would have further to cross on the way out, but Pasinler could always track and locate them if they drifted off course.

Something clipped him hard, sending him spinning. His suit corrected, but a warning icon now pulsed hard across his visual field. *Partial compromise of motive assist. Quickmatter repair processes instigated. Optimum functionality will not be regained for twenty minutes.*

He wrestled his arms and legs in the suit. Sluggish, but he could still do everything he needed.

"Are you all right, sir?"

"Nothing that'll slow me down, Thal." His words snagged on an unexpected silence. "Thal?"

"I'm back," she said, voice gravelly with interference. "Took a hit to my helmet. Comms dropped and recovering. I'm good, but I only have a partial feed on my visor display. Am I still headed in the right direction?"

"Yes, you're on target. You should be feet down in about five seconds."

"Adhesive grapples pre-armed. Here I go . . ." She grunted, hitting hard, buckling at the knees. The tethers flung out from her hip and wrists, securing Thalia to the rock before she rebounded back into space.

Dreyfus touched down a metre from her. He grappled, then released all but the hip tethers. He swept a hand across the blank visage of her helmet.

"Do you see me?"

"Wait a moment. I'm switching to transparency." A soft-edged portion of the front of her helmet de-opaqued, her face floating behind a layer of foggy glass. Thalia blinked against the brightness. Epsilon Eridani was behind Yellowstone, but the scattered light of the Glitter Band would still have been dazzling. "Glare shade isn't cutting in, sir. I doubt I'd be much use in a fight."

"It'll be better inside," Dreyfus said.

He guided her into the dock, their tethers retracting as they committed to entry. They both fitted, but with scarcely any room to spare. Thalia touched the belly-pouch, reassuring herself that the precious cargo was still safe.

"That was worse than I expected, sir. If we'd been wearing m-suits, we'd have been shredded alive. It was the right decision not to use them. That *was* the reason, wasn't it?"

Dreyfus said nothing.

The lock was old, rugged and cooperative. They huddled inside as the outer door closed and air flooded in from reservoirs. Dreyfus eyed the ambient sensors on his own visor overlay, glad to see that the air was building up to normal pressure and with tolerable gas ratios.

He glared at the inner door until it opened, low-level lights and systems displays coming on in a room only a little larger than the lock itself. They drifted inside, orientating themselves until they were facing each other, squatting in near-weightlessness on what would have been the floor, had the rock possessed any significant pull.

Dreyfus undid his helmet, setting it down next to him. Thalia did the same, masking a wince as she moved her arms. She took in a breath of air, then gasped at the coldness. Dreyfus nodded, sharing her reaction. His lungs felt as if someone had shoved a sack of ice down his windpipe.

"I'm afraid luxury wasn't on the agenda when they designed these places. With luck, we won't be here long enough to freeze." Dreyfus leaned past Thalia to reach a fold-out console, tapping his way through sub-menus until he found the list of executive privileges. Although the router was not Panoply property, it fell firmly within the organisation's sphere of responsibility. As with any similar facility, there were deliberate backdoors to allow Panoply to usurp some or all of the functions, temporarily or permanently.

"Nettles..." he began, typing cautiously.

"Wave Under," Thalia finished for him.

"Thank you. Just testing your preparedness."

"Of course, sir."

Panoply's executive access codes were refreshed on a three-month basis, but in recent years he had become lax at committing them to immediate recall. This failing nagged at him in the small hours, but he never did anything about it while awake.

Dreyfus unclipped the whiphound, turned on its torch function and handed it to Thalia.

"I'm about to shut down all power, including life support. Be ready to put your helmet on again if there's a pressure drop."

Dreyfus completed the command sequence, waiting in suspense as the systems continued functioning for several seconds, until with a hard mechanical thud everything went dead and silent, save for their own breathing and the quiet chug of their own suits.

"Now we turn off all suit functions," Dreyfus said. "All the way down, nothing to chance."

They tapped the commands into their sleeve panels, disabling every single mechanical and cybernetic component in their equipment, including all quickmatter repair processes. The suits complied, becoming instantly silent and heavier. Now their occupants' every movement, no matter how slight, became both more sluggish and more costly of effort.

The suits' system readouts, status lights and recognition markers had all gone dark. The only source of light in the room was the whiphound, pinning Dreyfus and Thalia within a cone of yellow. The boundaries of the chamber had receded, as if they now floated in a much larger void, filled with air turning staler with each pained breath.

"You may wonder why we need this level of precaution," Dreyfus said.

"I assume you have your reasons." Ghosts of breath haunted the space beyond her lips. "I don't like to say it, but there must be people you don't necessarily trust, high in the organisation."

"I trust most of them. Aumonier certainly. The other seniors, very little reason to doubt." He paused. "What I can't trust is Panoply itself. It's been compromised, infiltrated at a high level by Aurora."

Thalia nodded gravely. "I'm...alarmed, but not really shocked, after everything that's gone on today. Once she broke free of the Clockmaker, she could direct her energies wherever she liked, including breaching our own logical defences."

"She didn't breach them," Dreyfus contradicted gently. "I let her in. Years ago, and knowing full well what I was doing."

A frown pressed into her forehead. "Sir? I don't understand."

"I'm the one who gave her access. The Search Turbines, primarily, but from there I don't doubt that she was able to extend her snooping into many other areas of Panoply."

Thalia mouthed: "Why?"

"We struck a bargain. She supplied a critical lead on the Wildfire emergency, helping us avert the crisis, in return for my allowing her access to our records on the Clockmaker."

"You wouldn't have done that, sir," Thalia asserted, as if he had to be mistaken, misremembering his own past.

Dreyfus prepared his answer. "I did it. People were dying and I saw no other way. It was not my intention to weaken us, or endanger the greater security of the Glitter Band. My calculation was that access to our systems wouldn't greatly increase her power. We knew less about the Clockmaker than she thought we did. I believed that the bargain was worth striking; that at the end of the day, saving lives in the here and now mattered more than some abstract fears about one machine intelligence triumphing over another in the future." He shrugged inside the iron coffin of his suit. "I even allowed myself to think the Clockmaker had run rings around both of us, outfoxing Aurora even as she thought she had the upper hand. Back to the same old stalemate, my crime neutralised. Years passed and Aurora and the Clockmaker seemed equally balanced again. Until Catopsis upset everything."

"Catopsis failed."

"I made it fail." He nodded, reinforcing his culpability. "It was me, Thal. Aurora alerted me to the threat against herself—the threat against that stalemate. I couldn't expose Catopsis directly, not without too many questions being asked about my connection to Aurora. But I could drip-feed enough clues to Ingvar to make her pick up the investigation and run with it."

Again, that frown. "That was the original investigation, though—the one from four years ago, not the one that got Tench killed."

"I still instigated it. I put her into a position where working inside Panoply was untenable, hence her shift to fieldwork—where you were her mentor."

Thalia swallowed. "And after? Did you drive her to reinvestigate the case?"

"No," Dreyfus answered. But he searched her eyes for signs that she believed him, wholeheartedly and without question, and did not find the assurance he sought.

Understandably.

"But you're still to blame, in some way."

"I am. She was only doing what came naturally to her: refusing to let something go. I should have known that she wouldn't rest, and that it might put her in harm's way."

"I know that you'd never act against Panoply, unless there was no choice."

"There's always a choice. We don't always see it clearly in the moment, but there's always a choice."

Thalia was silent, shivering slightly within her suit. "Why are you telling me this, sir?"

"Because someone else needs to know. I don't know what's going to happen to us now, but I do know that I've carried this alone for too long. I can't go on being the only one who knows. She's been using me, Thal."

"Using you? You mean blackmail?"

"Aurora also has her claws into Valery, making her suffer if I don't do what she wants."

Thalia had the look of someone about to open a box of horrors.

"And what has she wanted?"

"There's how it was put to me, and how it actually played out. After Ingvar's death, Aurora led me to think she'd become aware of the nature of Ingvar's investigation. She wanted me to continue it: to identify the location of the revived Catopsis and shut it down, to save her own skin and preserve the equilibrium between her and the Clockmaker." Dreyfus sniffed, a cold icicle forming on the end of his nose. "That was a ruse, though. She already knew exactly where the operation was happening, because she'd been the one making it happen."

Thalia nodded her understanding. "To trap the Clockmaker."

"I was just there to bask in her glory: to bear witness to her finest hour. My entire investigation was a charade. There was no need for me to retrace Ingvar's movements. Aurora could have led me to Carcasstown directly."

"But that would have been too easy. You'd have known something was amiss."

"Yes. I had to feel as if I was investigating, turning over a stone at a time—while the whole time she was looking over my shoulder, coaxing me on, until she finally led me to Carcasstown."

Thalia leaned in. "Did she kill Ingvar?"

"Not directly. Ingvar's thoroughness meant that she got too close to exposing Carcasstown, and the operatives there decided to get rid of her. They tried once, killed Mizler by mistake, and then came back for a second go at Ingvar. It doesn't excuse what they did, but they were sincere in their belief that they were going to snare both intelligences. They didn't know Aurora was running the show."

"Then she *is* responsible for Ingvar's death," Thalia insisted. "And Sparver's—"

"Not Sparver," Dreyfus said quietly, as if there were still a faint chance of their being overhead. "That's the part that doesn't fit."

"I don't follow."

"Aurora didn't orchestrate his death. It had no connection with the elements behind Catopsis, either." Dreyfus stared at his colleague. "It was

something else, Thal. Something she didn't do, doesn't understand and can't explain."

"She told you this?"

He understood her scepticism. "She could lie to my face and I wouldn't know it. Here's the thing, though: she can't hide her ego. It's monstrous and it won't be denied, but nor will it let her take credit for an act that wasn't hers, and which doesn't fit into any of her plans. She didn't kill Sparver. Something *else* did, and that's why we're here." He paused and indicated the dark mass of the recording, faintly outlined by the glow from the whiphound. "Inside there is something Sparver thought was vital enough to die for. He understood the parameters of our investigation and how it connected to Aurora, even if he didn't know she was behind Catopsis all along. I trust his judgement. He learned something and he wanted us to learn it as well. Something I think Aurora doesn't know."

"All right," Thalia said, her mouth creasing as she half-followed. "But Asset 227...it *was* part of Ingvar's investigation, wasn't it? So even if it wasn't the location of Catopsis, she must have considered it a plausible candidate?"

"That's what I thought."

"And?"

"I'm beginning to think I was wrong. It's something else Ingvar was interested in—which Sparver badly needed us to know about. Something we can learn here and continue to keep from Aurora." Dreyfus addressed the whiphound. "Confirm recognition of an evidential cache within your sphere of detection."

The whiphound blinked confirmation.

"Can the cache be accessed and read?"

The whiphound blinked again.

"Prepare an audiovisual playback of all compatible traces from the adjacent unit, in timestamp order starting five minutes prior to the final entry. Play back but do not store this information. Confirm that you understand this instruction."

The whiphound blinked.

"Commence," Dreyfus said.

The whiphound's cone sharpened to a fidgety projecting beam, throwing moving patterns of coloured light onto the ceiling. A scratchy, breathless soundtrack accompanied the visual playback. It was Sparver, talking to himself.

"Another of those shows up, try to give me a *little* more warning."

Dreyfus tensed at his friend's voice. Thalia met his eyes, a wordless parcel of grief, loss and anger passing between them.

From the visual feed, replicating the view Sparver would have had from his suit, it was clear that there had just been some sort of altercation with a security robot. The machine lay in broken and severed pieces, weapons muzzles still smoking, holes blown in surrounding walls, floor and ceiling.

Sparver was rolling his whiphound in his gauntlet, checking it for functionality.

"Where was this?" Thalia whispered.

"The sub-levels of a structure he found in Asset 227: some kind of large private mansion. He knew the missiles were coming and he was trying to find his way out through an exit shaft in the basement."

The view pitched around, Sparver's attention drawn to one of the holes punched into the structure. He had noticed a hollow space beyond it, instead of the scabby bedrock exposed by the other damage sites.

He peered deeper in, his suit light delineating ranks of curious mannequins: upright, fully clothed bodies stretching away down the length of the hidden chamber in two opposed rows.

Sparver used his suit to enlarge the opening. Although he employed amplification, the wall flaked away readily, as if it had never been more than a flimsy partition. He created a gap large enough to admit his suit and stepped through the ragged doorway, walking to the nearest of the mannequins. Each was shrouded by a tubular transparent enclosure with a domed top, with a grey pedestal at the base.

"Like dolls still in their wrapping," Dreyfus remarked.

A new voice burst in on the recording: Dreyfus himself, communicating with Sparver. A quick exchange as they established that Sparver had no more than three minutes to make use of the escape shaft he had already identified.

Dreyfus bristled at the sound of himself. He had mentally replayed the conversation many times, relying on his memory of events. Now that he was confronted by the recording he sounded brusquer, snappily impatient with Sparver.

Sparver's visual feed tracked along the ranks of mannequins. Inside each glass container was a different human form, covering a spectrum of genders and ages.

While Dreyfus argued for Sparver to leave—the margin down to two minutes—Sparver was speaking aloud, working an idea through with Dreyfus as his audience.

His idea, based on the other things he had already seen in the mansion: Tench had gone out of her way to obscure the identities of anyone or anything that might be connected to the mansion. She had vandalised statues and paintings, and erased the faces of the robot mannequins she

had encountered in the upper levels: the main rooms, parlours and hall-ways of the mansion, not the spartan sub-levels where Sparver now found himself.

Not because she was in the grip of a spree of manic destruction for destruction's sake, but because there was a truth here which Tench wished to conceal.

Or protect from the wrong eyes.

But she had missed this one room, behind its hidden partition. And now Sparver was intent on using the time remaining to him to document its contents, because he believed in Ingvar Tench, her instincts and her judgement. What she had seen in this mansion was of vital importance. It had to be documented, preserved for the right witnesses.

Now Dreyfus watched the parade of faces behind glass, even as he heard his own voice buzzing from the past, making one last bid to persuade Sparver to save his own life, now he understood why Sparver had declined.

The recording played itself out. The whiphound's projection stuttered to whiteness.

Whiteness and silence.

CHAPTER THIRTY-SIX

The cold was eating into their bones, the air musty with their own exhaled gases, each new breath slowly murdering their minds.

They could not leave immediately.

"You recognised those faces, sir," Thalia said, observing Dreyfus with a peculiar stillness, as if she had passed through the cross-currents of shivering into some treacherous calm beyond.

"I did. I've seen them in the public records, as well as our own files. Anyone with the slightest interest in the history of the Eighty would have made the same connection."

"My cases have never involved the Eighty, sir," Thalia reminded him.

"The Nerval-Lermontov family," Dreyfus said. "It was their faces on those mannequins. Enough of them, anyway. The others, I'm guessing, were figures close to the family. Household employees, relatives, close business associate. Childhood companions."

"Aurora's family. The ones who decided to have her scanned and uploaded as part of the Eighty." Thalia frowned: either a headache due to the bad air or her own confusion. "Why are there mannequins of them inside a mansion inside a rock we'd never heard about?"

"That's an extremely good question."

"Do we have a theory?"

"Ingvar did," Dreyfus said. "She believed that she knew what it meant and why it had to be concealed. She couldn't just blow it up, so she had to make repeated visits, concealing a little more of the connection each time. Not from us, but from Aurora. That's why it was in our list of places to visit: not because of Catopsis, but because it interested her for another reason."

"What would have led Ingvar there?"

"Her doggedness. Her interest in Catopsis must have led her to a deeper enquiry into the origins of Aurora . . . and ultimately the Nerval-Lermontov estate. She must have examined their assets, the chains of shell companies

and mirrors, until her usual thoroughness led there. Tench being Tench, she looked inside."

"And found mannequins." Thalia shook her head, unsatisfied. "Why would she lift a finger to protect any of that, sir? So the family got up to something shady in Asset 227. That's not our concern—and we've certainly got no reason to help them cover up their misdeeds."

"I agree. She had no reason to act in the interest of the Nerval-Lermontovs. Which means she was protecting something else." Dreyfus was silent for a moment. "Or someone."

"Someone?" She stared at him. "Who are you thinking of? Not Hafdis, surely?"

"There's no one else that seems to have mattered to her as much as Hafdis."

"Let me get this straight, while we can still talk freely. You're saying that this empty mansion full of mannequins which Sparver found has some connection to Hafdis?"

Dreyfus felt like a man stumbling along a darkened path, seeing only the barest distance beyond his own faltering steps. Nothing had prepared him for this connection between Aurora and Hafdis which Sparver had found, but now that it was there, he accepted it wholeheartedly. The rock in which his friend had died was a Nerval-Lermontov asset, and if his reading of her was correct, Aurora didn't know about it.

"There's only one reason I can think of that a family like that would go to the trouble of creating that chateau and filling it with lookalike robots."

"Please enlighten me," Thalia said.

"It must have been a set of surrogate surroundings, designed to mimic reality. I can't check now, and I'm not about to when we get to Panoply, but my guess is that Sparver's recordings of that mansion will bear a very strong resemblance to the real Nerval-Lermontov household, as it was half a century or so ago. It'll be a painstaking copy, accurate in every essential detail."

"Because...?"

"Because they got scared. They'd committed to having their beloved daughter's mind scanned and uploaded via an experimental process, one that offered the promise of immortality, but with the very real downside that her mortal body wouldn't survive. They were willing to take that chance, for the glory and the prestige. But they wanted an insurance policy."

Thalia picked up the thread of his reasoning and followed. "Create a duplicate of Aurora, as a backup. A copy in case the scanning process didn't work out. A...clone, I suppose. Was that even legal?"

"Not then, and not now. But they'd have had ways and means. It had to be kept totally secret, of course, from the authorities, and from the real Aurora. They wouldn't want her to know that she was no more than an expendable prototype, ready to be cast into the fires, with a stand-in waiting in the wings if things didn't work out."

"Then she didn't know about the clone before the scanning process..."

"And she'd have remained ignorant after the fact, if the family did a good enough job of protecting its secret. Which, evidently, it did. Until Ingvar Tench found it."

"A human, unearthing a secret that even Aurora couldn't uncover?"

"It makes perfect sense to me. Aurora was keen to keep as much distance as possible from her human origins. She not only didn't know the full story, she had no interest in looking for loose ends. And even if she had...there's a limit to her omniscience. Tench and Sparver had to go inside that rock to find the truth of it."

"The rock ended up killing Sparver, sir. Do you think Tench set that up to happen?"

"No. We'll never know for certain, but it's much more likely that Sparver triggered a self-destruct system put in place by the Nerval-Lermontovs, in the interests of avoiding too much outside scrutiny."

"Tench was there before him, though."

"Unlike Sparver, though, she already had an inkling she was tangling with a dangerous, powerful family legacy. She may have been more careful, aware of that tripwire, or just luckier. Either way, she was able to get in and out on more than one occasion, doing only as much damage as she needed to in order to hide the connection to Aurora and whoever was meant to grow up in that place."

Thalia brooded. Dreyfus waited, pleased that he had found the outline of an explanation for Sparver's recordings, even if the implications of that theory remained uncertain, prickling with disquiet.

"If you're thinking Hafdis is somehow the copy, sir..." Thalia stopped, leaving him to finish the thought.

"No, that doesn't work," Dreyfus said, the stumbling path all but obscured again. "Because we didn't just take Tench's word that Hafdis was her daughter. I was there when Lillian Baudry took a sample from Hafdis and ran a match on it."

"I didn't mean to shoot the theory down in flames, sir."

"It's good that you did. But we still need to know why Tench tried to protect that secret. And Hafdis..." He trailed off, fighting a gathering fog at the edge of his concentration. "Something still doesn't add up, Thal. I just can't quite see it."

Thalia looked at the blackened husk that was all that had been preserved of Sparver.

"What about the rest of it, sir, aside from the last three minutes? We
owe it to Sparver to preserve his testimony."

"It'll be read out and archived when we're safe from prying eyes." Sensing her fears, he added: "When, not if. There's a way through this, and
we'll find it." He shut down the whiphound, satisfied that it would retain
no memory of the playback or their conversation, and began powering
his suit back up again, issuing permission for the repair processes to
recommence.

Thalia mirrored him, dabbing commands into her sleeve matrix. "What
now, sir?"

"We return to the corvette. We say nothing of what we've seen or discussed in this room, not even to Pasinler. You and I know something
about Aurora that she doesn't, and I'd like to keep it that way until we can
use that information against her."

Thalia scooped up the husk and tucked it into her utility pouch.

"I don't know how we'd begin to do that."

"Nor do I." He dredged up a smile. "Something will come along, though.
It generally does."

Dreyfus returned to suit air, gulping down the fresh flow until he felt
his headache lighten and his thoughts come more easily. A few million
expired brain cells was a price well worth paying for Sparver's information. He would miss them a lot less than he missed not living under a
tyrannical machine.

They returned to suit comms and Dreyfus restored power and light to
the room, not because they needed either to survive, but because it would
make their egress much more straightforward.

"Is your suit still malfunctioning?"

"Nothing I can't manage until we're back inside the ship, sir."

"Good. I'll lead you."

Thalia had one more thing to say, though, before they passed back
through the lock and fell back within range of the corvette and the Glitter
Band's wider communications network.

"You had to tell me about Aurora, sir, and how you helped her get into
our systems. I understand that."

"I assumed you would."

"I can't forget it, though—not something that serious. Then again, I
don't think you were counting on my forgetting it."

"I wasn't," Dreyfus said.

The outer lock opened. Dreyfus eased himself out, his suit still cumbersome with its motor functions not working properly. He offered a hand to Thalia and let her follow him.

Dreyfus emerged into open space, ready to sight onto the distant objective of the corvette and spring off in something like the right direction.

But the corvette was right over him, angled like a striking eagle.

"Damnation, Pasinler! I told you to retreat to a safe distance! You've got live refugees to think about!"

A face rippled into existence before him, interposed between Dreyfus and the rock.

"Don't blame Pasinler. There was nothing he could do about me."

The coldness of the room was still in his bones. "You've won," Dreyfus said, accepting the inevitable with only a flicker of surprise. "Congratulations. I wondered when the gloating would begin."

"I haven't come to gloat. I'm close to victory, but I'm not there yet." Her face, transparent enough that he could see right through it to the threatening form of the corvette, and her voice drilled into his head.

Dreyfus maintained his hold on Thalia. "What's stopping you?"

"What were you doing in there, Dreyfus? I'd very much like to know. You went to some lengths to make yourself inscrutable to me and I don't like that at all."

"I'm sorry you feel that way."

"I know Ng's carrying an evidential device, the kind left behind after the activation of your Vienna Protocol."

"It seems like you already know quite enough."

"Now that I know it exists, I very much want to know what's inside that artefact."

"So read it."

"I can't, not remotely. You'll surrender it to me, or save us both the bother and tell me what it contained. What was so important that you went to these lengths?"

Dreyfus and Thalia were standing now, their faces angled up at the foreshortened prow of the corvette. It looked very much like a raptor's flesh-tearing beak. The weapons ports were open, promising dark annihilation.

"It's all right," he said to Thalia. "She won't risk attacking you while we're together. Not when she's so keen to keep me alive as a witness to her brilliance."

Thalia's tone offered a verdict on that thin reassurance. "I guess that depends on how well she rates her control of those weapons, sir."

"She's good, but she's not a risk-taker."

"I'm not," Aurora answered. "And I'm not going to shoot either of you.

Why would I need to, when I have so many other channels for persuasion? I'm in Hospice Idlewild, hurting Valery this very instant."

Aurora's face miraged, rippling into the semblance of his wife, her features contorted in a sudden spasm of agony.

The sight of her was a knife-twist deep into his guts.

He held his nerve.

"Nice try. Only I asked Sister Catherine to make sure her implants were removed."

Valery's tormented face mocked him with his wife's voice. "Do you have evidence that she complied with this request?"

"I don't," Dreyfus admitted. "I trust that she honoured it, all the same. She's a decent woman, Sister Catherine. There's more kindness in her fingernail than in all of you. If she knew something mattered to me, she'd do it."

"You're putting a lot of faith in human nature."

He nodded in his suit. "More than you'll ever understand."

The floating face became that of Aurora again. "All right then. I'm reducing the life-support functions of the corvette. Pasinler and the refugees are already unconscious, but now I'm beginning to do some irreversible damage. Tell me what was in the recording."

"What if I decided that the lives of those people in the corvette mattered less than holding a tactical advantage over you?"

She scoffed. "I know you too well, Tom Dreyfus. You'd be lying to yourself."

"Not when I have to balance a hundred million other lives against your madness. I'm not saying I like the choice, but it's a consideration I'm willing to make."

"I can begin to do bad things to any number of habitats. Do you want to have that on your conscience?"

"I've a feeling you'll do bad things anyway."

Aurora seethed. "Your unwillingness to speak of the recording already tells me more than you realise. There's something in it that you think you might be able to use against me. Some information weapon or suchlike. Perhaps a distilled, weaponised shadow of my former adversary. Fine; I'll explore the possibilities and decide for myself what it's likely to be. Then I'll explain to you the myriad ways in which it won't work."

Thalia opened the belly-pouch. She extracted the recording.

"You want it so badly, Aurora? Then have it. We'll find another way."

She tossed the recording away, at an oblique angle to the rock's surface, so that it headed off into space without impacting the corvette.

Dreyfus stared, unmoored from everything he thought he knew about his protégée.

"Thalia? What have you just done?"

"Nothing that can't be put right again, sir." She sounded much calmer and more self-possessed than he was expecting. "If you can, go to full transparency. Turn off all your suit functions if you need to—she might still be able to fake what we're seeing even if we think we're just looking through glass."

Dreyfus took Thalia at her word. He skipped straight to the shutdown procedure, replaying the steps he had taken only a short while before. His suit went through its litany of warnings, then succumbed to his will. Comms and life support dropped out, leaving only the rasp of his own breath. His visor cleared of data, and Aurora and the corvette blinked away. The ship's real counterpart was visible now, murky through breath-fogged glass, but much more distant: still holding station just as he had instructed Pasinler to do.

He waved his arms, beckoning the corvette to move in to collect them.

He tapped the sleeve controls and powered back up, fearless for the moment.

"Well done, Thalia," he said, as soon as comms returned.

"My suit was still glitching after that impact, sir. She couldn't maintain the illusion through my damaged visor. Once I saw the real ship still out there, I guessed she didn't have that much control over it."

"Or she'd have brought it closer," Dreyfus said, marvelling at how a piece of bad fortune had corkscrewed into good, however transiently. "By now one or both of us would likely be dead, and she'd be chasing after that recording."

He restored his suit functions, and Aurora had not returned. Her gambit exposed, it appeared that she was throwing the cybernetic equivalent of a sulk.

"Do you think Pasinler and the others are all right, sir?"

"If she couldn't operate the corvette, chances are she couldn't damage life-support. She'll be trying hard to penetrate our systems, though —they're just a bit harder to crack than those bulk carriers. Whatever advantage we may have now..."

"We'd better use it while we have it."

Pasinler was alive, and so were the evacuees. The corvette was functionally intact; all Pasinler had been aware of was Dreyfus and Thalia emerging from the rock close to the stipulated thirty-minute time limit. Dreyfus wasted no time in telling Pasinler to track the recording. In fact it had only drifted a kilometre or so from their position by the time the corvette detected it.

"We can grapple, I can send out a drone, or someone can go back out through the lock and recover it."

"None of the above," Dreyfus answered. "If you've still any rounds left in those guns after the job you did on the rock, I'd like you to concentrate fire on it."

"I have rounds."

"Sir," Thalia said, wrenching off her helmet. "What about the rest of it? We've no idea what else Sparver might have seen or how significant it is."

"I know, and we'll carry that to our graves. This is the only way, though. We know she has at least partial control of our comms and information systems. Bringing the recording back aboard is too much of a gamble, as is letting it drift until she finds it. I'd rather burn that evidence than allow her a way into it."

Thalia processed his words. "I guess it did its job."

"Sparver did his, and it wasn't wasted. We're not dishonouring our friend, Thal. Anything but that. We're respecting everything that he was and everything he stood for. This is what he'd have wanted."

"On your mark," Pasinler reported.

"Do it."

The guns burped. A flash pulsed somewhere off to port, and the work of destruction was complete. There might be a shard or two of data still out there, but Aurora had next to no chance of recovering any of it, much less of grasping the whole of which it had been a part.

What mattered was in their heads—of which they could say nothing, for now.

"I suppose you'd still like to continue to Panoply?" Pasinler asked.

Dreyfus thought of Hafdis Tench, and the enigma of her identity that he had still not resolved to his satisfaction.

"I would."

CHAPTER THIRTY-SEVEN

As they returned home, Dreyfus watched the feeds with a sense of un-reality. Across the Glitter Band, nothing had really changed in the last twenty-six hours. Lives went on as if it was just another busy day around Yellowstone. The flow of human business continued, with no more than the usual jitters and recoveries in the markets. Physical commerce and civilian traffic moved between the ten thousand worlds as freely as it had ever done. Polls were tabled and tallied, information surging through the networks. The clamour of discourse was louder than usual, but it had been that way for months, with the rising pressure of the Mizler Cranach crisis.

If anything, there were tiny grounds for optimism where that particular difficulty was concerned. Following Thalia's visit to the lemurs, the local official called Minty Green Grass had issued a Band-wide public statement to the effect that the lemurs had been persuaded that the original attack on their community had not been instigated by the hyperpig Cranach.

"I thought my visit there was a disaster!" Thalia said, astonished by the news.

"It seems your earnestness won some friends after all," Dreyfus said. "They just needed a little time to come around."

It had still been a crime, Minty had been clear, but not one committed out of revenge for some past misdeed. Mizler had been innocent, the lemur asserted, and, if anything, had done all in his power to limit the severity of the attack.

"Far from repudiating him, it is our desire that his selflessness be com-memorated in some permanent fashion," Minty had declared. "And in the light of our reassessment of what happened—in no small part due to the diligence of our friend Prefect Thalia Ng—we would call on all reasonable parties to turn from the path of vengeance and recrimination. The pig community did not act against us. Those who have taken arms against pigs in some misguided notion that they were defending our honour... we must ask that they desist. And to those who have been harmed by pigs in the senseless escalation that followed...we would ask that you see

306

their actions for what they were: nothing more than the understandable, if misguided, consequences of that initial, ill-founded act of retribution. Blame need not be attributed, except to the perpetrators of that first attack against us. We who were most injured say this: we have confidence in Panoply as it seeks to shed light on that crime. And we have confidence in the good sense of pigs and humans alike, to step back from the brink."

It was a valiant effort, Dreyfus had to admit, though it was never going to put out all the fires in one go. Still, he clutched at such crumbs of hope that were tossed his way. Panoply continued to track each outbreak of the escalation, and while it was far too soon to draw any lasting conclusions, things had certainly not worsened in the last fifty-two hours. The arrests and interrogations in light of the Salter-Regent tip-off were having a moderating influence, too, with some of the louder agitators falling suddenly silent and attempting to distance themselves from the perpetrators of the atrocity at Mercy Sphere. As loyalties fractured, bad actors were almost stumbling over themselves to incriminate former friends and allies. The next few days were likely to prove critical—or rather, would have done so, if every other aspect of civilisation was not now in considerable jeopardy.

"It might seem inconsequential in the light of what we're dealing with now, Thal," Dreyfus said. "It's not. Every little bit of good matters, even more so when the lights might be going out at any moment. I have every reason to be grateful to you for getting me out of Carcasstown, no matter what Aurora says about her plans. The rest of the Glitter Band should be grateful to you for exonerating Mizler Cranach and convincing the lemurs. I know your father would have been very proud of you."

"Thank you, sir." Thalia had declined another spell in the surgical suite, content to nurse her bruises and reflect on what had happened between their leaving and returning to the corvette. She pressed a bulb of coffee into Dreyfus's hand. "Have you had that head wound looked at?"

"It can wait." Dreyfus accepted the coffee gratefully. "I've been monitoring the feeds. There's almost nothing that we wouldn't see on a normal day, whatever that is. A few concerned ripples after the destruction of Carcasstown, but nothing resembling mass panic."

"A habitat gets blown up, and no one cares?"

"If it had been a major population centre, deep in the Glitter Band, there'd be more of a reaction." He sipped, the coffee scouring the inside of his skull like some kind of steel-bristled industrial polisher, then raised his voice: "What's your take on it, Aurora? I know you're listening in. Don't be shy. We'd love to know your plans for the rest of us."

No answer came, but he did not believe for a second that his query had gone unheard.

She was here. She was everywhere.

When they were close to Panoply he abandoned the feeds, went to speak to the evacuees and briefed them on some of the security and quarantine measures they could expect upon docking. There was a certain amount of grumbling, especially when Dreyfus informed them that they were unlikely to be allowed to leave the asteroid, at least until the present emergency was concluded. He resisted being drawn into arguments with any of the evacuees who wanted firmer assurances than that.

"You're alive," he reminded them. "That's more than can be said for the people who were still in Carcasstown when you undocked. They either died being turned into human mincemeat by the Clockmaker or became a cloud of atoms when Abacus exploded. Tell me which you'd prefer to being my guest."

Their final approach was slower than he liked. Too many other Panoply ships were coming and going from the docks, creating a backlog for the bulky corvette and its specialised berthing needs. It was understandable. Ships of all classes were still making sure no elements of the Clockmaker made it across free space to another habitat. Though it had been several hours since the last reported interdiction, the net could not be relaxed too soon. There were also scattered pockets of survivors to be dealt with, people who had got out in lifepods or suits, and needed rescuing. That, on top of all the other things Panoply needed to be doing across the Glitter Band, from calming tensions between humans and pigs to the merely everyday work of prefects, which could not be paused.

Once they had docked, Dreyfus emerged from the ship and found Jane Aumonier waiting for him, her arms folded, her look expectant. Dreyfus made sure of two things: first that Thalia was taken for a proper examination, and second that his guests, willing and otherwise, would be looked after.

"I'm told Mirna Silk, Under-Supervisor Krenkel and Doctor Salazar made it aboard my cutter?"

"Yes, and you can explain how that happened when we have a spare half hour. I'm sure it'll be most illuminating. What do I need to know about the evacuees on the corvette?"

"Some of them may offer witness testimonies relating to the Clockmaker, but that's the only respect in which they are of any interest to Panoply."

"I'll see that they're made just as welcome as the other three. We're mopping up other stragglers as I speak, but I'm afraid there'll be far more casualties than survivors. You did well with these." Her look sharpened.

"What happened out there, Tom, besides the obvious? Other than routine comms, I'm in the dark."

"The Clockmaker's finished. Aurora isn't."

Aumonier nodded, gloomily unperturbed. "I figured the mood would have been a little more upbeat if we actually had something to celebrate. How bad is it?"

"I don't think we'll know until she makes a move. There are things I'd like to discuss with you in private."

"Fine, we can proceed directly to tactical, if you're sure that head of yours will keep. The other seniors are monitoring the Carcasstown clean-up, as well as the fallout from Minty's statement. Do you think Ng has earned a promotion?"

"Almost certainly." Dreyfus rubbed at his bruises, thinking also of the confession he had made to Thalia, and how it now stood between them. "I'll brief the seniors shortly. First, I need a higher degree of security than the tactical room offers. Can we meet in the cube?"

"I'll requisition immediate use. Are there any other arrangements you need?"

"Nothing for the moment. I've a feeling I could do with a wash first."

"I won't argue with that," she said, her nostrils tightening.

Dreyfus and Aumonier faced each other across the blank table in the blank-surfaced interviewing cell. It was an odd juxtaposition, almost like a formal Panoply interrogation, except that their roles were fluid, each with as many questions as the other.

Dreyfus meshed his fingers, staring down at his hands as if begging for mercy before his one god.

"Now that the Clockmaker has gone, Aurora is able to move through our information systems with almost complete impunity. She can spread herself around or concentrate herself, and our own countermeasures can't do a thing about it."

"From this precaution, I presume you have reason to think Panoply is at least partially compromised?"

"Yes, and she knows we're aware of that. Every conversation we have outside this room should be with the full knowledge that she's listening in, and knows we know it."

"Is it merely a case of eavesdropping?"

"No. It extends to the direct manipulation of some of our information protocols."

Aumonier lifted a hand. "Such as?"

"She can distort some things, such as the information fed through to our suits. Any sensory modality is likely to be susceptible, so from now on we'll need to rely on direct observation and face-to-face chains of command."

"You're saying that anything on a visor or a screen or coming through an earpiece might be adulterated?"

"Yes, if it suits her immediate purpose. She tried it on with Thalia and me, trying to mask the fact that she didn't have control of our corvette and its weapons."

"So in demonstrating one capability, she inadvertently exposed a weakness in another area?"

Dreyfus had to admire Aumonier's ability to winkle a nugget of good news out of the least promising material.

"It's not an advantage we can count on indefinitely. We know that she managed to gain control of those bulk carriers, as well as much of Carcasstown."

"Civilian-registered bulk carriers don't operate under Panoply level four security protocols, and as for that habitat..."

"Agreed, and she had time to put her takeover of those ships in place, as well as Carcasstown. It was all mapped out well in advance, to play me like the fool I was."

Aumonier lifted an eyebrow. "Save the self-flagellation for later. As far as I can see you've done a good job of not making a bad situation far, far worse. Do you think she'll gain control of our ships anytime soon? Panoply itself?"

"She'll be trying to. The fact that we've held out for as long as we have —even if it's just a few hours—encourages me that she can't crack us as easily as she'd like. That doesn't make us invulnerable, just a tougher problem than those civilian assets. We have a window of advantage, nothing more."

"This eavesdropping capability worries me. Do you know how she found an in?"

"I imagine it was only ever a matter of time," Dreyfus sidestepped.

"Doubtless it was." Aumonier regarded him silently. "Yet in all this you've said nothing about our understanding of her that she won't already know, and that we couldn't have talked about freely elsewhere in Panoply. Therefore, there's something else. Something you wish to share with me that she can't yet be aware of."

"Thalia recovered Sparver's evidence package."

"Yes, we were in contact. Do you have it with you?"

"I destroyed it, after we'd seen enough to make a vital breakthrough."

"This had better be good."

He told her what he had deduced from Sparver's evidence, of the likely link between Asset 227, the Nerval-Lermontovs and a biological backup copy of their daughter.

"That is...*something* of a leap," Aumonier commented.

Dreyfus shrugged, denying nothing of her assessment. "Yet the evidence fits. Including the existence of Hafdis Tench."

"You're saying..." Aumonier pressed a finger to her temple. "You're saying...Hafdis? *Hafdis?*"

"Is a second, purely biological, instantiation of Aurora."

She stared at him for a few seconds. "Sent here to do what?"

"Only Hafdis can answer that."

"But she didn't just pass herself off as Ingvar's daughter. She passed every check on her identity."

Dreyfus nodded. "I was there when she was tested for a familial connection to Ingvar. The test indicated a fifty per cent match, strongly supportive of the claimed relationship."

"You seem to be intent on undermining your own theory of her origin, unless you're suggesting that Ingvar was always a Nerval-Lermontov as well."

"She wasn't," Dreyfus said. "I'd stake my life on it. We've still been blindsided, though. We still have Ingvar's body, don't we?"

"Of course."

"Run a genetic test on it. My hunch is that it won't be a match to either Hafdis *or* Ingvar."

"When you stick your neck out like that, there's usually a reason for your bullishness." She leaned back, nodding thoughtfully to herself. "All right, I'll have the body tested. Is that something Aurora could interfere with, either now or in the past?"

"Only if she understands what we're doing and which outcome to influence. She won't risk interfering for the sake of it."

"She must know about Hafdis, surely?"

"I don't think she does. I think that's why Ingvar went to the trouble she did, to erase as much of the connection to the Nerval-Lermontovs as possible. And why she raised Hafdis as her own. Hafdis herself may know nothing about her real nature, but *we* know what she is."

Aumonier regarded him with a friendly professional interest. "In which case...how do you propose to proceed with Hafdis?"

"Softly, softly," Dreyfus answered.

Dreyfus visited Thalia in the medical section, pleased to hear from Mercier that her injuries were well on the way to healing.

"They're keeping the news from me, sir," Thalia complained. "They say I've had enough stress and anxiety for one day. I don't think they understand that not knowing isn't helping me."

Dreyfus had collected a bulb of fruit juice for her. He set it by her bed, smiling in sympathy. "I'd make sure you were the first to hear, Thal. The truth is there's nothing to report, beyond the ripples spreading out from your intervention with the lemurs."

"Good ripples, I hope?"

"From what I can gather. Random outbreaks of common sense and tolerance all over the Glitter Band. You'd almost think we were learning to get along better."

"I'm sure we'll get over it, sir."

"Indeed we will. Incidentally, the Supreme Prefect has noted the effectiveness of your various interventions. The word 'promotion' may even have crossed her lips."

"I wasn't even sure she *liked* me, sir, let alone thought I was worth promoting."

Dreyfus allowed himself another smile, thinking her sentiments echoed his own, at various times in his career. "Beyond that, there's nothing else you and I can discuss freely, and nothing much to report on that angle, either." He thought about his last conversation with Jane Aumonier, and the question of Hafdis. "Although we're going to push."

Thalia seemed to grasp his meaning.

"I wish I could be there when you do."

"You've done enough for now. I'm quite sure you'll be busy, preoccupied and worried before long. The universe normally obliges us in that fashion."

"Did they fix your head, sir?"

Dreyfus scratched at the reknitted skin around his scalp, still itchy and inflamed. "A few more scars and bumps to add to the collection. I wondered when I'd lose my youthful beauty."

"I'm glad we didn't die in there, sir. I feel I've still got more to do."

"I feel we all have," Dreyfus replied.

"Sir," she broached, after a silence.

"Yes?"

"About the other thing...the matter you confided in me."

"Go on, Thal."

"It can wait, sir. There's a lot to be dealing with here and now. But it can't wait forever."

"I know that," he said, nodding his reassurance. "And I'd expect nothing less."

He sought an assurance from Mercier that Thalia would not be allowed to argue her way out of resting, then went to see the three evacuees who had made it out of Carcasstown on his cutter. They had been given adjoining rooms of their own, but were waiting for him now in a small reception lounge where water burbled through a channel cut through the floor, tumbling over smooth, olive-coloured pebbles. They had chairs and a low table set with drinks and food. Dreyfus remained standing; it was strictly a courtesy call and he wanted to rest as soon as he was done.

"They told us you made it out," Mirna Silk said, meeting his gaze with a blush of shame. "I didn't want to leave you in there, not knowing what would happen."

"If I could have forced you, I would have. Your lives mattered individually, but it was doubly important that we preserve any expertise related to Abacus and the Catopsis program."

"I'm glad I got to tag along, then," said Krenkel.

Dreyfus beamed at the man. "I have good news for you, Under-Supervisor. Your family have been traced. They made it out of Carcasstown alive and well."

Several years' worth of concern lifted off Krenkel in an instant. "They're here?"

Dreyfus raised a hand, damping down his expectations. "No, they made it to one of the habitats in the upper orbits. They're with constables now, being well looked after. You have my word that you'll be reunited as quickly as possible. Though with the pressure on our ships and personnel, that may not be for some days."

"Do they know I made it out?"

"Yes, they've been informed, and reassured that you're here as a guest, not because of any difficulty with Panoply."

"Can I speak to them? Or at least send them a message? We've got whole new lives to start building now."

"I'm afraid not, just for now. We're limiting communications to the bare essentials. The only news we can rely on right now is anything conveyed to us by direct means, and that means there's a moratorium on nearly all transmissions."

Mirna Silk leaned in.

"What's the purpose of this moratorium?"

"So that we know what we can rely on, and what we can't," Dreyfus replied. "Even if that means we're down to a trickle of information channels, it's better than questioning everything else. It's not so bad. We have command and control protocols for just this sort of eventuality, so our day-to-day operations can still continue largely unaffected."

"Day-to-day, after everything that's happened?" she asked.

"The Glitter Band doesn't stop needing us just because Aurora has prevailed," Dreyfus returned. "If we were that dispensable, there'd be no need for Panoply at all."

"What has she done since Carcasstown blew up?" Doctor Salazar asked.

"Demonstrated that she's still here, still active and still intent on damage. She's infiltrated some of our systems, but not others. I wouldn't say we're winning, but we're not out of the game just yet. When you're rested, Doctor Salazar, I'm going to allow you access to some secure documents of ours. They're hermetically isolated records, so Aurora can't access them in any fashion."

He had piqued the man's interest, but there was a spark of suspicion with it. "Documents about what?"

"I'll explain," Dreyfus said.

CHAPTER THIRTY-EIGHT

Panoply's vote-monitoring algorithms were the first to register the change. Without any warning, all active and pending ballots were suspended. Across the Glitter Band, ten thousand polling cores went into offline status, unable to accept any further instructions. Nearly as much data continued to flow between the habitats as before, but now no part of it had anything to do with mass democratic participation. No one could vote on anything, from the tiniest matter to the largest. It wasn't even possible to table a proposal for a possible vote further down the line.

In Panoply, exhausted prefects scrambled to restore functionality to the polling cores. Jane Aumonier observed her colleagues' efforts with a detached fatalism, certain that they would fail, but equally confident that all possible measures had to be taken.

All orthodox solutions were exhausted within the first five minutes. Aumonier went to her weightless sphere to gauge the public mood and ponder her reaction. She floated there, silent and pensive, assailed by a barrage of colours and symbols, the feeds swelled and contracted as her custom algorithms assigned weighted significances.

There was, to begin with, surprisingly little consternation. Lulls in voting were not unheard of. The individual habitats were also not unaccustomed to the sudden loss of polling privileges. Citizens, if they noticed at all, assumed that it was just the prefects doing some unscheduled maintenance. The more nervous parties might worry that they had been put into some kind of lockdown, without the usual grace period. Only administrators were likely to have the slightest inkling that the outage was unusual. But even then, they would need time to coordinate with other habitats and pool their observations.

Only then, minutes into the shutdown, would a clearer picture begin to form.

Aumonier monitored an uptick in public and private comms, squeezing abstraction bandwidth. In line with this, activity at docking ports began to heighten, with demand peaking for shuttles and taxis. People did not necessarily know that they would be safer elsewhere, but the urge to do something was driving a nervous exodus. They knew something was up.

Requests for clarification were piling up. Panoply was expected to have answers.

Aumonier had nothing—at least nothing that was likely to go down well—but she still had to make some kind of utterance.

"This is Supreme Prefect Jane Aumonier," she said, recording a short statement that would then go out across the Glitter Band. "We are aware of the current outage and are doing all in our power to restore functionality to all polling cores."

True, in the strict letter of the word, even if she knew "all in our power" was about as empty a phrase as she could imagine.

She played back her own words, winced at their ineffectualness, then transmitted them anyway. Ten thousand Jane Aumoniers stared out from the feeds, replicating her appearance across public and private media, in the real world and via abstraction. In every home, every square, in the visual feeds of millions of citizens, she would be seen and heard.

She watched her face melt on the feeds.

Each Aumonier was transformed into a vision in gold and green brocade, a child-woman on a wooden throne, staring out at her subjects with liquid blue eyes, serene and commanding.

Instead of her own voice, Aurora's rang out of the feeds.

"Dear people. Please do not be alarmed. All is well. All will continue to be well." She smiled demurely, adding a nod of misplaced humility. "I am Aurora. You need not fear me. I want only the very best for all of us." Her fingers rubbed the wooden scrollwork on the tips of her armrests. "There'll be no need for voting now, so I've lifted that burden from you. You had to make hard choices in the past because I wasn't there to make them for you. That's all over: you'll live easier, more carefree lives without that pressure."

Aumonier, listening in, grew colder.

"No more worrying about voting. No more worrying about the future. It's all taken care of. And all you need do is...carry on as normal." She offered her palms guilelessly. "Live your lives. Communicate. Travel. Indulge in love, commerce, entertainment, games, sport, whatever gratifies you. Everything that was good yesterday will continue to be good tomorrow, and ever onwards. Better, even, because all the things that were not so good are now *my* concern, not yours." She angled her head, smiling sweetly, as if contemplating a basket of puppies. "I'll have more to say in a little while. There are some other things we'll be able to do without. Until then, savour your first hours of freedom from the drudgery of responsibility.

You'll find that things will be much nicer now. And we're all going to be very, very good friends."

Aurora's image vanished, leaving only the usual migraine of jostling feeds and analytics. Aumonier tried to push her message out again, but it was like throwing stones down a bottomless well. She listened for a splash, a plop, a ripple, anything. Nothing came. She had no means of addressing her subjects.

Perhaps because they were no longer hers to address.

Aumonier gagged on a cough. The classroom was hazed in dust as prefects and analysts worked with the crudest of tools to smash away wall cladding, stripping the room's inert-matter surroundings back to the bare rock substrate of the centrifuge ring.

Furniture, display devices and all forms of monitoring and surveillance had already been gutted in the hour since she gave the first instruction to prepare the space. Immense tangles of froptic cable lay severed and twitching on the floor, where they had been wrenched out like fish guts. The cables, laced with quickmatter, were making a vain effort to repair themselves. The process gave Aumonier a spasm of nausea, as if she were witnessing the death throes of some huge but pitiful monster.

"It'll take more time," Dreyfus said, his face grey from sweat and dust. He had been helping with the effort, swinging a hammer at the cladding. "And even when we're done, it won't be as secure as the cube. If she has access to microphones within a few hundred metres of this room, she may still be able to intercept conversations."

"It'll still be an improvement on the tactical room. I thought of gutting that, but I wouldn't mind having it in one piece for when we're on the other side of this mess."

"This is a good compromise," Dreyfus allowed, before breaking off for a coughing fit of his own. He made a vague effort at batting away the dust. "I've got technicians working to give us eyes and ears in here, but it'll take a few hours."

"Won't those channels be susceptible to Aurora?"

"Not if we go old and crude. The technicians are digging through construction files to have the quickmatter forges make simple cameras, microphones and displays, things that can be wired up very quickly and which run on analogue signal protocols."

"She'll be ahead of us there as well."

Dreyfus nodded gloomily. "The best we can do is have the technicians take each item apart once it's fabricated, to make sure Aurora hasn't slipped anything into the construction files. So far so good. These are

317

simple objects, just a few basic components with little room to hide concealed devices. We can use similar methods to coordinate our built-in defences, if it comes to that."

"Keep up the vigilance. We get tired and slipshod, but she has limitless patience."

"I'm well aware. What did you make of her transmission?"

"I didn't like any part of it. Especially not the part about 'getting rid of some other things.'"

"We must be somewhere near the top of the list of things she might want to get rid of."

"But no overt threats just yet." Aumonier reached out and scuffed dust from his eyebrows. "If she could turn *us* against *us*, she'd have done so already. Returning operatives report that ships and weapons are behaving normally. We can't entirely trust the comms of anyone still outside Panoply, but so far we've seen no sign that she's co-opting our resources."

"Let that remain the case." Dreyfus dropped his voice to a gruff whisper. "I've spoken to the three who came back in my cutter. Krenkel isn't a concern, but I'm still hoping the other two can be useful to us in certain ways. Especially Doctor Salazar."

"How so?"

"Now that Bacchus, Breno and Haigler are all dead, he may be the only person in this system who has any understanding of the principles behind the latency tracking. Aurora was ahead of us, but that doesn't mean the method was entirely without merit. The first time Catopsis was tried, it nearly snared her."

Aumonier shook her head bleakly. "She won't fall for it again."

"No," he agreed. "Catching her a second time is totally out of the question. But at the very least I'd like a means of sensing her movements. With your permission, I'd like to open the seals on the original Catopsis program."

"And allow Salazar access to them? With the likelihood of Aurora's eyes peering over his shoulder?" Her eyes flashed concern. "That's a bit of a risk, wouldn't you say?"

"We'll only permit him access to hardcopy documents, under Pangolin, and only in the cube. What he sees and reads in there stays in his head. He takes no materials in or out. If he has an insight, he can share it with us, but we limit all opportunities for Aurora to spy on the process."

"It seems like a very long shot, even with those guarantees."

"Salazar won't trust us entirely until he feels we're on the same side—and that will only happen when we give him a bone to play with."

She studied him with her usual shrewdness. "Have you already promised him something?"

"Just a teaser."

"One day you'll make an assurance I can't endorse, Tom. I bow to your instincts in this matter, though; you've had far more interaction with Salazar than I have. If you think he can do something for us, so be it. Have Mercier screen him for Pangolin suitability, of course. It would be a shame to give the man an aneurysm just as he's about to help us."

"Thank you," Dreyfus acknowledged. "And concerning Mercier: did you get anything back from the corpse?"

"Yes, although I don't think it will surprise you. There's no match to either of the DNA records you mentioned." She lowered her own voice to a conspiratorial hush. "How is that even possible? We know for a fact it's Ingvar's corpse, unless it was somehow substituted in the few hours before you secured the scene of her murder."

"It's hers," Dreyfus said. "And the sample you took will have been her genuine genetic material. The forgery is in our own files: the archived pattern supposedly derived from Ingvar at the time of her induction into Panoply. It was altered, perhaps as long as four years ago."

Aumonier grasped his logic. "Changed by Ingvar herself, knowing there'd come a time when we checked the relationship between herself and Hafdis."

"She had the means to alter her own entry undetectably," Dreyfus replied, as the crashing and banging from the tear-out work served to smother his words. "The match with Hafdis had to look real. She'd have taken a real DNA sample from Hafdis to some grey-market bloodcutter, then had them stitch in fifty per cent foreign DNA, creating a template for a parental DNA pattern that never existed in reality."

"What about the assumed father of Hafdis, Miles Selby?"

"He may have existed, he may have had some contact with Ingvar, and he may have left the system at the time the records state. It's highly unlikely he had anything to do with Hafdis. Just a name, to throw us off the scent."

"Ingvar would've been exposed the moment we re-tested her own blood against that pattern."

Dreyfus nodded. "She'd also have known that the odds on that ever happening were pretty small. She was one of us, a highly trusted insider known to all the seniors. Why would her identity ever have needed verifying?"

"A risk, all the same."

He accepted her point. "But one worth taking, to protect Hafdis."

"We were played," Aumonier reflected dolefully. "Again."

"And now I have no reason to discount my first hypothesis. Hafdis isn't her daughter."

"Softly or not, we're speaking to her. I want to find out how much of this is real, and just as importantly how much she knows about herself." Aumonier scratched a payload of grit from her eyes. "Only then will I be in a position to decide if she's useful to us, or something that needs to be burned alive in a heartbeat." She looked at him warningly. "There won't be any middle ground, Tom. Ingvar Tench has arranged for a cuckoo to be planted in our nest, and I want to know why. We proceed on the assumption of malice, until we have answers. We're at war now."

CHAPTER THIRTY-NINE

Doctor Salazar looked down at his forearm, where a fading blemish marked the spot where Mercier had injected him with the pre-booster. Warily, he lowered his yellow sleeve back down, leaning back into his chair.

"And what now, exactly?"

"In about six hours you'll be ready for the main Pangolin shot. You'll feel a little nauseous between now and then, but nothing too uncomfortable. Just rest, drink the therapeutic cocktail at the intervals I specified and allow the pre-booster to lay the temporary neural groundwork. Once I've satisfied myself that you're safe, I'll administer Pangolin." Behind his antique spectacles, Mercier's eyes conveyed seriousness tempered with some faint but genial concern for his new patient. "You'll be best sleeping after that. The effects of your first Pangolin shot can be disorientating and not always pleasant. You won't feel quite yourself."

"Nice of you to mention that now."

"It does get easier with time," Dreyfus said. He stood to the side of the table, arms folded, watching the process with weary detachment.

Salazar lifted his eyes, hooded with scepticism. "And all this so I can look through some musty old files of yours?"

"The work you were doing with Abacus built on what had already been done for Catopsis. All I'm asking is that you use the Catopsis files as a springboard to recover as much of the later progress as you can." Dreyfus leaned in slightly, planting his palms on his knees. "Mirna seemed to think you were the best, Aristarchus. Why don't we see if you can validate that high opinion of hers?"

"I can't promise anything."

"I'm a realist. I'm not expecting you to." Dreyfus switched his attention to Mercier. "That six hours contains a generous margin of safety, doesn't it? See if you can knock it down to four."

He called for the cube to be reconnected.

*

Dreyfus felt himself moving through a version of Panoply that felt subtly and threateningly unfamiliar, as if he had not quite woken from a nightmare. More than thirteen hours had passed since Aurora's initial statement, with no further clarification of her terms. Outside, life continued, but not according to any reasonable definition of normality. Dreyfus had monitored a selection of feeds himself. While their authenticity could not be guaranteed—there was always a chance that the data-streams were being manipulated by Aurora—he had a feeling he was seeing the unvarnished truth. She had nothing to gain by dressing it up. The effects of her speech were all too apparent. After the initial spike in demand following the loss of polling, there was now a marked dip in inter-habitat communication, commerce and travel. The citizens were sitting tight, trusting that in the absence of new information, doing nothing was the most sensible policy. The only exception was a modest flow of shuttles, taxis and private craft attempting to ferry people down to Chasm City and the other major settlements on Yellowstone. Aurora's intervention had been confined to the Glitter Band, so there was a certain logic in assuming that the planet offered a safe haven. The flow was small, though, because almost all entry permits were being denied, and any ships trying to make an unauthorised sprint for the surface were being interdicted in low orbit or, in worst cases, shot down in the atmosphere.

Dreyfus forced down any thoughts of recrimination. Had there been an equivalent exodus from Chasm City, the Glitter Band would have been equally zealous in policing its borders.

Hestia Del Mar had left him a message, to be picked up and returned at his convenience.

"Dreyfus," her recording said sternly. "This official silence is doing none of us any favours. Nature abhors a vacuum, and so does the public mood. We're getting anxious down here, waiting for Panoply to tell us it has everything under control. What is Jane Aumonier doing?"

"And a very good day to you too, Detective-Marshal," he answered. "I wish I had better news. The Supreme Prefect has attempted to address the citizenry, but all our usual channels of mass communications are being denied us. I don't even know if this reply will reach you. We're being allowed to carry on as before in some ways, but not in others. It all depends on Aurora's ever-changing mood. Rest assured, nonetheless, that we are exploring all possible avenues toward a restoration of the old order."

Her reply flashed back within a few seconds. "Well, if you're being spoofed, Dreyfus, Aurora is doing a very good job of conveying the tenor of a man at the edge of his wits. That suggests to me that we have an unadulterated channel of communications, for now."

He smiled through his tiredness and fear. "The mice are being allowed to squeak and play so long as they don't cause trouble."

"I'd rather not be a mouse, given the chance. Presumably you are investigating a range of informational countermeasures, or is that not something you can speak about?"

"I don't think it matters what I speak about," he said, sighing. "She knows our capabilities much more thoroughly than we know hers. In so far as you have influence, Hestia, I'd advise you to get your superiors to put Chasm City into an informational quarantine as quickly as you can. It was too late for us—she was already in our networks—but you might have a little time."

"I very much doubt she has overlooked us, Dreyfus, or that she's going to be content to let this little pocket of civilisation run amok while she lords it over the Glitter Band. We'll be next in her plans for conquest. Then…what? The Ultras, and beyond? The whole solar system? Why would she ever stop?"

"She'll only stop when she feels too attenuated and slow," Dreyfus said. "I think you're right, Hestia. Everything here is a prelude to a larger take-over of human civilisation around Yellowstone, and at least as far out as Marco's Eye, Idlewild and the Parking Swarm."

"In which case, I sincerely hope you have a plan for defeating her."

"We're taking steps," he answered, leaving it purposefully cryptic. At this point, he sincerely wanted Aurora to be listening in. It would suit him very well to reinforce the notion that Panoply was in possession of knowledge hidden to her, even if they didn't know what to make of it.

Just that one fact could be the grit that irritated her into making a mistake.

"Dreyfus, I meant to ask. Your colleague, the one you sent on that personal business. Did she make it back all right?"

Gratitude slid a tear into his eye. "Thalia was hurt quite badly in Carcasstown, but she's safe now." *Or as safe as any of us are*, a snide, silent voice added.

"I'm pleased. From what little interaction we had, she struck me as competent and thorough. Your standards are higher than I realised. Tell her that if she ever desires a more challenging work environment, her talents would not be wasted in Chasm City."

"I'm sure that will go down well, Hestia. Her heart's in Panoply, though. Her father was one of ours."

"Then your gain is our loss. Concerning the item that you had her retrieve... was all satisfactory?"

"More than satisfactory, thank you."

"Good. One day I hope you'll do me the service of explaining what that was all about. I can only imagine it pertains to the present situation?"

"A little."

"Then you've probably already said too much. Very well. Convey my sentiments to the Supreme Prefect. Tell her that we will attempt to use our surface-to-orbit channels to indicate that Panoply's silence is an involuntary condition and measures are under way. Do you think that will help?"

Dreyfus imagined his silent eavesdropper, hoping that some tiny portion of her intellect was raging in impotent fury at the notion of something she did not and could not know.

"It certainly won't hurt."

Hafdis was in her room, confined to quarters along with all of Panoply's civilian guests. She had taken the restriction on her freedom without complaint, accepting that there was nothing personal in it, purely a matter of safety and efficiency while much of the infrastructure of the asteroid was hastily repurposed.

Dreyfus found her watching the public feeds, switching from one stream to the next. It did not look like she was distracted to him, more a methodical need to drink in as much information as she could, through as many possible channels.

"Take it all with a pinch of salt, Hafdis," he warned her. "Without first-hand confirmation, we can't be sure how much of it's reliable."

Hafdis toggled the feed to one from a world that he recognised, the interior of a rolled-up cylinder, splintered with angular swatches of green, blue and red. "Feinstein-Wu, Prefect Dreyfus. I've been watching the public announcements put out by the constables I worked with every day. I know these people better than I know anyone. I believe in their reactions, and how they're handling the public mood."

"Which is?"

"Everyone's absolutely terrified. Despite what she told us, no one's going about their lives as normal." Hafdis switched between sub-feeds, displaying her effortless familiarity with the public surveillance modes of her own habitat. "Look at the lakeside. It's practically deserted, and yet the schedulers have arranged fine weather. The place should be teeming. I'd be there if I wasn't here, or on duty. Mother used to take me to the terraces for ice cream."

Dreyfus moved to one of the few items in the room that had not come with Hafdis and her modest amount of luggage. It was the black box they had found in Ingvar's quarters, with its jumble of mementos. Unbidden, he opened the lid and dug around until his fingers closed on the image of a small girl by the lakeside, her legs in the water.

"Like this?" he asked mildly.

Hafdis detected his coolness. "Yes, exactly like that. Why are you asking me?"

Dreyfus put the image back.

"I have a request, Hafdis. I'd like you to come down to the cube with me, to undergo a further part of your candidacy training."

"In the middle of...whatever this emergency is?"

"There's no better time to see how you cope with elevated stress, especially when the lives of friends are at stake. One other thing."

"What?" she asked tersely, undoubtedly picking up on his tension.

"Do nothing and say nothing that might arouse the interest of Aurora. We've done all that we can to block her options for monitoring us, but we still can't afford to take unnecessary chances."

She gave him a sharp look. "Why would Aurora care about me?"

"Accompany me to the cube," Dreyfus said.

They left her room. Hafdis went along with meek compliance, head lowered and her demeanour that of a student summoned to detention. It was not exactly the best display of normality, but Dreyfus was content that she wasn't making a spectacle, thereby begging the question of where he was taking her and why.

They reached the cube. Jane Aumonier was already waiting inside, by prior arrangement. While Hafdis took a seat at the table in the interviewing room, Dreyfus indicated for the duty prefect to disconnect the connecting bridge, leaving the cube fully isolated.

He sat down next to the Supreme Prefect, facing Hafdis.

"I'm sorry I needed to lie," Dreyfus said, with only the barest dusting of remorse. "As you correctly intimated, this would be a slightly odd time to be concerned with your candidacy. I'm afraid it's not that at all."

Hafdis looked to her hosts. "What's this really about?"

"I'm afraid we need to ask you some difficult questions," Aumonier said.

"They concern the story we've been presented with, about your relationship to Ingvar Tench," Dreyfus stated.

Hafdis flinched. "There's no 'story.' She's my mother."

"Did your mother..." Aumonier paused. "Did Ingvar Tench speak to you about Aurora?"

"Yes, from time to time." Hafdis frowned hard. "Why are you talking as if she isn't my mother? What aren't you telling me?"

Dreyfus went in with a direct question. "Are you certain that she was your mother, Hafdis?"

She snarled out her answer. "Yes, of course I am! What kind of a question is that?"

"One I needed to ask. Do you have any reason to believe that she was your mother, beyond simply accepting what you've been told?"

"I don't understand why you're asking me these things. Or why you needed to drag me here to do it."

Aumonier glanced at Dreyfus, nodded minutely. "Hafdis, I'm going to be blunt with you. Perhaps uncomfortably blunt. We know for a categorical fact that you're not Ingvar's biological daughter, or even a close relative. We also have every reason to doubt any familial relationship to Miles Selby, the man the records claim was your father, When we checked your DNA, we were comparing it against an internal document that had already been adulterated. Ingvar altered it so that we'd accept you as her daughter in the event of her death. It was clever and nearly foolproof. Most likely we would never have looked any deeper, but for one thing."

Hafdis's anger had bled away now, leaving a thin substrate of fear. Dreyfus felt it as surely as if her blood was his own.

"What thing?"

Dreyfus answered: "Our friend Sparver found a connection between Ingvar's work and the family of Aurora Nerval-Lermontov. Ingvar worked hard to protect that connection. Our belief is that she only did so to protect you, and the truth about what you are."

"I don't follow."

Aumonier laced her hands, ready to deliver the verdict. "We think you're a Nerval-Lermontov. Specifically, a close genetic copy of Aurora Nerval-Lermontov herself. The girl who became a god. A mad god."

Hafdis shook her head in unreasoning denial. "No. That's . . . insane."

"I admit we can't prove it," Dreyfus said. "To do that, we'd need access to Nerval-Lermontov genetic archives, which the Common Articles won't allow and which the family would never surrender willingly. What we have is a chain of connections: Ingvar's interest in Catopsis, which was a program to contain Aurora. The environment in Asset 227, a simulacrum of Aurora's childhood surroundings. And Ingvar's intense need to mask this connection."

"I know what I am," Hafdis asserted, yet with cracks fault-lining her assuredness. "I know *who* I am."

"You may think that you do," Aumonier said, not without a certain sympathy. "What is true, and what we remember to be true, aren't necessarily the same things. You were already the product of one set of barely legal technologies. It's not hard to imagine that your memories are similarly artificial. The mementos, your childhood memories of time growing up in Feinstein-Wu, may be carefully created fictions."

"Why?" she exclaimed, spitting out her indignation.

"Only Ingvar could answer that completely," Dreyfus said. "And I'm sure her reasoning was as sound as it was humane. What we're left with is speculation."

"You've speculated enough! Whatever secret she was protecting to do with that family, it's nothing to do with me."

"We can get to the bottom of this," Aumonier said. "There are techniques available to us. We can trawl your brain structure and use reliable methods to weed out false memories from authentic ones."

Hafdis settled her hands on the table, as if inviting them to be cuffed. "So trawl me."

"We can't," Dreyfus said, drawing a faint reproachful glance from his superior. "Not because it wouldn't work, but because we can't be sure who might be monitoring the results."

"The question on our minds," Aumonier said, "is whether your presence here is useful or detrimental to Aurora."

"Since I'm not what you think, it's a meaningless question."

Dreyfus leaned in, his tunic creaking from the strain. "Since we know what you are, Hafdis—and I'll keep calling you that out of respect for Ingvar—there are two possibilities. You're either here to serve Aurora, undermining us from within, or you're the one thing we might be able to use against her. It's rather important that we decide which."

Hafdis folded her arms, fixing them with a basilisk stare. "And if you end up deciding I'm here to work against you?"

Aumonier sniffed. "You'd remain under our protection. The terms of that protection might look a lot like solitary confinement, for the rest of your life."

"With what's going on outside, maybe that wouldn't be so bad."

"Ingvar protected you," Dreyfus said. "Unless her judgement was off —which would be the first time in her life—it's because she knew you weren't a threat. She didn't want Aurora learning about you, and following

327

Catopsis she was unwilling to share her intelligence with Panoply. She acted alone. She rescued you from that simulacrum in Asset 227, raising you as if you were her own. That can't have happened more than four years ago, which means virtually everything you remember prior to adulthood was false."

"Wouldn't it have seemed odd to you that she suddenly announced she had a fully grown daughter?" Hafdis countered.

"The way Ingvar kept her private life to herself, none of us knew you existed until after her death," Dreyfus replied. "She would have altered her private records when you came into her life, probably at the same time she changed her genetic profile. She was thinking ahead, imagining there'd come a day when we had to accept you as her own." He pressed harder against the table, its edge cutting into his belly. "All of that tells me she cared, Hafdis. Whatever you really are, you mattered to Ingvar. The personal effects alone tell us that. And it wasn't practicality that made you take that hair-clasp from the box. It was a link to Ingvar, the woman who'd sheltered you, the woman who'd given you the nearest thing to a mother's love."

Hafdis regarded him with granite indifference. "Not the nearest thing. The exact thing."

"There are still options for trawling," Aumonier said darkly. "The isolated equipment we used on Devon Garlin..."

"You mean that museum piece that nearly burned his brain out?"

"If she won't crack by other means..."

Dreyfus looked back to Hafdis, expecting fear but meeting only a thundercloud of affront and defiance.

"You won't do that," she said. "I know you won't. Whatever you think I am, you've still got your cherished principles. Mother believed in them, and she made me believe in them as well. You're better than this, both of you."

The room shuddered gently. Dreyfus got up and went to the outer door, where he noticed that the connecting bridge had been pushed back into place, the cube no longer physically isolated from its surroundings.

He had asked for thirty minutes with Hafdis. They were nowhere near that, which could only mean that the Supreme Prefect's attention was needed elsewhere.

And urgently.

"We'll continue this," he promised Hafdis, as they prepared to leave her in the cube.

Two competing emotions vied within him. Shame, that he might be inflicting cruel treatment on a complete innocent, someone that not so long ago he had ushered into his protection. And determination, that there was a facade here that would crack with only a little more persuasion.

I know you're lying, Hafdis, he told himself. *The question is, do you?*

CHAPTER FORTY

Aumonier and Dreyfus arrived at the newly designated tactical room. The place was still an improvised mess, with coiling cables stapled to surfaces, bare rock grinning through gaps in wall cladding, dust loitering in lazy veils, but at least now it could begin to function in its designated manner. One main table had been arranged: not quite as large as the original, but good enough under the circumstances. The table was circular, with a clear area in the middle. Tang and a handful of analysts were coming up with the next best thing to the Solid Orrery, leaning over the table and positioning coloured markers with long-handled sticks. Dreyfus appraised their handiwork, noting the major features. Yellowstone was a half-sphere, the Glitter Band a ragged ring of lesser markers, Panoply a black orb on a stalk. There was no hope of representing all ten thousand habitats, let alone tracking their relative movements with any sort of accuracy, so the analysts were making do with a couple of dozen representative habitats, their coded markers all bearing familiar names. Every now and then they needed nudging by tiny amounts, as the ensemble ticked around Yellowstone.

Prefects and analysts were already pressed around the table, as well as several smaller ones dotted around the room. Around the walls, and scattered haphazardly on the tables, feeds flickered with ghost images and random blasts of static. A handful of displays were still showing the information threads arriving through the normal network channels, crisper and clearer than the improvised ones, but open to manipulation by Aurora. Anything capable of listening in on the room had been removed, except for a diplomatic channel Aumonier had the option of opening and closing at will.

"Well?" she asked, out of breath after their dash from the cube.

"A repeating announcement from Aurora," Clearmountain said, tearing himself away from one of the table-mounted feeds. "Call it an interim policy statement. I thought it was best that you heard it directly, while she's still transmitting."

"Thank you, Gaston." She raised her voice above the hubbub of conversation and still ongoing technical work. "Quiet, please! Let me listen. Run it from the start, please."

Lillian Baudry handed Aumonier one of the improvised displays, a bulky thing connected to the table by a data-umbilical as thick as an elephant's trunk. Aurora's face stared out from the display in flattened profile, her lips moving, words buzzing out from a tinny speaker.

"Dear people. We're off to a bad start, I fear. I asked you to go about your lives normally, did I not? If you did this and let me worry about everything else, I promised that all would be well." Her tone gained an edge. "Well, it seems that wasn't enough, judging by your actions."

"Actions?" Dreyfus breathed. "No one's done anything!"

Aurora was still speaking. "Some of you evidently don't think much of my promises. You've been leaving the Glitter Band, heading to Yellowstone. I've been watching your ships as they leave. A few more of you have been trying to strike out for elsewhere in the system. I've let this stand until now because I understand that we can't build a basis of trust overnight." She paused, shook her head regretfully. "Frankly, though, enough is enough. I've done nothing to any of you, and yet you reward my good intentions with baseless suspicion and acts of open defiance. Well, let me make my position clearer."

Dreyfus braced himself. He knew something bad was coming.

"There'll be no more movement in or out of the Glitter Band. The exodus flights stop this instant. Because I'm mindful that the wise majority of you haven't attempted this transgression, I'll continue to allow free movement within the Glitter Band. In fact, I may soon be encouraging it." She smiled coyly. "We'll say more about that in time." The face glossed itself in to a mask of serenity. "For now, let's start anew. Put these early mistakes and differences behind us. Let's see if we can do that, shall we? Because you really don't want to see my firmer side."

The feed began to repeat itself.

"When did this begin?" Aumonier asked.

"Ten minutes ago," answered Baudry. "I made the call to pull you out of the cube the moment it began."

"Do we think it went out Band-wide?"

Tang replied. "To the best of our knowledge, ma'am. We're getting it on primary, secondary and tertiary feeds. It's even coming through on some of our analogue channels. She's making sure no one misses it."

Dreyfus said: "Can we track those movements she's talking about?"

"Only by channels that may be compromised, sir," Tang replied. He leaned in over the table to adjust one of the markers. "No reason to think we're not seeing an accurate picture, though."

Aumonier probed: "And what is that picture?"

"If she was hoping to damp down the exodus, ma'am, it's having exactly the opposite effect. We're tracking waves of ships detaching from habitats throughout the Glitter Band, not just in the lower orbits." He conferred with one of the other analysts. "More than a hundred since she made her announcement, ma'am, and that's excluding any departures that look like part of the normal traffic patterns. The first ships of this new wave will penetrate Yellowstone control space within the next ten minutes."

"They'll be denied entry permission," Dreyfus commented. "But I very much doubt that'll stop them."

"Estimate the number of people on these ships," Aumonier said.

"Between ten and twelve thousand, ma'am. It's a negligible percentage of the total population."

"But a trickle can become a flood, if not checked." Aumonier scratched at her neck. "The irony is that they likely won't find any long-term sanctuary in Chasm City."

"It's not the exodus that bothers her," Dreyfus said. "It's the disobedience. She's promised them paradise on a plate, and they've spat it back at her."

Aumonier nodded her agreement. "Maybe because they recognise a barking-mad lunatic when they see one. Even in the form of a cybernetic demigoddess. Keep tracking those movements, Robert."

A supernumerary produced coffee, lukewarm but drinkable. Dreyfus and Aumonier took their bulbs and squeezed into positions next to each other around the table.

"There's nothing we can do," Dreyfus said. "Even in peacetime we'd have no real powers to stop those ships. And even if we stopped them, we'd only be doing her work for her."

"Perhaps running for the hills really is the best move," Aumonier answered. Then, in a quieter register: "What did you make of her, Tom?"

"Hafdis?" He was glad for the distraction from Aurora's latest proclamation. "I hoped she'd crumble at the first prod."

"If it's a front, it's a good one. I wasn't serious about going in with a trawl, but I didn't see a flicker of concern about it when I floated the idea."

Dreyfus presumed it was safe to discuss their guess now that the new tactical room had been swept of listening devices, but he still opted to keep his remarks indirect.

"If the memories feel real to her, she won't find it easy to let go of them."

Aumonier cradled her coffee as she mused: "Four years at the utmost, Tom. That's how long she's been living under this guise. Forced amnesia is one thing: you know all about that."

"It's one thing to be aware of an artificial gap in your memories," Dreyfus acknowledged. "Another to be taken in by a whole set of false memories stitched over the same events. I've heard of that kind of mnemonic engineering being successful, but it needs time, expertise and occasional reinforcement."

"We don't know what kind of condition she was in when Ingvar found her. For all we know there were already holes in her memory, waiting to be plugged. It's still a stretch, though, to think of Ingvar achieving all that with the little which was at her disposal. And what about the public records in Feinstein-Wu? They'd have needed altering too."

"I won't say that it was easy," Dreyfus replied. "Still, if you had to pick a place to create a daughter out of whole cloth, it is about the best habitat available. They live very modest lives there, with the minimum of abstraction. I doubt it was beyond Ingvar to access their records and create a backstory for Hafdis, with a father, birthday, education and so on."

"It also fits with the idea of protecting her, by giving her a life in a place where people aren't in a rush to embrace the wilder philosophies of the rest of the Glitter Band."

"And yet," Dreyfus said, "she was the one who voiced the idea of coming to us, not the other way around."

"If she's what she claims, it makes a certain sense. Her mother just died, and she's always wanted to walk in her footsteps. Ingvar's done a very good job of schooling her in the idea that she can have a life as a prefect, too. What better time to come to Panoply?"

Dreyfus rolled the coffee bulb. "It also makes sense if she's exactly what we suspect. She's lived under Ingvar's protection for four years but was always prepared for the next phase, knowing there might come a time when Ingvar's enemies move against her. All of a sudden, she's at risk of exposure."

"So, she talks her way into Panoply. We oblige because she's the only living link to Ingvar. And we practically fall over ourselves to indulge her plans to become a prefect."

"At which point she gains a degree of protection, as well as potential access to our information-gathering systems," Dreyfus agreed. "It still begs the question: why run to us? She's had four years to get ready for this. Even on a constable's stipend, wouldn't that be enough time to put aside the funds to run elsewhere?"

"Out-system? Not likely, unless they pay their constables quite exorbitantly."

"Almost anywhere else in the system, then. Plenty of holes to hide in. Plenty of opportunities to change her face and name. A new set of false memories. Even a full genetic re-skin. Or just declare herself to the Mendicants and live a happy, carefree life in Hospice Idlewild."

"She did none of that. She just came to us," Aumonier said. "Which brings me back to square one. She's acting the way she would if she really *was* Ingvar's daughter. But we know she's not."

"What's our next move, Jane?"

"I'm considering it." She set down her bulb, leaning aside to allow Tang room to slide one of his markers into a new position. "What it won't be is softly, softly."

The flow of émigrés continued for the next thirteen hours, unchecked. Panoply could be quite sure that the exodus was real, though the exact numbers of passengers involved was debatable. Apart from the feeds, which might or might not offer a reliable version of events, Panoply still had its own ships and operatives dispersed throughout the Glitter Band. When they returned home, the operatives provided undeniable eyewitness testimony that the reported events were at least broadly believable. They had seen the exodus ships with their own eyes, not through displays or visors. They had tracked large numbers of them as they scuttled between habitats and the atmosphere of Yellowstone.

Panoply had also tracked interdiction measures put in place by the Yellowstone authorities. These had provided something of a deterrent initially, as ships turned back rather than being repulsed or destroyed as they tried to make their way to the surface. After a while, though, the flow had overwhelmed the planet dwellers' efforts and the interdiction measures had been quietly suspended. According to Panoply's best estimates, around two hundred and forty thousand citizens had probably made it safely to Yellowstone. They were not likely to be receiving the warmest of welcomes, but they undoubtedly considered it a great improvement on living under the questionable sovereignty of a deranged artificial intelligence.

Dreyfus hoped they enjoyed their temporary liberation. He imagined it might be quite short-lived. Aurora would be testing Yellowstone's network vulnerabilities, looking for a hole to squirm through. Eventually she would find one, if it had not already happened.

The flow was easing, minutely. This was not because of any lack of desire on the part of the émigrés, but because the supply of shuttles and ferries was beginning to dwindle. Once they made it down to the surface, the majority of the ships were staying put. Only a small number of robot vehicles were making repeated return trips, and this was insufficient to meet demand. Private ships and larger cargo haulers were still present in orbit in huge numbers, but few of them had the capacity to carry many passengers or endure atmospheric entry. They were remaining docked, with inter-habitat traffic now experiencing an almost total shutdown.

Dreyfus hoped Aurora might detect the tailing-off and let bygones be bygones. While her injunction might not have been followed immediately and to the letter, the shortfall in ships was having about the same effect over a longer period.

Hope and expectation were not the same thing.

"How are you feeling, Doctor Salazar?" Dreyfus asked, in the brusque tones of someone not tremendously interested in the answer.

"As if every synapse in my brain has just been torn out and stuffed back in through my nostrils, like a pile of wet noodles. As if every blank surface in this room is straining with possibility, like a balloon about to burst." He examined his hand, staring intently at the hairs on the back. "As if there's a universe of scripture crawling beneath my skin, trying to force its way out through my pores. As if I need to see symbols or else I'll drown in my own incomprehension. My head hurts. My eyes ache from too much looking." He regarded Dreyfus with distant hostility. "You know all this. You've all been through this."

Dreyfus sat down at the table and slid a compad onto the empty surface. "I'm sorry that it's been hard on you. Believe it or not, it's nothing personal. I just needed to have you in a receptive condition as quickly as possible."

Salazar regard the compad, which was so far displaying only a shimmering grey rectangle. "If you still think I had anything to do with those deaths, those friends of yours, you're wrong."

"I don't think you were culpable. Not of that particular string of crimes, anyway. I do think you were likely a brilliant but intellectually vain man whose ego was easily stroked. Did it never occur to you to question the things that were told to you about Midas Analytics?"

Defiance flashed in his face. "Are you going as hard on Mirna Silk as you are with me?"

"Mirna Silk had her failings, but she wasn't the one turning a blind eye several thousand times a day." Dreyfus sighed, easing back into his chair. "What's done is done. I'm going to extend you the courtesy of believing that you never had any idea where Abacus was leading." He nodded to the cube's sealed door. "Technically, you're a free citizen. If we weren't in the middle of an emergency, I'd offer you the chance of returning home. The trouble is, home may not mean much if Aurora continues extending her reach over us." He slid the compad nearer to Salazar, tapping it so that the grey rectangle resolved into a pane of blurred hieroglyphics. "So help us. If we can't beat our enemy, we can at least get an idea of her present capabilities and movements. These are the confidential files on Catopsis, constructed from recovered documents, interviews and trawls with the main perpetrators, after Ingvar Tench had exposed them. Look at the compad."

"I'm looking at it," Salazar snapped. "All I see is a blur of..." He paused, frowning deeply. "Wait. Something's emerging."

"The Pangolin booster is decoding the enciphered text directly into your visual cortex. You're reviewing some of the most operationally sensitive material anywhere in the system." Dreyfus nodded encouragingly. "It'll become clearer with practice, the effort less taxing. This is all you get, though. We'll allow you access to some simple mark-making tools and a physical recording medium so that you can formulate ideas for communication with other prefects and analysts, but no direct record of the document ever leaves this room. There's simply too much risk of Aurora outfoxing us."

Salazar scrolled down, his eyes flicking across the blurred document. Dreyfus had his own active Pangolin boost, but the internal decryption process was critically dependent on the stereoscopic viewing angle, meaning that only glints of meaning jabbed out at him from his side of the table. It didn't matter: he had studied all the documents at his leisure four years ago, and understood almost nothing of the mathematics.

That was for people such as Salazar.

"I understand the principles being outlined here," the man said, spooling through the document with increasing speed. "But only because they're so simplistic a child could understand them. We were as far beyond these ideas as...well, I'm not even sure if there's an analogy that would help you."

Dreyfus summoned his patience. "I know that this is rudimentary, compared with the methods you employed at Midas. Or thought you were employing. The key thing is to replicate the advances you've already made once already. You can do that, can't you? There can't have been an army of you working on it or the secret would have been blown long ago."

"We were few in number," Salazar answered. "We had time, though. And resources you're not allowing me in this room."

Fearing he might not like the answer, Dreyfus ventured: "How much time, to go from the raw ideas of Catopsis to the improved model running in Abacus?"

"Six months, easily. Six months of fearless, exhausting work."

"I'm not sure we have six months, Aristarchus. Right now, six days might be a luxury."

Salazar truncated a laugh, doubtless seeing sense at the last moment. "I don't think you have a realistic idea of what's possible here, Prefect Dreyfus. Yes, I know this theory...probably better than anyone alive. I can't just...magically recover all that lost work, though. No one could."

"But if anyone were to try, I'd put money on you succeeding," Dreyfus said.

"And if I fail?"

"You'd still be a free man, and I'd still allow you to leave without too many conditions. She's already out there issuing demands, though. I'd make the most of that liberty while you still have it."

Salazar said nothing. After a few moments, he bent his attention back to the compad, continuing to scroll. Dreyfus watched his lips move silently, the hunched acolyte reciting a wordless prayer, before turning to leave him to his labours.

Fifteen hours after her last proclamation, Aurora's face filled the displays in the makeshift tactical room again. Prefects and analysts had been waiting for it, filled with a sense of anxious inevitability. Silence fell across the room, tea and coffee bulbs were set down, coughs suppressed.

"Dear citizens," she began. "I made a simple request, in the hope that we could start anew. I wasn't asking for much: just a cessation of the exodus. I was tolerant to a fault, even after I clarified my position. I allowed time for good sense to prevail; time for reflection from wiser minds. I assumed that would be sufficient, and that the doubters among you would eventually turn to the light. I offered you kindness and freedom; you—some of you —have spurned that impulse to generosity." Coldness sheened her face. "So be it. These fifteen hours have been more than sufficient for a display of contrition, but I've seen nothing of the sort. I must therefore resort to the stick, instead of the carrot."

Dreyfus tensed. Aumonier, Baudry and Clearmountain seemed not to have breathed since the start of her statement.

"I believe in total honesty," Aurora declared. "There are things I can and cannot do. Presently, I can't reach into your heads and punish you through the direct manipulation of your implants. If I could, I would, because that would be the kindest and most efficient way to punish those acting against my desires. I also lack the means to control more than a handful of your ships, beyond the simple measures I already took with those bulk carriers. Nor is it within my gift to do anything really calamitous with your habitats. I can't, for instance, make one habitat veer out of its orbit, endangering millions. Those safety-critical propulsion systems are locked out of network access by design, and you should congratulate yourselves on that piece of forward-sightedness."

"If that's an admission that she didn't have anything to do with Asset 227," Aumonier whispered to Dreyfus, "it fits with your theory that it was a Nerval-Lermontov booby trap."

"Small consolation."

Aurora was still talking. "There are things I can do, however. Measures you perhaps should have locked out of my control when you had the chance. Take environmental housekeeping, for instance. There are thousands of habitats that depend on precise regulation of mirrors and solar shields for power, illumination and temperature maintenance. Among those thousands, there are hundreds with security vulnerabilities that allow me to alter the basic parameters of mirror angle and shield cover. Need I be clearer?"

"Dear Voi, don't do this," Aumonier breathed. "Not to my children."

"No one's going to be boiled alive instantly," Aurora said. "I'm firm, but not heartless. I can, however, begin making your conditions very uncomfortable. I'll start with a random sample of habitats, drawn from the larger pool to which I have housekeeping access. The following will see temperature rises of ten degrees per hour: House Chivilcoy, the Guardo Katsina Spindle, Carousel Salamina-Riki, Hospice Idlewild..." She lingered over the last, it seemed to Dreyfus, savouring his imagined reaction. "Safonovo-Ruteng, the Tikvin Hourglass..."

She went on, listing twenty habitats in total, before drawing breath. "The following, meanwhile, will experience temperature decreases of the same magnitude and at the same rate. Carousel New Madrid, the Droznen Tyranny, the..."

She completed her list: twenty habitats which would bake, twenty which would freeze. "These corrective measures will continue while there is *any* movement of citizens beyond the Glitter Band, based on such criteria as I deem appropriate. I think that is a very fair and balanced response. Now that I have been forced to resort to persuasion, though, I will go one step further. We have a mutual problem, citizens, and now seems as good a time as any to stamp on it." She smiled complicitly, as if the threats she had just uttered were the work of another life, a distant misunderstanding that they could all put behind them. "That problem is Panoply. No more than a minor thorn, but even a thorn can be irritating.

338

I wish Panoply to be neutralised. Commencing immediately, upon pain of further measures, its ships and employees will withdraw from active operations. They will return to their asteroid without delay. I expect this process to take no longer than forty-five minutes, but I will allow sixty out of some misplaced sense of charity."

"She's not done," Aumonier interjected.

"Of course she's not," Dreyfus agreed under his breath. "Thyssen needs to be ready to handle the influx, all the same."

"Notifying the docks," Baudry said, cupping a hand to her mouth.

"That will take care of the immediate difficulty," Aurora was saying. "We shall go further than that, though. In one hour, knowing that its forces are de-clawed, Panoply will be subjected to a massed attack by the free civilian forces of the Glitter Band. I said that I'd encourage movement between habitats. This is my proof. You have weapons, citizens, this I know. Now you may use them with impunity against our common foe. You've been under the heel of the prefects for too long. This is your moment of liberation."

"She wouldn't," Clearmountain said.

"She just did," Aumonier answered.

CHAPTER FORTY-ONE

A handful of cutters and corvettes were the first to return. Dozens more followed, flashing in from every corner of space around Yellowstone. Aumonier had ordered them all to come back in, using every channel available to her. As the crews were debriefed, it became clear that her instructions had not been blocked or distorted in any way. Clearly it suited Aurora that the Supreme Prefect's will be acted upon without question or delay.

Dreyfus went weightless and followed one of the service shafts all the way to the surface of the asteroid. He bobbed out with his head in a clear dome, able to swivel around and take in the view without mediation. Ships clotted the space around Panoply, cutters and corvettes organised into defensive pickets. A couple of the larger deep-system vehicles were arriving on-scene as he watched, their drives so bright that he had to lift a hand to his eyes against the glare. Stark shadows and highlights oozed across a sealike landscape of tumultuous crests and deep troughs, as if the asteroid were restless, awaiting its trial.

Panoply mustered far too many ships for them all to roost at once. Normal operations only functioned on the understanding that a sizeable fraction of the fleet was on active duty, with the locks, docks and berthing facilities already functioning at close to capacity. It was a puzzle Thyssen and his colleagues played expertly—so effectively, in fact, that few had ever pondered what would happen if all the ships came in at the same time.

Aurora knew this, Dreyfus was certain. She had issued a demand that she was confident it was impossible to satisfy. The best that could be done was to concentrate the ships as close to Panoply as possible. She would not take that as any sort of compliance with her wishes, but then she had never expected those wishes to be met.

Dreyfus returned to the interior. That had been his last chance to look outside with his own eyes: technicians were busy sealing off these service shafts, detonating pre-installed charges to collapse the tunnels.

He went to the docks, meeting with the crews of the last few ships to make it into the asteroid. A handful of these operatives had been close enough to one or more of the forty habitats to verify that the coercive measures were more than just a bluff. They had monitored the movement of mirrors and shields, and tracked temperature variations consistent with Aurora's threat. Although there had been no direct observations of the interior conditions, the feeds painted a similar picture. Even a few degrees of rising or cooling temperature were enough to spark panic, over and above what had already been there. This time, though, the citizens had almost nowhere to go. The shuttles, taxis and ferries that might have got some of them to safety had departed during the first exodus.

Dreyfus checked in on Doctor Salazar, finding him alone in the cube, the grey shimmer of the compad still before him. Spread out across the table was a score of glossy white sheets, some of them blank, some of them scrawled over with a mass of jagged marks. Salazar had a stylus in his hand, gouging a black line across one of the sheets. The symbols and annotation Salazar was committing to the sheets suggested some desperate internal mania, but Dreyfus understood better. The first time under Pangolin made for a difficult adjustment, the new neural structures interfering with visual expression, even the very rudiments of written language. That semantic confusion faded after a few doses, but Salazar was still in the full and merciless grip of his first exposure.

It was cruel to expect the man to function under such pressure; crueller still to expect him to reconstruct the work that had taken months the first time around.

"Take a rest from it," Dreyfus said.

Salazar had been so deep into his concentration that he jumped at the voice, unaware until then that he had a visitor.

He twisted to face Dreyfus, wearing a mask cut from equal parts exhaustion and desperation.

"You want to know what she's up to, don't you?"

"It'll help in the long run, once we've weathered this immediate crisis. We have to get through this first, though. She's sending ships against us—anything in the Glitter Band that's armed and willing to take a swing at Panoply." Dreyfus nodded at the bristling sheets. "Have you made any progress?"

Salazar swept his arm across the chaos. "Does that look like progress?"

"I can't ask more of you than you're already giving, Aristarchus. I was hard on you before, and I apologise. You were played, Mirna was played, I was played. Breno and the other conspirators don't get my sympathy— they were willing to kill to protect their operation—but I don't think you have any blood on your hands."

"I don't. Now that you've given me this task, though, I can't let it go." Salazar nodded emphatically, finding some inner fortitude. "I'll continue. If we're about to be attacked, this work is just the distraction I need."

Dreyfus wanted to argue, but he understood perfectly well how good it could be to have a distraction in a time of peril. "I'll have Mercier keep an eye on you, all the same. When he insists on rest, you listen. Besides, that Pangolin boost will start fading before long, and you can't go straight under another until you've built up a tolerance."

"I can start to see my way through," Salazar said. "It's not there yet—there's so much I need to reconstruct, and so much of that wasn't my direct work—but I can see the outlines. A few days...maybe?"

Dreyfus lowered a hand on the bony ridge of his shoulder. "Whatever you can do for us, Aristarchus."

Back in the makeshift tactical room, Tang and his colleagues were rapidly running out of markers to reflect the ever more complex and changeable picture. They were attempting—and mostly failing—to track a growing concentration of civilian spacecraft, mostly private vessels, departing habitats and moving on approach trajectories for Panoply. The ships were moving cautiously, but their intent was clear.

"I can't even blame them," Aumonier told Dreyfus. "They're acting in rational self-interest. You might almost say it's laudable, being prepared to throw themselves against us, rather than allowing those forty habitats to suffer."

Dreyfus opted not to argue, but he wondered which fraction of their motivation stemmed from altruism, and which from a long-frustrated ambition to give his organisation a bloody nose.

"How close are you going to let them get?"

"A little nearer, once I've petitioned their better natures. Then we'll see."

Dreyfus almost laughed. "Better natures? Good luck with that."

"I live in hope. Speaking of which, how is our captive cybernetics theorist managing with that impossible task you've set him?"

"He can see his way through. A few more days, he thinks."

"Good. The instant he has something we can implement, Tang can liaise between Salazar and our own network analysts. If I can just see her shadow, I'll at least know where to cower."

"It would be nice to do more than cower."

"It would be nice to live." She broke off from him to go live. "This is Jane Aumonier, Supreme Prefect of Panoply. We're tracking several civilian space vehicles moving with apparent hostile intent in the direction of Panoply."

Dreyfus raised an eyebrow. Several? It was more like several dozens, perhaps as many as a hundred. On reflection, though, he saw what Aumonier was up to. Panoply probably had a much better grasp of the size of that threat than any of the individual elements making it up. If they knew their real size, they would be emboldened, not deterred. Aumonier wanted to plant a seed of doubt in the mind of anyone thinking of taking on her forces, making them question their true strength.

"I understand your thinking," she added. "But I have to tell you, it's misguided. This won't buy you any favours from Aurora. Once she's dealt with us—at whatever cost to your own lives—she'll pick another enemy, then another, until there's nothing left of any of us but a few rats scrapping over crumbs. Withdraw your ships and weapons, and I promise there'll be no sanction against anyone involved in this action." Aumonier left that olive branch hanging, then proceeded with the rest of her statement. "Understand that I'll defend Panoply to the last atom. If a ship or part of a ship comes within a hundred kilometres of this asteroid, if a solitary weapon is turned on us, if so much as a single warm photon grazes my home, I will act with the full force permitted me under the Common Articles. There'll be no quarter given, no half measures. Your founders vested this power in me; don't be at all surprised when I exercise it."

"Well spoken," Dreyfus said, as her words sped out into the networks.

She nodded fatalistically. "Do you think it'll achieve the slightest good?"

"No. But it needed to be said, all the same."

Tang and his colleagues studied feeds and shuffled markers. "Thirty-three cutters, fifteen corvettes and three cruisers now standing by," Tang reported.

"How are our comms holding?" Aumonier queried.

"Intact, so far, and your transmission appears not to have been blocked. With the ships this close to Panoply, we're able to coordinate with short-range secure channels. They're slow, but the crews of those ships all have their orders. They know not to go in heavy."

"I hope I'm right, Robert," Aumonier replied. "I never thought I'd be put in a position of authorising open warfare against my own citizens. The best I can hope is that a few warning shots will blunt their appetite for a full-on engagement."

"Any sign that they're turning back?" Dreyfus asked, scraping the barrel of his optimism.

"Nothing definite, sir. A few of the stragglers seem to be having second thoughts, judging by range and velocity tracking, but the majority of those civilian ships are still moving as before." Tang conferred with a subordinate, some quick exchange passing between them. "Estimating that the first of those vehicles will be inside our hundred-kilometre margin in three minutes."

Dreyfus nodded gloomily. "A bit late for a change of heart, then."

"Bring our own defences to quick-reaction posture," Aumonier said.

Distant processes rumbled through to them. Dreyfus had been through enough drills to visualise the weapons uncorking themselves around the skin of the asteroid, gun barrels, missile launchers, tracking systems and countermeasure dispensers popping out of armoured emplacements. None of it was subtle and all of it would be visible through the windows of any ships still foolish enough not to have turned around.

"Robert?"

"Two minutes to contact, ma'am."

"Signal all corvettes to fire two fish apiece, set to detonate at ten kilometres, range from thirty randomly selected targets. Medium yield."

"Medium?" queried Clearmountain. "Is this the time to be showing restraint?"

"If we don't, Gaston, you can be reasonably sure no one else will. Medium yield will suffice. Close enough to make my point, but not to damage."

Tang relayed the order, then reported: "Fish away, ma'am. Running clean. First detonation in three, two..."

Around the room, screens overloaded as the missiles detonated at the agreed ranges.

"Thirty detonations, ma'am. Waiting for range and tracking updates on the hostiles."

"Don't keep me in suspense," Aumonier said.

"Three fallbacks, ma'am—possible light damage to one vessel. The remaining hostiles—eighty-eight vehicles—are still closing. Ninety seconds to contact."

"Let's press my point a little more forcefully. Two more up the tubes, same yield, as close as they can get them without actually kissing metal."

"Thirty fish away, ma'am."

The tortured screens flared again, brighter this time. A few of them stayed overloaded, their surface-mounted sensors burned out by the nuclear flashes.

"Tell me I just punched some late sense into them, Robert."

"I wish I could, ma'am. Six are definitely turning back, possibly with damage. That still leaves eighty-two, moving as before. Some of them may have damage preventing them from changing course, but it's impossible to be sure."

"I'm afraid they lost the right to the benefit of the doubt about a minute ago. Time to contact?"

"Thirty-two seconds. Thirty..."

"Crews to coordinate destructive fire on twenty of those ships, beginning with the nearest. Maximum yields on all warheads. If I can persuade sixty-two of them to turn back at the expense of twenty, I'll take that as a win."

"Crews confirm target selection and weapons readiness, ma'am. Interdiction in six seconds, five..."

"Voi forgive me for what I'm about to do," Aumonier intoned.

Dreyfus shook his head. "They're the ones who need forgiveness."

They waited for news to return. If he sought confirmation that it was not as desired, all that Dreyfus needed was the increasingly grim faces of the analysts as they collated the reports.

"Sixteen of the twenty targeted hostiles down, but four appear to have come through relatively unscathed, thanks to countermeasures of their own. Eleven others have begun braking and steering. Fifty-one remain committed and are engaging in free return fire across a range of weapons modes, mostly directed-energy and kinetic."

That—in so far as it went—was the limit of the good news. Now Tang announced a corresponding toll of losses and damage inflicted on Panoply's forces. The lightly armed and minimally armoured cutters had come off the worst, despite their weight of numbers. Because they were fast and agile, they had been at the front of the defensive response and were the most easily picked off by long-range civilian weaponry. Five had been lost completely, depleting the force to twenty-eight vehicles. Two corvettes had been damaged beyond operational effectiveness, leaving just thirteen useful craft. The three cruisers remained intact.

"Authorise all crews to respond with maximum force," Aumonier said, regret drenching her words. "Surface defences to engage. I want that wave stopped dead in its tracks before I lose another prefect."

Dreyfus felt it. The guns churned, sending bowel-loosening vibrations through hundreds of metres of solid rock, through insulation and magnetic barriers, through the superconducting bearings of the entire centrifuge ring.

"Nine hostiles destroyed outright," Tang announced. "Forty-two still tracking as operational and committed. Three more cutters lost. Corvette and deep-system assets intact."

"Instruct the cutters to fall back and use Panoply for protection," Aumonier said. "I won't lose another. The corvettes and cruisers can hold the line. Maintain continuous defensive fire until I say otherwise." She had barely finished speaking before the entire room jolted, every prefect and analysts within it flung sideways, just-settled dust coughing back into the air, makeshift displays crashing from their fixings. Dreyfus grabbed hold of the nearest fixed object, ancient training kicking in as he anticipated the worst. Bearing failure leading to catastrophic centrifuge lock-up: the entire moving mass of rock no longer spinning within the asteroid, but crunching to a sudden, bone-breaking halt.

But the bearings held, as did the artificial gravity caused by the centrifuge's spin.

"Ferris's bones. What the *hell* was that?" Aumonier snarled as the prefects and analysts scrambled back to their positions. "Did one of those ships just ram us?"

Half the displays were dark, with the remainder stuttering slowly back to life. Dreyfus watched the analysts hastily repositioning the markers that had been knocked loose, trying to regain at least a partial picture of Panoply's surroundings.

"Pell reports..." Tang paused, squinting to hear a badly attenuated audio signal. "Pell reports...foam-phase munitions." He gulped, sickened disbelief scribing itself across his face. "They're using foam-phase warheads against us, ma'am. One of their missiles got all the way through!"

Dreyfus shuddered. Short of nuclear or antimatter devices, there were few more potent horrors from the annals of space war. That these deathly instruments should be turned against Panoply, let alone possessed by the civilian citizenry in the first place, struck him as an almost personal affront to his values.

"Damage, Robert?" Aumonier asked, with a dangerous mildness of tone. Dreyfus knew it well. Whoever had committed that crime had just entered the codex of sinners who could never be redeemed.

Images formed on a handful of the still-functioning displays, sent back by the Panoply assets shrouding the asteroid. The foam-phase warhead had blasted a deep new crater across the brow of the pumpkin-faced rock, a throbbing red depression cutting fifty or sixty metres deep into the surface.

"One to one point five per cent of our total mass, ma'am."

"We can't take many hits like that," Baudry said.

"I agree, Lillian. Prioritise interception of those missiles above all other considerations. Then find the ship, or ships, responsible and rain all hell on them. If there's anyone left alive who thinks that was a good idea, they'll have the pleasure of me flaying them alive—"

The room shook again, but the jolt was not as severe as the first time. Dreyfus looked warily at the analysts, calibrating the next dose of catastrophe.

"They got close that time, but our anti-missile guns took out the warhead a couple of kilometres from the surface," Tang said. "The blast has damaged the surface defences across that whole sector."

"If you felt like tossing me a crumb of good news, Robert, it wouldn't go totally unappreciated..."

"I wish I could, ma'am." Tang hesitated, caught on some awful threshold. "There's something big coming in, ma'am, from beyond the Glitter Band. Cruisers have just alerted us."

"Big?" Clearmountain quizzed.

But Dreyfus had no need to wait. "Ultras."

Baudry looked disgusted. "I shouldn't be surprised. It's not like those posthuman degenerates to miss out on a scrap, especially when we're the punching bag."

"Let's...keep an open mind, shall we?" Dreyfus replied. "It's not as if our defences would be much use against a lighthugger, anyway. Can we get an identification on the ship?"

"Just waiting on Pell to relay a visual and cross-match it against our records," Tang said. "Ah, wait. No need for that. The vehicle is broadcasting its registration profile across the usual traffic control channels. The ship in question is...*Shades of Scarlet.*" He looked around the assembled seniors. "Have we done business with them before?"

"I have," Dreyfus said.

The room shook twice more, with confirmation arriving that Panoply had received one direct and one indirect hit from a second pair of foam-phase warheads. The indirect explosion had knocked out sensor and weapons-targeting systems across another sector, while the direct strike, although doing far more damage to the fabric of the rock, had not had an immediate detrimental effect on their defensive capability.

While all this was going on, two more cutters had been lost, one more corvette, and the cruiser *Democratic Circus* was reporting mild impairment after a glancing strike from an energy weapon.

"Incoming from Pell," Tang announced urgently. "Visual on *Shades of Scarlet* indicates multiple anti-ship weapons systems deploying across her hull."

"Put a nuke up them while we can," Clearmountain said.

"Wait," Aumonier snapped, before there was any risk of his suggestion being miscommunicated into an operational fact. "We've spent decades cultivating friendly neutral relations with the Ultras. Aurora isn't their fight, just yet. Why would they throw everything away just to side with a bunch of common rabble they'd look down on at any other time?"

"They're a law unto themselves," Baudry replied. "This is the price of our diplomacy: a knife in our back the moment we're weakened."

"Harbourmaster Seraphim wouldn't allow any one ship to take unilateral action against us," Dreyfus said, desperately hoping that his instincts, and his reading of the man, were not leading him astray. "Those weapons aren't necessarily being aimed at us."

"If you're wrong about this, Dreyfus, you've just written your epitaph," Clearmountain said.

"A constructive contribution might not go amiss, Gaston," Aumonier put in.

"Pell reports..." Tang paused, frowning hard. "Pell reports...massive directed strikes from *Shades of Scarlet*, concentrated on...concentrated on our aggressors. Total loss of four hostiles...no, five. Make that six. Reprisal strikes under way, but now they're having to split their fire between us and the lighthugger."

"Press the advantage," Aumonier said. "Everything we have."

"Ten hostiles down. Twelve. Remaining units are breaking away! All remaining foam-phase warheads tracked and interdicted, ma'am. The attack is over!"

"It's not over," Aumonier intoned, a mountain of resignation in her voice. "She's just landed her first blow, that's all. There are thousands of other armed ships out there that can be turned against us, if she can persuade enough people that it's in their interest."

"Incoming transmission from *Shades of Scarlet*, ma'am." Tang sounded apologetic. "They're asking to be put through to...Prefect Dreyfus."

"Let them speak."

An Ultra appeared on half a dozen screens, face blurred by transmission interference. Dreyfus stared, measuring the barely human form against his limited experience of Ultras to date, and particularly the four he had been asked to consider during his most recent trip to the Parking Swarm. This gargoyle, he was reasonably certain, was new to his acquaintance.

"I'm here," Dreyfus said, angling one of the room's makeshift cameras onto his face. "To whom do I have the pleasure?"

The voice that emerged from the screens sounded like mercury being gargled from the bottom of a bucket.

"Captain Remanso of *Shades of Scarlet*, Prefect Dreyfus. We didn't have a chance to talk before. Had we done so, I would have been sure to thank you for your earlier intercession."

Dreyfus felt that honesty was the best course in nearly every situation.

"You're under a misapprehension, Captain. I thank you for your intervention in our little local difficulty here, but you should be aware that I advised Seraphim to find your senior crewmembers guilty. It was up to him what he did with that opinion, but I wouldn't want you to think I'd ruled in your favour."

For all that the visage facing him was alien and—until then—thoroughly inscrutable, Dreyfus detected a sly amusement playing out on the face of the Ultra.

"There was no misapprehension, Prefect, but your reputation for candour was clearly not exaggerated. We had a little local difficulty of our own, you see. An internal reorganisation of our command structure, following a vote of no confidence in the actions of my predecessors, Triumvirs Nisko and Pazari. Their disreputable conduct brought the good name of our ship into jeopardy, as you rightly found."

"Then...I am pleased that matters were satisfactorily resolved," Dreyfus said, conscious that the other seniors were looking on with no small measure of astonishment. "And I think it may fall upon me to convey the thanks of the Supreme Prefect, and Panoply as a whole, for your timely intervention."

"We did what we could, Prefect. Now, though, considerations of safety and commerce oblige our return to the Parking Swarm. I hope that our modest display of deterrence will suffice, for now?"

"I hope it will as well," Dreyfus replied.

"You have a plan, should wiser minds not prevail? There would be no winners should our ships be forced into all-out war against half the Glitter Band, even if we were acting to defend Panoply."

"A plan is in hand," Dreyfus said.

"And there goes your reputation for honesty," Captain Remanso said, not without a dry measure of sympathy. "Good luck, nonetheless, Prefect Dreyfus."

"Thank you," Dreyfus said, deflated and relieved in the same breath.

The screens had barely cleared of the Ultra captain's face before another formed, one all too familiar to the assembled prefects and analysts.

"We'll call that a draw," Aurora declared magnanimously. "And it *was* a good fight, while it lasted. I'll give you credit for that. Kudos for that helpful little intervention from those Ultras you all secretly despise and fear. Nothing's changed, though. I can keep turning up the heat, and the cold, in more habitats than you can name. The advantage of fear, and terror, is all mine. And I intend to press that while I can, Jane Aumonier." She brightened, as if an exciting new idea just formed in her head. "Or would you like me to stop it?"

"What would it take?" Aumonier asked.

"Your head. Or the whole of you, whichever you prefer." Aurora nodded, letting her demand sink in. "Give me Jane Aumonier and the pain stops. You have until those people boil or freeze. Your choice."

Aumonier said nothing for a few moments. She looked around at her colleagues, taking in their stricken expressions.

"You want me?"

"I'd have thought I was plain enough, even for you."

"And what if I said I don't believe you'd ever keep to a promise? I'd give you my head on a stick if I thought it would achieve anything."

"It won't," Dreyfus said.

Aurora had heard him. "The problem is, dear Dreyfus, that if she does nothing, the people in those forty habitats—including Hospice Idlewild—will most definitely perish. Whereas if she surrenders herself to me, there's at least an outside chance I might keep my word. Not the best odds, I'll grant you, but even Jane Aumonier can see that backing a lame horse is better than no horse at all."

"Take me instead," Dreyfus said. "You've no quarrel with the Supreme Prefect."

"Ah, but you and I have entirely too much history. Besides, I want the figurehead. I want to publicly decapitate Panoply."

"We'll still be here," Dreyfus insisted. "You'll have achieved nothing but an act of pointless cruelty."

Aurora looked affronted. "You don't even know my plans for her."

"I know you."

"Then you should know that I can be merciful, as well as severe. Did I allow you to die in Carcasstown? Did I let Ng perish?"

"We both know I'm not standing here out of the goodness of your heart, Aurora."

"Enough, Tom," Aumonier said, laying a hand on his sleeve. "She's right: she's stated her case clearly enough. It's me or nothing. And while I doubt that it'll help any of those people—or anyone else in the Glitter Band, for that matter—I can't simply stand by." She turned to her seniors, looking at each of them individually. "My mind is made up, friends. Please don't try to persuade me otherwise."

Baudry's lips moved, but no sound came out.

"What, Lillian?"

"I was just wondering...since your choice is made...would you consider...?"

"Resignation, and reassignment of the role of Supreme Prefect?"

"I was going to say, would you consider some form of...euthanisation?"

350

Aumonier shook her head briskly. "Thank you for your kind concern, Lillian, but I strongly suspect Aurora wants a warm, talking body, not a corpse. Something she can play with, like a doll, until she pulls me apart in a fit of rage and boredom."

Dreyfus swallowed, his throat tightening. "We can still consider drugs. Something to take the edge off, whatever comes."

"I'm surprised you're not trying to argue me out of this, Tom."

"I know you better than to try."

Aumonier returned her attention to the screens. "You'll have me, Aurora. In a suit, if not on a plate. What you do with me is up to you. I insist on time to make my final arrangements, though."

"You can have as long as you like, Supreme Prefect. The only clock ticking is the one measuring out the lives of those people. How long you let them suffer, and to what end, is entirely down to you."

"Provided no attack on Panoply is ongoing, I'll emerge from one of the surface locks in...well, you'll be expecting me."

"I shall indeed, Supreme Prefect."

"Kill the feeds," Aumonier said, making a chopping gesture around the room. "Everything for now. The ships can handle themselves, and if those fools try to lob a few more foam-phase missiles at us, I've a feeling we'll know about it anyway. She's going to be in my head before long; the least I can do is have a holiday from her madness for an hour or two."

With the screens and feeds neutralised, the room seemed darker than before, darker and smaller and more oppressive.

"None of that was a bluff, was it?" Clearmountain asked rhetorically. "You're really going out there."

"I've nothing left to play, Gaston. If I'm the pawn she wants right now, she can have me." Then she nodded forgivingly at Baudry. "That was sharp of me just now, Lillian, and I apologise. Your consideration was well meant. That said, I wasn't wrong to raise the possibility of a formal transition of power. I'd be remiss in my responsibilities if I neglected it, while I have the time. I'm appointing you and Clearmountain as Joint Acting Prefects Supreme. This will provide Panoply with an unbroken chain of authority in the hours after my departure. Once matters are resolved...whatever *that* means...you may proceed with a formal process for appointment of a permanent Supreme."

"No," Clearmountain said flatly. "I refuse this appointment, Supreme Prefect."

"As do I," Baudry stated.

"I can still resign. You'd have no option but to fill my boots."

"But you won't, and they know it," Dreyfus said. "You're our Supreme

Prefect until your heart stops beating. That's one thing we get to decide on, not her."

Aumonier waited a moment then nodded, accepting the verdict of her colleagues.

"I still have formal business I'd like to complete, in the privacy of my own quarters. It needn't take more than a few minutes. Before then, though, I'd like to surrender myself to Aurora with at least one question fully satisfied." Her features gained a familiar determined set, one that might almost have been reassuring. "She's going to give me the truth if I have to wring it out of her. Take me to Hafdis."

CHAPTER FORTY-TWO

Dreyfus and Aumonier took their places opposite Hafdis in the cube, now vacated by Doctor Salazar on the medical instructions of Mercier. For a minute they said nothing, did nothing, waiting for her to fill the silence. She looked disconcerted more than alarmed, as if she were expected to play a role for which she had not been adequately briefed.

"A prefect told me we were under attack," she said at last, nodding to the door. "I heard and felt it in here, but then I don't suppose we were as fully isolated then as we are now. Has the attack finished?"

Dreyfus cleared his throat. "Aurora moved against us. I don't know if you were given all the facts, but there are forty habitats out there being put through two different kinds of hell, with thousands of people suffering needlessly because of Aurora's need to assert her supremacy over us."

"But the attack stopped?" she asked, her eyes inviting good news.

"It's just a lull," Aumonier answered. "The Ultras intervened once, but that's no lasting solution. Aurora can keep turning the pressure up on the Glitter Band, turning even the mildest, most law-abiding citizens against us. I don't blame them for acting under such coercion..." But her mouth creased, her own sentiments disgusting her. "No, I *do* blame them. There are a thousand of us, one hundred million of them. What sort of citizenry turns against its own protectors, when we've done everything possible to defend their rights?"

"Aurora isn't trustworthy," Dreyfus said. "That's beyond question. When she issues an ultimatum, though, we're obliged to act as if she might honour it. Anything less would be an abandonment of our most cherished principles."

For the first time Hafdis seemed to grasp the severity of the moment. Her voice darkened. "What sort of ultimatum?"

"She's demanded me," Aumonier answered, laying her hands on the table. "If I hand myself over, then there's at least a possibility that she'll stop interfering with those habitats. The people inside them can't hold out for much longer. Hours, at best, for the majority of them. Depending

353

on a roll of the dice, they die of either heat exhaustion or hypothermia. Neither's a good way to go, and I won't have that on my watch."

"She won't keep her side of the bargain," Hafdis said, with a surprising confidence.

"I know," Aumonier acknowledged, dipping her head. "That truth is practically written in the stars. I have to go along with her game, though. She'll betray us, but at least then we'll have the fact of her betrayal to throw back in her face. She'll have lost what little bargaining credibility she has."

"And where does that leave Panoply?"

"We'll adapt to the changing crisis," Dreyfus offered. "We'll adhere to our obligations under the Common Articles. Until we're down to our last prefect, our last drop of blood. There isn't one among us who won't uphold that commitment."

"Bold words, from an organisation with a proven history of saboteurs and turncoats."

Dreyfus chilled. "All of a sudden, I don't think I'm talking to Hafdis Tench any more. Is this the point where you finally drop the mask?"

She shrugged, indifferent to his provocation. "There's never been a mask to drop, Dreyfus."

Aumonier studied her with a reptilian focus, barely blinking. "The act always had to fall apart at some point, didn't it? You couldn't argue with the falsified DNA records. It was just a question of how long you maintained your denial. You're exactly what we suspected: another face of Aurora Nerval-Lermontov."

"When did the false memories begin to break down?" Dreyfus asked.

She smirked at his misapprehension. "There never were any. I've known exactly who and what I am from the moment we first set eyes on each other. You just didn't have the imagination to accept that someone could play their part that well, that convincingly." Then the smirk softened, becoming something fonder. "Ingvar schooled me well."

"You call her Ingvar now, not your mother," Aumonier said.

"Because she was never my mother."

"Did you engineer her death?" Dreyfus interrogated.

"I loved her," she countered, with a venomous edge. "She may not have been my mother, but she was everything to me that a mother would have been."

Dreyfus had pushed deliberately. This was the reaction he had been hoping for.

"She really protected you, then. Knowing what—who—you are?"

"From the moment she found me on that rock, she knew everything.

354

They put me in there as a form of insurance: to be raised in an environment similar, if not identical, to the surroundings of my erstwhile counterpart. I came to adulthood in that chateau, with only robots for company."

"We're going back more than half a century," Aumonier said.

"Yes." Hafdis nodded. "And when I came to fruition, so to speak, I became an embarrassment, and then a problem to be hidden away. I was put on ice, placed in hibernation, with only the robots to tend to me. The links between Asset 227 and the Nerval-Lermontov family, obscure as they already were, were further obfuscated. My family made every possible effort to forget about me and what I represented. Asset 227 was abandoned to its fate, the house falling into decay, the robots failing one by one, until there were just barely enough to monitor my hibernation. Decades went by. The ties were buried so thoroughly that only someone as dogged and resourceful as Ingvar Tench could possibly have unearthed them."

"What motivated her to look for you?" Dreyfus asked.

"She wasn't looking for me. She didn't know I existed. Her work on investigating Catopsis had led to a general interest in Aurora's background, which in turn meant looking into every possible loose end connected to her family. She was...relentless. If there was a single loose end, a single transaction that couldn't be accounted for, you could rely on Ingvar to pursue it doggedly, all the way to the answer. A thousand would have given up before she did. It simply wasn't in her character to let go."

Aumonier leaned in, her hands still on the table. "And when she realised what you were?"

"Instead of seeing the worst in me, she saw the best. Just because I was a copy of Aurora didn't mean I was bound to turn into her. My counterpart wasn't a monster, not until they made her into one. The Eighty was the crucible in which she was formed, not her childhood. And I've never been through the Eighty."

"That makes you good?" Dreyfus asked.

"It makes me neither good nor bad, Dreyfus. I'm a blank slate, a human canvas with all the possibilities thereof."

He glanced at Aumonier. "Why did you wait until now before admitting this?"

"Ingvar went to a lot of trouble to protect me. One thing she made sure I understood was that my identity wasn't to be shared by anyone I didn't trust beyond the slightest shred of doubt."

"She was afraid of what the world would do to you," Dreyfus said, nodding slowly. "Afraid of what Aurora's enemies would do, including the Clockmaker."

"I'm a weapon," she replied. "I've always known that." She reached behind her head, removing the hair-clasp so that her curls tumbled down. In the same continuous fluid movement, one that was so natural that Dreyfus barely had time to detect its wrongness, she brought the sharp tip of the clasp into contact with Aumonier's left hand. "Don't flinch, Supreme Prefect. Mother gave me this clasp for a reason. There's an extremely powerful nerve toxin embedded in the needle. She obtained it from a black-market weaponeer, knowing I'd have cause to use it eventually."

Dreyfus made an urgent stilling motion with his hand. Aumonier tensed, but she made no attempt to withdraw.

"I'm likely going to die today, Hafdis," she said calmly. "What is threatening me going to achieve? I might decide that your toxin is by far my best option."

Hafdis was as poised as a statue. "You won't, though, because you're Jane Aumonier. You know that your duty lies beyond Panoply, with Aurora. You'll do nothing that jeopardises that." Barely moving her head, Hafdis dipped her eyes to the table. "Dreyfus, go and make them reconnect the corridor so that we can leave the cube. Supreme Prefect, get up from your chair very slowly and carefully. I'll get up from mine in the same movement."

"This isn't going to get you anywhere, you know."

"Do as I say. Ingvar told me the effects of that toxin are excruciating and irreversible."

Aumonier flashed a look to Dreyfus. "Do it, Tom. If I leave this room, then I'm one step closer to the surface. Somewhere along the way she'll make an error."

Dreyfus moved to the outer door and signalled the attending prefect through the window, making a spooling gesture with his fingers. Slowly the connecting bridge advanced back toward the cube.

He returned to the room. Aumonier and Hafdis were both standing now, with the needle still pushed against the Supreme Prefect's skin. He could see the flesh dimpling down, almost as if it were eager to yield, inviting the toxin to storm its human host.

"If Ingvar had a plan for you," Dreyfus said, "I'm not sure how this fits. We're your friends, not that thing out there. What do you think she'll do: welcome you like a long-lost sister?"

Hafdis said nothing until the bridge had reconnected, providing free passage back into the rest of Panoply.

"The Sleep Lab," she said, urging Aumonier to walk.

Aumonier twisted her head around, the fine scar around her neck whitening. "What do you want with me in there?"

"I think we both know."

Dreyfus moved ahead of the pair as they advanced along the bridge, detesting his complicity but determined to clear the way of any prefects who might try to intervene. Time and again he had cursed the labyrinthine layout of Panoply's interior, the seeming perversity of its designers in making it awkward and confusing to get from any one part of it to another. Now the corridors and junctions flowed past, the journey compressing, as if some treacherous tide was intent on sweeping the Supreme Prefect to her destiny in the Sleep Lab.

They moved through the outer annexes of Medical. Prefects and supernumerary staff detected the trio's arrival, saw in Dreyfus's demeanour the extreme inadvisability of meddling, and retreated back into nooks and hollows so that there was not the least chance of hampering Hafdis and thereby provoking her hand.

They passed into the green womb of the Sleep Lab.

Hafdis guided Aumonier along the glass cabinets, past rank after rank of clocks and pieces of clock, an arsenal of dreadful things, past the many iterations of the scarab until, with a terrible finality, they arrived at the cabinet that contained only one exhibit.

The last scarab. The final product of her finest minds: the one scarab that was complete and functional.

"No," Dreyfus said, as his understanding crystallised. "Not that, Hafdis. Not ever again."

"Open the cabinet, Supreme Prefect. With your other hand, naturally."

Aumonier reached out, palming the alloy panel next to the cabinet. The glass screen whisked up and away.

"Take it out," Hafdis instructed.

"I swear I'll take your toxin over this."

"Do it."

Aumonier used one hand to extract the scarab from its fixture, her fingers trembling as the innately evil object responded to her touch, ticking and twitching.

"You said its inputs were available for programming. Was that correct?"

"Yes," Aumonier said, her voice little more than a rasp.

"Place it on me." Hafdis waited for her words to drill home. "I said *place it on me*. I'm wearing it, not you."

"Hafdis…" Aumonier began.

"Do it. I won't ask again. Fix it onto my neck." Hafdis emphasised her instruction by increasing pressure on the needle. Aumonier winced as it bit deeper.

"I think you should do it," Dreyfus whispered.

"I think she should," Hafdis agreed.

Something broke in Aumonier, some last defence crumbling. Still with the needle pressing against her skin, she lifted the scarab into place on the back of Hafdis's neck. It clasped on reflexively, and Hafdis let out a tiny gasp as the neural taps drilled into her spine.

She let the hair-clasp drop from her fingers.

"I'm sorry..." Hafdis started, shivering before regaining some brittle composure. "I'm sorry I put you through that, Supreme Prefect. I knew you'd never consent to this otherwise."

Dreyfus bent down and picked up the hair-clasp. He held it tentatively, eyeing the needle. "Was there ever any toxin in this, Hafdis?"

"You've already taught me several things, Dreyfus. One of them was how to improvise my way out of a difficulty."

Aumonier swung Hafdis around to face her. "I don't know why you've done this. But you're right that I'd never have willingly agreed to this."

"This is the only way, Supreme Prefect. Trust me; I've given it more than a little consideration."

Aumonier persisted. "We're in the grace period where it might just be feasible to remove it, Hafdis. It allowed me one hour to achieve complete isolation from human contact. The same delay will apply with that unit. Once that hour is up, we won't be able to remove it or reprogram it."

"I won't be asking you to do either."

"Then what?" Dreyfus asked.

"You can track Aurora, even now. I know about the latency metrics Grigor Bacchus developed for Catopsis to detect her and trace her activity. Ingvar made sure I was fully informed. All of that work...it's all still applicable. She'll move and behave in different ways, now that she's no longer limited by the Clockmaker, but her activity can still be tracked using those same analytic methods." Her eyes locked onto him, burning with wild conviction. "When the scarab was fixed onto Jane, it was primed to kill her if she slept or came into close contact with another human being."

"And now?" Dreyfus asked.

"The triggering criteria will be different. Not human proximity, this time, but Aurora's activity. You'll use the latency metrics. Set the detective threshold very low, so that any intervention by Aurora—any movement or activity on her part—leads to my instantaneous death. It doesn't matter where in the system I am, or where she is—whether she's concentrated or dispersed. She only has to breathe and she'll kill me." She nodded, the scarab flexing against the movement of her neck, but not relenting its hold. "We make this happen, and then we inform Aurora. We allow her

358

time to understand what I am and what would become of me if she were to trigger the scarab."

"You think she'll act to protect you, at all costs," Aumonier said, marvelling. "By disappearing herself."

"It's a calculation, Supreme Prefect," Hafdis acknowledged. "A managed risk. Either she will see herself in me and decide that I'm the last link to her former innocence, something to be valued and defended, a reminder of all that could have been—and perhaps still could—or she'll bat me away like a bad smell. Really, though, what choice do you have? You have no weapons to turn against her, no adversary to hold her in check, nothing else that she wants badly enough to make her play nicely. It's me or nothing." She straightened, the scarab relaxing closer to her neck with a series of tiny ratcheting clicks. "This, or damnation. Now take me to Grigor Bacchus. We have urgent work to do."

"Grigor Bacchus is dead," Dreyfus informed her.

Aumonier nodded gravely. "Tom's right. Lovro Breno is gone as well; with the right persuasion, he might have helped."

Hafdis took this news with disarming equanimity, as if she would have been disappointed not to have been set a last obstacle.

"Then you'd better dig up someone else who understands these metrics. And be quick about it."

"There's Doctor Salazar," Dreyfus said.

"What of him?"

"I've been encouraging him to reconstruct the work that was lost when Abacus was destroyed. No one's better placed to understand those latency metrics, or to implement the triggering thresholds. He needs time, though. He's just one man, undergoing his first taste of Pangolin."

"Can he do it?"

He evaluated his answer carefully. "Mercier instructed him to rest. There'd be a reason for that. And he wasn't close to reconstructing the work—he still needed days, at the most optimistic estimate."

"He doesn't have days," Hafdis said.

CHAPTER FORTY-THREE

They put Hafdis into an m-suit, set for full transparency, so that there could be no ambiguity about the presence of the scarab. Then Dreyfus and Aumonier donned suits of their own and went with her out through one of the main locks, each of them wearing a tether that allowed them to drift a few hundred metres out into space.

For Dreyfus, it was his first opportunity to inspect the damage done to the rocky outside of Panoply with his own eyes. He surveyed the toll of impact points, both minor and major, and the large, still-glowing depression where the worst of the foam-phase strikes had hit home.

"It feels like a gut punch," Aumonier commented, reading his thoughts. "After everything, this was how we were rewarded. My own children, spitting in my eye."

"You'll get over it," he said dryly. "You get over most things."

"Are you all right, Hafdis?" Aumonier asked.

"Yes, I'm perfectly comfortable. I was looking forward to the day when you let me try on one of these suits. Granted, I didn't anticipate quite these circumstances."

Aurora's face appeared before Dreyfus, faintly translucent and shot through with a shoal of distant habitats and slow-moving spacecraft.

"It's very good of you to accompany her, Dreyfus and whoever the other prefect is, but I only asked for the Supreme Prefect. Or did you feel you needed the moral support of your friends, Jane Aumonier?"

Their tethers reached their limit, snapping tight. Dreyfus, Hafdis and Aumonier came to a halt, floating three abreast.

"The Supreme Prefect was willing to go along with your proposal," Dreyfus announced, watching the face for tell-tale responses. "Foolish as that may have been."

"I don't care for your use of the past tense, Dreyfus."

"There's been a change of plan," Aumonier announced. "You're not getting me."

"Another lamb to the slaughter, in your place? How admirable."

"No," Aumonier said. "Hafdis, perhaps you ought to explain. By now, Aurora will have detected the scarab fixed around your neck. She won't need reminding who and what was the mastermind behind it."

"You feign ignorance of me," Hafdis said, speaking boldly. "Although I don't doubt for a second that you know who I am."

"Ingvar Tench's daughter. Yes, now move along. Your mother was at least resourceful enough to be of use to me."

"She wasn't my mother. My mother was your mother. I'm a Nerval-Lermontov."

The denial was instant and vicious. "No."

"We may not look alike, but that's just camouflage. Mere skin and bones. I was created in your image, Aurora. When our parents sent you to be scanned and uploaded, there was a part of them that feared the outcome. Feared failure. Feared that they were putting family glory above the welfare of their beloved only daughter. Therefore I was created, so that if the worst happened to you, not everything would be lost."

"No! I won't abide this a moment longer. Surrender yourself, Supreme Prefect. Cut the cord. Drift out to me, and we'll put this foolish little gambit behind us."

"You've got an hour," Hafdis declared. "Actually a little less than that, but for a being of your immense power and speed, I'm sure it'll be ample time."

Now she snarled. "Ample time for *what*?"

"To be gone. To vanish from human affairs. The scarab is linked to an algorithm monitoring latency metrics throughout human space around Yellowstone."

"The Catopsis algorithm? I could break it in my sleep, if I slept."

"Not that one. Doctor Salazar worked to reconstruct the improved algorithm implemented as part of Abacus."

"Abacus was a feint. I made it."

"But the algorithm was genuine—the human minds behind it made it so. It was authentic, and Salazar has only bettered it in the time available to him. You can't evade physics, Aurora. To exist at all, you can't avoid imposing a drag on our network resources. You can create noise and echoes and all sorts of confusion to attempt to mask your presence, but Salazar's methods will always weed you out. They can't destroy you, but they can at least know you. And when his algorithm goes live, which it will do in less than sixty minutes, I become your hostage. Or you become mine, depending on how you look at it."

Now Aurora's denial was a shriek of impotence and fury. "No! This is not—"

"Shut up," Hafdis said mildly. "We've heard more than enough from you. Now I get to speak. The *other* Aurora. The one who hasn't been damaged. The one who still gets to breathe and feel, the one who still understands love and loyalty. The one who can still hurt. The one who can still die."

"Give me proof. Give me one tiny reason not to send a carrier hurtling into you right now."

"I've given you something more powerful than proof," Hafdis replied. "What you have now is doubt. Like it or not, you can't dismiss the possibility of me. It's all entirely plausible, given what we both know of our family. The greed, the hubris, the cowardice."

"Panoply will furnish corroborating data," Aumonier said. "The operational logs of my operatives, including Ingvar Tench and Sparver Bancal. The tangle of ownership records relating to Asset 227, which—if pulled upon firmly enough—lead to the Nerval-Lermontov estate. Genetic records, verifying everything Hafdis has said. It will all be surrendered for your inspection, in the next thirty minutes."

Dreyfus took up the thread. "You'll rightly point out that almost every record is questionable on some level. That will still leave you with that nasty little kernel of doubt, chafing away. You won't be able to ignore it. And even for you, with your limitless speed and cleverness, those minutes are going to speed by. I'd get to work now, if I were you. You've got an awful lot of harm to undo."

Hafdis spoke again. "If the latency metrics sense you, the scarab will kill me. If the metrics sense any attempt to interfere in their function, the scarab will kill me. Beyond that, all normal functionality will be returned to the Glitter Band: abstraction and voting rights will be restored, and you will release your grip on those forty habitats. There's no negotiation on these principles. You either comply or face the consequences for the one part of you that hasn't been tainted."

"We're not denying you a choice," Dreyfus said. "In fact, you've got several possible courses of action. You can brazen us out and see if we mean what we say. Perhaps your last link with flesh and blood really doesn't matter to you that much and you're willing to take a gamble that you can outwit us. I think it does matter, though—or else why would you have taken such pains to remind me that you're not like the Clockmaker, that you still remember being alive, being human, being a girl?"

Aurora seethed. "Don't imagine that you can understand what does and does not matter to one such as I."

"Oh, I can chance a guess or two," he said. "Do you want to know about your other choices? You can hide here, in this system, and bide your time, waiting until you've summoned the nerve to re-emerge. Perhaps you'll be content just to wait for Hafdis to die of natural causes, which will happen one day. She's young, though, and there's no reason for her not to live for another couple of centuries. That's a problem for you, because the thing you really fear, the thing that may mean the end of you, is going to hit sooner than that, isn't it? A century, maybe sooner. And waiting and hiding…that's not exactly a risk-free strategy, even in the short term. You'll guess at the parameters of Salazar's latency algorithm, but you won't know it in its entirety. And in not knowing, there's always a chance that you might trigger it accidentally, just by existing. Perhaps you're willing to bank on your superiority, though? Or you could just eliminate all the unknown variables and yourself. Remove all possibility for error; remove all possibility of ever harming Hafdis, by deleting yourself completely." He looked at her searchingly. "You *could* do that, couldn't you, or am I overestimating your capabilities?"

"Tell her the last option," Aumonier said gently.

"You can leave," Dreyfus said. "Just go. Find some other solar system to play with. There are ships leaving all the time. I'm sure, with your ingenuity, you could bottle yourself into one. Become a stowaway on a lighthugger, haunting its data architecture. Be quick about it, though. You wouldn't want to trip over the algorithm on your way out the door."

Hafdis touched her hand to the back of her neck, fingering the scarab through the membrane of her m-suit. "Dreyfus is right. There's much less time than when we started."

"You're not me, you worm. You couldn't ever *be* me."

"Perhaps not," Hafdis answered. "But I know what I *can* be. Something that's closed to you for all eternity: *alive*. I'll go through my life with this thing on me, and there won't ever be a day when I forget that it's there or fail to remember what it could do to me at any moment." She nodded back at Dreyfus. "Not a day in that very long life I might have ahead of me. That won't be every second of my existence, though. There'll be lots of time when I just get to be me. Within the Glitter Band, I can move anywhere and do anything I like. I could even become a prefect, if I want it badly enough."

Then she nodded to the two agents of Panoply who had accompanied her out into space. "I think we've stated our position, don't you?"

"Adequately," Dreyfus agreed.

"Reel us in," Aumonier said.

The tethers tightened behind them, hauling them back to the waiting sanctuary of the asteroid. Aurora was still screaming at them as they retreated, but Dreyfus let the noise wash over him, no more worthy of his consideration than the mindless howl of some distant dying star.

While they waited for the consequences of their ultimatum to play out, Dreyfus went down to speak to Aristarchus Salazar.

As a final precaution, he made sure that they spoke in the cube.

"If you've come to chastise me for failing, Prefect Dreyfus, you're preaching to the converted. Nothing will ever excuse my weakness in being suckered into Abacus, but at least I had the defence of gullibility. Here, I don't even have that." He spread his hand across the white sheets, still hectic with his markings. "I was close—I could see the goal. I needed more time, though. Far more than an hour!"

"I haven't come to chastise you," Dreyfus said, sitting opposite the harried data theorist. "That wouldn't really be fair, given the difficulty of the task I set you. We always knew it was a long shot, although that doesn't mean you won't keep working on the problem, once you can tolerate another dose of Pangolin."

Salazar gripped air with his fingers. "But everything depended on me! This one chance for redemption! You made it perfectly clear, Dreyfus. You needed that latency algorithm there and then!"

"We did," Dreyfus admitted. "I was wrong, though. What we needed was the idea of it: the possibility that it might be real."

Salazar looked up sharply, some dark comprehension breaking through. "The idea?"

"Hafdis showed me the way. I believed in her hair-clasp, for just long enough for it serve the purpose she needed."

"I don't know what that means."

"It means you're the hair-clasp, Aristarchus. Aurora knows about you, and she knows that you had a hand in shaping the latency tracking behind Abacus."

"Well, yes," he allowed. "But I don't see..."

"It's enough. Aurora can't tell if you succeeded, but by the same token there's no way for her to know that you failed. Only three people in the universe know that."

"You and I..." Salazar began, lifting his fingers to count.

"And the Supreme Prefect, Jane Aumonier."

Salazar frowned, some fraction of his understanding lagging behind the rest. "But what about the one wearing the scarab?"

"Hafdis doesn't know," Dreyfus answered gently. "Hafdis can't ever know. You, Jane Aumonier and I have to keep a secret: a simple matter of never discussing these events. For Hafdis it's different. She has to play the role with perfect conviction, at least until we know Aurora is no longer a concern. That might be tomorrow, or it might be fifty years from now.

Until then, the only way to make sure Hafdis plays her part is for her to think that the algorithm is real, functioning in exactly the way she imagines."

Salazar asked him: "Then what *is* real? What's the true triggering criterion for the scarab?"

"There isn't one. The inputs have closed, and now there's no possibility of altering the programming. Short of someone trying to remove the scarab by force, she has nothing to fear from it."

"But she doesn't know that!"

Dreyfus nodded solemnly, standing up and bidding Salazar to join him. "And she can't, ever. Not until the day we're absolutely sure that we're free of Aurora. That's the burden she has to carry, Aristarchus. I wouldn't exactly say it's one she's chosen, but she forced us into placing it on her. That part, at least, she was prepared for long ago. She's been ready for whatever was asked of her, and I think Ingvar Tench would be proud of what she's done."

"I still failed," he said mournfully.

"You succeeded by existing," Dreyfus replied. "The fact of you is enough. That's no small thing, Aristarchus. You've nothing to apologise for now." He patted the man on the back. "Come. It's been a long day for all of us."

"Is it over?"

Dreyfus scraped up a smile. "Ask me again tomorrow."

CHAPTER FORTY-FOUR

Thalia was already awake, and he was glad of that. He would not have felt good about disturbing her, even for this.

"They won't let me out of the infirmary, sir, not even to observe," she said, as if he had come down to chastise her for a lack of commitment. "Some of the news reaches here, but it's hard to find out much without a compad."

She was sitting up on a couch, her injured shoulder bulging through the fabric of her dragon-patterned gown.

"That's on the mend?" Dreyfus asked, passing her a bulb of tea he had collected on the way.

"Mercier says I'll be able to go back to my quarters tomorrow, then resume light duties if I so wish. I'm not to think about field work for at least a week." She sipped on the tea, her customary politeness masking whatever deficiency of preparation it might have had. "That's very kind of you, sir. They don't really know how to make it down here."

"It might be a little premature to be making plans for field duties," Dreyfus said, easing into a seat next to Thalia. "We can hope for a return to normality, of course—no harm in that—but it'll be some while before we stop looking over our shoulders." He looked at her with a fatherly interest in her progress. "How much have you managed to keep up with?"

"Just the bare bones of it, sir. That there was an attack against us, then some kind of ultimatum concerning the Supreme Prefect. Are you able to tell me what actually happened?"

He smiled, rummaging through the chaos of his thoughts for some kind of order. Some narrative that made sense to him, and which might satisfy Thalia. Even if it could never be the whole truth.

"Hafdis has placed herself in jeopardy to save both the Supreme Prefect, and not inconsequentially the rest of us. Aumonier is fine: she was willing to throw herself on the fire, but in the end that was never needed. Now Hafdis is under the scarab."

Horror broke on her face. "No!"

366

"It's not as awful as it sounds. The scarab's fixed to her, but it's not impinging on her freedom in any significant way. She can still be with people, move around, do as she wishes. She's not in any discomfort, and she can sleep whenever she likes."

"But to do that to her…"

"We didn't," he corrected gently. "It was Hafdis, doing it to herself. Her idea, her execution. I think it was always there, a contingency to be put into place if all else failed. I don't doubt her mother had some say in that, too."

"Then Ingvar was her mother, after all?"

"In all the ways that matter."

Thalia sipped her tea, brooding. "How does it help us, for her to be wearing that thing?"

"It gives us a point of leverage over Aurora, something we never had before. No weapon was ever going to work against her, so the only thing left was love. By which I don't mean our love for her, or her love for us; there was precious little of either."

"Then what?"

"Aurora's love for what she once was, and what she lost. Call it yearning, call it regret, if love doesn't fit. Hafdis is the last living link to that, and Aurora would sooner disperse herself than risk the end of what she used to be. That's the calculation, at least."

"You think she'll end herself, rather than hurt Hafdis?"

"We offered her a get-out. It's not necessary that she terminates herself, just as long as she makes herself scarce. She can do that." The chair creaked as he adjusted his bulk. "I'm not sure I'd have rejoiced at her destruction, even if that had been an option. She's something rare and dangerous, something capable of great cruelty but also great cleverness. Who's to say we won't have need of her, somewhere down the line? I think I prefer the notion of banishment to execution."

"You could argue that we've just passed a problem onto some other people—perhaps even put them at serious risk."

"Maybe they'll be cleverer than we were. Maybe she'll have learned a thing or two along the way. Maybe the ship she bottles herself into runs into a speck of interstellar rock at nearly the speed of light and she becomes nobody's problem ever again."

"Aren't you concerned that she'll just try and trick you?"

Dreyfus had arrived at a juncture, the first of several lies he needed to negotiate. It was why he had purposely chosen to sit next to her, rather than facing her: so that she would not see his face too clearly, and the strain that he was certain would show.

367

"No. So long as Hafdis keeps living, it can only mean that Aurora is gone. Either hidden—and therefore harmless—or entirely vanished from the system. I don't care which. If the scarab kills Hafdis, then we'll know that Aurora has betrayed herself. That won't happen, though."

"Can you be sure?"

Dreyfus calibrated the earnestness of his nod. "I have complete confidence in the work of Doctor Salazar and his predecessors. We'll know soon enough if she intends to comply with our terms, anyway. She's holding forty habitats hostage by tampering with their thermal regulation. The moment they start returning to normal, I'll have confidence that she's seen the light. The Supreme Prefect is waiting on eyewitness data as we speak. I doubt that we'll have long to wait."

"I wish I could be in the tactical room, watching this all play out."

"You'll get your share of dramas, trust me. Do you remember Mirna Silk, the woman in charge of Midas Analytics?"

"Yes, although we only met briefly."

"She's an interesting case, Thal. She was suckered into that whole mess, but she's not without talent in her own right. We could send her scuttling back to the Glitter Band with her tail between her legs, or we could put her gifts to real use."

"What are you suggesting?"

"When you're ready to resume those light duties, I'd like you to assess her for suitability to work within Panoply. Not as a prefect, necessarily, but an analyst. She has an ability to understand the flow of wealth that I suspect may outshine even machines like Abacus."

"Money's not really our concern," Thalia pointed out.

"No, but where money flows, so does trouble. I just think Mirna might be the sort of bright spark we could find a use for, and that you might be the bright spark to shepherd her. Give it some consideration, anyway. I've left a memo for the Supreme Prefect, so she'll have time to think about it as well."

She looked up guardedly. "Wouldn't you be a better fit for that, sir? I mean, assessing and mentoring Mirna Silk?"

"Even if I were, Thal, there are a couple of question marks over my immediate career prospects. I need to put those behind me before I can... move on."

Thalia ruminated between quiet sips of her tea. "Sir, I've been thinking while I've been down here, and especially in light of what you've just told me about Aurora. If it's true, and she really isn't going to be a threat to us anymore..."

Dreyfus interrupted her gently. "You're going to say that any historical actions I took which might have compromised our security with respect to Aurora are now...moot?"

Thalia looked stricken. "I wasn't sure how to put it."

"However you put it, it's the wrong way to think. I was responsible for those actions when I took them, and I'm ready for them to be accounted now." He had chosen his own words with immense care: not for him to be held to account, but for his actions to be accounted. It was nearly the same thing.

Nearly but not quite.

Thalia ventured: "You still want me to go to the Supreme Prefect?"

"It's not about what I want or don't want. It's about the right thing to do. Which you've always known, Thal, as did your father."

Her hand trembled on the bulb. She seemed to retreat deeper into the patterned gown, cocooning in on herself, oppressed by the conflicting emotions pressing in on her: duty to Panoply, gratitude and concern for Dreyfus. "It might be bad for you, sir."

"It might." He shrugged. "It's not all on you, though. There's a reckoning coming for me anyway. I contravened the direct orders of the Supreme Prefect when she told me not to speak to Grigor Bacchus."

"He was involved, sir."

"Tainted. Not the same thing." Dreyfus wished he could lessen the moral burden on the other prefect, the young candidate he had shaped into the effective and loyal operative he now considered one of the organisation's finest assets. "Whatever testimony you provide won't decide my fate, Thal, but it will be the right thing for you, and the right thing for Panoply."

"It would feel like a betrayal," she said, in a small and sad voice.

"The only way you'd ever betray me is by failing to live up to your principles." He smiled as he grunted his way out of the chair. "Which you won't do. I've not the slightest shred of doubt about that."

"I...need to think about this, sir. The best way to present it."

"You've time," he said. "A day here, a day there, won't make your testimony any less valid."

"I'm sorry," she said. "That it's come to this, I mean."

"You've nothing to apologise for, Thalia Ng," he said, preparing to be on his way. "You've been the best of us, and it's been my very great privilege to consider you my colleague and friend." He jabbed a finger at her. "Now rest. No one's earned it more than you."

Aumonier, Clearmountain, Baudry, the other seniors and analysts, waited in the makeshift tactical room for the first of the direct reports to come

369

in. Aumonier had already seen the advance indications, but since these filtered through to her via channels that were at least theoretically open to manipulation, she had placed the least possible stock in them. She would not permit her hopes to soar, and then be crushed by cold reality.

"First eyewitness debriefing arriving from Thyssen now, ma'am," Tang informed her. "Two cutters, close enough to verify changing conditions in a sample of the forty habitats. It seems..." He was pressing an earpiece into his skull, frowning hard. "It seems..."

"In your own time, Robert."

"Prefect Sherrod reports mirror and sunshade configurations defaulting to normal aspects. External temperature indications suggest a convergence back to nominal levels. They're not out of the woods..."

"I wouldn't expect them to be."

"...but the warm ones seem to be cooling, and the cold ones warming back up."

Aumonier closed her eyes once, opened them again. Not exactly a prayer of thanks, but not infinitely distant from one either. "And abstraction and Band-wide comms?"

"Trending to normal on all metrics. I mean, normal for a state of emergency, with widespread panic and mass evacuations still ongoing..."

"I understand." She swapped tentative smiles with her colleagues, all of them in the room. "We can't say she's gone, not just yet. What we can say is that she's doing a very good impression thereof." She scratched at the lingering itch in her neck. "I'll take that for now. It's better than anything I imagined possible twenty-six hours ago. Someone should inform Dreyfus that the risk to Hospice Idlewild is diminishing. He'll want to know for Valery's sake." Then her expression clouded, some prickling intuition taking the edge off her elation. "Where *is* Dreyfus?"

Dreyfus had told Thyssen a lie, perhaps the last one of his career. He had asked for immediate use of a cutter, telling the man that he was throwing himself into the eyewitness effort, going out to corroborate the flood of reports already arriving. It was a good, plausible story and Thyssen had accepted it without complaint. He had not even questioned the need for Hafdis Tench to go with him.

Instead, Dreyfus had steered directly for Hospice Idlewild.

It was, in a sense, not entirely a lie: no prefect had yet ventured as far out as Idlewild, and someone needed to do the work of verifying that Aurora's hold on the place had slackened. That was not really uppermost in his considerations, though. He already believed that the worst was over.

"I won't keep you here for long," Dreyfus reassured Hafdis, as the cutter locked on for approach. "I just thought it might be useful for you to meet the people who have been so generous to my wife over the years. I've not always valued their kindness, if I'm being honest. They've rarely faulted me for that, though." He smiled inwardly, thinking of the occasions when he had indeed been found wanting. "What I have been sure of is that they'd always be there for me. You've a difficult path to walk now, Hafdis, and although I know you're strong enough—just as Ingvar knew you were—it won't hurt to know that there'll be friends to turn to."

"I presume I can count on you, Dreyfus?"

He said nothing, concentrating on the final approach to Idlewild.

They docked. Sister Catherine was there to meet them, leaning onto her stick more forcefully than ever, the support bowing improbably beneath the featherweight burden of her bones.

"You came," she said, nodding once. "I am pleased. And who is this?"

"Candidate Tench, one of our newest and brightest." He bowed to the Mendicant. "Hafdis, this is Sister Catherine of the Holy Order of Ice Mendicants. Don't be put off by the craggy exterior: there's a heart of gold under all that armour."

"And you'd know, would you Dreyfus?" Catherine probed grumpily.

Dreyfus beckoned a confiding hand to Hafdis. "It's always Dreyfus until the ice breaks, then I'm Tom. Until the next time, when we go through the whole elaborate charade again. How is she, Sister Catherine?"

Catherine beckoned the two of them on. "Good, all things considered. No more fits, and we removed the implants according to your instructions. That was a curious business. Nothing quite like it has ever manifested in our other patients, even the ones receiving similar treatment, with more or less the same kind of harvested implant."

"I doubt you'll ever see a second case, Sister."

"Let us hope not." As they walked further into Idlewild, following one of the winding trails, Catherine shot a glance at Hafdis. "Is there a reason for that odd attachment, Candidate Tench? It must be terribly uncomfortable."

"It is, Sister. I'll get used to it in time, though, I'm sure."

Catherine's look veered to Dreyfus, sharply quizzical. "She's a strange one. Is that the way of recruits into Panoply now?"

"Hafdis has the weight of the world on her neck," Dreyfus said, taking a perverse delight in being cryptic. "I've suggested that she might find friends here, Sister. She may have need of them."

"Can she garden?"

"She can learn," Hafdis answered.

"Well, if you find yourself at a loose end between the pressing engagements of Panoply, you know where to find us now. Is she coming all the way to Valery, Tom?"

He smiled. There it was: the calculated shift in her register from brusque inhospitality to the thawing promise of warmth, even if the frost was still upon her. "I thought she'd like to get a sense of the place, Sister. Also, there's a little business Hafdis and I need to sort out between us." He nodded at his puzzled companion. "Nothing complicated, I promise."

By turns they arrived at the walled hamlet of low, white-painted buildings and gardens where Dreyfus had last seen his wife. Hafdis took a polite but distant interest as Catherine showed her the various efforts toward the cultivation of herbs and ornamental flowers, as well as some of the re-education and rehabilitation work going on in the open areas, where Mendicants sat with their patients, coaxing small miracles from damaged minds. Hafdis clearly had her mind on other matters, though. Dreyfus could not blame her in the slightest.

"I'm going to go through and see my wife in a moment," he explained, sitting her down at a vacant table by one of the flower beds. "And this is for you."

He set his whiphound down on the table.

Hafdis regarded it with curiosity and suspicion. "Why would I want that, Dreyfus? I'm not even sure they'll let me continue candidacy training, now that they know what I am."

"They will. What you are is measured by your deeds, not some family background over which you had no control." Dreyfus rolled the whiphound over to her. "It won't operate for you. What it will do is preserve an evidential testimony. It's something I learned from Ingvar Tench."

Her eyes narrowed. "What testimony?"

"Mine. I have a number of things I need to get off my chest, Hafdis, and I thought you would be the ideal custodian for them. You'll be taking them back to Panoply aboard my cutter."

"Why not you?"

"Because I'm not returning." Dreyfus watched her reaction, nodding slowly as her understanding showed. "Take this to Thalia Ng first, if you don't mind. She'll know how best to handle it, and I want you to pass on my personal gratitude for her service and friendship." Then he raised his face, looking her hard in the eyes. "Hafdis, there's another reason I want you to listen to this and convey my sentiments back to Panoply. There are things I need to tell you about Ingvar."

"Bad things?"

"Not exactly. She was exemplary, to the end."

372

"Then what?"

"I bear some responsibility for the things that happened. Including her death. I can offer justifications for my actions, but it's not for me to be the arbiter over whether I was right or wrong. That's for Panoply, and the people who will eventually hear my words, to decide. Not me." Dreyfus paused, gripped by a sudden, swift terror that he was on the brink of something irrevocable. Yet he continued. "I'm done as a prefect, Hafdis. Whatever their verdict, I can't return to my old life. This path you're on now, I'm afraid you'll have to walk it without me. You'll do well, though. I've never had less doubt about anything in my life."

"As long as *she* still has doubt..."

"Then I suppose we'll be all right, for the time being." Dreyfus leaned back, cleared his throat and began speaking for the whiphound. "This is Tom Dreyfus, late of Panoply. I wish to state the following facts for the formal record..."

The whiphound captured. Hafdis listened.

Dreyfus watched Sister Catherine hand Hafdis over to one of the other Mendicants for the long, meandering walk back to the docking hub. Just before they passed out of sight, Hafdis turned back to him, nodding in some last silent exchange, and then it was just her back, with the scarab glinting off her neck, before he lost sight of her for ever.

After that, he went to see Valery.

She was sitting up in bed, already forewarned of his arrival. Her smile of recognition lit him up, brightening walls that were already as white and spotless as a new conscience.

"I'm sorry I had to leave," he offered, clasping her hand in his.

She studied the new scars he had gained since their last meeting, her eyes quizzical.

"The red wooden...bridge," she managed. "The bridge. Walk me to the bridge."

He wondered how much she remembered of their walk when Aurora had taken control over her. Something, perhaps. But not enough to deter her from a second try.

"They took the implant out of you," he said, marvelling. "But something's made a difference. You're speaking as well without it as you did with it."

"It isn't..." She paused, the strain written on her face. "Easy."

He realised the effort it had cost her, just to express that simple idea about the bridge.

Still, it was progress, and he snatched at it with all the eager-hearted willingness of a drowning man thrown a lifeline. They talked, Dreyfus making most of the conversation, but Valery filling in with great determination, each word costly, each its own miraculous reward. There was so very far to go, Dreyfus thought, but the immensity of the journey before them should not detract from the terrain they had already conquered.

"He's here," Sister Catherine announced quietly.

Dreyfus turned, mentally arming himself for his first physical encounter with the Ultra.

"Captain Remanso," he said, rising from the bedside. "It's very good of you to come, at such short notice. Might I ask...?"

"*Shades of Scarlet* will depart in thirteen hours, Prefect," the mercury-gargling voice responded. "The reefersleep berths are ready for you both. My shuttle stands by."

Dreyfus nodded, the bare scraps of a plan still yet to settle fully in his mind. "And your likely next port of call, beyond this system?"

"Fand, if my advisors can agree on it. After that, most likely the Pattern Jugglers of Groombridge 1618. However matters fall, you have my personal guarantee of safe transportation to one of the Juggler worlds, for you and your wife."

"I can't pay," Dreyfus clarified, fearful that there had been some misunderstanding.

"You have done so already," the captain answered. "Harbourmaster Seraphim was most insistent in that regard. We stand in your debt, not the other way round. This...small favour that I may do for you is nothing against that."

Dreyfus nodded, almost crumbling with gratitude. "It might be prudent to leave before very long, Captain Remanso. I'm afraid I'm no longer part of Panoply, despite this uniform. I hope that they'll think well of me, but I can't guarantee that there won't be some attempt to call me back to answer for my actions."

Remanso swatted aside his concern. "Your little ships would have difficulty outrunning my shuttle, let alone *Shades of Scarlet*. I will keep a careful watch on movements between the Glitter Band and Hospice Idlewild, but I would image you are safe for an hour or two." The gargoyle face turned to his. "How long did you have in mind?"

"Not long," Dreyfus said. "Perhaps half an hour, if Valery is strong enough. Just time for a little stroll before we leave."

extras

orbit

meet the author

Barbara Bella

ALASTAIR REYNOLDS was born in Barry, South Wales, in 1966. He studied at Newcastle and St. Andrews Universities and has a PhD in astronomy. He stopped working as an astrophysicist for the European Space Agency to become a full-time writer. *Revelation Space* and *Pushing Ice* were shortlisted for the Arthur C. Clarke Award; *Diamond Dogs* was shortlisted for the British Fantasy Award; *Revelation Space*, *Absolution Gap*, and *Century Rain* were shortlisted for the British Science Fiction Award; and *Chasm City* won the British Science Fiction Award.

Find out more about Alastair Reynolds and other Orbit authors by registering for the free monthly newsletter at orbitbooks.net.

if you enjoyed
MACHINE VENDETTA

look out for

EVERSION

by

Alastair Reynolds

From the master of space opera comes a dark, mind-bending adventure spread across time and space, where Doctor Silas Coade is tasked with keeping his crew safe as they adventure across the galaxy in search of a mysterious artifact.

In the 1800s, a sailing ship crashes off the coast of Norway. In the 1900s, a zeppelin explores an icy canyon in Antarctica. In the far future, a spaceship sets out for an alien artifact. Each excursion goes horribly wrong. And on every journey, Doctor Silas Coade is the physician. But only Silas seems to realize that these events keep repeating themselves. It's up to him to figure out why and how. And how to stop it all from happening again.

Chapter One

Footsteps rescued me from my nightmare. They were approaching with urgency: hard soles thudding on old, creaking timbers. I came around seated at my writing desk, face pressed to the pages of my manuscript. I lifted my head and pinched at the gummy corners of my eyes. Pince-nez spectacles were before me on the desk, slightly askew where the force of my slumping forehead had borne down on them. I straightened them out, fixed them to my nose, and splashed water on my face from a cork-stoppered earthenware jar.

The footsteps ceased. A knock sounded at the door, followed by the immediate sound of the door being eased ajar.

"Come in, Mortlock," I said, swivelling in my seat, feigning the impression of being disturbed from innocent business.

The tall, stooping midshipman bent his head and shoulders into the low-ceilinged cabin.

"How did you know it was me, Doctor Coade?"

"You have a manner, Mortlock," I said pleasantly. "Everyone has a manner and I remembered yours. Sooner or later, if we are not first shipwrecked, I expect I will know the manner of everyone on this vessel." I made a show of blotting the manuscript, even though the ink was hours-dry on my last addition. I was in the process of closing the leatherbound covers when my eyes alighted on the little machine-engraved snuff box that was still on the desk, open to reveal its contents. A cold horror of discovery shot through me. "How is that tooth?" I asked, a touch too hastily.

Mortlock tugged down his scarf to touch the side of his jaw. It was still slightly swollen but a good deal less inflamed than it had been four days ago, when I had dealt with an abscess.

"Much better, doctor, sir, thank you very much."

"Turn about. Let me see your profile."

382

Mortlock did as he was instructed, affording me the precious seconds I needed to spirit the snuff box safely into a drawer. "Yes," I said, nodding. "Yes, very satisfactory. Continue with the tincture I gave you, and you should feel a steady improvement over the coming days." I looked at him over my spectacles. "Your company is always welcome, Mortlock. But is there something else besides the abscess?"

"It's the Coronel, sir. He's had a bit of a bump out on deck. Out cold, he was, and now he's back with us but he's striking out, wriggling and cussing in that native tongue of his..."

"Spanish, is I believe the term for it. Or at least the form of it endemic in New Spain." I relaxed slightly, believing that Mortlock had made nothing of the snuff box nor its sudden disappearance. "What was the nature of the injury?"

"A block came down on his bonce, hard as you like—knocked him clean to the floor." Mortlock made an emphatic chopping motion. "We were changing tack, looking for that gap in the cliff, and the Coronel just happened to be in the wrong spot when a rope snapped. There was a bit of blood, but his head hadn't gone all soft as if it had been stoved in, so we thought he'd be all right if we just sat him up and let him have a nip of rum, sir..."

I shuddered to think of the poor man's injury being poked and prodded by men who could barely read, let alone perform a competent diagnosis. "Bring him to me immediately, Mortlock."

"What is it, do you reckon?"

"I dare not speculate. But if he has suffered concussion, even in the absence of a skull fracture, there may be elevated intracerebral pressure." I reached beneath the desk for one of several elegant boxes which I had brought with me. "All haste now, Mortlock!" I continued, raising my voice spiritedly. "And be so kind as to communicate to Mister Murgatroyd, or Captain Van Vught himself, that it would be extremely helpful if the ship were to maintain a constant heading for the next half an hour."

"The Master might grumble about that, doctor, if it slows down our search."

I nodded sombrely. "He is bound to. But I shall remind him that it is his man-at-arms that I shall be striving to save."

Mortlock departed, his footsteps ringing away. I sat still for a moment, collecting myself, and reflecting on that irony that I had first hidden one pretty box and then disclosed another. Both were finely-made things; both in their way vital to my work. The box I had concealed contained opium snuff, self-administered with the intention of dulling myself into dreamless oblivion. The other held a French-made trephination brace of impeccable manufacture, but which I had never had cause to use on a living subject.

I feared—no, hoped—that this state of affairs was about to change.

"Are you ready for this, Silas?" I asked myself aloud. "Your first real test, on this voyage? Your first real test, of any sort?"

I opened the lid on the trephination brace, imagining the college examiners casting their doubtful gazes upon my hesitant efforts. Stern-faced men in black, men with London manners, veterans of troubled voyages and bloody engagements, men for whom cutting and sawing was as effortless as breathing, men to whom screams were merely the peculiar music of their profession. What hubris was it that made me think that I could ever join their ranks? I was a West Countryman without connections: a poor, provincial surgeon out of Plymouth (but of Cornish blood, as I reminded all who would listen), forty-four (and therefore long past the age at which most surgeons made their first voyage), a mere Assistant Surgeon (yet the only surgeon of any kind) on a fifth-rate sloop under a Dutch captain. The captain was kind, but his ship was old, his crew tired, their provisions threadbare, and the terms of our charter questionable in the extreme.

This was how I meant to make my way?

The gleaming parts of the trephination brace waited in snug recesses of purple felt. The metalwork was engraved, the handles of ebony. Such beautiful artistry, for such brutal ends. My fingers quivered as I reached to extract the drill-like components.

Suppressing a spasm of shame, I retrieved the snuff box and took a hasty pinch in order to settle my nerves and banish the last traces of the nightmare. It was a habit that was becoming all too familiar, especially as we ventured further north along the Norwegian coast. Matters had worsened since leaving Bergen, with the nightmare repeating itself with increasing regularity. I had been taking more and more snuff to counter its effects, with diminishing success.

The nightmares were like nothing I had endured before setting foot on *Demeter*. In them I found myself staggering along a barely-lit stone passage, clad in hood or mask or helmet, gripped by the terrible intimation that I myself was dead, merely a shambling corpse, with empty sockets and grinning jaw. I could not identify the cause of these torments, other than to speculate that being con-fined for long hours in my cabin, with only books, potions and sur-gical instruments for company, my mind had become unhealthily focussed on the thin membrane which separates the living from the dead.

My one hope lay in the failure—or should I say abandonment—of our expedition. Perhaps, as we scoured endless dismal miles of Norwegian coastline, looking for a glimpse of something that only one man truly believed to exist—and he not exactly the most sober or reliable among our number—and as the days grew colder, the seas rougher, the ice more abundant, the stores more depleted, the ship more worn-out, the general morale weaker, the lugubri-ous Dutchman more openly sceptical of our chances—perhaps I might yet be saved by our turning home. It was a coward's hope, as well I knew. Yet in the grip of the equal miseries of seasickness and dysentery, not to mention every other common hardship of sea-borne life, I should gladly have proclaimed my cowardice to all who would listen.

I had hidden the snuff box again by the time the injured Coronel was brought down to my room. In those minutes I had also pre-pared the main table, sweeping it free of books, journals and man-uscript pages, and made sure my other instruments and remedies were to immediate hand. Coronel Ramos was in a state of consider-able agitation as the midshipmen press-ganged him into the room, for even in his confused condition he was bigger and stronger than any of them. It took four to get him onto the table, and they had a struggle to make good his restraints as he thrashed and twisted like some muscular eel.

"He was unarmed while agitated?" I asked Mortlock, who was one of the four assistants, and the only midshipman I knew by name.

"That's the lucky part, doctor. He's always polishing that flint-lock of his, and he had it in one hand and a cleaning pipe in the other when the block came down, and it made him drop the pistol. Mister Murgatroyd got hold of it before it got washed through the gunnels, but I think if he hadn't, and the Coronel had still had it in his hand, you'd be digging a bullet out of one of us."

"Let us be thankful for small mercies, then."

Since the wound was on the back of his head, I had dictated that they secure him to the table face down. He had bled profusely, so I swabbed the affected area as gently and thoroughly as I could, being careful not to depress the bone until I had determined to my satisfaction that there was no serious fracture. My examination was helped by the fact that Ramos was quite bald, not just about the crown but around his whole blocky, boulder-shaped head. Some hair still grew, but he shaved it away each morning, sparing only his beard and moustache, which he maintained with the same devotion shown to his armaments.

"It doesn't look too bad," Mortlock offered.

"There is no penetration of the skull, nor any fracture that I can detect. He is made of stern stuff, our Coronel. But the impact has knocked his brain about, causing his present distress. There is likely a build-up of pressure—blood or cerebral fluid—which must be relieved by means of trephination."

Mortlock's eyes drifted to the exquisite French brace, poised in its now-open box.

"You're going to drill into 'im with that Froggy thing?"

"It is the only thing that will save him." I looked to the four men who had come in with the Coronel. "It will likely cause him some discomfort, and you must be ready for that. But I am confident that the procedure will work, if we proceed speedily." I pushed my spectacles back up my nose, countering their habit of drifting to the tip. Rolling up my sleeves I took the brace, and settled myself into the most comfortable and stable position for the procedure.

Master Topolsky and Milady Cossile burst into the room without warning. The former was a cloud of black, the latter an apparition in yellow. I glanced up from my preparations, squinting through a loose lock of hair.

"What is this?" asked Topolsky, heavily clothed, wet and windswept from being out on deck.

"A medical emergency, Master Topolsky."

"The doctor's going to drill into 'im," Mortlock explained, with as much eagerness as if he had just graduated to the position of Assistant Surgeon. "His brain can't breathe in and out, see, so it's squeezing his thoughts."

"A most commendable summary," said Milady Cossile, her fingers steepled. "I expect Mister Mortlock will soon be composing the standard monograph on the subject?"

Mortlock looked at me doubtfully.

"Is the young gentlewoman being sarcastic again, doctor?"

I nodded sympathetically at the midshipman, who was straining every muscle to hold Ramos still. "Pay her no heed, Mortlock. You are doing very well."

"Is there need for this?" asked Topolsky, looming over the table. "The Coronel is a hale man with the common vigour of his kind. He just needs a little rest, not to be drilled into like a brandy cask." His tone sharpened. "We still have need of him, Coade!"

"And my purpose is to ensure that he remains at our disposal, Master."

Ramos muttered something from the table. It sounded like *trece* to me, the Spanish for thirteen.

He was not a true-born Spaniard but a citizen of New Spain. He had been a soldier—hence his title—but he now owed his allegiance to no army or king, and offered his services for hire to men such as Topolsky. I knew very little about him, for Ramos was a taciturn man, quite the opposite of his boisterous employer. But we had spoken now and then, usually in the quiet moments between watches, when one of us might encounter the other on deck, pensively watching the sea.

Some political or religious difficulty—more than likely the same thing—had forced him to leave the Americas: I understood a little of it, piecing together such crumbs of biography as Ramos chanced to offer during our nearly silent communions. Turning against his father, Ramos had developed sympathies for the independence movement led by the Jesuit Hidalgo.

"Better men than I have found themselves before the Court of Inquisition," Ramos had confided to me. "But I had the means to leave, and they did not. It does not make me brave, merely astute."

Now this softly spoken giant—Ramos said that he owed his size and strength to his mother, who was of *criollo* descent—lay on my table, whimpering and foaming at the mouth. I was glad that his face was averted, facing the floor, because I could not have stood to look into his eyes as I began to work the brace.

"*Trece*," Ramos murmured. Then, after a pause: "*Cinco.*"

I applied firm but steady pressure on the brace, while turning the handle at a slow, constant rate. The three-tipped bit was already biting into bone, etching a coin-sized groove. Mortlock kept glancing at my work then tearing his gaze away, while the three other midshipmen seemed incapable of mustering even a glance. I did not blame them for that: trephination was hardly something to be encountered in the normal life of the sailor.

"A question of terminology, if I may?"

Sweat was already in my eyes. It was the first time I had found my cabin anything other than intolerably cold since leaving Bergen. I paused in my work and pushed my hair and spectacles back again.

"By all means, Milady Cossile."

"*La vigilia...*" Ramos said, on a note of rising concern. "*La vigilia! La vigilia...de...*"

"Concerning the procedure you are employing." Milady Cossile still had her fingers steepled, tapping their tips against her lips between utterances. She had perfect lips, I thought. Not even the brush of Gainsborough could have captured their fullness. "I have encountered the term trepanation as well as trephination. Would you presume that the two forms are etymologically related?"

I resumed my drilling. "I cannot say that I have given the matter much consideration."

"But still—would you presume?"

"I suppose I might."

Even with my eyes focused on the drilling site, I still detected Milady Cossile's gleeful response to my answer. She skipped forward, clapping delightedly, her feathers bouncing jauntily, before re-steepling her fingers.

"Then you would presume incorrectly, Doctor Coade! The two forms are etymologically quite distinct! I am surprised you were not aware of this."

I continued with my work.

"Do enlighten us, milady."

Ramos said: "*Trece…cinco. Trece…cinco! La vigilia de piedra! La vigilia!!*"

"Trepanation derives from *trepanon*, which in turn derives from the Greek *trupanon*, meaning an instrument for boring. Trephination—or *trephine*—derives instead from the Latin, in particular *tre fines*, or three ends. Whether the latter term was first coined by Fabricius ab Aquapedente, or John Woodall, a century later, is a question yet to be settled."

I looked up from my work and nodded. "Thank you, milady. I am sure we are all most enlightened."

"Never mind enlightenment," Topolsky said, leaning very close in to the drill site. The Russian was a stout, pot-bellied man of about forty, with a wide, cherubic face, densely circumscribed by a curly mass of beard, sideburns and fringe. He had the sort of twinkling, searching, jocular eyes that suggested an agreeableness of temperament lamentably absent in the man himself. "Will he live? We need this brute, Coade! Our expedition cannot proceed without him! He may not be learned, and his manners distinctly those of the New World rather than the Old, but who among us understands the placement of gunpowder like the Coronel?"

"I agree entirely," I said. "And if you value him as much as you say, you might refrain from projecting spittle into the wound site."

Topolsky swore at me in Russian, his lips largely hidden behind the prodigious eruption of his beard, which was as voluminous and roomy as Ramos's was neat and manicured. His hair glistened and smelled faintly of perfumed oils. Regaining something of his usual composure he continued: "Your reputation is satisfactory, Coade. I only wish that this were not the time to put it to the gravest test."

"In my experience, Master, serious accidents rarely happen on a convenient schedule." Suddenly I felt the opposition to the brace lessen as I bored through the last, sliver-like layer of bone. I had an image in my mind's eye: the tip of a drill bursting through the underside of a layer of ice, into the dark water beneath. Ice as bone, water as dura and brain. "We are through. Master, if you might assist: that small implement like a sugar-spoon? I must lever away the bone fragment. Had there been more time I might have attempted to form an osteoplastic flap, but..." Abandoning my commentary I put away the brace and closed my fist around the tool Topolsky had passed me. To my immense relief the coin-sized section of bone levered away willingly, and with it came an immediate expulsion of thick, sticky blood from a severe epidural haematoma.

"It's like raspberry jam, doctor!" Mortlock declared excitedly.

I smiled at him. "But perhaps a tad less palatable, even with your mother's best bread and butter." I watched Ramos for a minute, until I had convinced myself that there was a definite easing in his distress. "That must work," I declared. "It is, in any case, all I can do. To go beneath the dura would kill him. Medicine has done what it can, gentlemen—the rest of his fate is between Ramos and his god."

"His god," Topolsky muttered contemptuously. "Can you

imagine such a debased deity? Half Papist nightmare, half what-ever Inca savagery came down to him from his mother." Laughter lines creased the skin around his eyes and mouth, as they did when he was pleased with an observation he had either uttered or was about to utter. "Better no god at all, I might venture!"

The expulsion of blood was easing. I did not think there was continued bleeding under the skull, although it would likely be many hours or days until we could be assured of his survival. Longer still before we knew that Ramos would recover entirely. I was not so sanguine, for I had seen and read about the lingering influence of concussion and other maladies of the brain on otherwise healthy men. If he carried only the physical scars of this day, he would be fortunate.

if you enjoyed
MACHINE VENDETTA
look out for

TRANSLATION STATE

by

Ann Leckie

Qven was created to be a Presger Translator. The pride of their clade, they always had a clear path before them: Learn human ways and, eventually, make a match and serve as an intermediary between the dangerous alien Presger and the human worlds. The realization that they might want something else isn't "optimal behavior." It's the type of behavior that results in elimination.

But Qven rebels. And in doing so, their path collides with those of two others. Enae, a reluctant diplomat whose dead grandmaman has left hir an impossible task as an inheritance: hunting down a fugitive who has been missing for over two hundred years. And Reet, an adopted mechanic who is increasingly desperate to learn about his biological past—or anything that might explain why he operates so differently from those around him.

As the conclave of the various species approaches and the long-standing treaty between the humans and the Presger is on the line, the decisions of all three will have ripple effects across the stars.

extras

Enae

Athtur House, Saeniss Polity

The last stragglers in the funeral procession were barely out the ghost door before the mason bots unfolded their long legs and reached for the pile of stones they'd removed from the wall so painstakingly the day before. Enae hadn't looked back to see the door being sealed up, but sie could hear it for just a moment before the first of Aunt Irad's moans of grief rose into a wail. One or two cousins heaved an experimental sob.

Enae hadn't cried when Grandmaman died. Sie hadn't cried when Grandmaman told hir she'd chosen the time to go. Sie wasn't crying now. Which wasn't necessarily a problem, everyone knew what expressions you should have when you were following the bier to the crematory, everyone knew what sounds a close relative made, and Enae could sob and wail if sie'd wanted to. And after all, among all these aunts and uncles and nuncles and cousins, Enae was the one who'd lived with Grandmaman for decades, and taken care of her in her old age. Sie had been the one to arrange things in the household these past ten years or more, to deal with the servants—human and bot—with their very different needs. Sie still had all the household codes and bot overrides, and the servants still looked to hir for orders, at least until Grandmaman's will was unsealed. Sie had every right to walk at the head of the procession, right behind Grandmaman, wailing for all the town to hear, in these quiet early morning hours. Instead sie walked silent and dry-eyed at the back.

Grandmaman had been very old, and ill-tempered. She had also been very rich, and born into one of the oldest families in the system. Which meant that the procession to the crematory was longer than one might have expected. There had been some jostling in the entry hall, by the ghost door, Aunt Irad turning up a half hour early to position herself at the front, some cousins attempting to push her out of her place, and everyone eying Enae to see how sie'd react.

None of them had lived in the house for decades. Grandmaman had thrown most of them—or their parents—out. Every year she would hold a birthday dinner and invite them all back for a lavish meal, during which she would insult them to their faces while they smiled and gritted their teeth. Then she'd order them off the premises again, to wait until the next year. Some of them had fallen away in that time, sworn off Grandmaman and any hope of inheritance, but most of them came back year after year. It was only Enae who had actually lived in the house with Grandmaman, Enae who, one might think, would be the most affected by Grandmaman's death.

But for the past week Enae had let the aunts and uncles and nuncles and cousins do whatever they'd wanted, so long as it didn't trouble the household unduly. Sie'd stood silent as Aunt Irad had changed the cook's menus and stood silent when the same aunt had raged at Enae because sie'd told the cook to disregard any changes he didn't have resources for. Sie had done and said nothing when, the very first day of the funeral week, an actual fistfight had broken out between two cousins over who would have which bedroom. Sie had remained silent when sie had heard one uncle say to a nuncle, *And look at hir, fifty-six years old and sitting at home sucking up to Grandmaman,* and the nuncle reply, *Well look at hir father's family, it's hardly a surprise.* Sie had walked on past when one cousin had surreptitiously slid a small silver dish into his pocket, while another loudly declared that she would be making some changes if she were so fortunate as to inherit the house. And in the meantime, sie had made sure that meals arrived on time and the house was kept in order. That had been the trick, all these years, of living with Grandmaman—keep calm, keep quiet, keep things running smoothly.

Grandmaman had told Enae many times that sie was her only

remaining heir. But she had also said—many times—that Enae was an embarrassment. A failure. As far as the Athturs had fallen since Grandmaman's days—look at all those grandchildren and great-grandchildren and nephews and nieces and niblings of whatever degree abasing themselves to win her favor in the desperate hope that she'd leave them something in her will—as pathetic as they were, Enae was worse. Nearly sixty and no career, no friends, no lovers, no marital partners, no children. What had sie done with hir life? Nothing.

Enae had kept calm, had not said that when sie had had friends they had not been good enough for Grandmaman. That when sie had shown any sign of wanting to do something that might take hir out of the house, Grandmaman had forbidden it.

Keep calm, keep quiet, keep things running smoothly.

At the crematory, Grandmaman's corpse slid into the flames, and the funeral priest sang the farewell chants. Aunt Irad and three different cousins stepped forward to thank him for officiating and to suggest that they might donate money for future prayers for the Blessed Deceased. Enae could feel everyone else glancing toward hir, yet again, to see hir reaction to others acting as though they were the head of the family, the chief mourner, the now-Matriarch (or Patriarch or Natriarch, as the case may be) of the ancient family of Athtur.

"Well," said Aunt Irad, finished with her loud and obvious consultation with the funeral priest, "I've ordered coffee and sandwiches to be set out in the Peony Room." And marched back toward the house, not even looking to see if anyone followed her.

Back at the house, there was no coffee and sandwiches in the Peony Room. Aunt Irad turned immediately to Enae, who shrugged as though it wasn't any of hir business. It wasn't anymore—technically, Grandmaman's will would have taken effect the moment her body slid into the flames, but the habit of ordering the household died hard. With a quick blink sie sent a query to the kitchen.

No reply. And then someone dressed as a servant, but who Enae had never, ever seen before, came into the Peony Room and coolly informed them all that refreshments had in fact been set out in the Blue Sitting Room and their collective presence was requested there, and then turned and walked away, ignoring Aunt Irad's protests.

In the Blue Sitting Room, another complete stranger sat in one of the damask-upholstered armchairs, drinking coffee: a lanky, fair-skinned woman who smiled at all of them as they came in and stopped and stared. "Good morning. I'm so sorry for your loss."

"Who the hell are you?" asked Aunt Irad, indignant.

"A few minutes ago, I was Zemil Igoeto," said the woman as she set her coffee down on a mother-of-pearl inlaid side table. "But when the Blessed Deceased ascended, I became Zemil Athtur." Silence. "I don't believe in drawing things out. I will be direct. None of you have inherited anything. There wasn't anything to inherit. I have owned all of this"—she gestured around her, taking in the Blue Sitting Room and presumably the whole house—"for some years."

"That can't be right," said Aunt Irad. "Is this some kind of joke?"

Grandmaman would have thought it a joke, thought Enae. *She must have laughed to herself even as she was dying, to think of the looks on everyone's faces right now.* Everything had seemed distant and strange since Grandmaman had died, but now Enae had the feeling that sie wasn't really here, that sie was watching some sort of play or entertainment that sie wasn't terribly interested in.

"Fifteen years ago," said Zemil Igoeto—no, Zemil Athtur— "the Blessed Deceased found herself completely broke. At the same time, while I had plenty of funds, I wanted some way to gain access to the sort of influence that is only available to the oldest families. She and I came to an agreement and made it legally binding. In, I need not tell you, the presence of authorized witnesses. I would purchase everything she owned. The sum would be sufficient to support her in excellent style for the rest of her life, and she would have the use of all the properties that had formerly been hers. In return, on her ascension to the Realm of the Blessed Dead, I would become her daughter and sole heir."

Silence. Enae wasn't sure if sie wanted to laugh or not, but the fact was, Grandmaman would *very* much have enjoyed this moment if she could have been here. It was just like her to have done this. And how could Enae complain? Sie'd lived here for years in, as Ms Zemil Athtur had just said, excellent style. Enae couldn't possibly have any complaints.

"This is ridiculous," said Aunt Irad. She looked at Enae. "Is this one of the Blessed Deceased's jokes? Or is it yours?"

"Mx Athtur has nothing to do with any of this," cut in Zemil. "Sie had no idea until this moment. Only I, the Blessed Deceased's jurist, and the Blessed Deceased herself knew anything about it. Apart from the witnesses involved, of course, whom you are free to consult as confirmation."

"So we get *nothing*," said the cousin who had declared her intention to make changes once she'd inherited.

"Correct," said Zemil Athtur, picking up her coffee again. She took a sip. "The Blessed Deceased wanted to be sure I told you that you're all selfish and greedy, and she wishes she could be here to see you when you learn you've been cut off with nothing. With one exception."

Everyone turned to look at Enae.

Zemil continued, "I am to provide for Mx Enae Athtur, with certain stipulations and restrictions, which I will discuss with hir later."

"The will," said a cousin. "I want to see the will. I want to see the documents involved. I'll be speaking with my jurist."

"Do, by all means," said Zemil, and Enae felt the itch of a message arriving. Sie looked, and saw a list of files. Documents. Contracts. Contact information for the Office of Witnesses. "In the meantime, do sit and have a sandwich while the servants finish packing your things."

It took some time, and a half dozen looming servants (who, once again, Enae had never seen before), but eventually the aunts and uncles and nuncles and cousins had left the house, picked their luggage up off the drive, and gone elsewhere, threatening lawsuits all the while.

Enae had remained in the Blue Sitting Room, unwilling to go up to hir room to see if hir things were still there or not. Sie sat, more or less relaxed, in a damask-upholstered armchair. Sie badly wanted a cup of coffee, and maybe a sandwich, but sie found sie couldn't bring hirself to get up from the chair. The whole world seemed unreal and uncertain, and sie wasn't sure what would happen if sie moved too much. Zemil, too, stayed sitting in her damasked chair, drinking coffee and smiling.

At some point, after the house had quieted, Grandmaman's jurist arrived. "Ah, Mx Athtur. I'm so sorry for your loss. I know you loved your grandmother very much, and spent your life attending to her. You should be allowed to take some time to yourself right now, and grieve." He didn't overtly direct this to Zemil, sitting in the armchair across from Enae, but his words seemed intended for her. Then he did turn to her and nodded in greeting. "Ms Athtur."

"I am fully aware," said Zemil, with a faint smile, "that I'm tasked with providing for Mx Athtur, and I will."

"I would like some time to read the relevant documents, please," said Enae, as politely as sie could, and braced hirself to argue with an angry refusal.

"Of course," said the jurist, "and I'll be happy to go through them with you if you need."

Enae, at a loss for some reason, said, "Thank you."

"You'll see, when you read it," said Zemil, "that I am obligated to provide for you, as I said. How I am to provide for you is up to me, within certain parameters. I have had years to consider what that might mean, for both of us."

"Your provisions will meet the requirements of the will," said the jurist, sharply. "I will be certain of it."

"I don't understand." Enae suppressed a sudden, unexpected welling of tears. "I don't understand how this happened." And then, realizing how that might sound, "I didn't expect to inherit anything. Gr...the Blessed Deceased always said she would leave her houses and money to whoever she wanted." *Watch them gather around my corpse when I'm gone*, she'd said, with relish. *Ungrateful, disloyal while I lived, but watch them come the moment they think they might get something from me.* And she'd patted Enae's hand and made the tiny huff that was her laughter, near the end.

"As I said," said Zemil, "the Blessed Deceased was facing bankruptcy. Her income had declined, and she had refused to alter her way of living. It took several years to negotiate—our ancestor was stubborn, as I'm sure you know—but ultimately she had no choice if she was to continue living here, in the way she was accustomed to."

Enae didn't know what to say. Sie hardly even knew how to breathe, in this moment.

"I wanted the name," said Zemil. "I have wealth, and some influence. But I'm a newcomer to wealth and influence, at least according to the oldest families. An interloper. Our ancestor made sure to tell me so, on several occasions. But no longer. Now I am an Athtur. And now the Athturs are wealthy again."

Another unfamiliar servant came in, to clear the food and the coffee away. Enae hadn't eaten anything. Sie could feel the hollow in hir stomach, but sie couldn't bring hirself to take a sandwich now, knew sie wouldn't be able to eat it if sie did. Grandmaman's jurist waved the servant over, muttered in her ear. The servant made a plate with two small sandwiches, poured a cup of coffee, handed both to Enae, and then took the rest and left the room.

"Have you dismissed the servants?" Enae asked. Sie'd meant to sound casual, curious, but hir tone came out rough and resentful.

"You are no longer the housekeeper here, Mx Athtur," Zemil replied.

"I was until this morning, and if I'd known people were going to lose their jobs I'd have done what I could for them. They've worked for us a long time."

"You think I'm cruel," said Zemil. "Heartless. But I am only direct. No servants have been dismissed. None will be who perform their jobs well. Does that satisfy you?"

"Yes."

"I will do you no favors," Zemil continued, "leaving you in any misapprehension or uncertainty. As I said, what I wanted in this transaction was the Athtur name. There will be some reluctance on the part of the other old families to accept my legitimacy, and that will be made more difficult if you are here as an example of a true Athtur, one who so loyally cared for hir Grandmaman for so long, and rightfully ought to have inherited—in contrast with my false, purchased hold on the name. But I am also obligated to support you. Understand, I bear you no ill will, and I have no objection to providing for you, but I need you gone. I have, therefore, found employment for you."

"Ms Athtur . . ." the jurist began, reproachfully.

Zemil raised a forestalling hand. "You may stay here for another month, to complete the time of mourning. And then you will take a position with the Office of Diplomacy. Your assignment is already arranged. You will find it congenial, I assure you."

"You could just leave me my allowance," said Enae. "I could move out."

"Would you?" asked Zemil. "Where would you go?"

"I have a month to figure that out," sie replied, not sure sie had understood anything anyone had said for the past five minutes, not even sure what sie, hirself, was saying.

"Let me tell you what your position would be in the Office of Diplomacy. You have been appointed Special Investigator, and a case has been assigned to you. It is a situation of great diplomatic delicacy. Perhaps we should discuss this in private." She glanced at the jurist.

"I'm not going anywhere," he said, and crossed his arms very decidedly.

"You don't work for Mx Athtur," Zemil pointed out.

"No," he acknowledged. "In this matter, I represent the interests of the Blessed Deceased. And consequently, I will be certain that her grandchild is appropriately cared for."

"If she were here . . ." began Zemil.

"But she's *not* here," said the jurist. "We have only her expressed desire, and your agreement to that."

Zemil made an expression as though she'd bitten into something sour. "All right then. Enae, you've been assigned..."

"Mx Athtur," said Enae, hardly believing it had come out of her mouth.

To Enae's shock, Zemil smiled. "Mx Athtur. You've been assigned, as I've said, to a matter of some delicacy. Some years ago, the Radchaai Translators Office approached the Office of Diplomacy to request our help in tracking down a fugitive."

Radchaai! The Radch was an enormous, multisystem empire, far enough away that no one here in Saeniss Polity felt immediately threatened by them—especially now, with the Radchaai embroiled in their own internal struggles—but close enough and powerful enough that Radchaai was one of the languages the well educated often elected to study. The Translators Office was the Radchaai diplomatic service. Enae felt the itch of files arriving. "I've sent you the details," said Zemil.

Enae blinked the message open, read the opening summary. "This incident happened two hundred years ago!"

"Yes," Zemil agreed. "The Office of Diplomacy assigned an investigator when the request first came in, who decided the fugitive wasn't here in Saeniss Polity or even anywhere in this system, and what with one thing and another the matter was dropped."

"But...how am I supposed to find someone who's been missing for two hundred years?"

Zemil shrugged. "I haven't the least idea. But I rather imagine it will involve travel, and a per diem on top of your wages. On top of your existing allowance, which I have no plans to discontinue. Indeed, the Blessed Deceased was quite miserly in the matter of your allowance, and I believe I'll be increasing it." She turned to the jurist. "There, are you satisfied?" The jurist made a noncommittal noise, and Zemil turned back to Enae. "Honestly, no one cares if you find this person or not. No one expects you to find anything at all. You're being paid to travel, and maybe look into an old puzzle if you feel like it. Haven't you ever wanted to leave here?"

Sie had always wanted to leave here.

Sie couldn't think. Not right now. "I've just lost my grand-mother," sie said, tears welling again, sie didn't know from where. "And I've had a terrible shock. I'm going to my room. If..." Sie looked Zemil directly in the eyes. "If it still is my room?"

"Of course," said Zemil.

Enae hadn't expected that easy acquiescence. Grandmaman would never have tolerated her acting all high-and-mighty like this. But what else was sie supposed to do? Grandmaman wasn't here anymore. Sie blinked, took a breath. Another. "If your people would be so kind as to bring me lunch and coffee there." Ridicu-lous, sie was still holding the sandwiches the servant had handed to hir, but sie couldn't even imagine eating them. Not these sand-wiches, not here, not now. "And I'll have supper in my room as well."

"They'll be happy to help you any way you wish, as long as you're here," said Zemil.

Enae rose. Set hir untouched food back onto the sideboard. Sie turned and nodded to the jurist. "Thank you. I...thank you."

"Call me if you need me," he said.

Sie turned to Zemil, but found sie had no words to say, and so sie just fled to hir own room.

Follow us:

f /orbitbooksUS

X /orbitbooks

▶ /orbitbooks

Join our mailing list
to receive alerts on our
latest releases and deals.

orbitbooks.net

Enter our monthly
giveaway for the chance
to win some epic prizes.

orbitloot.com